# CRIMEU(

# THROUGH THE PAST DARKLY

## A Murderous Ink Press Anthology

✶✶✶✶✶✶✶✶✶✶✶✶✶✶✶✶✶✶✶✶✶✶✶✶✶✶✶✶✶✶✶

# CRIMEUCOPIA
## THROUGH THE PAST
## DARKLY

First published by Murderous Ink Press
Crowland
LINCOLNSHIRE
England
www.murderousinkpress.co.uk

Editorial Copyright © Murderous Ink Press 2024
Base cover artwork © Lazyskel-AI 2023
Cover treatment and lettering © Willie Chob-Chob 2024
All rights are retained by the respective authors & artists on publication
Paperback Edition ISBN: 9781909498587
eBook Edition ISBN: 9781909498594

Acknowledgements

To those writers and artists who helped make this anthology what it is, I can only say a heartfelt Thank You!

And to Den, as always.

# Contents

*The Confession first appeared on the *Yellow Mama* website, Issue 88, July 2019
**On the Side of the Angels first appeared in *Ellery Queen's Mystery Magazine*
January/February 2022 Vol. 159 Nos. 1 & 2 Whole Nos. 964 & 965.

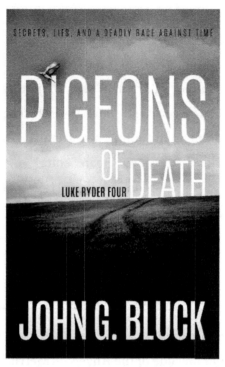

SECRETS, LIES, AND A DEADLY RACE AGAINST TIME

# PIGEONS OF DEATH

LUKE RYDER FOUR

## JOHN G. BLUCK

**A HIGH-STAKES GAME OF MURDER AND ESPIONAGE, WHERE LOVE AND LOYALTY ARE TESTED AT EVERY TURN**

Mark Spicer, a renowned thoroughbred trainer, meets a chilling end at his own gala, victim of a sinister plot. As the investigation unfolds, Deputy Luke Ryder, posing as a stable hand, navigates the dangerous currents of illicit drug trade and unbridled ambition. Entrusted with unraveling the truth, Luke's quest is complicated by his attraction to the enigmatic Carmen, Spicer's widow, whose own secrets threaten to unravel the fabric of their burgeoning affair.

Amidst the opulent backdrop of horse racing and the shadowy corridors of drug cartels, Luke's mission pits him against a network of corruption extending far beyond Kentucky's rolling hills. With each step closer to justice, Luke and Carmen find themselves ensnared in a deadly cat-and-mouse game, where the stakes are life and death.

Will Deputy Ryder uncover the truth before it's too late, or will the shadows of deceit claim their next victim?

Find details of all 4 of the Luke Ryder series here:

*https://www.amazon.co.uk/dp/B0C7Y3GXNG*

# It Was In The Year Of....
## (An Editorial of Sorts)

When you get a good piece of fiction, it's hard to pass it up, and we always try and see if we can make it fit in somewhere.

The trouble comes when it's a period piece. Yes, sometimes you can sneak it in, under the guise of it being 'sort of' Cosy/Noir/Narrative/Whodidit/Whydidit (etc) orientated. However, sometimes you know you're left with two choices: Either reject the piece because it doesn't fit — or see if a new anthology project can stand on its own two feet, take on the world, and win.

And no, not every piece in this is a Cosy — some might be considered as such, but some are Cosy Noir (and yes, Aunty Jean, such does exist), Historical/Period Drama, Historical Private Eyes, Narrative Crimes, and a whole spectrum of the Crime fiction sub-genres — going from 420 BC through to AD 1969 — a decade in itself which could easily fill several volumes on its own.

So, as with any good investigation, we start with the earliest point in our timeline — from the adept stylus of *Gary Thomson*'s Cos-based *The Wedding Cup Mystery* at the renowned Healing Temple, Asklepion.

From there, *Edward St Boniface* gives us what some may say is a piece in the Unreliable Narrator style as Simon Magus Iscariot recounts his meeting with a particular Nazarene, in his piece, *Judas*.

From AD 30 we skip over to France and the Middle Ages — AD 1305 — as Terry Wijesuriya talks about *The Death of a Parfait*.

235 years further on, and we are privy to the nefarious machinations that lie behind *The Queen's Judgement*, as recounted by historical interpreter *Frances Stratford*. From there we jump a few years further along, and *Dennis E. Delaney* takes us to The New World at the start of the Elizabethan Era, and shows that when all else fails, *A Pragmatic Solution* is all that's called for in order to fix things.

From the 16th, *Joan Leotta* jumps us to the 17th and Italy, as she explains why *The Confession* will always ease a troubled conscience.

*Hope Hodgkins* picks up the torch and slides us into the 19th Century, recounting a tale from the shadows, in *Darkness Becomes You,* before letting *Karen Odden* explain why she might have to licence *Her Dangerously Clever Hands.*

*J. F. Benedetto* kicks off the 20th Century by presenting his *The Canadian: Death in the Chinese Darkness,* and *S.B. Watson* continues with *The Problem of the Disappearing Heart.* And from there we jump into the 1940s for *Hal Dygert,* who has *Something to Tell,* and *Merrilee Robson* who is *On the Side of the Angels. John G. Bluck* lets us know that in 1946 it was *Cold in Chicago,* and *David Hagerty* closes out the decade with his *Itching Hands and Aching Hearts.*

Moving further along the timeline, we have a quartet from the 1950s, starting with *Avi Sirlin* telling us about *What Lies Buried,* which leads us to *Karl El-Koura* who explains just how complex *A Rehanging at Nine* can be.

Jump forward 3 years, and we find the welcomed return of *Penny Hurrell,* who says she's *A Good Judge of Character,* before *Kai Lovelace* presents some social comment, even though he insists it's *Only a Story.*

From the Dawn of Rawk'n'Roll we spin into the 1960s as we approach the end of this timeline with a triptych of pieces from that decade.

*Cop and Robber* allows *Maddi Davidson* to regress to 1963, a popular timeline year, and shortly afterwards *J. Aquino* explains why his hero is happy he did not *Shake Hands with the Devil* in 1966.

And closing out both this anthology and bringing our Crimeucopia timeline to an end is *Kirk Landers,* who lets us know what actually happened in *The Parking Lot* that night in 1969 and, more importantly, why.

So, as we replace the lids on these 21 evidence boxes, and stack them back on the Historical Crimes Archive shelves once more, we hope you'll find something that you immediately like, as well as something that takes you out of your regular era comfort zone — and puts you into a completely new one.

Because, in the spirit of the Ye Olde Murderous Ink Press motto:

*You never know what you like until you dust it off and read it.*

# 420 BC
# The Wedding Cup Mystery
## Gary Thomson

"Kallipos has worked his painter's genius again," marvelled Eleon the physician at the entrance to the Healing Temple of Apollo. A slave attendant gathered locks of packing fleece from the base of the waist-high amphora, gleaming heaven black in the sunlight. "The god will surely respect this dedication."

His friend Zenodoros grumbled. "A lecher and bully, buying penance for himself."

Eleon frowned. "He's also endowing a fund to keep the vessel filled with olive oil, for patients at the purification baths."

Two painted figures decorated the amphora: A seated Asklepios, son of Apollo and god of medicine, warmed to the attentions of his daughter, Hygiea, goddess of good health. In her right hand a temple snake extended his thick body and sniffed the air.

A bumble of newly arrived pilgrims rose over the Temple's courtyard. Priests barked directions to marshal the crowd. A soldier clumped by on worn crutches; soiled head bandage flopped across his forehead. Zenodoros called to him. "Bias, we saved you once from a sword slash. You're into tavern fights now?"

The soldier looked up, hesitated, then patted his head. "Aye, sir, ugly wound... campaign against the Boetians. Keep your needle and stitches close by, so's I'm ready for those Spartan dogs when this truce falls apart." He gripped his crutch and hobbled into the crowd.

Beyond the reception yard a slave lad came running toward them.

"Kallipos would serve the god more nobly if he offered some financial help to these poor souls who risk the journey here to Cos."

Zenodoros said. "Most barely able to pay for their sea passage and treatments." Eleon stiffened as the running figure knocked an elderly man to his knees.

"None have been turned away, my friend. Ever. Master Hippocrates would sell his robe before denying anyone a healing service."

The panting runner stood before Eleon. "Sire... the *gymnasion*. In the equipment room. Murder. The painter. Kallipos. "

∞

Kallipos's naked body lay crumpled over the stone flags. Blood pooled along his neck. A bag of high jumpers' training weights butted against his right thigh. Eleon recognized the purple scar that grooved Kallipos's right calf. He himself had treated the wound recently.

The gymnasiarch Kimon paced beside the body. "A slave attendant come to fetch javelins for the arena found the victim. Claims he heard no commotion, nor did he see anybody leave the room."

"There was noise a-plenty here last evening. Kallipos was killed after the watchman's round, it seems." Eleon placed his hand on the victim's neck. The skin was cold to his touch. "The assassin could have exited the grounds unseen along the path to Hermes's sanctuary." Eleon lifted Kallipos's right hand into his own: the index and middle fingers were severed at the first knuckle. "What do you make of this?"

Kimon studied the bloody wound. "By holy Zeus, it's a mad dog at work, to mangle his archery fingers." He looked at Eleon. "He was shooting in competition only yesterday."

"The army surgeon, Zenodoros, sent him to me a while back. Kallipos was cut from a mishandled arrow, and ranting that Zeno wasn't to touch him, he was a quack and would poison him." Eleon stood musing with his hand along his chin. "Did he have any enemies from the competitions?"

"Rivals, for sure. But no blood feud haters. One, Herodes of Kalymnos, always wanted to beat him – and badly." Kimon spoke slowly, as if he were ticking off scores from a tablet. "Kallipos is living with Praxilla and her boy, she lost her husband in the war."

Kimon snugged his purple robe about his shoulders. "Everyone scrambled for his vials. For their daughter's marriage perfumes… Most of the athletes here are wearing one of his olive oil flasks."

Eleon made to drape an empty sand bag over the body. A flash of light stopped him. "Hello, what's here?"

Carefully he moved Kallipos's right knee and dislodged a ceramic cup, slender and elegant. Its hallowed use was to hold a new bride's baptismal water. He examined the wedding scene painted along the side: Aphrodite leading a procession of singing women.

Inside lay two finger pieces, icy blue. He stifled a retch.

He turned the vessel over, read the inscription on the base: *Kallipos painted me.*

⸎

"A woman's life is bound by waiting, Eleon of Rhodes. She waits for her father to choose her a good husband; she waits for love between them to grow strong." Praxilla, wife of Itys, spread her hands over her lap. "Sometimes, in despair, she waits for the Daughters of Night to call her toward the River."

Her pinched face told of her living in a house empty of joy. "Queen Penelope had her loom, to mark her time. And I had Kallipos." She rolled her eyes. In exasperation or sufferance? Eleon wondered. "He was a generous provider, and for that I was grateful. He kept me from the shame of selling firewood in the agora day by day. But always in my heart I was waiting for my husband to return from his battlefield."

"You've had no word, even since this peace treaty?"

"Nothing. We heard his cavalry unit was badly mauled at Olynthos. But there was no account of his death, no body, no appearance in a field hospital. It was as if the gods had carried him into their presence."

"What was your son's reaction to Kallipos living with you?"

Praxilla looked away toward the street.

"Telamon went inside himself, into silence and bitterness. He cursed this intruder in my bed and called on the Furies to drive him mad."

"Would he be capable of this homicide?"

Praxilla shook her head. "He would never disadvantage me that way. There is none other male relative who would oversee our safety and welfare."

"Where can I find him, for a quick word?"

"He's off with Xanthos, the horse trainer, where he is learning about riding and caring for horses. To follow in his father's service, and make him proud." She eased Eleon toward the door. "I'll tell him this hard news tonight."

◯◯◯

Zenodoros leaned over Herodes's elevated left leg and eased a bronze probe around his patient's calf wound. "No inflammation, adjacent muscle appears strong and healthy. Slight odour, as of overripe apples. Firm signs of healing." Close by, Hippocrates heard each comment with approval, seeing confirmed his own long held belief: the best school for surgery was an army battlefield, amidst spilled guts and severed limbs.

Eleon handed Zenodoros a bone forceps. With deft movements he separated ridges of muscle to examine exposed bone. "Here we are... what we came for." Zenodoros closed the forceps around a bone splinter, then lifted both into a nearby bowl. "These wounds don't end with the peace. Sword cuts, if they don't kill you, can smash a bone to pieces."

The two left Eleon to wash the wound and apply a fresh dressing.

Eleon worked the sponge soaked in nitre and vinegar along the perimeter of the wound. Herodes eyed him closely. "It's the constant pain. How often have I wanted to saw my leg off with a knife."

"And take your archery comps sitting down?"

Herodes smiled grimly. "Now that Kallipos is dead, there's not much incentive to shoot. More's the loss, that."

"How far back is it, this bad blood between you?"

Herodes leaned on his elbows. "I was good at it, physician. Painting the athletes' victory pots. Could've made a strong living one day, with my own workshop and artisans. When Kallipos started seeing what I was capable of he sacked me. Slagged me and my work in front of the hired help, shouted I had no eye for the scene painted over the clay."

Eleon reached for the roll of bandage. "Why didn't you set up your own business?"

"Wanted to. But I was called up for war service. 'Fore I could turn around I was facing Thracian archers in the north."

Eleon tied off the bandage. "Come back in six months. Before you go, I must ask if you were in the *gymnasion* the eve of Kallipos's assassination."

Herodes shook his head. "Me and my mule Argos was at the harbour, carting pilgrims from the ships to the Temple. Some of your priests must have noticed us."

◄○►

Zenodoros filled the doorway of the *gymnasion* Treatment Room. "These herbals are for you," he called to Eleon. From a leather bag he withdrew three clay jars, and voiced the writing on each lid. "Yarrow, garlic… and silphium. Sent from the temple *pharmakoepia* with me, since I'm off to the baths."

Eleon finished a line in his treatment notes. He looked up from his desk. "Before you go, I want to hear your suggested treatments for wounds here." Eleon tapped his finger over his forehead. "What have you learned about *amnesios* from treating these wounded soldiers? Different causes? Effects on behaviour?"

Zenodoros warmed to his subject: He told of fear and chaos in the midst of carnage. Thunder of clashing shields and armor, piercing screams of the wounded. "I saw men who convinced themselves they were walking dead in Hades; others who lost power of speech, and recall. We couldn't treat their agonies in the field. Only later could we try to make them whole again."

Eleon followed the account with fascination. "Hippocrates and his physicians are trying new treatments to restore these soldiers' lost memories."

"We're moving beyond the old ways of bloodletting, or dream therapies with the temple snakes. Now empathic doctors will ask of the patient gentle, leading questions. Encourage him to seek out these missing fragments of experience, talk of their reality, and so restore them, defanged, to his psyche."

A fleeting memory tumbled into Eleon's head. "Why did Kallipos rage against your treating him for the arrow wound?"

"I knew him, in Miletos. My daughter, Amynta, worked for him, as painter's model for the portraits on his high-end amphoras and wine goblets." His eyes brightened in pride and admiration. "She was his Aphrodite, his Ariadne, sometimes his Hecate if he had funeral urns to paint."

"She was fortunate indeed with her prospects."

"Not with the troubling conditions in his studios. Overcrowded, foul air from the paints, his abusive outbursts. I was continually after her to leave his employ."

Eleon thanked Zenodoros for his summary. "Now I must acquaint myself with a young horseman. And hope his memory is intact."

⊠⊠

"He was a deserter...."

Telamon, son of Itys, began his denunciation of his father. "First, from his military unit. Then from his family." He studied the padded stave in his hand, his cadet's substitute for a future battlefield weapon

"At first I thought he was wandering as a stranger somewhere. Like Odysseus lingering in the Isles of the Blest." The lad's dark eyes softened; the re-called animosity drained from his face. "I told myself, he's wounded, unable to make his journey home."

"And you felt his loss even more when Kallipos came into your mother's life."

"It was my kinship duty to protect my mother. He did not belong in our house. If I were my father's true son I would have plunged a dagger into his throat, and freed my mother. But his removal required a man for the doing." His voice trailed off.

"You have the means now. Weapons training, size and opportunity. Did you? Seize the chance to rid yourself and your mother of this contagion, as you saw Kallipos?"

"There was no need, physician. My mother spoke with the oracle in Hygeia's sanctuary. She found another answer than murder to her distress."

"Do you remember the prophetess's words?"

"Clearly. She said: *What Poseidon has taken, he shall give back; that day the true one shall reveal himself.* Shortly after, my mother's troublesome dreams ceased. She took to walking along the hill beside the harbour. She craved a sighting of my father's inbound ship, and him walking down the gangway, coming home to her... to us."

Eleon acquainted Telamon of the effects of *amnesios*. "Perhaps your father is safe in a soldier's barracks somewhere where rest and time will restore his memory. Then Earth-Shaker will provide as the oracle foretold." He bade the lad return to his training precinct.

⊗⊙⊗

Eleon approached Hygeia's sanctuary at the Temple of Apollo. He wanted to hear the oracle's version of Praxilla's consultation: Did she ask for additional guidance, or details about time unfolding?

He stopped at Kallipos's amphora. A slave was polishing the shoulder with light strokes of lamb's wool. The strong confident face of Hygeia held him. He imagined Amynta's similar poise in her work with Kallipos.

The painted figures took on a silent reality: Asklepios, seated upright, a trusted father basking in the love of his daughter; Hygiea, calm and assured in her divine mission to guide humanity toward abiding health. He saw that fixity of purpose in her grip on the snake's midsection. The curled fingers summoned a cold memory.

He followed the penetrating gaze of the serpent, away from the amphora and over the terrace. In the courtyard three patients lounged on a stone seat, chatting in the warmth. On the right, Bias leaned his chin onto the top of his crutch. A clean bandage covered his head.

A voice sounded in his head: *The fingertips, Eleon. Gathered in the bridal cup. A defamation? A portent? Or an atonement?*

He half ran down the terrace steps toward the three gathered soldiers. He wanted a direct word with Bias.

&#9731;&#9731;&#9731;

Hippocrates led Eleon into Surgery Theatre on the northwest corner of the second terrace. There they found Zenodoros, directing a slave attendant in assembling his surgical instruments, steel probes, and linen bandages. He gave off examining the edge of a scalpel and welcomed his visitors. "Time to remove an arrow head from Aktor's shoulder," Zenodoros offered. "He came in from Paros three days ago. Suffering pain since the war ended."

Hippocrates dismissed the slave; he turned to Zenodoros. "Not if Eleon's allegations against you hold truth. Not if you have violated your oath to do none harm in your capacity as surgeon."

Zenodoros's expression hardened. "You should explain yourself, sir."

"Bias provided a few details from Miletos," Eleon said. "The lamentable situation with your daughter and Kallipos."

Zenodoros closed his eyes and inhaled deeply. He tapped the scalpel blade on the table edge. "Did he tell you the whole story? How Kallipos seduced Amynta? That he promised her marriage, abruptly forswore himself, and drove my anguished daughter to suicide? Did he tell you all that, and did he mention a father's blind rage ensuing?"

"Why did you not kill him then?" Eleon said. "At that moment following your daughter's ruin?"

"No, he had left the city two days before her untimely death. Later I learned he had set up business here. I had no urgency; the god would lead me to him in good time."

"And so you found him, one evening, in the *gymnasion*. He was unaware that you were stalking him, to settle your blood debt."

"The training area is quiet near closing time. I watched Kallipos carry his archery gear to the equipment room. The god was calling me to revenge. No slave attendants were about." Zenodoros hesitated, calling details from his memory. "Still, he put up a strong fight."

"The bridal cup beside the body. It was Kallipos's gift to your daughter?"

"I kept it all these years. To honour her memory. Now it will serve as a black charm to lead his soul to the Dark Regions. He will wander there, incomplete and reminded forever of his loathsome actions."

"The fingers in the cup," Eleon continued. "They fooled us at first, we mistook them for Kallipos's archery fingers. But they were his painter's fingers. You were cursing his foul work with your beloved daughter."

Zenodoros smiled tightly. "It's doubtful the city magistrate will pursue a trial. I was acting as the law demands, in protecting my family's welfare."

He brushed his fingers over the probes and bandages. "Now, sir, I beg permission to continue with Aktor's surgery. He's a loyal soldier; his pain is longstanding. I can remedy his suffering." He seemed confident in his request. "That too is part of my vow, to help the sick according to my ability and judgment."

His interrogators held silent, each hesitant to answer soon. Hippocrates said, "Since we're in the house of the god, Asklepios shall determine - through Hygeia's priestess." He raised a brow to Zenodoros. "She serves a compassionate goddess. Do not pack away your implements yet."

# AD 30
## Judas
### Edward St. Boniface

*'And supper being ended, the devil having now
put into the heart of Judas Iscariot, Simon's [son],
to betray him.'*

John 13:2 (King James Version)

I meet the Nazarene coming out of the not very grand house of a minor
Jerusalem merchant where I've been informed by Herod's spies he
currently resides. It is early in the evening. He is clearly on his way
somewhere when I put myself wordlessly in front of him.

Neither of us speaks but the glance he gives me is eloquent. A long
time has passed since the execution of John the Baptist, his friend and
something of a mentor. Herod had ordered it while consumed by lust
for Helene, but it was really at my instigation and one of my greatest
hidden *coups*.

Capitalising on it took subtlety. Using Helene impersonating
Herodias' daughter Salome dancing a wild dervish was a masterstroke,
provoking lustful Herod to swear he would give her anything that was
in his kingdom for the asking. Best of all, no obvious gain for me could
be attributed.

John saw through myself and my power and this affronted me. Worse,
he foretold the new power that would supplant the Goddess and Her
rule. So I could not permit him to live.

Prevented nothing, of course. The Nazarene who inherited John's
maddeningly pacific movement stands at ease before me now. Gestures
with that irritating calm of his towards a nearby tavern and I find myself
following him in where I intended to command and interrogate.

At the back as though by providential intercession there is a booth of rough-hewn boards as seats and a rude table empty. With a dip of dismay I see most of the Nazarene's followers are here. At the sight of me they stop short and stare in amazement and intense hostility.

Afraid despite myself I am instinctively poised to defend but of course my shadows are absent. No command I invoke will induce them to come near this man I seek to harm and destroy as I did John. But he gestures in the slightest way and they leave us alone.

> SIMON MAGUS ISCARIOT: *"I don't see my son over there among your followers and he hasn't been in Jerusalem for awhile. Have you zealots tired of or done away with him? I wouldn't put it past this rabble you run around with, Nazarene."*

I'm being deliberately and needlessly provocative, of course. Characteristically like the followers of the Baptist before him the Nazarene's hangers-on are generally submissive and obnoxiously law-abiding. I can't get Pilate to make an example of them and can't get too vocal lest Tiberius hear about it and send his assorted human ghouls after me again.

> JESUS CHRIST OF NAZARETH: "Master Simon, your son is the most invaluable of my disciples. His intellect and sensitivity and competence are equal to your own with a somewhat differing emphasis. I count him not merely as a follower but as friend."

No; it's really not going my way today.

> SMI: *"Evasive, eh?"*

> JCoN: "Forgive me, that was not meant. Judas your son currently sojourns near the Dead Sea. At least until recently, today was meant to be the last part of their journey. He is with several of my trusted other disciples imparting the gospel and assisting healing of the sick and afflicted. I believe they are due back in the next day

or so, conditions permitting."

SMI: "*Herod permitting, you mean.*"

JCoN: "We have conversed upon Herod before, Master Simon. He is a man divided and placed in an impossible situation as king of Judea. I am not one of those who revile him in the marketplace or take pleasure in his plight. That burden he carries would torment even stronger men than himself. I believe he largely conducts himself and his politics for the greater good of Judea and Israel."

SMI: "*You think either he or I care about your flowery diplomacy? You don't have the power here.*"

JCoN: "None of us have power here. Herod's temporal power is circumscribed by Rome. His religious influence is limited and corrupted by exceptionally bad counsel. By your own version of religious influence using fear and brutal example, if I may speak freely."

SMI: "*No you may not, Nazarene. I know the nature of power because I exercise it, and so does Herod. Rome doesn't want trouble any more than either of us do in our respective domains. And make no mistake that I am an overlord in mine. You have taken my heir from me and I want him back.*"

JCoN: "Master Simon…"

SMI: "*Don't do that fake politeness mincing thing, curse you! Talk to me man to man while I'm still willing to be more or less diplomatic myself!*"

JCoN: "Simon, then. As you point out you are indeed an overlord. Of many lands in Samaria which you have taken by terror of your powers through magically induced famines. Amongst the cast out spirits you also have a place, although one considerably more problematic and vulnerable. But conscience by itself you cannot rule, and Judas has made his choice."

SMI: "*I even heard he was acting as your treasurer or something.*"

JCoN: "That is indeed so. Judas has a rare gift of discretion and prudence. With an understanding of money he has volunteered for the role of keeping our movement's meagre finances solvent. He grew up in an educated household despite the affliction you visited upon him."

SMI: "*I knew it wouldn't take you long to get back onto that. I've explained that possession of him by a minor demon was a catastrophic mistake. Exorcism was not possible.*"

JCoN: "But transference was, Simon. You could have taken the demon into yourself and conquered it but did not."

SMI: "*I'm a busy man. I didn't have time.*"

JCoN: "Judas suffered dreadfully but has made considerable progress in his healing with us. Over that time we have mutually discovered him to be a trustworthy and quite reliable man of figures. That is an essential skill that most of us lack, being simple men. Every sesterce and shekel counts in our movement's work since we largely subsist on charity."

SMI: "*Yes, I see you beggars in the streets of Jerusalem and Judea and Samaria everywhere I go now. 'Come To Jesus, Come To Jesus', all day long. It's like listening to mules braying. You've even scraped a few coppers against provincial Roman garrison soldiers. I heard something about you advising a* Centurion *no less at one of your grubby meetings the other day. You had better watch yourself because neither Herod nor Pilate like suborning of their troops. Or sedition."*

JCoN: "All men have souls, Roman soldiers and lepers alike. We are all of us wounded by the world in many and diverse ways and seek healing. Wealth and status or poverty and obscurity make no difference to me. Sometimes it is possible to help and sometimes, regrettably not."

SMI: *"You're no simple man like you make out, either. This story of a carpenter's son become the Son Of Man or whatever else they say, I don't buy into it. I've travelled the world and I know. Power and knowledge like yours come only from much study and application. Plus a great deal of travel too. And there are only a few places in the world where you can get it."*

JCoN: "Terrible events followed my birth when our present king's predecessor perceived a threat to his rule and caused all infants born in the year of and just prior to Augustus' taxing of the empire to be massacred. My parents fled to Egypt with me. We lived among the large Hebrew community at Alexandria. It was there I received the first part of my education as you perceive it."

SMI: *"Wait a minute. You surely didn't attend the Library there? That's not possible. I've thought I heard a low level of Greek sophistry in your speeches, but..."*

JCoN: "Patriarch Philo generously helped us. With the Patriarch's kind patronage after a few years I was able to attend the Library as a student, yes. When I was twelve we were informed it was safe to return and I accompanied my family back to Judea. I saw the Temple at Jerusalem. Afterwards I went back to Alexandria with my mother and remained there until my final graduation from the Library."

SMI: "...*Philo?...*"

JCoN: "I knew him as an old but kindly man. In fact he was my guardian on my return since my father needed to build his business in Galilee up again after the long years of near poverty in Alexandria. You too are a graduate of that fine Library, are you not?"

This really is not going the way I'd anticipated. Force myself to stop staring stupidly at the Nazarene as his words ring abrasively through my mind. I'm giving myself away again.

Philo who rivalled me in the secret study of sorcery when we were novice students at Alexandria. Philo who stole Master Satureus' affections away from me. Philo, the very nemesis of my youth.

SMI: "*Philo...*"

That little catamite pseudo-intellectual Philo himself, grown into a pompous patriarch, had nurtured and supported and funded the boy who had become this threat to me. Who had become the Nazarene subverting by his very existence all my plans. Did Philo foresee this? Could Philo have *known*?

JCoN: "You knew him also?"

SMI: "*I knew him.*"

JCoN: "Generally I do not go by appearances among men. It is the spirit and the soul that most influence and reflect character. Yet the physical resemblance of Judas to yourself is so striking. Despite myself I cannot help but be reminded that you yourself look appreciably younger than your own son. And that is not because of the possession he suffered under for so many years."

SMI: "*You excelled at your sophistry classes. Say what you really mean.*"

JCoN: "After my graduation and before my eventual return to my native Judea I also travelled widely, Simon."

SMI: "*Frankly I couldn't wait to get away from all the catamites and four-cornered men that passed as tutors there. Only a few of them had real talent like Satureus.*"

JCoN: "I heard stories of this master during my time. His brilliance and tragic and unexplained early death. Interestingly your name was frequently mentioned in connection with him. Curious how they remain very strong in the Library's folklore even after more than a whole generation passing. Yes, the closeness that develops in an all-male academic community can be excessive. Particularly one so influenced by the Greek cultural example and mores. But I was not myself inclined towards the Greek passion."

SMI: "*In my experience you have to swing both ways to see the whole picture.*"

At this he stares briefly at me and chuckles suddenly, attracting the attention of his followers. Hadn't thought he was the type to appreciate a ribald joke with undertones.

JCoN: "Judas is so much more serious but he has the beginnings of your effortless conversational gift. Satureus lived and died in Augustus' time. You must have been a boy and then a young man during that era. By now you are certainly over sixty and actually look younger than both Judas and myself. You must have made an early start in sorcery and forbidden knowledge at Alexandria."

SMI: "*Since they don't teach the kind of things you've learnt at the Library proper either I'd already guessed you knew about the catacombs.*"

JCoN: "I always wondered if the Simon Antonius so often described as knowing too many things he should not had intimate knowledge of the catacombs. Of course I too came to know them with a small group of other boys who were inducted into a secret society that shared the knowledge of how to enter the catacombs undetected. A society that had begun some years after you left, I believe."

SMI: "*Don't suppose that little spider Philo hosted the meetings, did he?*"

Now the Nazarene does laugh, and heartily. But this time it is covered up by the noise of the tavern which has become busier. Not even his followers glance over, they are completely self-absorbed over something and muttering among themselves.

JCoN: "Intuitive, Simon. Normally we used the egress located behind the altar of the temple to Serapis."

SMI: "*Credit where credit is due. I found that exit myself and put it back into operation secretly. I had real audacity and don't mind letting you in on that little secret. I was the first and real pioneer of what was hidden down there.*"

JCoN: "Surprisingly Simon, at least perhaps to you, all of us knew this. The Patriarch Philo freely admitted you had both been young rivals towards gaining restricted knowledge. And that you had first found the way in. But we could never draw him out on just what extent you did make use of all the treasures of knowledge there."

SMI: "*A great deal more than Philo, whatever he did or*

*didn't imply. I'm willing to bet he didn't tell you everything about our...rivalries."*

JCoN: "Both of you admired the great scholar who was Satureus. He mourned his master tutor to us many times and declared that had he lived he too would have commanded the Library."

SMI: *"Master Satureus commanded far more than that from me."*

Something in me catches at the memory of Satureus. Beautiful in body and mind and spirit, the greatest of the translators living and teaching at the Library in his time. Didymus Chalcenterus, for many years the head of the Library, had also employed him in his great re-translation and expansion of *The Aeneid*.

Many said that at least half the work on that was Satureus'. That Old Bronze Guts, as we boys called Didymus, had never given Satureus proper recognition. Fine memories.

Much happier than what I later did to Satureus, body and mind and spirit, in vengeance for turning away from me and favouring Philo. Destruction I had also intended for Philo himself which he maddeningly avoided.

Nearly break my wine goblet in my suddenly clenched fist as the remembrance and renewed fury almost overwhelm me.

JCoN: "Too many good and great men pass out of the world before their time."

SMI: *"Philo's still hanging on. Suppose he tells more than a few unflattering stories about me, but I could give you a plethora about his little peccadilloes, as he describes them."*

JCoN: "Whenever the name of Simon Antonius came up he was disapproving and reserved, but I believe scrupulously fair-minded. He spoke of you as an exceptionally gifted boy. Intellectually there were few pupils at the Library who could compare with you. In fact the Patriarch told us you had so impressed the great poet Ovid on a visit you were granted a private audience and shown books then proscribed by Augustus himself."

SMI: "*The old…Philo actually admitted that? Simon Antonius is flattered.*"

JCoN: "As for your morals and inclinations and motives he could not have been more condemnatory."

SMI: "*Consistent, at least. He was content to remain a dusty old scholar and just capitalised on his age and being rooted in one place to get that patriarchy thing conferred on him. I went out into the wide world to find real knowledge and power. Now I'm an overlord in my own lands.*"

JCoN: "In fear both of Herod and Tiberius?"

SMI: "*Don't tempt my wrath any more than you already have, boy.*"

JCoN: "After graduation and my leave-taking from the Patriarch I also travelled. Like yourself I met both the Egyptian Atenites in their secret stronghold and later the Persian Magi at their mountain fastness. Many times I felt as though I followed in your footsteps. Tyre had particularly much to say of you and what you left them with."

SMI: "*Phalixar's hospitality is especially good if he likes the cut of your jib and you can handle the really dirty work. He pays a lot better than Herod.*"

JCoN: "Indeed I have heard tales. The Patriarch also told us you have the uncanny ability to find your way into and flourish in the most improbable settings."

SMI: "*If you mean Samaria that brings us back to the*

*issue of your encroachment on me."*

JCoN: "Neither myself nor my followers have ever wished you harm, Simon."

SMI: *"You pollute my lands and all of Samaria and Judea and clear out to the Syrian border with your blasted missionaries, but that's not what I meant. What I really mean and you well know is my son. Judas is not meant to be one of you subversives. All of you are only going to end up in prison or crucified anyway, I promise you that. He is a young man come into his nativity and that brings responsibilities. As his father I will require him to learn his role in overseeing my estates."*

JCoN: "That will never happen, Simon."

SMI: *"You dare to disrespect and defy me about my own son?"*

JCoN: "No, I mean no disrespect. However, in truth you have been no father to poor Judas and he has entrusted his destiny to us."

SMI: *"As his father I claim him by right."*

JCoN: "As a man born free and without obligation he may choose his own companions and he has chosen us. This cannot be undone."

SMI: *"I could have you all taken and Judas forcibly returned to me. Pilate and Herod would assist me in this as but one favour due to my service."*

JCoN: "Pilate and Herod would both patiently tell you to close the door on the way out of their offices, I think. Forgive me for speaking plainly again Simon, but if you wish my death and those of my followers you will have to effect rather more subtlety."

SMI: *"It can be arranged. Return Judas to me,*

*Nazarene."*

JCoN: "You must convince him to return to you of his own free will."

And there it is. I am stymied for I know of no way to do this. Judas is useless to me as a son but an enemy I cannot tolerate in the midst of the Nazarene's close disciples. It's maddeningly irresolvable.

SMI: *"Fine. You steal my only son from me and will not return him. But you also seek to take away my followers and break my hold on the faithful of Samaria."*

JCoN: "Ah, yes. Your Gnosis."

He does turn and look directly at me now. A penetrating gaze that gives me the uncomfortable impression he looks both into my past and future. Sees my soul as only one with the true vision like an Oracle may and remind myself my own power pales before this man.

SMI: *"It's a lawful faith. This movement of yours seeks to purloin my followers."*

JCoN: "Theft and coercion are not our way. Nor are magic tricks and curses and clever horrors to impress the easily led. Truth will always draw the intuitive away from lies."

SMI: *"You dare to suggest the Logos and Ennoia to be lies…"*

JCoN: "Hardly, for I have studied those wise principles with great attention. I have read your book, your *Great Pronouncement*, Simon. It is the product of an ambitious and capable and unscrupulous man who seeks power over the dominions of body and soul in the worst imaginable manner."

SMI: *"All in THE APOPHASIS MEGALÊ is truth, Nazarene."*

JCoN: "You blaspheme when you claim godhood,

Simon."

SMI: "*Words such as blasphemy are air.*"

JCoN: "Living truth is what they are. You know as I do we are surrounded by a spiritual universe. Sacred and profane utterances are noticed and those who make them are known to the invisible places."

SMI: "*I'm not one of those simple provincials who follow you and can't be impressed with those nicely vague and expansive half parables.*"

JCoN: "The parables of which you have heard are a necessary means of encompassing difficult and complicated truths into stories that can be repeated. Few of my followers can read or write. Much must be invested in stories of symbolism which can be told around a campfire or a supper table. Works such as yours are pompous mistruths designed to impress the powerful and learned but pedantic scholars. And I must say this but you subvert and profane the truth of the Gnosis."

SMI: "*Ever been to my temple?*"

JCoN: "An impressive edifice, but in truth a Lunar temple in disguise."

He keeps surprising me, this Nazarene, when he should not. That knowledge he just casually expressed is of truly ancient provenance.

SMI: "*All right, I admit that. You clearly know the secrets. Particularly during the full moon, with certain invocations, the spirits will speak forth there from the darkness.*"

JCoN: "Demons and revenant spirits and exiles even from the Well Of Souls speak forth there from the darkness you have deliberately created. Voices from the netherworld echo all through it."

SMI: "*Nice to know someone in the know also appreciates the success.*"

JCoN: "Whatever you may think you have learned, each time you commune with such diabolic entities they look into your own soul. You have given away far too much of yourself and are too well known."

SMI: "*The useful ones are worth it.*"

JCoN: "Was Thakallos worth it?"

Suddenly I feel very cold in the overly hot and sweaty and smelly tavern.

SMI: "*…meaning what?*"

JCoN: "I did not think you knew the name of the devil who possessed Judas for all those years. A simple enough matter to banish it from him if you had."

SMI: "*How…how could you…*"

JCoN: "When I recognised the genuine possession infesting Judas I commanded the devil in the name of the Father. It must obey such incontestable words and required little effort to send it back to the darkness in disgrace."

I really wish he hadn't said that.

SMI: "*Always good to know who your friends are.*"

JCoN: "Had you but wished to ask instead of confronting and attempting to intimidate and threaten me I would have told you all of this before. You consider me your enemy but I am not."

SMI: "*Fact remains, you are keeping my son from me and taking my followers away as I've described. Just what do you really intend with this dangerous*" *movement of yours?"*

JCoN: "To bring about a rebirth in the soul of the world around us."

SMI: *"And you'll do that just how?"*

JCoN: "By invoking my Father in the right manner at the appointed time after many suitable preparations. It will require a certain sacrifice."

SMI: *"Virgins normally work best I find, in case you're wondering. It's more difficult to find them around these days, so you may have to go looking with your minions. Don't think I missed the less than subtle reference of you describing yourself as the Son Of God there, either. Now who's blaspheming?"*

At this he smiles enigmatically and I am disturbed despite myself.

JCoN: "We are all that, Simon. Each of us is a divine creation inhabiting a temporary envelope of flesh on its journey through time. The world is cruel and we become brutalised and cruel with it. Forgetting and ignoring our true divine origins."

SMI: *"Was that the Persian Magi or the Egyptian Atenites talking?"*

JCoN: "Prince Siddhartha, I believe."

SMI: *"The Fat Guy In The Sky, that's what they call him colloquially over in Cathay and the nastier parts of Khmer. Mind you, most of that really transcendent stuff is available in the scrolls kept in the Lower Catacomb at Alexandria, just beneath the place where old Didymus used to keep the quality literary porno stash. Don't suppose Patriarch Playmate Catamite Philo told you youngsters about that."*

JCoN: "Again you intermix the sacred and the indecent with unexampled skill, Simon."

SMI: "*You're not the son of God.*"

JCoN: "I am a man given gifts such as you have. Both of us have been given the knowledge and understanding and opportunity to do good. You have succumbed to the hunger for power and the lure of Mammon. This will not lead you to a lasting glory."

SMI: "*In fact I could introduce you to Mammon himself, if you like. I conjured Him up once when I was having a particularly difficult time with Tiberius' spies in Athens last year.*"

JCoN: "I think not. Enough of his influence is evident even at the Temple here in Jerusalem."

SMI: "*I've also got stuff you could use against Joseph Caiaphas that would break him in half. Raise the mob and the zealots up together howling for his blood.*"

JCoN: "Joseph Caiaphas has a role of his own to play."

SMI: "*Potions? Aphrodisiacs? Drugs?*"

JCoN: "Not today, thank you."

SMI: "*Judea isn't big enough for both of us. There is more to this than you know.*"

JCoN: "Simon, the age of the Great Goddess passing, which we both sense, does not mean her death. And you cannot serve both her and the Evil One."

Not again.

SMI: "*How did we get from the Gnosis and its threat to you and your followers all the way to a mythical being like that?*"

JCoN: "Your Lunar temple is unquestionably a shrine to Her. The lotus symbolism cunningly worked into the sculpture-work of the atrium told me this at once. I did quite like the subtle touch that all the lamps in the place were intentionally on the model of the lamp of the Muse

Clio."

SMI: "…*uh, you're overstating it but there are some details in there like that, yes. And why not, the place celebrates knowledge and the light of reason too.*"

JCoN: "It is a place of darkness. Much worse a darkness than that which the Great Goddess illuminates in Her many incarnations. I and my followers do not seek to destroy Her, Simon."

SMI: "*You lie, I've heard all your priests declaiming against the old ways.*"

JCoN: "The old ways serve us no longer. The Roman empire is only the latest and most powerful incarnation of a profound slavery of the human body and imagination in materialism and worship of money. If the spirit of humanity is to flower there must be a new hope for the future that can envision a better way."

SMI: "*You're a puerile fool. We have only the present. Every day from dawn until dusk is a fight for survival for mankind. The common herd will never be lifted out of it. They are not worthy to be lifted out of it. Matters were always thus in our world and it is ordained to always be.*"

JCoN: "No, Simon. Humanity itself has created the impasse we currently inhabit. Hope for the future must be towards a state in which we are not perpetually frightened and oppressed and forever turning upon each other."

SMI: "*Man is predatory. We were so in the wilderness long before civilisation appeared. This is the rightful and established order of things. It gives order to our lives.*"

JCoN: "Civilisation is good and necessary yes, but it need not be predatory in this way."

SMI: *"No other way is possible, boy. You have to decide to feed yourself today. Claptrap about hope and tomorrow could be a better day will just get you into beggary and the early grave of the mendicant."*

JCoN: "Change is difficult from one form of philosophy to another. It is a thing of centuries. But I believe the soul of humanity can be healed from its current affliction. Or collectively we will forever be imprisoned within the lies of irrational superstition and materialism and mutual hatred."

SMI: *"Hatred. Now there's something I understand. You talk grandly of idealism and the love of Man. But you still resolutely keep my son captive with whatever hypnosis you employ while claiming you do it for the greater good. Stone the crows boy; I'm going to get you crucified if I can."*

JCoN: "And how would that help you in the here and now?"

SMI: *"Removing a threat and making an example they will fear."*

JCoN: "As with John the Baptist?"

SMI: *"Him again! Goddam it, he paid the price for insulting a king. It was Herod's stupid and incompetent folly like the rest of his reign as Rome's little pet jackal!"*

JCoN: "We both know your role. So enfolded are you in your own lies you are hardly aware of their contradictions of themselves. Having made a victim of me if you were successful in your machinations, who would be next?"

SMI: *"Well, your followers of course. But once their leader is gone they'll just turn away from you and fall apart. Factions will break up your movement and it won't take long to drive wedges between them once you're down in the cold, cold ground where you belong.*"

He smiles at me almost sadly.

JCoN: "And when you succeed with all of that, what of Judas?"

SMI: "*He will inherit all I have built.*"

JCoN: "Including the demons of your temple?"

SMI: "*Everything. But before that I will make him choose of his own free will between us to show you that your hold on him was nothing more than the lies of a pretentious charlatan.*"

JCoN: "Your opportunity to do this has come."

He gestures and I see Judas himself entering the tavern, dusty and tired but elated. He is with several other of the Nazarene's accursed disciples whom I recognise. Pious Peter is among them, one I really hate for rebuking me not long ago in Samaria. Darkness has fallen outside in the meantime. Judas looks around but sees neither of us initially since we are away from the dim light of the lamps.

Some high spirited conversation ensues. Cheery words pass between him and the disciples who have been here all evening. Then he does catch sight of the Nazarene and rushes over gladly, stopping dead in his tracks when he recognises me sitting there also.

SMI: "*Hullo; Son.*"

JUDAS ISCARIOT: "I...what are you doing here?"

SMI: "*Is that how you show the respect due your father and lord?*"

JI: "My lord, my master, my brother, I cannot meet him here. Not in front of the brethren. Forgive my rudeness but I cannot remain."

Judas hastens away before I can react. I make to rise and rush out after him. Incredibly however the Nazarene puts a gentle restraining hand on my own. Against my own will I feel my impetus to demoniac fury subside and I remain in the stark tavern silence that follows my action.

Unhurriedly he makes a sign of peace to his disciples and all returns to normal.

SMI: "*He dares. In public he dares defy me!*"

JCoN: "Judas appears to have made his decision."

SMI: "*Truly you have bewitched him. I suppose I can hardly be surprised.*"

JCoN: "No, Simon. Judas is a man torn apart. Of all my disciples he is both the most gifted and remains the most divided within himself. Ultimately he will face the hardest decisions and make perhaps the greatest sacrifice of all of us. Know this, however. Implicitly I trust him."

SMI: "*Then you're an even greater fool, Nazarene. Judas is weak and will always be weak. Had he not been possessed he would have accomplished nothing but a dreary mediocrity and I have no pity in me for that. He will fail you in a worse way than he has failed me.*"

JCoN: "Those do not sound the words of a caring father."

SMI: "*Damn you boy; what would you know of raising children?!*"

JCoN: "Enough not to possess them of devils, sorcerer."

That does it. I leave the booth and that maddeningly imperturbable Nazarene conniver behind me. Push strenuously through the pious crowd of the tavern, driving them back with a special look I reserve for my worst moods among my followers and house servants.

For a moment I watch the tableau as I briefly turn in the cramped doorway. Utter devotion to him is on their faces. Fanatical devotion to his merest word. I see not a trace of weakness or the indecisive among them.

Judas is nothing but a mass of indecision and weakness. He is also perhaps the Nazarene's greatest friend and trusted confidant from what the man himself has just unwisely and inexplicably told me. And I know how or can find the way to break Judas, treasurer of the Nazarene; for he is mine.

I go out into the crowded and noisy Jerusalem night. A new and peculiarly simple plan is forming in my mind. Replacing all those monstrously complicated and unpromising stratagems and complicated plots and unlikely conspiracies of before.

Knew those would not work. One plan is clear now with a single instrument which only I control. It will involve simply Joseph Caiaphas otherwise.

And Judas.

# AD 1305
# *Death of a Parfait*
## *Terry Wijesuriya*

The sun was slowly climbing to its zenith. An eagle wheeled far away, over the valley. Another came into sight from the scattered clouds. As Pierre watched, more eagles came into view, circling and dipping around a particular place. He whistled sharply, and his dog ran around to join him.

"Keep an eye on them," he said, nodding at the eagles. The dog barked as if to show it understood, and sat at attention on a low outcrop of rock overlooking the herd. Pierre leant back again and rested his head on his hands. He was a man of average height, in his mid-twenties, lean and made of untiring muscle. His black hair curled around his head, and his tanned, clean-shaven face was defined by his sharp nose and wide mouth, that habitually split in a big smile. He let his mind wander, keeping both ears open for any variation in the sounds his sheep made, as they grazed their way slowly along the mountainside. The day was heating up, and Pierre was grateful for the rough shade afforded by the scrubby trees he sat near.

He was almost dozing when he heard a shout from across the ridge. "Pierre!" a voice called. "Pierre Maury!"

He sat up. "What is it?" he called back.

"It is your turn to make the pie," the voice came again. "And quickly, I am starving!"

"You are always starving, Jean-Magre," Pierre said, good-humouredly, as he came to his feet and started for the hut. As he walked, he glanced to where the eagles had circled. They still remained there, not getting closer to the ground. Pierre's gaze dropped to the mountain track that came up from the village. A man was climbing slowly up the winding path. He was undoubtedly heading for the shepherd's hut, as there was nothing else up there, except perhaps the path to the Spanish side of the mountains. Pierre watched him for a bit, then headed into the hut to collect the ingredients for the pie he would make, enough for his group and the man who was coming visiting them.

The pie was cooked by the time the man had climbed up near the hut. Jean-Magre and Jean-Gros left their flocks with the dogs and joined them on the flat area where the hut was sited. The shepherds eyed the man with interest. He was a stranger to them, a fairly uncommon occurrence for their society. His clothes were not new, but they were made of the best material. His hands were beautifully shaped, free from marks of hard labour and slightly ink-stained. His fair hair fell around an open, friendly face, and he had a small, neatly-trimmed golden beard. He presented a stark contrast to the shepherds, dressed in their coarse garments with sun-tanned faces and darker hair. The two Jeans presented a humorous contrast, Jean-Magre short and thin, with a small moustache, and Jean-Gros tall and big, capable of picking up one fully-grown sheep under each enormous arm.

"Friend, you're welcome to share this pie with us," Pierre said, sitting down on the ground with the pie.

"I thank you," the stranger said, sitting down with alacrity. The others didn't blame him, there was nothing to whet the appetite like the mountain air and the smell of one of Pierre Maury's famed pies. They all ate, sitting in companionable silence. Jean-Magre was on his third piece of pie when the stranger finished eating, took out a linen handkerchief and wiped his lips. He drank some of the wine Jean-Gros passed him, and then looked expectantly around the company.

"I came up from the village," he said.

"Oh yes," Pierre Maury nodded. "And was all well there?"

The man sighed. "It was not," he said, finally. "The parfait has been murdered."

The shepherds received the news in shocked silence. "The goodman who lived with Raymonde Laborde?" Jean-Magre asked.

"The same," the man said.

The shepherds exchanged glances. Pierre turned to the man again. "Pardon me, but we do not know your name," he said.

"I am Francois Duval," the man said.

"And you are not from Occitanie," Pierre asked, but it was more of a statement.

"Indeed not," Francois agreed. "I am from up north. Just passing through, as I go on pilgrimage."

Pierre nodded. "To Santiago di Compostela?" he asked.

"Yes, as a matter of fact," Francois said.

"You will pardon these questions, but the parfait was known to us," Pierre said.

"Quite," said Francois. "In these days we cannot always speak openly about that which we most wish to discuss," he said, looking out over the valley. He seemed to miss the quick glance shared among the shepherds.

"So, you too understand the need to be, shall we say, circumspect about certain matters?" Pierre asked. The two Jeans leant forward, eager to hear the scholar's answer.

"Of course," Francois said, turning back towards them. "There are those in the big towns, and even here in your village, who do not see things the same way we do."

"Oh," said Pierre. "You need not worry about our village, everyone is of the true faith except the old woman who owns this flock, and she will not bring the inquisitors on us."

Francois seemed mildly surprised. "Have you no priest, then?" he asked.

"We share the one from the village in the next valley," Jean-Magre explained.

"Now tell us more about the parfait's death," Pierre requested.

"He was killed, stabbed in the heart by night as he lay in Raymonde Laborde's house," Francois said.

Pierre shook his head, sadly. "Who would kill the goodman?" he asked.

"They do not know, in the village. They said that the parfait had been up to visit you in the past week, and perhaps you would know something about it." Francois said, watching the shepherds keenly, though he managed to seem disinterested.

The shepherds exchanged another glance.

"I should go down to attend to matters," Pierre said.

It was on the tip of Francois' tongue to ask what matters Pierre would have to see to, but he choked the question back, afraid of making Pierre suspicious. Pierre turned to Francois. "Will you be returning to the village?" he asked.

Francois thought for a moment. "Yes, I will," he said. "I will delay my pilgrimage until this matter is cleared up." "That is very generous of you, to do such a thing for a man you do not know," Pierre praised. For an instant, Francois feared that the shepherd had tumbled to the truth about the fictitious pilgrimage, but then he saw that Pierre was being sincere. Being a man who wouldn't hesitate to give his entire wealth to a friend or stranger in need, Pierre naturally attributed such altruism to those he met.

"Let us go down the mountain as soon as we can, then," Pierre proposed. "I will return, Jeans, once things are settled to our satisfaction."

"We will head south, Pierre Maury, you may join us there. Bring Pierre Laborde if he has recovered," Jean-Gros said.

⊠⊖⊠

Dusk caught them as they descended the mountain. Francois wanted to stop for the night, afraid of missing his footing in the dark, but Pierre assured him of his help and friendlily encouraged him down the mountain. They were at a particularly tricky stretch, with far too many loose stones and opportunities to break his leg for Francois' liking, when all of a sudden, they heard a sound behind them. Pierre looked up quickly, frowning. There was no moon, and the stars gave just enough faint light for Francois to see Pierre's expression. He also turned, but could make out nothing on the black mountainside. There was a quiet rumbling sound, and Pierre said, "Get off the path."

He spoke quietly and unhurriedly, but something in his voice made Francois scramble to obey. The rumbling grew louder. Francois missed his step and landed heavily on his twisted foot. He made no sound other than a quick intake of breath, but Pierre realized what had happened and came back. He half-carried, half-dragged Francois further away from the road, with the rumbling sound growing louder.

"Is it an avalanche?" Francois asked, gasping with pain as they hurried along. "Rockslide," Pierre said. He stopped when they reached a large rock which jutted out of the mountainside. As they stood in its shelter, the rockslide reached them. The main direction of the slide seemed to be the road, and they remained out of danger in their shelter. Pierre knelt down and felt Francois' ankle, wrapping it up tightly with a length of cloth he tore from the edge of his tunic. The pain eased, and Francois accepted the food Pierre handed him from his satchel. They slept sitting under the rock, for Pierre said it was too dangerous to venture out in case the rockslide hadn't ended.

At dawn the next morning, Pierre slipped out of the shelter without waking Francois. When Francois emerged, he looked in disbelief at where the road had been. It was a litter of stones, completely impassable. Pierre had climbed up, and was frowning.

"How shall we get down?" Francois called, waving at Pierre. Agile as a mountain goat, Pierre came leaping down the stones. "There is something funny about this rockslide," he said, reaching Francois.

"Like what?" Francois asked. Pierre shook his curly head, still frowning.

"We shall have to use one of the sheep tracks," he said. "It's not a hard matter, but it will take some time. Can you walk?"

Francois found that he could hobble along slowly, and they set off.

ᗧᗤ

Pierre Maury and Francois reached the village in the late afternoon. Life was going on as usual, despite the death of the parfait. They stopped at the house of Pierre's brother, ate a meal with his family, and then made their way to the house of Raymonde Laborde. Her brother, Pierre, also a shepherd, sat outside. He had been ill and thus unable to go into the mountains with the flocks as usual. He had a long lugubrious face, heavy brows and moustache, and eyes that seemed sunken into his face.

"Pierre Maury!" he cried, catching sight of his friend.

"Pierre Laborde!" Pierre called. "We have just heard the sad news."

Pierre Laborde did not look too sad. "He was no good for my sister," he said. "But one must not speak ill of the dead."

"Who could have done such a thing?" Pierre Maury asked. Laborde looked shifty, and, casting a suspicious glance at Francois, who remained slightly out of earshot and seemed to not be listening, whispered something to Pierre.

Pierre was suitably shocked. "What? Inside your sister's house?" he exclaimed.

Laborde nodded, gravely.

"Let me tell Francois," Pierre said. Catching Laborde's frown, he hastened to reassure him. "Francois too is a true believer. You need not fear him."

Francois came forward and Pierre introduced the two men.

"My sister has just discovered," Laborde said, "that the parfait had much money hidden under the floor of the bedroom."

"I thought that parfaits were not supposed to have worldly possessions," Francois said, puzzled.

"They are not," Laborde said. "This man was no goodman, he used his position to ask money from everyone. And in this village, we have suckers enough who gave their all to him."

Pierre looked suddenly guilty, and turned away slightly.

"You needn't hide your face, Pierre Maury, we know that you gave him all the money you owned," Laborde said. Pierre blushed. Francois looked at him with renewed interest.

"Yet," he said, "it is good to tithe to the ch-goodmen."

Laborde shook his head. "It is good to help people," he corrected. "But these men, the goodmen and the churchmen, they only have greed in their bellies. They use the power of God to threaten and blackmail all the people who have nothing."

"Don't say that, Pierre Laborde! The parfait taught us many things, and if he wanted some money in return, what is that?" Pierre said.

"It's alright for you, Pierre Maury." Laborde said. "You only have yourself to please, and that girl in the village across the mountains when you visit her. There are others in this village who cannot afford the money they have given to the parfait."

"So do you think it could have been one of these people who murdered the parfait?" Francois asked.

Pierre's eyes widened. "Now, that is an idea," he said, glancing admiringly at Francois.

Laborde shrugged. "It could be," he said, noncommittally.

"We should ask whether anyone noticed anything unusual, or if anyone held a grudge against the parfait," Francois suggested. He bounced on the balls of his feet, eager to get moving.

"A grudge against the parfait?" Pierre asked, wonderingly.

"Yes," Laborde said. "I know who to start with- the priest. He will come visiting soon."

"How do you know?" Francois asked.

Laborde looked cagey. "Oh, he is a great friend of Bartolomeu Leclerq. He often comes to take a meal." Francois nodded. "Let's talk to him. Did he by any chance hold a grudge against the parfait for having heret- I mean, different ideas from him?"

Pierre threw his head back and laughed uproariously. "The priest? No, no, not he."

Even Laborde gave a small smile.

Francois looked from one to the other, puzzled, but neither offered to explain matters so he smiled as well.

❂❂❂

The priest was being entertained at Bartolomeu Leclerq's house, so it was to there that the three men repaired. They heard the party long before they reached the house, and all three entered. The Leclerq family, the priest and three other villagers sat around the room, eating many different foods, the aromas of which rose up to tantalize the newcomers.

"Pierre Maury! Pierre Laborde!" Bartolomeu called. "And a friend we do not yet know! Sit and join us," he said.

Pierre introduced Francois, and the three men helped themselves to food.

The conversation, which had been animated, flagged and died down as the local men and women and the priest eyed Francois, doubtfully.

"Oh!" said Pierre, at last noticing the change in atmosphere. "Francois too is one of us. You can speak freely in front of him."

At once, it seemed as if everyone in the room relaxed. "Let us continue," the priest said, but he watched Francois with narrowed eyes.

"If God is so good, how can there be evil in the world?" Bernadeta, Bartolomeu's wife, asked.

"The parfait told me that that is because there are two gods," one of the village men explained.

Francois forgot to eat, leaning forward and drinking in the conversation instead.

Pierre interrupted. "You know that I too enjoy these discussions, and I knew what the parfait taught," he began. "But we want to know about the parfait's death."

A more effective way to stop the conversation couldn't have occurred to Pierre if he had tried.

Everyone looked at Pierre. Bernadeta shook her head. "He was killed by a stranger to the village," she said, with an air of finality.

"Has a stranger come to the village?" Pierre countered.

The priest cleared his throat. "He has," he said, lifting a hand and pointing at Francois.

There was another silence, and Pierre ate a bit faster so he could get as much food inside him before the fight he believed was inevitable broke out.

Before anyone could say anything, however, the door opened and a lady, dressed in widow's clothes and looking angry, came in.

"Is this the home of Bartolomeu Leclerq?" she demanded.

"I am he, your ladyship. Why do you wish to see me?" Bartolomeu said courteously, stepping forward.

"I have come to this... village... because a parfait has been killed," she said, haughtily.

"That is so," Bartolomeu said, but he seemed puzzled.

"I have come because I am his lawfully wedded wife, and any property he has left behind is now mine."

∞∞

Pierre Maury, Pierre Laborde, and Francois sat outside Raymonde Laborde's house. She came outside, almost threw some bread and cheese at them, and then returned into the house.

"She is upset about the wife," Laborde said, apologetically.

The men chewed in silence for a while. "The lady last night said she hated the parfait," Pierre said, reflectively.

"My sister was also on her way to that feeling," Laborde said.

Francois swallowed the last of his cheese and sighed. "It seems to me, that the question is not who wanted the parfait dead, but who *didn't* want him dead!"

"Basically," Laborde said, listing things on his fingers, "it could have been a villager who felt he had cheated them out of their money, it could have been a churchman who wanted him out of the way, it could have been this lady from the city, it could have been an old enemy he made before he came here. It could have been anyone."

"It could have been your sister, or your sister's husband," Francois said.

Laborde sat very still. "She left her husband years ago," he said, gazing fixedly at the chickens which had come out to peck at worms across the road.

"He might still feel anger or jealousy," Francois said, mildly.

Laborde said nothing for a while. Then he swung on Francois. "How do you know she was married?" he demanded. "You are not from around here."

Francois seemed taken aback at the ferocity with which Laborde asked his question. "I, uh, heard someone speak of it the other day," he said.

Laborde's eyes narrowed. He turned away again. Then he abruptly got up and left, swinging off down the road.

Francois and Pierre watched him go. "Did I upset him?" Francois asked.

Pierre turned to him, surprised, and then laughed. "Oh, that is rich!" he said, shaking with laughter. "You are a one. You make a man upset and then you ask so mildly if you have upset him!"

Francois was discomfited by Pierre's laughter. He wasn't sure whether the man was angry or not. It took a few more moments for him to realize that the shepherd found the situation genuinely funny.

Francois looked at him, and finally, reluctantly, grinned back, a little shame-faced.

"I didn't mean to," he explained. "I only was listing possible suspects."

Pierre shook his head. "He is overprotective of his sister," he told Francois. "That is why he reacts badly. Let's follow him, and you can beg his forgiveness." He came to his feet and set off down the road in the direction taken by Laborde.

As they walked, a little boy came running up to them, and spoke to Pierre. "Your brother Jean wishes to see you in the sheep pen," he said. "He said for you to wait there for him."

"Alright," said Pierre, changing the direction of his steps. "Will you come with me, Francois?"

"I think I'll go and search for Pierre Laborde," the scholar said. The little boy shook his head. "No, Jean Maury wants to speak with you as well, sir," he said.

Francois was puzzled. "Are you sure?" he asked.

"Of course!" the little boy said, and then he ran off.

"That's a bit funny," Francois commented, as he and Pierre strolled in the direction of the sheep pens. The pens, which held the sheep when they were brought back to the village, were located at the far end of town, beyond the last houses. "Why should your brother wish to see me as well, and why meet us here when we could meet at his house?"

Pierre shrugged. "It is probably some whim of his," he said, airily. "Jean is always acting on whims."

They reached the pens. They were deserted. There was a small shed built at one end, and the two men went to it and stood by it, waiting for Jean.

Suddenly, Francois felt uneasy. "There's something wrong here, Pierre," he said, quietly.

"It must be just our imaginations," Pierre said, also sounding concerned.

The next moment, something struck the side of the shed right near Francois' head. They turned to look, and saw a gleaming knife, thrown with such force that it had sunk three inches into the wood.

"Get down!" Francois said, shoving Pierre down and following him so that the slats of the pen provided some cover.

They lay there for a few minutes, but no other knives came.

Finally, Francois knelt cautiously and looked around. Nothing happened, so he came to his feet and began searching the area for any clue of their assailant. There was nothing. He turned to return to the village itself. "Come on, Pierre," he called.

"But Jean wanted us to meet him here," Pierre said.

"I think that was a plan to lure us out here," Francois said. "Let's go to Jean's house and ask him if he ever sent that message."

Jean expressed surprise when he heard of the spurious message. He said that he had never asked them to meet him, and, moreover, why would he ask them to meet him at the sheep pens when they could have met at his house?

Pierre and Francois went out to the river where the children played, and soon found the small boy who'd brought them the message. "Who told you to bring that message?" Francois asked him.

"Jean Maury, of course," the boy said, impatient to return to his swim.

"Did Jean Maury come and ask you himself to bring that message to us?" Pierre asked.

The boy screwed up his face in an effort to remember. "No, not him," he admitted. "It was someone else who told me that Jean Maury wanted to see you."

"Who was it?" Pierre asked.

"Why, the priest," the boy said, and as Pierre and Francois looked at each other, he skipped away and rejoined his friends.

∞

"Why would the priest want to kill us?" Pierre asked, as he and Francois walked through the fields to the village. Francois shook his head. "I haven't the slightest idea. Maybe it wasn't him?"

"Someone tried to kill us on the mountain," Pierre said, casually, as if mentioning last year's wool yield.

"What?" Francois yelped.

"Yes, the rockslide was started by someone. Natural rockslides come in a different way," the shepherd explained.

"But why? Who?" Francois asked.

Pierre shrugged. He cast a longing glance up at the mountains behind the village. Their tops were golden in the evening sun, and he could catch glimpses of the sheep on their slopes.

"I lift mine eyes to the mountaintops, whence will come my deliverance," Francois said, under his breath, following Pierre's gaze.

Pierre turned to him. "That is true, is it not? The deliverance which comes from the mountains," he said, sighing contentedly.

Francois was startled. "Actually, the deliverance comes from God. God is on the mountaintops," he said.

"But don't you think that God *is* the mountaintops?" Pierre inquired, ingenuously.

Francois felt uneasy. "That sounds like a bit of a misunderstanding," he began. Then he caught sight of Laborde on the path in front of them. He faced two men on horseback. Francois recognized the two men and began running. Pierre did not, but also ran. They reached the three men.

"Ah, Francois," the older man on horseback said. He had a grey beard, and wore the robes of a priest.

"Your Grace," Francois said, bowing.

"Your Grace?" Pierre asked, astonished. "This man is the Bishop?"

The bishop glanced at Pierre. Then he turned back to Francois, dismissing the shepherd.

"Have you done what you came here to do?" he inquired.

Francois was very conscious of Pierre and Laborde's eyes on him.

"We wondered why you took so long to return," the bishop continued, his eagle eyes boring into Francois'.

"Er, yes, your Grace," he stammered. "I will report to you later."

"See you do," the bishop said.

"Excuse me, sir," Pierre addressed the bishop, who was turning his horse to leave. "Did you send Francois to investigate the parfait's murder? That is very good of you, to take trouble for a man you did not know."

Laborde made a move towards Pierre, as if to stop him from talking. Francois had turned pale.

"My good man!" the bishop said, hardly liking to look at Pierre. "Pere Francois is here to find all the heretics."

The horses cantered away.

✂✂✂

Laborde found Pierre halfway up the mountain. He was sitting on a rock, staring into space across the dusk-filled bowl of the valley. Laborde sat down heavily next to him, and tried to control his breathing. "You are not well," Pierre said, concerned. "You should not have come up here."

"You ran so fast," Laborde complained.

Pierre seemed to remember, and turned anguish-filled eyes towards him. "I have betrayed everyone in the village," he whispered. "We will all be heretics and some will be burnt."

Laborde said nothing, for what Pierre said was true.

"However," he said suddenly, "it was Francois- Pere Francois- who betrayed our trust. He led us to believe that he too believed as we do."

Pierre shook his head in dumb suffering. "It is on me," he said, brokenly. "I told everyone he was safe. Everyone."

Laborde shook his head. "I think you may have been right," he said.

"How?" asked Pierre.

Laborde shrugged. "It is just an idea."

They sat in silence.

"So what will you do now?" Laborde asked.

"Join the Jeans," Pierre said, promptly. "My sheep need me."

"I'm heading back to the village," Laborde said. "And since you yourself accepted blame for telling Pere Francois all this, maybe you should also return, to see what can be done."

Pierre sighed. Then he got to his feet. "Let's go," he said, holding out a hand to Laborde.

Just before they got to the village, a small boy came running up to them. "Pierre! Pierre! The man Francois has been stabbed! He asks for you!"

The Pierres looked at each other. They broke into a run.

Francois lay on the road, surrounded by villagers. Bernadeta was tending to his wound, stanching the flow of blood with cloths. Pierre dropped to his knees by Francois' head.

"Francois- my friend. Who has done this?" he cried. Before Francois could reply, the priest stepped forward.

"I did," he said. The crowd gasped. "I have tried to kill that man twice before," he added. The crowd gasped harder.

"Because that man is a stinking priest! He is a spy of the church! And he killed the parfait."

There was stunned silence. Francois was gasping in pain, but still managed to ask, "But you yourself are a priest, are you not?"

"I am a priest, but I have discovered the truth! I believe in the two gods," the priest said.

Francois smiled. "Finally," he said, tiredly. "It makes sense." He slowly closed his eyes. Then he reopened them. "But I tell you this, priest. I did not kill the parfait. Was it not you who killed him?"

The priest frowned. "I did not. I swear by the two gods-"

"Yes, alright," Francois interrupted. "I guess we are no closer to knowing the truth. Perhaps we will never know who killed him."

"Will he die?" Pierre asked Bernadeta, quietly.

"No, it is a flesh wound. He will be weak but he will recover," she told him.

"That's too good for the likes of him," the priest shouted. The crowd began to stir and mutter.

Jean Maury spoke up. "We only have the word of the priest that he is in fact a spy from the church," he said.

The priest looked black as thunder. "There are witnesses," he growled. "Pierre Maury, will you swear that this man is not a spy of the church?"

The crowd held its collective breath. Pierre Maury was an honest man, and he had never lied. Whatever he said would have great weight.

Pierre came to his feet. He met the eyes of the priest, on the opposite side of the crowd.

"This man," he said, pointing at Francois, "is not a spy of the church. He will recover and then he will continue his pilgrimage to Santiago di

Compostela. He will not return to the bishop yet, and when he does, he will not report anything because he did not notice anything."

The crowd was impressed. They slowly began dispersing.

Francois opened his eyes again and met Pierre's. He smiled gently, and then fainted away.

◈

Laborde accompanied Pierre up the mountain the next day. They bid each other farewell, for it would be a good six months before Pierre and the other shepherds returned to the village.

"Is Raymonde better now?" Pierre asked.

"Yes," Laborde said. "The lady agreed to return some of the villagers' money, and Raymonde has enough for herself." He paused. "Her life is much better now that he is gone," he added.

Pierre nodded, sympathetically.

"He beat her, did he not?" he asked.

Laborde's face darkened. "He tortured her," he spat.

Something in his tone made Pierre look at his face. He understood something he had not seen all this time.

"Yes," he said, hoisting his satchel onto his shoulder. "Her life is much better now that he is gone."

He shook Laborde's hand and turned, climbing up the mountain into the sun.

—oOo—

**Author's Note:** This story was inspired by, and based on *Montaillou: Cathars and Catholics in a French village, 1294-1324* by Emmanuel Le Roy Ladurie, trans. Barbara Bray (Penguin, 1980)

# AD 1540

## *The Queen's Judgement*

### *Frances Stratford*

Thomas Cromwell, Chancellor of England

March, 1540

No clock is more regular than the stomach and it was time for my midday meal, yet King Henry VIII insists justice moves by its own dial. So, as a good crown servant, Chancellor of England, and a score of other stolen offices, I arranged today's hearings in the Star Chamber at Westminster Palace as he asked.

Country-dwellers milled about the hall in a swirl of rough cloth and barnyard smells, craning their necks up at the blue ceiling with its spatter of gold stars that give the chamber its name. They spoke in hushed tones and gawped at King Henry and Queen Anne.

Peasants.

I shifted my bulk and willed myself not to yawn. The court sits only for today, I reminded my grumbling belly. The king rides out tomorrow and the Chamber will be closed.

Henry VIII sat enthroned underneath his purple and gold canopy, wearing his smug smile of power. The king enjoyed this theater of fairness. Peasants knew the Star Chamber as a place where any member of the kingdom can come and petition for justice if local authorities fail. Yet many rightly feared the justice meted out here because the Star Chamber sat without a jury. That left the law to darkness and to me.

Over the noise of the press, the king called, "What case next, Master Cromwell? My new queen is most interested in how the law works in England."

A lesser man would find the king's bonhomie grating. As a good servant, I endured all.

That is, I endured all except his new wife. Queen Anne looked at me, her homely face smiling.

I shuddered to think of the wager I had made and lost on her when I advocated the Cleves marriage.

The king respects beauty.

The queen had none.

Truly, the king's codpiece was more sacred than any cathedral I had stripped of its wealth. I knew now not to meddle with its contents. Anne of Cleves will have to go the way of the others if I was to retain my favor. I passed many judgments and careers in the Star Chamber. She was no different.

I pulled my miniver furred robe closer and scanned the paperwork, my assistant, Ben Paget handed me. "Your Highness," I kept my voice sepulchral, "the next case is Selwyn versus Meverell. The law that the Selwyn's are using to sue is the 'Statute against the taking of women' from 1487'."

The bailiff called the Selwyn family—mother, father, jilted betrothed, and daughter—and the abductor Gregory Meverell to the bar. There was a gasp as the jostling crowd caught sight of Agnes Selwyn. Her face was splattered with a greenish-yellow bruise that extended up to her eye. Even I, a man who had served as a mercenary in the Italian wars, stared for a moment. My assistant, Paget, prodded me by handing me the documents that contained the legal precedent.

I cleared my throat and addressed the hall, "The law states that the nearest male relatives of abducted women have the right to sue for felony abduction. The defendant, Gregory Meverell, attests that he and Agnes Selwyn were married. The plaintiffs, Agnes's parents and her betrothed, state that Meverell illegally removed her from the Selwyn home. Since Agnes Selwyn is her father's property, the Selwyn family now brings suit against Gregory Meverell for rape and abduction."

The queen, dressed in heavy crimson and silver brocade, looked at the king and asked. "Why this case here?"

King Henry raised his voice to address the room. He had a deep baritone that hushed the crowd. Even the reeking laborers stopped shifting and stood still. "My father, Henry VII, first of our dynasty, was very wise. If the local authorities cannot provide justice, the case comes to the crown in the Star Chamber."

The crowd cheered in praise of the king. Even the queen's newest little page, a street imp she had rescued, raised his cap. The bailiffs had to shout and waive their halberds to quiet the mob.

"The case also comes to the king because the family also owns lands jointly in Norfolk and in Essen in Cleves. Agnes Selwyn is heir sole to the properties." I added.

"*Ja*," The queen put her hand over the king's meaty paw. "This is good."

Henry VIII smiled at his queen, his blue eyes sparkly as the gems in his cap. You could almost believe he didn't hate her, for the kindness he showed her in public.

But I knew better. Behind Queen Anne's back he had given gifts of furs, jewels, and even land to Mistress Kat Howard…. Rather than play at justice here in the Star Chamber, the queen should stick to the needlework she loved so much. Only then might she avoid the fate of the other unwanted wives before her.

Always one to put on a good show, King Henry declared, "For the queen's mercy, we would like to know more of this case."

I nodded. "According to the law male guardians—that includes husbands, fathers, and fiancé—are guaranteed they regain any loss of power over the abducted woman's body. After all, her body is theirs to dispose of as they see fit."

A gap-toothed man in the crowd murmured his agreement, saying the king's law is just. A lady beside him, in a linen cap and stained apron, shook her head and retorted "For who?" in a thick northern accent.

I continued. "Forcible abduction and marriage, such as Master Meverell is accused of, may nullify the betrothal contract and transfer ownership of," I ran a finger down the parchment, "Agnes Selwyn to Gregory Meverell from her father and fiancé William Brewster."

Susan Selwyn, the mother, cried out. "My daughter! You ruined her pretty face!"

Meverell roared, "You lie!"

The guards pressed their pikes into a few stomachs and called the room to order.

"Why was this case not done in the village?" the queen asked in her halting English.

I flipped through the crisp paper, translating in my head from Latin. "The land on which the crime took place was in dispute. The crown recently awarded the estate to Mistress Katherine Howard...." With the hopes the money will get her into the king's bed, I thought.

The queen nodded and looked fondly at Kat Howard who stood beside her throne.

*Jesu*, I groaned inwardly. She's as dull-witted as Thomas More after his beheading.

I turned to the witnesses. "Are you the Selwyn family?"

The wife stepped in front of her daughter and answered, "Yes, your lordship."

My assistant Ben Paget leaned forward and whispered, "She sent her accounting books showing service to the crown. Inside was a bribe."

I smiled. We would make quick work of this case. Good too because hunger had given me a grinding pain behind my eyes.

"I speak for the family," Goodwife Selwyn continued. "My husband speaks little English and has settled property on Agnes in both England and in Cleves. I gave both documents—the English and the German—to the good Chancellor's office."

I scanned my desk and saw this was so. I nodded at her to continue.

"This greedy monster broke my daughter's jaw when we gainsaid his marriage proposal!" She pointed with a reddened, trembling hand towards Meverell and pulled it back quickly. The jerking movement of her hand was odd. Must be a peasant affectation, I thought.

"Bring forward the betrothed," I demanded.

A small blond man with a pointed beard stepped forward. "I am William Brewster."

"Were you precontracted to Agnes Selwyn?" I asked in my severest voice. A voice that could make dukes tremble.

Rather than answer, Brewster shouted at the abductor. "You befouled my betrothed!"

"Shut your noise you! Answer the Chancellor!" the bailiff warned Brewster. The crowd laughed.

The king laughed as well at the bailiff's audacity. "And you, Sir Noise? Are you the lady's intended?"

"Yes, Your Majesty. And he," Brewster pointed to an exceptionally ugly man in the custody of a country constable, "stole my bride!"

Meverell was a hulk of a man with a shock of black hair and a face that looked as if it had been stitched together by a blind tailor's apprentice—color and proportions all mismatched. I had met a few like him in my younger days in military service. Before the Reformation— my Reformation—pocky priests taught that a man's evil soul showed in his appearance. In my military experience, men such as Meverell knew how ugly they were and had worked harder to prove themselves.

Meverell rose. "You lie! Your Majesty, I have evidence—"

The mother wailed loudly drowning Meverell out. The disputed bride, Agnes, cowered.

Even I, a man not known for his sympathy, could tell her weeping increased her pain.

The bailiffs yelled for quiet and pushed at the crowd with their staves.

Best to move this along. I picked up the scissors I always had at my desk and sliced open the sealed marriages contract between the fiancé Brewster and Agnes.

"My lord Cromwell," the queen asked looking towards the battered girl, "does she have *zwei*, I mean two marriage contracts?"

She did. The first contract her parents negotiated with Brewster was actually two documents, one in English and one in German. There could be some confusion there.

No matter. I got to keep the bribe either way.

"She does your Majesty," I answered. The crowd murmured excitedly and pressed forward towards the bar at this revelation.

My assistant Paget pointed to the marriage papers presented by her abductor, John Meverell. I read and saw all was in order for the Meverell marriage, signatures in the right place, witnesses, a priest even copied out their vows.

Paget leaned in and prompted me, "The 1487 law states that women must remain married to their abductors if the marriage was legal. Yet, if Agnes Selwyn had a precontract, the law might not consider her a single woman when Meverell stole her."

It was ambiguous legal ground. I looked up at Meverell who fumed in the bailiff's custody. He was so ugly, it was unlikely he would get a bride without stealing her.

Still, I believed it was a professional courtesy to rule in favor of those who bribed you.

"We are good servants of the crown, your Majesty," Goodwife Selwyn, disrupted my musings. "We are all neighbors, Brewster, Meverell, and us. Together, we provide food, ale, and mules for Your Majesty's army. By joining our family with Brewster, we hope to increase our service to our new leaseholder…..Mistress Howard."

Kat Howard preened, and the king looked towards her over the queen's head. He licked his lips, barely concealing his lust.

Inwardly, I smiled. Goodwife Selwyn came not to play.

"Do two contracts say same thing?" the queen asked, her syntax as broken as her marriage.

She's trying to be competent even with her limited English, I thought. Well, ability was a thing the king respects as much as beauty.

The goodwife answered the queen. "Your Majesty, Meverell wanted our girl and our business and would not take no for an answer. After the betrothal to Master Brewster was finalized, he stole our Agnes!"

"Does Mistress Agnes have a true precontract?" the king asked, his voice rising. Having at one time married his brother's widow, I knew Old Harry considered himself an expert on precontracts and how badly they could go wrong.

Meverell cried out, "All she has is mine now! She's my wife!"

"*Mein Esel!*" the father wailed in German. "*Mein Schatzi!*"

The queen perked up, hearing her native language. She looked to the king. "May I?"

King Henry waived his heavily ringed hand and nodded in assent. The crowd clapped and the king smiled at his own ability to stage manage the performance of justice.

Rapidly in German, the queen questioned the Selwyn father.

Goodwife Selwyn and Brewster exchanged panicked looks, or so it appeared to me.

Truly, the Star Chamber was more than some peasants could handle. All in all, Agnes Selwyn should be grateful that Brewster was still in the market for soiled goods.

The queen turned to the king. "This man bought the *esel,* I mean the mule, from my brother's stables."

The king nodded and stared hard at me. "Yes, there are many who prize mules from Flanders."

The queen continued. "He says the marriage contract is different—English is different from German. He is most worried about his….mule."

The king smile returned. "This must be a most regal beast!"

A ripple of laughter ran through the courtroom.

Goodwife Selwyn chimed in, "Your Majesty, our business provides sumpter mules for the crown's use." She cast a look at her cowering husband. "My husband has a prized mule from Neustadt that would be given over to Meverell—along with all of Agnes's dower goods if Meverell has his way."

The queen smiled down at the Selwyn father and said. "The mule is dear to him and will only let him and Agnes to come near."

The crowd laughed and I covered my face to hide my exasperation and protect it from the sight of the increasing chaos in the room. This was like a pantomime show at the market cross.

But I knew the king adored this type of theater. "Animals are great judges of character," he mused. "I would hear from Mistress Selwyn about her ordeal."

Goodwife Selwyn cried noisily. "Your Majesty, Meverell broke my girl's jaw. She cannot speak!"

"Your Majesty—I did not hurt her!" Meverell declared. The palace guard cuffed him about the head and silenced him.

The king held up his hand. The Star Chamber fell quiet.

"Your grace?" the queen broke the silence. "Mistress Howard is one of my household." Her speech was slow and porridge-thick. "May I read the papers in German? I would like to be a good servant to England, a good queen, and a good mistress to my ladies."

A wave of approval skimmed across the crowd.

The king looked pleased and rose from his throne. "An excellent suggestion! I will take Mistress Howard to dine and see what she knows of her new lands. You and my Lord Cromwell go to the Queen's Council chamber and read both documents. We will reconvene after."

Well, at least I would get my midday meal.

The herald of the Chamber declared the session over and people began to walk towards the door into the palace lobby.

Just then, I saw Agnes Selwyn push past the barrier that separated the king from the petitioners. She was a tiny thing and moved as quickly as an eel, in spite of her painful injuries. Before the palace guards realized it, she was at the queen's feet. The queen bent to lift the girl up. Agnes Selwyn's wordless cries rent the courtroom.

I sighed. If I had a groat for every crying girl who did not want to obey the abduction law and marry her ravisher, I could stop taking bribes altogether.

⊠⊠⊠

## James Burbage
## Queen Anne's Page

Agnes Selwyn had a flair for the dramatic, as the Master of Revels might say. As I pulled her up from the queen's slippers, she managed to say something like "mule." Or so it sounded through the shattered bone.

"Mule?" I whispered back.

She nodded frantically before her mother gathered her up and dragged her off.

*Jesu.* This little lady with two perhaps-husbands wanted only the queen to know the word "mule." I was loyal to her majesty above all, so only the queen would know.

I knew Queen Anne had a soft heart for those in need. Months ago, as she drove through London in all her finery, she heard me singing for ha'pennies. My no-longer-a-boy cracking voice caused many on the street to jeer at my song. Her heart went out to me, and she brought me into the royal household as her page. Every day, the queen smiled as she saw me scurry about the palace, plumper, happier, and pestering the Revel Master for a place on stage.

Thanks to Her Majesty, now I can help this lady with her smashed face and only a mule for a friend.

I spoke softly in Her Majesty's ear. "I think the mule has something to do with this," my changing voice squeaked, and the queen smiled.

"Find the mule in stables," the queen whispered back, not wanting Cromwell to hear. "Tell me what you find—*schnell.* The court returns soon!"

"I will question this ass most closely, your Majesty," happy to do her service.

As a boy working to become an actor, I had been much impressed with the theater today in the chamber. I could learn a thing or two from Goodwife Selwyn. Her exaggerated crying, her whirlwind yelling, and overdone gestures were perfect for pantomime shows at the market cross. The castle guards even played their part, hustling the still-declaiming Meverell out the west door.

The Revel Master, the man responsible for all the entertainment at the palace, told me that actors learn performance begins and ends with the feet. So, with delicate steps, I sidled up to the cook stall. There, Agnes, her mother, the jilted betrothed Brewster, and one of the constables that had accompanied them from Norfolk, had stopped at a pastry seller for bread and ale. The seller hawked his wares with a loud Cheshire accent, dispensing food with one beefy hand and taking coins with the other.

I squatted down unseen beside the hawker.

The Norfolk constable handed over three pennies for bread and cheese from the cook stall. No one asked Agnes if she wanted milk or ale, poor girl.

Goodwife Selwyn ripped angrily at her chunk of warm manchet bread with one hand, the other she held oddly against her stomach covered deep in her sleeve. Grinding away at the chewy crust she declared, "The shillings we sent to Master Cromwell were well spent. He swayed the king more upon our part—even though Meverell has good papers recording the marriage rites."

"What of the contract in German?" Brewster asked. "And why did your husband mention the mule?"

Agnes rolled her eyes. "He's as thick-witted as the queen! That's why we did not tell him. We should go to the stables. He rode here on that infernal mule. Likely, he has brought the other papers with—"

The cook stall owner bumped me from my crouch as the number of customers crowded in. I landed with a hard "oof" near the Norfolk constable's feet.

The constable eyed me suspiciously. "What are you doing here, boy?"

"I am most sorry!" I rose and smoothed my doublet, pretending I was a bored courtier rather than a green page. My decision to improvise and treat the world as a stage needed more scripting. I did not want to let the queen down on this, my first real part. "I came to find myself bread and ale. I am young and just learning my way around the palace."

Brewster narrowed his eyes and Goodwife Selwyn hissed. "Do not lie to me, boy!" She cast an angry look at her cowering daughter. "What did Agnes whisper to you, imp?"

I turned towards Agnes. A look of terror passed over what had once been a pretty girl's face.

No scene partner there.

I lied quickly to the goodwife. "Naught but her cry of despair ma'am. The queen was moved and would be most glad if I could be of service to you."

The constable and Brewster exchanged glances. "What are you to the queen, boy?" Brewster prodded.

I pulled myself up to my full height which, in truth, was not very impressive. "I am her most loyal page and apprentice reveler."

Brewster dismissed me with a wave. "Away you rogue, we have court business to discuss."

Brewster was partly right. I was a street singer and a rogue. But I was loyal to Queen Anne. Though she had not been in England long, our good queen made a favorable impression on everyone.

Except for the one person who mattered.

It was time to improvise again. The revel master also told me good actors knew to say "yes, and…"

"Yes, Master Brewster, I have a low position at court." I leaned in closer, "And as such, the queen knows I can move about without notice. She wishes me to watch over Meverell the accused. She is most concerned to see justice done for you."

Agnes Selwyn looked up, horror in her eyes. Goodwife Selwyn stared her down. Then she turned to me. "That is most gracious of the queen!"

The constable interjected. "My deputy has gone with Mr. Selwyn and the queen. There's a groat in it if you can find Meverell in this crowd." He tossed me a coin.

"He's likely gone to Southwark. That's where the stews are. He'll look for another woman there." Goodwife Selwyn sniffed. She pointed towards the east exit.

Did she not see Meverell had gone west? Was she deliberately sending me on a merry chase? What papers might be hidden with the mule that Brewster spoke of?

This ass had much to teach me. With a doff of my cap, I took the groat and sped outside.

The press of the crowd was heavier than usual. When the king was in London, many loitered about for a glimpse of the great and the good striding in and out of the theaters of power. Poulterers brought squawking chickens into the kitchens. Carters hauled fragrant applewood for the fires. Clerks with self-imposed urgency ran around, caps askew, trying to catch their masters' attention. I followed my nose and made for the stables.

The Westminster stables were huge and packed. It would be hard to find one mule in the row of courtiers and other asses that lined the walls. I did not dare disturb a grimacing blacksmith as he quenched hissing iron in a barrel. A hay wain nearly pushed me down in a pile of manure in a rush to service a nobleman's train. In haste, I climbed a pile of saddles near one of the stall doors to get a better view.

I did not see the mule.

But I did see Gregory Meverell.

He skulked towards the back where there were smaller stalls. I climbed down and followed him. We had only until after the midday meal when the court reconvened. Whatever I could learn from the mule and report back to the queen, I would. I would repay her kindness, perhaps do some good for Mistress Agnes, and perfect my stagecraft.

With stealth, like a serpent in a Creation play, I approached the stall.

The mule was a pretty thing, with a dappled white and gray coat, and a saucy eye. Someone had paid extra for a small brazier of coals to warm him. Meverell was already in the stall. But if I expected the beast to give Meverell a kick or a nip, I was mistaken. He whispered softly to the animal, offering a crisp carrot. The beast nuzzled him and daintily took the carrot. When the creature settled with his provender, Meverell made to look through the saddle pack hanging on a wall peg.

What papers were in the bag that worried Goodwife Selwyn and Brewster?

I was so busy watching Meverell search, I did not hear the approach of Goodwife and Agnes Selwyn and Brewster. "Meverell!" Goodwife Selwyn yelled like a hunt master at a dog. "Now you will steal from us!"

Meverell looked up. "I want only what is mine!" He looked at Agnes. The girl gasped, unable to speak. Goodwife Selwyn yanked her daughter close.

Brewster lunged at Meverell. The men exchanged knocks and blows upon each other, with the bigger Meverell having the upper hand. The saddlebag fell from its peg into the hay.

In the fray, the mule kicked Brewster in the face. He flew back against the wall of the stable and landed with a thud against the brazier. Some of the fiery coals fell into the straw. Goodwife Selwyn cried "Fire!" as she attended to Brewster's injured head.

Agnes slipped from her mother's grasp.

Men from all corners of the stables raced to the stall, wanting to put the fire out.

In a flash, Gregory Meverell grabbed Agnes Selwyn by the hand and was gone in the crowd.

I grabbed the saddlebag.

ЄОСЗ
## Queen Anne

"I will leave you to it." Cromwell dismissed me, likely his belly demanding its late midday meal. I was a political wager he laid that did not pay off. Unable to attract the king and further his Reformation, I am of no use to him.

I twisted my sapphire and ruby wedding ring. My motto, engraved inside, was "God send me well to keep." Though the king did not want me to meddle with his codpiece—that was a pleasure saved for Mistress Howard—I meant to do good service to my new country. And keep my head by proving my worthiness.

I looked down at the blood-red ruby as it sparkled in the firelight. It was the fate of some women to be sold as property for the benefit of their husbands—or their families. I closed my eyes and bit my tongue. Such had been my fate. Yet perhaps it need not be Agnes Selwyn's. Her shattered face broke my heart. The man who inflicted those injuries did all short of death to silence her.

The men in the council chamber, Cromwell's assistant, the Selwyn *père,* and the second Norfolk constable, a pimply young man stood before me, they all looked expectant. The quiet of the queen's council room was a smaller stage than the theater of the Star Chamber. The applewood fire snapped in the grate, warming the chilled room with its sweet fragrance. Outside, I could hear the bustle of the street and lives clashing and melding in the city.

Agnes's father, Master Selwyn twisted his hat nervously. The rural constable scratched at his beard's patchy growth. The Chancellor's assistant Paget pawed distractedly at Cromwell's papers, ink, quills, and scissor on the table. My hands trembled and my golden wedding ring felt cold. The court sat only for today. I needed to make sense of this maelstrom of ink and paper if I were to prove to the king I could be of use.

And to save Agnes Selwyn a lifetime of marriage to her abductor.

"I'll start with the account books," I said with what I hoped was a regal voice. I opened and scanned its meticulous columns, indicating the price the crown paid the Selwyn's for fodder, blacksmithing, and repair of tacking. "Who keeps these records?" I asked Selwyn in German, impressed with their thoroughness and precision.

He shifted nervously. "I do not know that book. I keep the records in the stable to be accurate. There's so much coming and going—if I don't write it immediately, I might make a mistake."

Cromwell's assistant Paget looked up after my translation, his black clerk's cap askew.

"This is not your signature?" Paget asked Selwyn, pointing to the ledger columns.

Selwyn's cap twisting increased. "No. I brought my account books with me, your grace. They are in my saddlebag."

"How about here?" I pushed the marriage contracts—the English and the German—towards him. Master Selwyn looked and pointed at his signature. "*Ja.*"

"Let us look together at the two marriage contracts," I said. After some back and forth between Selwyn, Paget, and myself, we realized the German betrothal contract between Brewster and the Selwyns had significantly different provisions than the one in English.

"Is this usual?" I asked Paget.

He pressed his black spectacles onto his nose and squinted down. "It is not unusual to have the same contract in two languages if the heir will inherit property in two countries. However, if the German document is different, the confusion in the contracts may nullify the marital agreement between Brewster and Mistress Selwyn. Her marriage to Meverell may then be legal. The statute of 1487 would honor her marriage to her abductor."

My heart constricted. A young woman forcibly married to the man who beat, kidnapped, and raped her.

I touched the cool gold of my wedding ring to my cheek. Perhaps I could get more information about Agnes from her father.

The young constable looked out the window, distracted by some noise from the stable, more interested in the pageantry of the city than a village girl's fate.

"How did Mistress Selwyn get her jaw broken?" I asked her father in German.

"*Ach!* I was at Snettisham near the Norfolk coast waiting for a ship from Cleves when the constables found my Agnes and Meverell. Susan, my wife, said Meverell hit her with a horseshoe so she would not gainsay his story."

My heart beat faster and I felt a pressure rise behind my eyes. The court would reconvene in less than an hour. I needed to do something to prevent the oncoming tragedy. "What was Meverell's story?" He had not been allowed to say much in the Star Chamber.

Mr. Selwyn had wrung his cap into a twist and held it tight, his knuckles showed white. "Meverell says she went with him willingly. Someone else broke her jaw later, he knew not who."

"Where did you find Mistress Selwyn?" I asked the young constable who was still window gazing.

He scratched the back of his neck as if an aid to memory. "She and Meverell were walking through the churchyard, talking to Mistress Agnes's godmother."

The translation was quickly done. Agnes's father looked quite confused. "My wife said she was injured by Meverell that night."

"Perhaps the mule kicked?" I suggested to Master Selwyn.

"Never!" he scoffed. "Benny will allow only Agnes and me. He will not even let my wife near."

I turned to the young constable. "When did you see Mistress Agnes with her injury?"

"The next morning, after Goodwife Selwyn brought Mistress Agnes home."

Goodwife Selwyn lied in the Star Chamber. Why? Agnes was injured after she left Meverell. Who had done so?

Master Selwyn muttered "Susan's hand...." in German, but I knew not what he meant.

Before I could think more, my little page, James Burbage ran past the guards at the chamber door and dropped to his knees. "My lady! I have found something!"

Mr. Selwyn gasped, pointing to the satchel James held close to his chest. "*Das ist meins!*"

I stood and extended my hand. "Bring the bag here, James."

The boy leaped to his feet and made to do as I asked, but he tripped. The satchel went flying and ledger sheets and other papers fluttered like snow onto the flagstones. I tried not to smile. The boy was as sweet as honey, but nowhere near ready for the Revel Master to cast in a court masque.

Paget groaned and pinched his nose, as his master did when irritated.

Selwyn and James swept up the papers. They smelled of hay and leather. Selwyn rubbed his forehead and declared. "These are my records—in my hand. See how I have listed for hay, tack, shoeing—"

I waved him silent, mentally calculating the difference between the accounts Goodwife Selwyn presented to the crown for payment and the real numbers her husband kept. They were quite different. I showed them to Paget. Paget clucked as he scanned an ink-stained finger down the widely divergent numbers.

"Not the first time someone providing for the crown has committed fraud," he said.

It was all well and good to save the crown money; but it mattered little, I was sure, to Agnes Selwyn.

"My lady?" James piped up. "Despite what Goodwife Selwyn's said, the mule likes Gregory Meverell. I saw him pet the beast and give him a carrot as he searched the saddlebag."

I became more suspicious of Mr. Selwyn. "You said the mule could only tolerate you and Agnes."

Selwyn clutched his empty bag and mumbled to himself in neither good English nor German.

"Did you lie to the king in the Star Chamber?" Paget fumed. "That is a most serious offense."

Selwyn blanched white and stammered. "*N-n-nein!*"

"Bring me the bag," Paget demanded. "Let us see what other evidence of fraud against His Majesty you have hidden here." Little Burbage took the satchel from Selwyn and handed it over. Paget rummaged furiously inside. After a few moments, he gave up and threw the bag down. "It is empty."

Curious, I picked it up. I had spent many hours sewing and embroidering. I could see the bag was delicately worked with box corners, cinched edges, and stitched with a fine needle. It was skilled sewing for a laborer's bag. Curious, I touched the corners, but I found the leather did not give.

There was something sewn inside the bag.

"Master Paget, may I have Chancellor Cromwell's scissors?" The Chancellor's scissors were sharp and cut the fine leather quickly. Inside the box corners, I found paper. I took them out with trembling hands. They were small letters, no more than the size of a playing card. I scanned their contents.

They were love notes. "*My dearest Gregory... the law my mother has broken will be made to work for us....*"

There was no date, but one note was spotted with blood not yet turned brown with time. I touched my hand to my mouth and felt the cold metal of my ruby wedding ring.

"What is in those papers?" Paget asked. He rose from his chair and moved towards me.

Agnes Selwyn was using the abduction law for her own benefit.

My thoughts flew. With the conflicting marriage contracts between her family and the Brewsters, with the evidence of fraud against the crown, Goodwife Selwyn would likely face heavy charges of fraud and profiteering. Charges would have to compensate for nearly beating her daughter to death. Charges that would leave Agnes free to marry Meverell. Together, Agnes and Gregory would take all of the business. Brewster would get nothing.

*Clever girl,* I thought.

"Naught but stuffing for the corners," I replied to Paget. I tossed Agnes's letters into the fire.

Just then there was a flourish of voices in the outer hall. "Make way for the king!" I heard my husband's resounding footsteps and the stamp of halberds as he walked past.

"How fares the Selwyn matter?" the king boomed as he entered the council chamber with Mistress Kat Howard close behind.

Paget quickly explained the matter of fraud in the accounts to the king.

"This is most serious, Paget! No one defrauds the crown and walks away without severe punishment. And what of the precontract?"

Paget sighed and was about to speak but I cut him off. "My good lord, it would seem that there was no precontract. The documents in German contradict the English. Master Paget says they nullify each other."

The king sat down at the head of the council table, mulling the matter. Paget said nothing to contradict me.

I went and knelt beside the king. "My lord, in such matters as marriage, matters that touch a man so dearly, Meverell should get his choice, would you not agree? No man should be forced to marry a woman he does not love."

We held eyes for a moment. Loudly unspoken between us was the knowledge he had married a woman he did not love. Me.

My husband slowly nodded. "Indeed."

Master Selwyn twisted his cap and attempted to gabble a protest in German. I raised my hand and he fell silent.

"It is often the lot of women to marry men not of their choosing," I turned to look at pretty Kat Howard. "Mistress Howard is the leaseholder of the land in dispute. Is that not the unfortunate lot of women, Kat? To marry someone she does not love?"

Kat Howard dropped her eyes. In a soft voice, she whispered, "Yes, my lady."

The king then slammed his hand down on the table. "What the queen says is true. If the law favors Meverell, then the marriage stands. The Selwyns will have much to answer for—lying in the Star Chamber and fraud against the crown are most serious offenses."

The king rose and took my hand, hiding my wedding ring with his big palm. "The queen's judgment in this is most sound. Paget, make sure my Lord Cromwell knows the good service done here."

# AD 1590
# A Pragmatic Solution
### Dennis E. Delaney

The New World

October 1590

Major Nicholas Whitby and Woohabatabi, great Sougmou of the Wabanaki tribe, parleyed in the green grassy field between Little Creek and the fort palisade. Whitby, a tall, sturdy man of forty, with longish black-and-white peppered hair pulled back to a ponytail, gazed with lucid gray eyes into the determined browns of the elderly native. Each man, backed by armed soldiers, stood with unflinching resolve. Two hundred painted Wabanaki against seventy-four pale faced English colonists, and all but Whitby and Woohabatabi held weapons aloft, ready to war. Behind the Sougmou, warriors knocked flatbows with arrows that could fly death two-hundred yards with astonishing accuracy and awaited the signal; behind the Major, colonists loaded sixty-five arquebuses and nine long muskets. Two small but effective cannon on the fort battlements needed only the touch of a torch. The line was drawn. Whitby stood on his side of the board, Woohabatabi on his. The peace and friendship they had forged and maintained over the year threatened to end because of murder.

Dark clouds boiled in the sky and brilliant flashes etched the near forest in relief. Stephen Whitby, the Major's twelve-year-old son, a boy who made a hellbent effort to learn the Wabanaki tongue, translated the Sougmou's demand in English. The strange melodic language came easy to the boy. Major Whitby had seen time-and-again how much easier foreign languages came to children than adults, and Stephen, fascinated from the beginning by the dulcet tones of the Wabanaki, appeared almost preternaturally gifted. Consequently, the major insisted his son attend all-important meetings with the natives, but especially here and now, in the most important confrontation thus far between the two wildly different cultures, one that would determine the fate of both English and Wabanaki. Despite the gravity of the situation, his son's composure and performance made him proud. The Sougmou himself smiled down at the boy and shared a word with his remaining son standing beside him, commenting that the English boy spoke like a human being. Stephen did not translate this, wishing not to appear boastful, but then the Sougmou spoke again, this time directly at the boy's father.

"Robert Meechum must be delivered over to them," the boy translated.

"What will you have with him?" Whitby said to the old man. Stephen signed and spoke one word.

The Sougmou spoke briefly, and when finished, Stephen carefully translated his words. "For his crime, they will burn him on a pile of dry dung. I'm not sure if the latter was not simply an oath; however, it is not a request. If he is not handed over, they intend to take him by whatever means necessary."

The major held no illusion the colony could withstand an assault. Casualties on both sides would be catastrophic. Whitby scanned the leather-clad hoard. He'd led many successful military campaigns in the name of king and country and knew his business. He took everything into account, the sheer size of the opposing force, their weapons, the commander, their determination, and the ground upon which the battle would take place. Of his own men, he could count only five among them who were seasoned soldiers. Until the colonist's arrival in the new world, few had ever even gone hunting. Not the least of his concern was the weather. If it rained, and it appeared likely, the number of arquebus and musket misfires would be high, as much as thirty percent, particularly among men with no experience in warfare, giving arrows a distinct advantage. The initial volleys would allow them a chance to retreat behind the palisade and continue the fight from the battlements. The palisade would stop many arrows, and armor would deflect some, true, but not all, not nearly enough. He had seen an arrow pierce a breastplate and penetrate four inches further into a foot-thick hard oak behind it. Then there was fire, the Wabanaki could burn the fort to the ground, or failing that, they had simply to wait them out. There was not enough powder, not to mention food or water, to sustain them in a prolonged siege. Still, though outnumbered, he could not hand Meechum over. English punished their own.

He nodded at the Van Dyke bearded Captain Drake, his go to man in any action. Meechum grunted when Drake prodded him with the barrel of his arquebus. The shackled prisoner stumbled forward. He stopped beside Whitby and looked into the Major's cold visage with pleading eyes.

"It was my right," said Meechum, murderer of the Wabanaki hunter named Sharp Eye, youngest of the Sougmou's two sons. "The savage stole my knife."

If true, Meechum was well within his right. He himself had done worse in war, cut off hands, heads, to teach a lesson. But it was not true.

Whitby said, "You left it on a rock by the oyster bed where you had been shelling oysters, and the boy found it. Your own wife said as much."

"It was a bought marriage. She hates me. Besides, he attacked me with my own knife! I swear it on all that is holy."

"You would swear it before God?"

"Yes!"

"You think God knows not the truth? Sharp Eye was returning it. He attempted to explain this, but you gave him no chance and put a ball in his heart."

"I didn't understand him. It was an honest mistake. The way he came at me, I thought my life was in danger."

"You well understood, and belly laughed as he lay bleeding."

"That he did," said the Captain.

Whitby said, "Though you, Robert Meechum, deserve the fate our once good neighbors plan for you, I cannot hand you over, nor even apologize. Contracts and charters forbid it. We punish our own."

Meechum shuddered with relief.

"Let it be so," said Whitby.

As if commanded by the Major's words, thunder clapped and rolled heavily overhead. Meechum, and soldiers, Sougmou and warriors alike, all looked up. When their eyes lowered, they saw a long knife in the Major's hand, dripping blood, the very knife over which the coward Robert Meechum had murdered Sharp Eye. The looks of astonishment on their faces turned fearful. Meechum stared at the fort commander, his thick eyebrows knit, his down turned mouth petulant, his entire demeanor that of a woeful child, while blood sprayed from a long deep cut across his throat.

A strong gust of wind swept a fine red mist toward the forest. Meechum dropped to one knee, unable to tear his shocked and pleading eyes from Whitby's stony visage, blood whipping away in the wind, and then fell forward onto his face. He convulsed, reached out, and placed a hand on Whitby's boot, then became still. Whitby kicked the hand aside as he gazed into the eyes of the Sougmou.

The Sougmou wore a puzzled expression. Soldiers on both sides whispered among themselves. Stephen gasped and staggered back, as though he had turned down a blanket and discovered a large black spider on his bed. He nearly lost his balance, and but for his father's quick reflexes he would have fallen.

Captain Drake was the first to speak. "He was cousin to the Duke of Cornwall. I might add, favorite cousin."

Whitby said, "Which does not speak highly of the Duke's judgement." He then spoke loudly to all in attendance, "It is done, justice has been meted out. Let us speak no more of this." He put his hands on his boy's shoulders and positioned him to translate. The boy looked up at the Sougmou of the Wabanaki, and in a trembling falsetto, repeated his father's words.

"Thank you, Stephen," whispered his father.

Woohabatabi considered the dead man, and after a sigh, looked into Major Whitby's cold eyes. After a moment, he nodded, once. But he looked again at the dead man and spit. He muttered, "Piz wat," and turned away.

Whitby looked down at his son.

"Good for nothing," the boy translated.

Major Whitby nodded. The two men were not so unalike, neither wanted war, though both were prepared to do so regardless of the dire consequences.

It was finished. War averted, thought Whitby. For a few moments, he watched the Wabanaki's slow departure, then turned to Drake.

"Bury him in the road without a marker like any common thief or murderer."

# AD 1650
## *The Confession*
### *Joan Leotta*

They say you can find anything and everything in Naples. Last year, in a flea market on Spaccanapoli, the street that bisects the old center, I bought an inlaid wood puzzle box. When I got back to the hotel, I promptly dropped it on my tile floor, and it shattered. I tried to console myself over the loss of the box, reasoning that it would have been hard to fit it into my luggage, when I noticed that among the pieces of wood were some tightly rolled pieces of parchment. A different sort of souvenir. Love letters? I tried to read them, but the message was partly in Italian, partly in what looked like Neapolitan dialect, and likely from the 17th century, if the dates on the letters were real.

So, when I returned to New York, I contacted my sister's former Italian Renaissance professor, the well-known linguist, Giorgio Lupo, in Chicago and flew west to meet him very early on a clear November day.

On the phone he had said he was intrigued by the idea of these letters and agreed to do a basic translation over a lunch or two. Anything more, he would have to charge, he said. We met over pizza at Medici on 57th, Chicago pizza place near the university. We sat down, I peeled off my brown leather gloves, pulled the letters out of my navy-blue Chicago Pier day bag, and handed the letters to him across the table. When he lowered his eyes to the first page, studying the handwriting, I studied him. He was as handsome as my sister had told me — green eyes, sculpted strong jaw, curly black hair, olive skin that looked as if it were perpetually burnished by the sun.

"This would be a lot easier if I could work with the originals," he complained.

"I didn't want to carry them on the plane. If you think they are worth something, I will have you do a real analysis — for pay — of the originals."

"There is another sheet. A second letter." I handed it to him, but it fluttered to the floor. He bent to pick it up. He took a bite of pizza and then seemed ready to read.

His long, elegant fingers held the pages loosely, and after a deep sigh, no doubt directed at me, he began to read aloud in English, as if the small, crabbed writing and hundreds-year old syntax were merely a set of contemporary notes:

*Naples, 1650*

*Dearest Mama,*

*For years I hoped to honor you with my talent as an artist. But sadly, early in life, I realized my abilities are small in your field. So, mama, I write to you now, to tell you that thanks to a certain old woman here in Naples and the power of her concoctions, six years ago, with the help of God, I made sure that your enemy would not outlive justice.*

*I recall you telling me the story often, how Nonno was out, and no one came to your aid when you cried out as Tino raped you. And how in court, they squeezed your fingers with thumbscrews to test your truthfulness, boring down on your digits so that years later you still bore the scars of those cruel cuts. You told me that in spite of the pain you never stopped telling what was true. The pain and damage had almost cost your ability to hold a brush.*

At this point the professor stopped reading. "A sad story."

He looked up at me, green eyes glittering as if he had seen something valuable.

"Do you think it is the story of the famous woman painter, Artemisia

Gentileschi?"

He looked a bit disappointed. I suppose he thought that since I was not in the art field I did not know her.

"Ah, you've heard of her. Possibly it is written to her. But then again, anything that is found in Naples is subject to review. Naples is known for thievery."

I bristled a bit but said nothing. Our family originated in Naples.

He continued, "If you don't mind, I would like to send these papers to a friend who can test the parchment and the ink."

"Maybe after I hear all of what is in them. I don't have much money and before I could pay more than a lunch for something, I would have to be a lot more sure that these are from Artemisia and her daughter."

He sighed and continued to read:

> *I know that you won the case, but when Rome allowed that rat of a human to remain free, you and Nonno headed to Florence where you married Papa and where you won many good commissions from Medici. You once told me you often ate at the Medici table, and we laughed about tales you were not sure about where they told of dispatching their enemies by many clever means without waiting for the courts to decide.*

Giorgio looked up. "The letter seems to break off as if she were interrupted and it picks up again in a different ink."

I didn't comment. He continued:

> *Sorry, Mama. Papa came to visit. He does not like Naples. I like the chaos of Naples. The great families think they run it, but I think it is the old herb women who hold all the power, they create a different sort of order here in the shadow of the great volcano.*
>
> *I was on my way to see you when I encountered an old herb woman who seemed to know I had need of her services — even before I knew it. When she spoke, I recalled your tales of the Medici and well, I took some of*

*my savings and made a purchase from her.*

*A few days after that, dressed in some of Papa's old clothes I used more of my savings to make a trip to Rome. I told you and Papa I was going to stay with a friend on Capri.*

*Before leaving I had asked some Roman artists visiting Naples about Tassi and had learned where he was living. I took lodging not too far from the ugly area where he resided.*

*I told everyone I was looking for a painter to do my portrait. I made sure Tassi got one of the notices. He sent a proposal. I made an appointment with him for an early morning visit to determine if I would select him—so I said.*

*Slowly, on the appointed day, but well before the hour of the appointment, while the moon still lit the sky on morning, I picked my way through Rome's narrow streets descending into ever less salubrious neighborhoods until I arrived at Tassi's door.*

*I shouted out for him in a deep hearty voice. Tassi appeared at the window — slovenly awful. Although he was clearly upset that I had come so early, he agreed to come down and let me in and sent the half-asleep student to the market for some food.*

*He motioned for me to sit on the cleanest looking stool in the place. Then he pulled out two dirty cups. There was a bottle of cheap wine already on the table.*

*"Even this early, no, especially this early, I cannot drink that swill," I snarled at him.*

*I pulled out a fine bottle from underneath my cloak. "This wine is good for any time of day."*

*Tassi was happy to drink the more expensive offering while we talked about the portrait.*

*At first, he sipped from his filthy glass. Then, as the fine quality of the wine grew apparent even to his debauched taste buds, he gulped the rest.*

*"Can you make a little sketch for me, to show me your skills?"*

*He turned to his pile of pencils, papers, and paints. I switched glasses with him as if I had also drained mine and pretended to pour more for him as he returned with a sketch pad.*

*He put the pad and charcoal on the table and greedily gulped the other glassful.*

*In a slurred voice, he directed me, "Remove your cape so I can begin. Let me show you where to sit for the best light."*

*He moved me toward the window, still overshadowed by nearby buildings. He began to sway.*

*"More wine might steady you," I suggested. He nodded, grabbed the bottle, and guzzled a large amount. "The better to steady me," he declared in a sloppy slur.*

*"You were never steady," I replied in my own voice.*

*I stood and dropped the cape. Tassi saw the fullness of my bosom under the blousy shirt.*

*"Who are you?"*

*"You don't remember the love of your life as you declared her to be in court? They say I look just like her."*

*He peered more closely at me, then stumbled back. "No!" He tripped on the stool that had sufficed as chair and fell to the floor, striking his head on the table.*

*I leaned over him and whispered in his ear. "I am her daughter, her avenging angel."*

*I knew that the poison in the wine would take effect soon enough but smiled to myself that maybe fate had killed him for me with the table, absolving me from all blame and guilt.*

*Just to be safe, I gathered up the filthy glasses and my bottle. I put another two of his cups on the table and his bottle. I spilled some of its sour contents into his mouth—enough to mask the aroma of my better vintage.*

*Thanking God for the late sleeping habits of this undesirable neighborhood and the long distance the boy had to go to get to the market, I strode quickly back toward my lodgings.*

*When I got to a bridge, I consigned the wine and glasses to watery grave, knowing that the Tiber would never betray me or the belladonna I had add to the wine I brought. I changed to my own clothes, left a coin to pay for the room, slipped out the back and walked, a countrywoman with a basket to the coach station. I dropped the men's clothing on the steps of a church, knowing the beggars would appreciate them.*

*On the coach ride back to Naples. I began to fear you would not be pleased with my deed. I often heard you say to let God have his way. I was fearful you might not approve. But, Mama, perhaps Tassi died from the fall against the table, and I was merely allowed to watch? God will tell you, soon, for I know, my dearest Mama, that you are more ill than you have led me to believe. Only you know my secret, Mama, that you are avenged upon Tassi and not just in your paintings.*

*Tanti Baci, Tua figlia,*

*Prudentia*

The Professor stopped reading and looked up. This is pretty solid. If the letters are authentic…"

"You seem to have one more sheet in your hand. I'd like to know what that one says, Professor."

He obliged.

*Naples, 1650*

*Carissima Figlia, Prudentia,*

*So much happened to me in my life, so much good —
and so much sorrow. I wept when I received your letter.
No one has ever shown me as much love as you have, my
daughter, in taking up my cause, in battling for me as no
other, not even my father, not your father, not the
courts, not even the kings I painted for — as no one else
has done. I am sure God has forgiven you, if there is even
any blame at all that could be set on you.*

*My dear child, I shall keep your letter by my bedside
reading and rereading it until my life ends. When I soon
join your brother in the hereafter, I beg you to destroy
this note and your letter to me so that no one on earth
will ever come after you. It is dangerous to have made a
confession on paper. My hands still remember the
terrors of the ropes tied on them as I testified at my
rapist's trial.*

*Con molti baci and abbracci*

*Mama*

The gold flecks in Giorgio's eyes began to glitter again. "If we can authenticate this letter, there are people in the art world who will pay huge sums of money for it — a letter from Artemisia, in her hand and a letter from her daughter that seals the fate of Artemisia's rapist. Do you realize this could be worth millions?"

I replied with a question:

"Tell me professor, do you think it was right for Prudentia to avenge the rape of her mother?"

He smiled widely. It was the first time I had noticed the wolfish nature of his mouth. While he was reading, the full lips had seemed sensuous, not sinister. "Of course. Blood is blood."

Now it was my turn to smile. "I agree. Blood is blood. Mothers, sisters. Rape, murder, they should be avenged."

"Well, Tassi didn't murder Artemisia. In fact, some could say her rape put her center stage for a great career as an artist."

I cringed thinking about how the court had maimed Artemisia's hands,, how she had to live the entire rest of her life with the memory of his smarmy hands and more upon her. "Tell me, do you think that all of this applies to modern life as well?"

He looked puzzled. "Who are you? I wasn't sure I taught anyone named Fusillo last year."

I looked him in the eye. I didn't give him my name. "Maybe this is the story of you, my sister, and me."

"So, you're Annette Ruolo's sister, not the person you claimed to be. You made this all up, didn't you, you little idiot. Trying to get me to confess to something I didn't do! The Chicago police can't solve her case. What would ever make you think I did it, anyway?"

Professor Giorgio Lupo stood up, tossed the papers and his napkin on the table, and strode toward the door. Two years after my sister's death and he guessed who I was. He was guilty. I felt vindicated.

I slipped my gloves back on, grabbed my coat and bag and stood up as if to follow him and knocked over the table. The busboy came running over.

Looking upset I told him, "You go get a tray; I'll pick up the pieces. I'm so sorry I knocked things over."

"Do you want to follow your boyfriend out? I'll clean it." The busboy tried to push me aside.

I tried not to laugh. "It's ok. He is not worth it. Please let me clean this up. It will help me feel better. I don't think he ever cared for me." The boy turned away to get a tray, I began to stuff the Professor's plate pieces and utensils into the trash bag inside in my Chicago Pier shopping bag. When the busboy returned and handed me the tray, I scattered the broken pieces of my dish around on it and gave it to him. The waitress helped me up and handed me the bill. I paid cash and gave her a large tip for the busboy and herself. The restaurant didn't charge me for the broken plates.

I walked slowly out, holding my head high, pretending to hold back tears. After walking a block or so, I ducked into an alley and deposited my gloves, the plastic bag of crockery and after removing my purse, even the Chicago Pier bag, into the dumpster. It was worth the effort to make sure no one else would find or be harmed by the remains of amanita mushroom I'd sprinkled onto Giorgio's slice while he was picking up the manuscript page I'd dropped earlier.

Yes, I'd used a fake name for today's appointment. And I was wearing a wig in case anyone would later question who the professor had met, but I wasn't really worried. The mushroom powder was the perfect instrument. Professor Lupo would be mildly ill tonight, something he would probably attribute to the upset of my tricking him to meet with me. But in two weeks the poison will have done its job, by destroying his liver. He would sicken and die in pain.

Was I right to take justice into my hands? Like Prudentia, I questioned myself, but I was more sure because my sister wrote of his raping her in her diary — a book I only discovered a few months ago among things she had sent home—just two weeks before she died, two years ago. Her book confirmed he had raped her and she was pregnant. In her diary she wrote of her plan to confront him just before she went to the airport to come home. However, she never made it home.

She'd been suffocated, and her body left on the side of the road near the University. But the murder was only circumstantial in the eyes of the law. My sister's diary, his jumpy guilt, these were not legal evidence. He would never be charged. Even to charge him with her rape would be problematic since no one knew of it at the time. In the diary she had talked about his penchant for redheads with green eyes—green eyes like his own. I wondered how many other girls he had raped, and maybe even murdered.

My own smoldering Neapolitan blood made it difficult for me to accept that he could never be brought to justice. I went to Naples for comfort. I bought the painted wooden puzzle box in the market and dropped it while still in Naples on the elaborate but unforgiving tile floor of my hotel room. My own Italian was good enough to figure out the gist of the letters. I found an herb lady on Spaccanapoli, a street that is said to divide the old town in half. For me, the purchase bridged a divide between ancient and modern, an old cold case and new way one and opened a way to find justice. I followed the example of Prudentia. However, instead of belladonna, I brought special mushroom powder home with me and then to Chicago along with photocopies of the pages of parchment. Were the originals really from Artemisia and her daughter? Maybe.

A few hours after the flight I was on a plane back to New York and to Staten Island. I took a few hot dogs out back and lit my grill using the rolled-up paper. Neighbors waved. We New Yorkers are a hardy breed and backyard grilling wearing a coat — not that unusual. I waved back. Then, while I waited for the grill to get hot enough to char my hot dogs, I slipped the parchment pages into the flames, along with the fake ID I'd used to buy my ticket and the ticket stubs from my Chicago flight. The old parchment cackled wildly, and the ink seemed to dance along in the flames as it were a string instead of a liquid marking the page. Or was that just in my mind. I didn't care if the letter was really from Prudentia along with her mother's reply. I did hope that in some way, Tassi had been brought to justice, whether by the hand of God or one of his servants, just as I acted on His behalf in the case of my sister and her predatory professor, Giorgio Lupo. The letter of confession and Artemisia's reply were not worth anything to me now. They had served their purpose in guiding me to the way to avenge my dear sister. I was sorry to have had to toss the leather gloves and Chicago Pier bag, both gifts from my sister. But then again, tossing them was part of my gift to her, of avenging her. Before consigning them to the flames, I copied out a quote from Artemisia directed to Prudentia into my own diary, the only reference to my actions, of my day in Chicago:

> *"When the world has long forgotten me and my art,*
> *beloved child I hope that you will not forget me or the*

*trials I suffered and why though I cared very much for you, your brother, and your grandfather, I had to strike out on my own, be separate from your father, even from you and them, and be my own person."*
*Artemisia Gentileschi*

Note: Records on the death of Artemisia in Naples, differ on the dates of her death. Some say she died from an illness in 1653, others that she died of plague in 1656.

# AD 1849
## *Darkness Becomes You*
### *Hope Hodgkins*

#### I

The slender black-clad figure hesitated under the gaslight, where mist swirled. Behind her, the man retreated to a doorway where he waited, a motionless lump of snow. Soon the girl staggered on, a moth without a flame, into the night. Her broad-shouldered pursuer followed close after, his linen suit blending into the St. Louis fog. He moved with military precision, while his quarry stumbled to escape.

She would not live long, I thought.

"But my dear Ellen, come away from the window!" So spoke my employer Mr. Hamilton, flushed with drink and rumpled with desire.

I paused, my fingertips on the cold glass, sad to leave my cozy window seat. But the matter was urgent, so I jumped up and slipped around the dining table to the door. When Mr. Hamilton caught my hand, I showed him my dimples, though everything in me cried out to run down to the street.

"Checking on my pupil," I murmured. "I shan't be long."

I slid my hand into my underskirt pocket, where Mr. Hamilton's gift lay. Only a little effort, a smile and an eyelash flutter, had gained the emerald necklace.

Running up the staircase, I felt Mr. Hamilton staring open-mouthed, a fat man useless as a Joker card.

Before my bedroom mirror I hurriedly coiled and re-pinned my hair, reaching for Ma's old beaver bonnet and cape. In the candlelight my face was smooth, enchanting.

Darkness *is* becoming to most women. Mr. Hamilton said so. He said night-time turned my eyes to black velvet.

Mr. Hamilton said many things, some of them true.

"The most charming governess we've had, my dear."

Charming! What would he know of charms?

My mother taught me charms, with certain botanical remedies. But from my own discernment I knew this April fog, in the Year of Our Lord 1849, was a mist of marvels, a melting freeze smelling of new life but also of death—for the cholera was spreading in the city. The signs flamed in the sky and crawled on the skin of young Mae in the schoolroom, illuminating her pale hair and thin fingers. I barely remembered our French lesson, once I saw my pupil's fate etched on her brow.

Now I ran out the front door, over the wet cobblestones, calling in a low voice.

"Johannes!"

The man in the linen suit turned his head. Wisps of mist rose around his tight blond curls.

"Miss Ellen, don't you trust me? I do understand the need, though I don't like it."

"Wait till there's fewer people." I laid my fingers on his arm. "She won't be hard to catch."

"Does the master know?"

"Mr. Hamilton!" I laughed low in my throat, and Johannes frowned. Such a good man, Johannes. I revered his virtue, except in times like these.

Swiftly I rearranged my face, murmuring, "You know how slowly Mr. Hamilton moves. He has no idea his daughter has escaped. Dear Johannes."

My eyes ran over the muscles beneath the light suit, hardly suitable for cold—but then the weather was fine only last week.

Johannes looked towards Mae, who stumbled again.

"Let's hurry, Miss Ellen." He hunched his shoulders, a movement that in a lesser man would have been a shiver. "It's a terrible night to be out. We'll spare her that, at least."

I shook my head. "Find a quiet place. If she squeals—"

But Johannes had plunged back into the fog, because the thin figure was passing out of sight.

So young, so undeserving of death! I tried to rouse compassion in my heart, but these past nights had frozen me: the darkness and the cold sheets and the hot flesh. My hand slid into my pocket to clutch those glittering emeralds.

Deep in another pocket lay a small bottle. Mae refused to swallow my botanicals, or to eat the food I prepared so thoughtfully. Now she was attempting an impossible escape.

On Lafayette Avenue I overtook Johannes, nearly bumping into him under the maples.

"She's headed for the gardens," he said. "Where we picnicked last spring, and Miss Mae gathered so many daffodils. Like a leetle flower herself—"

"Watch!" I interrupted. "Where did she turn?"

We hastened over frozen mud streets. Lights glowed in windows where families dined, safe enclosed in their homes.

By the Commons Mae wavered, then plunged into the street. How *could* she move so fast, in that peculiar tottering gait of the sick or ancient?

We pursued flat-footed, conscious of lit houses and people who would hear a ruckus.

"If she knocks on a door, Miss Ellen?"

"She's too shy, even now."

I peered up at him through the dark air. When did I become "Miss Ellen" to Johannes?

Didn't he recall our childhood? As a small girl, I perched on our wooden steps on warm afternoons, peeling potatoes. Johannes, the neighbor boy, would bring his canary in its wicker cage to share its singing and brightness, like a yellow flower against the peeling gray walls. Everyone in our shanty town had cats for the mice, but a songbird was a luxury. Sitting on a lower step, Johannes would warble sweet German tunes of shepherds and love. As the sun dropped and shadows fell, I answered with ballads from my mother, about bloody outlaws hung at the crossroads: Johannes's sunshine to my world of shade.

Innocent children, we spent hot afternoons in the river bluffs, the air spicy with toasted barley from the fields. Once we found a cave, spacious and cool, a natural chapel. Johannes sang, *Das Leben ist gleich*, "This life is like a flying dream," and I felt spirits flap out around me from the dim recesses. You may say they were bats.

But at that moment I knew I saw what others did not. And I understood the future.

Still, in the cold streets I took Johannes's arm—a warm living log—as if for aid. Oh, the strength and vigor in that arm! If I had Johannes with me now—but calm, I must keep calm.

To continue my recollection: We passed ox wagons and fishmongers' empty reeking carts. A pair of drunkards reeled by, which induced Johannes to press my hand against his side. Which amused me.

Men love to think women weak, so long as it doesn't inconvenience them.

We approached O'Fallon's burial ground, the proper place for Mae, if she only knew!

We captured her in the Shrine of St. Joseph—still brightly lit, for holy service had just finished. As we hurried in, I fancied the busy priest looked at us with suspicion. I wanted to tell him he'd be busier still, soon. But we only smiled, slipping into a side chapel where Mae slumped in prayer, or pain.

"Our young mistress is so pious," Johannes remarked loudly for anyone to hear, as we pulled the exhausted girl to her feet.

It was true.

"But it's time for her supper."

That was not true. Mae would never eat again.

In the end she came meekly, laying her head on my shoulder in a weak way that tore at my heart. I mustn't soften, I thought, or her fragile spirit would haunt my dreams.

Besides, as we left the Shrine, Johannes's fingers intertwined with mine and I felt such joy that the mist sparkled around me.

Mae would join the other bodies in the shed.

Still, the fog presaged a dangerous warming trend. Soon those bodies would start to stink. Soon the Hamilton mansion would be shut tight, enclosed indeed.

The cholera epidemic was upon us.

## II

The deaths began in early winter: workers by the river, the butcher's boy, servants in a neighboring house. Nobody wanted to acknowledge the pestilence.

When old Mrs. Hamilton sickened, Dr. McDowell visited twice. But after the famous *médecin* mentioned cholera, Mr. Hamilton hastily assured his good friend that his mother was improving and her symptoms had softened.

Which left me, the clever governess, to nurse the old lady. I compounded medicines and dosed her thoroughly. I sat in the dim fusty room, watching her sweating face and her fingers picking at the coverlet.

I cannot claim I wept when she died, for my plans were falling into place. Still, I would have preferred that she pass away under the doctor's care rather than my tender attentions.

In truth Dr. McDowell was rumored to "burk" his patients: to hurry them into the next world so he and his students might resurrect and dissect their bodies. But I don't believe Mr. Hamilton ever suspected such a thing. He was surprisingly naïve for such an old groper.

For one need not see—as I did—the dark shadows hanging in folds, like smothering curtains, over Joseph McDowell's head: you only had to gaze into his insane bright eyes.

And beyond his gruesome diggings, Dr. McDowell cherished mad schemes for truly raising the dead: all St. Louis whispered how when his beloved young daughter died he refused to bury her. He pickled the poor girl in alcohol and placed her in a copper tube, which he hung in an upriver cave. The doctor claimed he could converse with his child, so long as she wasn't smothered under cemetery dirt.

Alas, to those ideas my gullible Mr. Hamilton was all too vulnerable.

I thought of strange Dr. McDowell as I watched at Mae's bedside. In the lamplight the girl's body moved in pain, convulsed, then fell back as if already dead. She refused the water I urged on her, though I intended no harm. Despite her frail body Mae had a strong spirit, stronger than her father's puling essence.

Spirits! Who should know spirits better than I? And believe me, despite the doctor's theory, applications to dead flesh—whether weight of earth or fumes of alcohol—make no difference to the eternal spirit.

Oh, I admit living flesh interests me more. Especially now!

But I must keep calm. After all, since childhood I have loved the comfort of enclosures.

On summer evenings Pa ran his card games, while we children played Red Rover in the street. When the neighbor children were called to bed I would crawl beneath our porch, to curl on an old blanket until the last whiskey-sodden mark stumbled from the house. How I cherished that dark hidden space!

By the time I crept inside—if I was lucky—Pa snored already at the fireside.

Yet I myself am the greatest gambler in all St. Louis. Pa called it improper for my sex, but he wasn't the one who went to market, bargaining for potatoes and salt pork. By age 10, with Ma in the grave, I learned to freeze my face and walk away, my eyes on the mud churned up by oxen. Three or four farmers would let me pass, but finally a man would sigh, "Well, little Ellie, bring me your dime."

It was always a man, never a farmwife. I learned that lesson early, too.

Do you think it was a bad childhood? St. Mary's orphanage was worse. We wore dingy linen frocks, and the odor of cabbage soup filled the hallways. There was no fire in our dormitory and the thin sheets barely covered our narrow cots.

Occasionally I wished that riverboat man hadn't pulled his pistol on Pa.

Now I had my safe enclosure, the rich Hamilton mansion. And fate had shut me into a tight smelly sickroom: even the pestilence, I thought, furthered my purposes!

Sitting at my pupil's bed, fondling bottles and curatives, I considered: what if Mae hadn't waded into Chouteau's Pond during the warm spell last week? I'd dreamed of tiny evil creatures in the water, seeking entrance to the soft human bodies that trespassed their territory. And yes, I should have stopped her; and yes, it was Johannes's admiring eyes on Mae's halo of hair that induced me to release her to her doom.

I have many tempting qualities, but golden hair is not one of them.

In the bedroom lamplight I looked down at myself. Mr. Hamilton's green stones sparkled across my bosom, brazen and potent, and why not? When, months ago, I first saw old Mrs. Hamilton wearing the emeralds—she was passing out the door, going to the opera house—those beauties drew me as if they were my own. Perhaps they were, by law; the thought made me smile.

In any case, the old lady had no use for them now.

Emeralds have virtue for dysentery, or so my mother said.

On impulse, I unclasped the necklace and fastened it round the unconscious girl's neck.

Lord, what a disastrous act! My only thought was to test their fabled power: if they cured cholera, they would be miracle workers indeed. True, underneath I felt a curious gentle pity.

At my touch Mae opened her eyes.

"A sip of water, dear?" I whispered. "You must be so thirsty."

The doorknob turned slowly and I straightened. The house was nearly empty. The cook had fled, and our young maid had succumbed that morning. Only Johannes, the factotum, and I remained to care for Mr. Hamilton and Mae.

True, Mr. Hamilton had looked in once, neck wattles trembling, to beg for protective remedies. Mr. Hamilton who, with his mother on her deathbed and then his daughter ill, had thought of nothing but my eyes and bosom, I thought with sudden nausea.

Not that I am like that archangel Johannes. I'm not unduly chaste, but I have good reason for keeping out of Mr. Hamilton's bed.

However this sickroom visitor was Johannes, his broad forehead creased with trouble.

"That little dark maid, dead too! You didn't say, Miss Ellen."

He stopped, staring at the emeralds which lay garish across Mae's nightgown. Did he know their priceless value?

"They're mine," I said quickly. "But they may work good charms against her illness."

Johannes hesitated, then took my hand. "You are so kind, Miss Ellen!"

"Ellen, not Miss Ellen."

He was silent, but I thought his eyes lingered on me. My white neck and dark eyes must be striking in the shadowy room.

"So far as the maid goes, Mr. Hamilton refused to call the doctor for a mere servant," I told him. "She was gone before I could dose her, poor skinny thing."

Mae flung out a restless arm, and Johannes returned his sad gaze to her.

"Shall I fetch Miss Mae a teaspoon of ice?"

"No, an entire pitcher of water!" I laughed. "She's dried out, and a body knows what it wants."

"Wants...what Mr. Hamilton wants...."

Johannes's voice trailed off as I looked up in surprise. His unhappy eyes met mine, and he muttered, "Not here. Come down to supper."

The tile-floored kitchen was not so grand as the Hamilton dining room, but the fire blazed hotter. Johannes put cold chicken, bread, and honey on plates and poured drink.

Then he leaned close to whisper.

"The master wants to follow Dr. McDowell's science and suspend Miss Mae in spirits, in a cave. For resurrection. It's crazy, Mi—Ellen. Isn't it crazy?"

For a moment I dwelt in a dream, Johannes so near I could feel his warmth, wine in my mouth and meat in my belly. Soon I would sit again at the polished dining table, silk on my back and the emeralds around my neck. And Johannes beside me, in the candlelight that became me so well: all I wanted, cozily enclosed. Yet I saw it only through a mist, like the cursed fog.

Now I know it was the precious stones that obscured my vision: emeralds, the gems most like passion, brilliant but opaque. How could I suspect what their foggy future offered?

I spoke fancifully. "Caves can be beautiful. My friend, do you remember our river cave, where we played as children? Take *me* there, if I die."

Johannes stiffened. "Like a pagan Indian? Don't you want a Christian burial, Ellen?"

"Doesn't God see us in the darkness," I countered, "as in the light?"

Johannes was not sure. His noble brow creased. Such a good man!

When I returned to my patient I found Mr. Hamilton kneeling by her bed, dripping with tears.

"She's all I have, Ellen, the last of my family," he moaned.

The fool! Should I have revealed my secret then? Instead I soothed him and petted him and sent him from the room.

Still, he had shaken me: could Mr. Hamilton have learned repentance at last?

### III

Mr. Hamilton's original sin was this weak puffy softness. It was his old mother who, twenty-five years ago, insisted that George Hamilton cast out his younger sister. The girl had given in to her admirer Elias Franklin one time too often—a time that engendered my humble self.

The joke is, my ma was the least carnal of women: slender, spiritual, rather like young Mae who blushed if a dog sniffed her in the street.

I must resemble my father.

As for my uncle Mr. Hamilton, he doomed my ma and me to poverty and labor while his family ate roast beef and slept in soft beds.

True, I learned and grew strong despite the injustice: at St. Mary's I studied geography, French, music—and botany, to add to my mother's wisdom. There's marvelous things you can do with plants.

Along the way, I learned men: how to move my body inside my clothes in certain ways that men understood. In ways that Mr. Hamilton, otherwise so stupid, understood.

Mr. Hamilton, the weakling, would never, never know that his daughter's pretty governess was in fact his niece! Mr. Hamilton, who wouldn't call the doctor when the sprightly little maidservant fell ill! Mr. Hamilton, whose sagging wet lips gasped with affliction too late, in his dying daughter's bedroom! Mr. Hamilton, who—but my spirits are raging overmuch.

*Du calme, du calme*, I must conserve strength.

Let me rehearse my story in orderly fashion.

Mae died three days ago. The priest gave the last rites, then departed in haste. A smattering of neighbors and friends gathered for the wake. They perched on carved chairs in the elegant Hamilton parlor, exuding uneasiness. The gentlemen drank whiskey but were not jolly. Several ladies held handkerchiefs over their faces.

To my fury, the guests scarcely touched the layer cake I had labored to bake.

Could it be they feared me or my food?

And how did my carefully laid plans go wrong? Perhaps my errors were due to exhaustion. In addition to baking, I had to wash and lay out the girl, dressing her in dove-colored silk with those green gems sparkling across her breast.

Oh, yes. After seeing the necklace on his dying daughter, Mr. Hamilton had wantonly, selfishly, decreed that Mae be interred with the emeralds. Despite having given them to me!

Even worse, I heard Johannes, gazing on Mae in her coffin, whisper,

"Farewell, little flower!"

At least Johannes would set eyes on her no more. Emeralds are also the color of jealousy.

This afternoon we departed St. Louis to carry Mae's body to this cave by the river—not *our* cave, Johannes's and mine, but one handily linked to Mr. Hamilton's farm properties ten miles off. There Mae was to be put, in imitation of Dr. McDowell's peculiar practices, in a copper cylinder filled with alcoholic spirits.

Having issued these decrees, Mae's grieving father took to his bed. Dr. McDowell diagnosed nerves. Johannes, with unusual cynicism, thought his master too timid to personally oversee his grotesque plan.

Only I know that Mr. Hamilton's malady is real. He will never rise from his sickbed. The cholera truly took his mother and his daughter. But if my uncle does not die from the cholera, I have ensured he will, nonetheless, die.

Do you think me revengeful? I merely seek restoration.

Riding in the wagon today, through chilly rain, I felt no cold. I propped my boots next to the coffin, to keep poor Mae from indecorous jostling, as my mind rehearsed my plans.

The pestilence soon will rage across the city, taking lives, filling boneyards, occupying the priests. I pictured red swollen eyes, rivers of tears—and I recalled Ma's drooping face, the sorrows of her life. All avenged, all recompensed, I thought as we jolted past the last shacks on the edge of town.

My claims were prepared, the papers locked in my trunk. The house might be brightened for Johannes and me—or sold, according to our wishes. According to *my* wishes.

First, however, those emeralds. The wagoner, hired from the village, would return to his humble abode. Johannes, pale and reluctant on his mule, would ride to his cousin's house to stay while the cholera raged.

My miserable belly cramps resumed, muddling my thoughts. Yet even if had the cholera, I knew the best remedies—above all water, which doctors seem curiously unwilling to allow its sufferers. If Dr.

McDowell himself were ill, he'd drink gallons.

I was smiling at the thought when the wagon bumped to a stop atop a rocky river bluff.

Mr. Hamilton's cave down below was pleasant enough, possessing a huge boulder for a door like Christ's tomb of resurrection. It took the carter, his boy, and Johannes combined to roll it away. This was part of Mr. Hamilton's plan for his daughter's security.

A workman had hung the cylinder from the cave ceiling with stout ropes. Now the men carried in the coffin, lifted Mae's body, and placed it in the container. Then we all trudged back and forth with jugs of spirits to fill the cylinder.

"Miss," the carter said at last. "Miss, should we say a prayer?"

The priest did that already, I thought with annoyance. The pain behind my eyes was growing, and I sweated even in this cold cave.

Nevertheless I recited some Latin doggerel: who was to know? Then I recalled my own words to Johannes, "Doesn't God see in the darkness?"

What might that mean?

Now Johannes was departing, pausing to touch my cheek tenderly.

"I *will* come to you, Johannes," I told him warmly. "Once the cholera has lifted."

That wouldn't happen for months, I knew, but I planned to see him sooner. I wanted Johannes above all. Almost above all.

"But—Mr. Hamilton," he said with doubt. "It's not seemly for you in that house, alone with a man."

Even Johannes occasionally observes more than one might think.

"He's an old grieving man. Also—" I detached my gaze. "I doubt he is well. If the cholera strikes him, he'll need nursing."

"Your sweet, charitable nature, Ellen! Still, I'd wish that you stayed at my cousin's place. The Hamilton house is cursed, despite its riches. Won't you come with me now?"

Dusk fell as I made the fateful decision. My plans were too long brewing to toss away. Above all, I must get those emeralds.

I looked into Johannes's clear blue eyes once more and I heard a ghost of a long-ago song, a boy's voice singing of true love. Then I turned away.

He was correct about the cursed Hamiltons. I planned to allay that curse, before entering the embraces of dear Johannes for good.

As Johannes trudged away, the waggoner moved near. "I can drive you to the inn, Miss."

His breath smelt of onions, and the village was only a half-mile walk. That was why I lied, "Johannes will bring me."

A sudden longing took me, to indeed ride back with Johannes, my arms around his warm waist.

A bluebird, poor solitary creature, perched on a twig above as a sign. But my way was set—by spirits, by my own willful heart, who knows?

I lingered beside the cave entrance as Johannes on his mule plodded away, along the narrow bluff-top path. Then I slipped back into the darkness.

Tiptoeing to the cave wall I found a stone, small enough to lift and large enough to elevate me. I rolled it next to the suspended coffin and climbed upon it.

The cylinder's cover was easy to raise. A reek met me, of rotting flesh and ethyl alcohol. I had to stand on tiptoe to reach into the strange coffin. My exploring hand felt something move in the water and I jerked back in panic, splashing liquid on my face.

Ridiculous: it was only Mae's body, floating loose in the spirits.

I lifted my skirt to wipe my face, gasping, then made myself breathe slowly. With the corpse shifting in the liquid, securing that necklace would be unhappily like bobbing for apples.

Mastering an urge to puke, I gritted my teeth and again thrust my hand into Mae's cylinder.

Voices approached: the carter and his boy, returning to collect the last jugs.

Quietly I continued fishing: a bootlace; a cold hand; a mouth and chin. Then, hanging from the neck, the emeralds!

Alas, I could not manage the clasp one-handed. I fumbled in the dark for a second stone, to make me tall enough to reach both hands into the noxious liquid.

You see, I do not easily relinquish my plans.

I did not relinquish them even as my brain noted with detachment a grunting and crunch of sticks and leaves, followed by deep darkness: the men had rolled the stone into place.

I should have shrieked. Did I pause because of the emeralds? Because Johannes trusts in my "good heart"?

Perhaps I truly believed I could push away the stone myself.

By the time I approached the entrance, wet necklace in hand, night had fallen. A slice of sky was visible above the huge stone, with one star among the clouds. I wouldn't smother in the cave. But I could not budge the rock, though I puffed and pushed my measly weight against it.

Then I did scream for a while, until the night-sky crescent turned dark.

Since then I've been sitting, sucking my bruised fingertips which taste of chalk and blood. No spirit or sign warned me, and the comfort of enclosures has failed me.

I see nothing but dizzying black, not even a green gleam from the cold stones in my palms.

Above, Mae swings in her copper casket.

Shall my beautiful flesh rot, too?

The carter is long gone. He thinks I returned to town with Johannes, while Johannes thought I would ride with the carter.

Johannes expects me in a few weeks, "when the cholera has lifted."

As for Mr. Hamilton, this morning I spooned a large fatal dose of Fowler's solution down his puling throat.

"Darkness becomes you," he used to say, in that elegant house so far away.

Perhaps, perhaps: if darkness becomes you, finally you become darkness?

# AD 1879
## Her Dangerously Clever Hands
### Karen Odden

London, 1879

The Metropolitan Police Divisions had known of the Wrens for years, but like their winged namesake, the all-women thieving gang from Whitechapel was quick to flit away, hard to catch, and prepared to move their nest as needed. They also prudently stuck to thieving—nothing violent, nothing vicious, mostly pilfering items worth less than ten pounds, even if it was hundreds of them each month around London, which meant it was the local divisions, not the Yard, who responded to their cases.

But one day, I entered the division to find three inspectors blocking the hallway with a newspaper opened too wide for me to pass. White and Bristow read avidly over Montrose's shoulder.

"What is it?" I asked.

"Oh, Corravan," White said. "You might know her. She's from the Chapel."

"Ugly murder," Montrose said.

I peered between them to see the headline: "Whitechapel Woman Fatally Stabbed!"

"Name's Margaret McHugh," Bristow said, peering up at me. "Heard of her?"

"No," I lied, shouldering my way around them. "Chapel's a big place, and I left near fifteen years ago."

"Poor thing," Bristow said. "Stabbed four times."

I stepped inside my office and shut the door.

I'd known Margaret McHugh as "Maggie"—now head of the

Wrens—since I was a boy, for she'd come into Ma Doyle's shop, like most Irish in that part of Whitechapel did, for their sundries. Ma once admitted to me that Maggie amused her, but she trusted Maggie only so far as she could reach into her pocket, which might not make sense to outsiders, but I understood. All the Wrens had special cavernous pockets sewn into their skirts, reinforced against their crinolines to support the weight of merchandise. One of Ma's friends' daughters had once stood in our kitchen and laughingly shown me how the pocket's wide opening could allow her to slip four pairs of gloves, two yards of ribbon, a pair of lady's slippers, and half a dozen handkerchiefs inside without a West End shop clerk suspecting a thing.

A knock interrupted my thoughts, and the door swung open. My usual superintendent Mr. Vincent was away, and his superior, a gimlet-eyed man named York, stood with his hand on the knob. "You heard about the murder? This woman McHugh?"

I nodded.

"You're Whitechapel Irish, a'n't you?" he said with distaste. "Why don't you take it?"

I bit my tongue and watched his mouth twitch. I knew what he thought of my race, and he was just waiting for me to rise to the bait and balk. "Yes, sir," I replied evenly.

"Victim lived in Coburn Street, number six." He turned on his heel, leaving the door wide open.

I took a cab to Leman Street and climbed out, about a quarter of a mile from her house. I liked putting my boots on the ground here because I could sense changes like a new odor in my nose. I wondered where the Wren nest was these days; as a precaution, it was never close to where the leader lived, so she could keep her work separate from her home. I also wondered if Maggie's murder was an internal matter or something else. If this was a feud among the Wrens, they'd close ranks, and I'd have a devil of a time convincing anyone to talk to me.

Maggie's house, on one of the better streets, was white-painted brick, with a wood door. I put my hand behind the black mourning wreath to find the knocker and struck it once; the door was opened by a maid, slender and young. Her face was pale, her brown curls pulled back, her eyes red-rimmed. "Good morning," she said, her voice quavering.

"Good morning. I'm Michael Corravan," I said, softening my voice. "An inspector from Scotland Yard. I'd like to speak with you, please. What's your name?"

Her brown eyes widened. "Katie Wells." It came out little more than a whisper. She closed the door behind me with a subdued click. She led me into the parlor. "Do you want to see the housekeeper, Mrs. James?"

"Both of you," I replied. "Is there anyone else in the house?"

"Nay, just us two. A charwoman comes in to help every other day."

Mrs. James, a sedately dressed woman of about thirty-five, entered the room, a silver chatelaine snug around her waist. She did not ask me to sit, so we all stood in the parlor. At first, Katie fidgeted with the ties of her apron, until Mrs. James gave an admonishing look, and Katie meekly dropped her hands to her sides. I asked the usual questions about how long they'd worked for Mrs. McHugh and what their routines were. Both women lived in the house, and Mrs. James had worked here twelve years, Katie seven.

When I asked if anything out of the ordinary had happened in the days before her death, any unusual visitors, or if Mrs. McHugh had seemed out of sorts, Mrs. James shot Katie a look that might have silenced her. But Katie's eyes were on me, and she didn't see it.

With some surprise, Katie said, "Why, yes, Mrs. McHugh did have a visitor."

"Two days ago," Mrs. James added, pursing her lips. "A woman named Mrs. O'Connell."

"She was very pretty, with long dark hair and green eyes," Katie said, a touch wistfully. "I don't think they were friends, though. It sounded as if they were having a row."

"About what?" I asked.

Mrs. James gave a warning cough, and Katie amended, "Well, it probably warn't a row exactly. We didn't listen in—"

"She means we could hear their raised voices," Mrs. James interrupted.

"Had you ever seen her before?" I asked.

Both shook their heads, and Mrs. James said, "When she left, Mrs. McHugh told me not to admit her again."

I looked to Katie for corroboration. "Aye, her face was red, and she was fidgety the rest of the day."

"Anything else you noticed about Mrs. O'Connell?" It was a common enough name in this part of Whitechapel.

"Well, 'twas odd," Mrs. James said. "Her dress was right fashionable, though her bonnet and shoes were old."

"There's one other thing," Katie said, her cheeks flushing, and she gave a quick look at Mrs. James before turning back to me. "I heard her say 'Damn Honora,' later that night."

I was writing in my pocketbook when I heard that, and I froze, then continued to push my pen across the paper, scrawling nonsense for a line or two and hoping I gave nothing away. But I knew that name.

If it was the same Honora O'Connell I'd known years ago in Whitechapel, I'd been a little in love with her, when she was twenty to my fifteen. It had been she who showed me the special pockets Wrens had in their skirts, one time when we'd played cards together in Ma Doyle's kitchen, and she'd taught me how to spot someone's tell and how to bury an ace up my sleeve for later. She had the prettiest dimples and a sly, approving wink for me when I mastered the sleight of hand. When I lay in bed at night, thinking of girls I might fancy, they all had her green eyes and dark glossy hair. But after I left the Chapel, I'd never seen her again. Had she left, to get married? And why would she fight with Maggie? They were Wrens together.

Feeling a poke of gratitude that Katie and Mrs. James had been so forthcoming—as I'd anticipated, they weren't Wrens—I asked a few more questions, took down their names, and left, pointing my boots toward Ma Doyle's shop.

Ma Doyle had adopted me, taking me in when I was thirteen, after

I'd kept her son Pat from being beaten to death in an alley. A cheerful, clever, competent woman, she had a way of offering a cuppa and sympathy without causing offense, so she knew a good deal about people who lived nearby. More than once, when I needed to know what was happening in the Chapel for my work, I'd gone to her first. As I reached the shop, I looked in the window and saw Elsie behind the counter. The shop held about half a dozen customers, some of whom I knew, others I didn't. I observed Elsie for a moment. She was just twenty—and prettier every year, with the braids that used to hang long down her back now coiled around her head in a way that made me think of a flower. There was no sign of Ma, so I started for the back stairs that led up to the living quarters above. I inserted my key in the lock and turned it, calling out, "Ma, it's me," as I stepped inside.

"Mickey," she said and presented her cheek for a kiss.

We sat down with our tea and thick slabs of bread and butter.

"Are y'here about your work or to visit with me?" she asked with a knowing smile that dented a dimple in her cheek.

I looked at her apologetically, and she patted my hand. "I'm only having a spot of fun. I'm glad for whatever brings you."

"I'll see you Sunday for tea, but this is work," I admitted. "Maggie McHugh was killed last night near her house."

"Aye, so I heard," she said indifferently and slipped her knife into the butter.

Surprised, I asked, "Am I not remembering properly? I know you didn't trust her much, but I thought you were friendly."

"With Maggie?" She looked up from buttering her bread. "Why would you say so?"

"Well, I've seen you talking and laughing with her in the shop."

She gave me a look. "I visit with everyone in the shop."

"True," I said. "Why don't you like her?"

She merely shrugged. "'Tis no matter. Haven't seen her in years, since she moved out of the Mews and started putting on airs of bein' respectable."

Ma was a fair judge of people and tended to get on with most, so I took note of her dislike.

"Ma." I sipped at my tea. "What ever happened to Honora O'Connell?"

While the mention of Maggie's murder barely raised Ma's eyebrow, this question made her skitter her teacup into her saucer with a clink and stare at me. "What on earth made you ask about Honora?"

When I hesitated, she shook her head. "You can't like *her* for Maggie's murder! She's in Swan River, in Australia!"

"What?" It was my turn to stare. "The penal colony? When? How did I not know?"

"'Twas after you left. And you didn't come back for a good while, if you recall."

I winced, knowing what my abrupt departure from Whitechapel had led to, the hurt it had caused the Doyle family.

"So why would you pull her name out o' thin air?" Ma asked.

"It isn't out of thin air. She might have been in Australia, but she's back now. She was seen by witnesses. Here in London."

She frowned. "She's warn't due back until October. That's the month she was shipped off."

"Sometimes they'll let them go a mite early, depending on if there's space in steerage."

She shook her head, slowly at first and then more firmly. "Honora wouldn't kill Maggie. I know her, Mickey. She wouldn't."

*People change,* I thought. *Especially in a penal colony.* But I kept that to myself. "Why was she transported? Was she picked up for thieving?"

She made a tsking sound, her tongue against her teeth, a sign I knew. She thought Honora had been dealt an unfair hand. "It was the worst of luck. Honora went out with …" She paused, thinking. "Eliza Bell, that was her name. A fool of a girl."

"A fool how?"

She sighed. "Ah, she was empty-headed. As many times as she was told not to smirk at the shopkeepers or sashay when she left a store with summat in her pocket, she couldn't help herself. So most times, she was the decoy." A shrug. "She was pretty."

I knew the importance of a decoy. Sometimes it took the shape of a young boy who pretended to steal a Wren's purse in the shop – and while she was screeching over it, a second Wren was quietly filling her pockets. Other times one Wren did a bit of flirting with the shopkeeper, to occupy him.

"Why would the Wrens keep a girl like that?" I asked. "Seems like they'd drop her faster than a hot coal."

She gave me a look. "She's O'Hagan's niece."

"Ah." Seamus O'Hagan kept the bare-knuckles boxing club where I'd worked until he ran me out of the Chapel for not throwing a match. O'Hagan had a straight line to James McCabe, who oversaw most of the crime here.

"So Honora was caught because of Eliza's foolishness," I said, and she nodded. "And this was seven years ago?" Seven was the usual sentence for thieving.

"Nae." Ma shook her head. "Fourteen. At her trial, the judge told Honora she had dangerously clever hands, and a dangerously corrupting heart, teaching a young innocent girl like Eliza the dark business of thieving. So he doubled the sentence and gave Eliza none at all."

I did a quick calculation: I was eighteen when I left Whitechapel, and I was thirty-two now. "Why, this happened *very* soon after I left," I said in surprise.

"Aye. Only a few weeks, if I remember rightly."

So Honora had served her sentence and returned. I wondered what kind of vengeance she had in mind for a sentence she probably felt she didn't deserve. And why Maggie might have been on the receiving end of her anger. And if Eliza might, too.

"Were you at the trial?" I asked.

"Nae. The trial happened almost straightaway, like they did back then, and it was the autumn Elsie had pleurisy. So I didn't know of it till later, from her mum." She winced with regret. "By then Honora was already on one of the ships. They had to fill 'em, you see, and they needed one hundred women for each."

"Women only?" I asked.

"Aye." She looked askance. "Couldn't put men and women together on a ship for six months, Mickey. 'Twas bad enough the crew were men."

"Ah."

"Once a ship was full, it left. She was gone 'afore I could say goodbye."

"Do you have any idea where I'd find her, where she'd stay in London now?" I asked. "I just want to talk to her." Ma bit her lip anxiously. "Ma, you know if she didn't do it, I'll make sure she isn't accused. I want the person who did it, not just the person easiest to blame."

"I know that!" She looked indignant. "I was just tryin' to think who she might have gone to. I'd have thought she'd come to me. Her mother was my dearest friend."

"I'm sorry she didn't."

"So am I," she said unhappily. "Let me ask 'round. Come back tomorrow, will ye? I'll find out what I can."

I thanked her, finished my tea, and kissed her goodbye.

⊗⊗

The next morning, I stopped into the Yard only long enough to report that I was attending Maggie's funeral. It had been announced in the paper for eleven o'clock, at Sacred Heart. I knew the church well, for many a night I'd hidden in the priest hole, eating stale bread and moldy cheese with other boys, before the Doyles took me in.

Funerals were one of the best places for discovering truths about people's lives. Mourners thought no one was watching, with everyone too wracked with their own feelings. But some people sobbed because they relished a chance to go into hysterics, some were stoic, some sincerely grieved, and some secretly gloated that the person was dead.

Rain drummed at the windows as I entered the church and sat near the back to watch. There weren't more than thirty people, but I saw two women who must've been Maggie's relations; they had the McHugh red hair and round chin. Nothing out of the ordinary happened during the mass, but at the end, a burly, slightly balding man approached one of the McHughs to say he was sorry, how Maggie had always been a fine woman.

She gave him a baleful look, and my instincts drew me closer, so I could listen.

"If you thought she was so fine, why didn't you marry her?" she demanded. "If you had, she'd still 'a been alive. That witch wouldn't 'a killed her."

He stood with his hat in his hands, blinking in bewilderment.

She turned and swept around the pew, as his mouth opened and shut like a trout.

I had a split second to make the choice between the two. She knew something, while he seemed not to know his arse from his elbow. So I hurried after Maggie's relation and approached her sideways, withdrawing a card from my pocket, with my name and Scotland Yard's insignia, almost like a gentleman's calling card.

"I'm Inspector Michael Corravan," I said as I passed it to her. "I'm looking into Maggie's death."

"Murder, you mean," she snapped. "Or you wouldn't be here, would you?"

"Are you a relation?"

"Her cousin." Her gaze went over my shoulder. "My sister Mary is too."

"I have questions for you," I said. "But if you'd like to answer them later, I can come by your house."

She weighed that for no more than a second. "I'll speak to you now. Not sure when I'll be home after this."

"Who was that man with the thinning hair?"

Her mouth pursed. "Sean Tooley."

"A friend of Maggie's?"

She grimaced. "Ach, you needn't bother with 'im. He wouldn't have nothing to do with 'er murder, the big, spineless, sad-faced oaf, more's the pity." Her voice faded toward the end, and I wouldn't have heard, if I hadn't been intent on every word.

"Why not?" And when she didn't reply. "Did he misuse her?"

"Nae. But … he …" She shook her head. "He lured her along, like, played with 'ffections." Her eyes drifted over my shoulder again, and I turned to follow her gaze. Her sister was beckoning urgently. "I must go. We have the graveside yet, in all this rain."

I watched her leave, put up my umbrella, and headed back to Ma's shop. It was late afternoon, when Ma usually sorted the day's shipments and parcels. With a wave to Elsie behind the counter, I pushed the door that led to the storeroom and entered. The tang of tea, coffee, brown sugar, and the cloying odor of tallow candles brought back my time as a boy, when I'd help Ma with the counting, tallying the sums on a square of slate. "Ma?"

She put her head around the corner, and her face brightened then fell in regret. "I haven't found Honora yet. But I put out word."

"It's all right," I said, dropping onto one of the wooden barrels. "Something else I want to ask. Who's Sean Tooley?"

"Ach, Sean." She winced, as if she felt sorry for him.

"He was at the funeral today," I said. "Maggie's relations didn't seem happy to see him."

She frowned. "Dunno why that would be. Maggie and Sean were friendly, so far as I know."

"What can you tell me about him?"

She plumped down on a barrel opposite. "Well, Sean grew up here, same as you. He's a foreman at the St. Katherine Docks." She paused. "He was sweet on Honora for years — and she was fond o' him."

That put a cold feeling down my spine. "And when Honora left?"

"Ach, it nigh broke 'im. Oh, he took up with this woman and that, but he never married. I suspect he couldn't stop comparing everyone to her." Her mouth twitched. "I'd say there was a time when you felt the same."

I grinned. Naturally Ma had noticed. "Well, she was beautiful and clever. And a great one to laugh. She taught me card tricks."

She chuckled. "Aye, she did." Then her smile faded. "Clever hands, she had."

"Did Sean ever take up with Maggie?"

Her expression changed to shock. "Good lord, Mickey. Is that what you're thinking? That Honora might'a killed her out of revenge over that?"

I spread my hands. "She went to Maggie's house, Ma."

She pursed her mouth and looked thoughtful. And in the silence, the door swung open, and we both turned.

Honora O'Connell stood before us, and I caught my breath. She was still beautiful, with green eyes and rich coils of dark hair, though her face was thinner. "Beggin' your pardon," she said, appraising and dismissing me with a glance. She stepped toward Ma with her hands out. "But I heard you wanted to see me, Mary."

"I did." Ma put out her arms, clutching Honora to her. Then she stood back and looked Honora straight on, their eyes speaking words I couldn't decipher. "Dear girl, I'm very glad you're home, safe and sound. I didn't think you were due yet."

"They credited my time on the ship down and let me go a mite early." She kissed Ma affectionately on the cheek.

"We'll have a proper visit later," Ma said. "But Mickey needs to talk to you. He's a Yard man now."

"Honora," I said. "I'm glad to see you looking well."

She turned and blinked rapidly. "Mickey? Corravan? Good lord." She came closer and peered at me. "Well, I see it now. You've changed a mite."

"I know."

A smile tugged at Ma's mouth. "I'll just step into the shop."

As the door swung to and fro behind Ma, Honora sat on one of the barrels and folded her gloved hands in her lap. *Mrs. James had been right*, I thought. I didn't know much about fashions, but it seemed to me her dress looked new, though her bonnet looked worn.

Her gaze ran over me. "So you're an inspector now? Last I heard you were running away from O'Hagan."

"I began in Lambeth, as a constable. Worked my way up."

"Ah." A flush that might have been from embarrassment came to her cheeks, but her chin came up. "Your ma told you where I've been?"

"Australia," I said. "Sentenced for fourteen years."

A slow nod.

"When did you return to London?" I asked, my voice casual, but she understood.

"Eight days ago." She cocked her head. "And you're here because you think I murdered Maggie."

I put up a hand. "Honora, I was assigned the case. I didn't choose it, and I had no idea you'd be involved. But frankly, I'm glad it's not someone else. We're friends, and I want to help. But I need to know what happened."

She looked indignant. "*Nothing* happened!"

I turned both palms out. "You were at her house, arguing two days before!" I wasn't going to let her lie to me. "The maid heard Maggie cursing you by name after you left."

Her eyes darkened. "I didn't kill her, Mickey."

"I didn't say you did. But what were you arguing about?"

Her expression flattened, and she crossed her arms over her chest. She gave a mirthless laugh. "Well, you and I might'a been friends once, but you're police now, that's sartin."

"For God's sake, Honora!" I burst out. Her face was hard, her eyes full of distrust. I stood and came close, reached to touch her elbow, but she shied away, and I let my hand fall. "If you didn't kill Maggie, you could only be convicted for it over my dead body. I swear it. I've no desire to pin it on you. In fact, if my superintendent knew just how far

I'd lean to your side, he'd take me off this case."

She gave a snort and a skeptical shake of her head. "Begging pardon if I don't believe you, but every police I ever knew lied to me." Her eyes were full of pain, and her voice dropped. "And worse."

Her tone carved out a dark place in my chest, and I sat back down on the barrel, curling my palms over the rim. "I'm bloody sorry about that, Honora." We sat in silence a moment before I continued. "But I'm looking at what's in front of us. And at the moment, you are the first and only suspect."

Her mouth tightened. "I had a right to confront her after what she done. Not that you'd understand."

"Honora," I protested, and then I stopped. I couldn't prove myself to her other than by playing a fair game, with honest questions. "Do you blame Maggie for your getting caught?"

"Course not." She gave a scornful look. "She warn't even there. If I was going to blame anyone, it would've been Eliza Bell."

"So why did you argue?"

"Maggie was my friend, and she didn't even come to my trial! She knew the police had caught me, and she could'a testified how Eliza warn't no innocent young girl that I'd corrupted. Eliza'd been thieving as long as I had, and ... other things besides." Her eyebrows rose.

"Like what?"

She shrugged. "Baitin', for one."

Setting up as a prostitute in a brothel and then drugging men and taking everything out of their pockets and off their fingers. Illegal, of course, but Eliza's crimes didn't matter to me.

"So Maggie could have helped you get seven years, instead of fourteen," I said. "What did she say?"

Her mouth curled in contempt. "She told me it would 'a been a risk to come. Except no other Wren would 'a said a word—and who else could've recognized her as one?" She shook her head. "I'd 'a done it for her, even if I had to disguise myself, or wear a veil, or dress like a boy."

"She was cowardly," I said.

"And disloyal." Her voice was thick with feeling. "I'd lie awake some nights in Swan River, achin' over her not caring enough to come." There was a world of hurt and anger in her eyes. "So, we argued the other day. But I didn't kill her. You think I'm going to do something stupid that will have me hung? I'm no fool."

To my relief, my instincts told me she was being truthful. "I know. Sometimes you'd save the ace for the next hand, even if it was burning up your sleeve. Being prudent, you called it."

She gave a grim smile. "Swan River was fourteen years spent learning to be prudent, putting my anger into stitches and hems. I'm not ruinin' what's left of my life over her wrongdoing."

"What are you going to do now? Will you stay in London?"

"Oh, aye." Her expression eased. "I've found a position. I worked for a dressmaker in Swan River, and the superintendent recommended me to one in Oxford Street. Wedding dresses, veils, fancy costumes. I start tomorrow."

"You made the dress you're wearing?"

"Aye." A wry smile tugged at her mouth as she plucked the skirt. "Stepped off the ship, looked about me, realized how I must look, and spent two days sewing. Knew I'd never get a job at a good shop if'n I was dressed like I was."

"Where are you staying?" I asked.

She hesitated, her expression wary again. "You can reach me through your ma." At my frown, she added, "I won't leave London, a'right?"

Likely she was staying with one of her old Wrens and didn't want to betray her, so I had to be satisfied with that. I gestured toward the back door. "Then you leave ahead of me, so it won't look like we've been talking."

"All right, Mickey. Tell your ma I'll come back later to visit."

As she stood, I asked, "Do you know where I'd find Eliza Bell now?"

She rolled her eyes to the ceiling. "No."

"One other thing. Who do you think will take over the Wrens now that Maggie's gone?"

Wren leadership was passed down from mother to daughter, and in the absence of daughters, to the second in command. Leadership carried more risks, but it was lucrative, as ten percent of the value of every pawned item was given to the head.

Honora shrugged. "Couldn't even guess."

But I remembered her tell. She didn't take her eyes off me, but there was the slightest head tip to the left. She was lying.

"Can you think of anyone who might want Maggie dead?"

"P'rhaps some other friend she betrayed."

I pulled the door open and watched her go.

Then I followed her. Left, right, left — then, around a corner that she took quickly, I lost her.

I paused and felt a rueful smile curve my mouth. Honora had known I was following.

&#128528;&#128512;&#128520;

I walked back toward Whitehall Place along the Victoria Embankment, up the broad stone steps, and through the rough cobbled yard behind the division, mulling my next step. It wasn't likely Eliza Bell would still be at the same address as fourteen years ago, but someone who knew her might. I wanted to know what she remembered.

The records room held books with the names of people we'd arrested. They were organized by year, so I began with the year 1861, the year of Honora's trial, pulling each book down off the dark wooden shelf and reading through the alphabetized listing. It might not seem difficult, except that sometimes names were added in later, in an addendum, or scribbled in the margins.

I looked through every book until the present year and found no mention of E or Eliza or Elizabeth Bell. I swore under my breath just as Barton stuck his head in.

"What's the matter, Corravan?"

"Trying to find a woman," I said dryly.

"The everlasting problem." He chortled and raised a finger. "The problem ain't finding a woman. It's finding the right one."

"Well, she isn't in here," I said, slapping the last book closed.

"Who're you looking for?"

"Thief and baiter named Bell."

"When was she arrested?"

"I guess she wasn't," I said. "But she should have been. She was an accomplice."

"Was she let off to turn witness?" he asked.

I blinked. The way Ma and Honora had told me, it seemed Eliza had been tried alongside Honora and "given nothing." But Ma hadn't been in the room, and Honora hadn't specified one way or the other. If there was no physical evidence of Eliza having committed a crime, she could've been turned.

"A good thought," I said to Barton and grabbed my coat. My first stop was the Home Office, which kept the Criminal Registers and the trial calendars. It took the clerk nearly an hour to find the notation and the indictment number for Honora's case. Armed with that, I went to the Old Bailey to look at the trial transcript. If Eliza had been a witness, her address would be on it.

There she was: Elizabeth C. Bell, of Russet Street, number eight.

The only defendant named was Honora O'Connell, with a shopkeeper Mr. Dross and Eliza as the sole witnesses. Mr. Dross identified the pair, and Eliza protested that she'd had nothing in her pockets and had only been in the shop to buy some ribbon.

But something odd caught my eye. In his testimony, Mr. Dross had called her "Eliza," though the judge had called her Elizabeth, as had been listed on the first page.

Instinct made me check Mr. Dross's address. Meryton Mews, number six.

I shuffled the papers back into their proper order and replaced them in the folder.

At that time, Maggie McHugh and her father had also lived in

Meryton Mews.

Coincidence? I rather thought not.

As luck would have it, an envelope had been slid partway under Eliza Bell's door when I arrived, and I gave it a gentle tug. It appeared to be a receipt of some kind, addressed to Mrs. E. Bell. Satisfied that I had found her, I replaced the bill and gave the door a sharp rap with the knocker. No one answered, and I rapped again.

"Comin', comin'!" I heard and the door opened.

A very pretty woman of about my age, with heaps of auburn hair, an upturned nose, and bright blue eyes looked up at me. "Yes?"

I glanced down at the floor. The envelope had vanished into her pocket.

"Mrs. Bell?" I asked, and at her nod, I said, "I'm Michael Corravan, an inspector at the Yard. I was wondering if I might ask a few questions."

A young boy was peering over the fence, and he hooted.

She hissed at me. "Not so loud! D'you want the world to hear?" She gestured for me to come in, and I stood in the foyer. Her home was decent, but the bench in the entry was threadbare, telling me that despite the respectable address, she strained to make ends meet.

"Do you remember a woman named Honora O'Connell?" I asked.

"Nae."

"You were in the Wrens together," I said. "Fourteen years ago."

She blinked, and her jaw jutted forward as she crossed her arms, but as I held her gaze, she pouted. "P'rhaps. Don't recall."

I put my hands into my coat pockets. "I read the trial transcript. If you don't want me to come around here every day, making it look like you're in trouble with the law, you'll tell me everything, including why you weren't tried with Honora."

She was silent, and I waited. Finally, her chest heaved with a sigh. "It was Maggie. She made the roll for the day and told me not to take anything from the shop."

"Maggie McHugh?" I asked, that cold feeling running down my spine again. "But she wasn't running the Wrens back then, was she?"

"When Jacinta were feeling poorly, sometimes she did."

I kept my voice even. "You were sent with Honora and told not take anything."

"Aye."

So Maggie had set Honora up to be caught. "Why would Maggie do that?"

She shrugged. "I dunno."

But I was beginning to assemble the pieces into order in my mind.

"Who will take over the Wrens now that Maggie's gone?" I asked.

"I dunno that neither. I'm not in it anymore. I'm respectable now."

*Probably due to money O'Hagan gave her,* I thought. Whatever I thought of the man, he was loyal, like most Chapel Irish. He'd take care of his niece.

"Thank you," I said and put my hand on the knob. "One more thing. Do you know Sean Tooley?"

Her face paled. "Get out! Just get out! And if you come round here again, I'll—I'll tell my uncle. He let you run off back then, but he still frets over you when he's in 'is cups."

"All right, all right." I left, letting her think she'd succeeded in scaring me off.

*What the devil was that about? Why so snappish about Sean Tooley? I* wondered. *Was Eliza one of the women he took up with "on and off," as Ma said?*

But I had the growing certainty that Maggie had wronged Honora beyond not appearing at her trial. My question was whether Honora understood the extent of it.

It was time to go see the man whom I suspected knew even less than I did.

⊰⊱

Sean Tooley wasn't difficult to find. I began at one of the Irish pubs frequented by dockworkers and found him at the third. "Over thar," the barman said and sent a thumb over his shoulder without even looking.

I went to the corner, and there he was, sitting with a newspaper and a pint. The light coming in at the window showed the lines on his face more harshly than the light at the church. I'd put him at five or eight years older than I, around forty.

"Mr. Tooley," I said.

He looked up. "Aye. 'at's me." He took in my coat, my hands, quiet at my sides. "You police?"

I pulled out a chair. "I wanted to ask about some friends of yours."

You can tell a lot about a man, his general level of guilt, by the way he responds to that sort of opening.

Tooley folded the paper and set it aside, clasped his hands, and landed them on the table, meeting my gaze. "A'right."

This man didn't have much to hide. Or he was very good at feigning.

"How did you know Maggie McHugh?"

"Ach." His face fell. "A turrible thing. We both grew up here. Knew each other since we were..." his hand gestured to somewhere around the table's height.

"Did you ever take up with her?"

He drew back. "Nae!" And then he shrugged. "Not saying we didn't have a pint together once or twice. But I didna care for her, not that way."

"And Eliza Bell?"

He stiffened and ran a hand over his chin. "Aye. We were friendly for a bit."

"And Honora O'Connell?" I asked.

His whole body stilled. "Why're you asking about her?"

"She's back from Australia."

His back thunked against the wooden panels behind him. "Wot?" It came out in a hoarse whisper.

Satisfied that he hadn't known, I said, "Only just back, a week ago."

"You seen her?" He tensed as if he'd jump up and run to her that very moment.

"Settle down," I cautioned him, and he swallowed and put his spine back against the panels. "And yes, I've seen her. Did you ever speak to her after she was arrested fourteen years ago? Get a letter from her, from Australia?"

"Nae. I couldna read then, so I doubt she'd 'a written."

"Did you care for her?"

His mouth twisted, and he looked down at his hands. When he looked up, his gray eyes were suspiciously damp. "Is she a'right? Healthy, I mean? Safe?"

My heart went out to him. If he didn't truly care for her, he would have asked different questions.

"She's fine," I said.

He drew a ragged breath. "And she's here in the Chapel?"

"I don't know where she's staying," I said. "But I'll get her word that you're asking after her, if you'd like."

"Thank'ee." His broad chest was rising and falling out of rhythm.

I guessed this was a man who had no idea at all that Maggie McHugh loved him — mostly because he loved Honora too much to notice anyone else more than in passing.

My second guess was Honora had known he loved her. And if she still loved him in return, this was another reason she wouldn't risk committing murder. She had a position and someone to love. What more reasons to live? What more reasons not to ruin it by killing an old rival—especially if she didn't even know that Maggie had sent her out with Eliza to be caught, to be sent away for years, maybe so Maggie might have a chance with Sean Tooley?

"Back when Honora was caught," I said. "Who was running the Wrens?"

He frowned, wary of revealing that he knew. "Why can that matter? She's dead."

"Honora's suspected of killing Maggie, and I think the reason has to do with whoever was in line for the head." I saw him hesitate. "I'm police, but I was born and raised here by Mary Doyle."

A flicker of recognition sparked in his eyes.

"Honora taught me how to play cards and slide an ace up my sleeve at Ma's table."

His eyes narrowed, and the left side of his mouth twitched. "Jacinta Wells."

I rose. "Thank you."

He put out a hand to halt me. "Is she staying?"

My mind had already leapt elsewhere, and it took me a second to realize what he meant. "Aye. She's taken a position with a dressmaker."

He released a sigh of relief. "She was always clever with 'er sewin'."

I left him smiling into space, his newspaper and pint forgotten.

Jacinta *Wells*. Katie *Wells*. It couldn't be a coincidence.

Maggie may have put on airs of respectability, but remarkably, she had Wrens living in her own house. I shook my head in surprise and headed back there.

&#9731;&#9731;&#9731;

Katie answered the door, looking calmer and more poised today. That wasn't suspicious, in and of itself. It had been another two days, after all, and as I had reason to know, the shock of sudden death does wear off.

Clearly she expected someone else, for she started, and her former air of timidity reappeared a shade too suddenly. "Do you want to see Mrs. James?" she asked, her eyes wide.

*Good lord*, I thought. *She should have been an actress, the way she could mold her expression.* "No," I said. "I want to talk to you."

She blinked but held her air of innocence. "All right."

I didn't let her direct me to the parlor. The light was better here, and I wanted to see her face. "Who is Jacinta Wells to you?" I asked.

She stiffened. "My late aunt."

"You know she ran the Wrens, back in the '60s, before Maggie did."

A long beat as she took that in, and then her eyebrows rose. "You can't possibly suspect her of Mrs. McHugh's death. My aunt died years ago."

"Did your aunt have any children?"

"No."

"And do you have any sisters? Any other cousins?"

This line of questioning shook her, but the only tell was a slight flare of her nostrils. "I didn't kill Mrs. HcHugh so I could run the Wrens, if that's what you're saying."

"Answer my question."

"I've an older sister Alice," she said with a shrug. "But she's respectable, same as I am."

"Where can I find her?"

"Putnam Street, number twelve."

As I noted it in my pocketbook, Mrs. James appeared on the stairs, her pale hand sliding down the banister, her eyes on me. "What's the matter?"

I turned to Katie Wells.

She looked up at the housekeeper and replied in a tone of mock seriousness. "He thinks my sister Alice killed Mrs. McHugh. So she'd be able to run the Wrens."

Mrs. James simply stared.

For the second time in as many days I watched two women speak to each other with their eyes. I needed to hear what lie had been concocted for this situation, and if both of them told it.

"Look here," I said, rising and standing between them. "You can avoid any unpleasantness if you tell me what Honora and Maggie fought about. This house isn't large enough for you not to have heard *something* they were saying."

From the second-to-last step, Mrs. James looked down at me and began with a seeming reluctance. "They were friends, from a long time ago, only Honora was jealous of Mrs. McHugh on account of Sean Tooley."

Katie explained further: "Mr. Tooley was in love with Mrs. McHugh. He'd come round and ask her to go for a pint or they'd sit in the parlor together, and anybody could see it, the way he looked at her, though she didn't think of 'im that way."

"Ah," I said and put an expression of belief on my face. "But why was this a problem for Honora?"

"Because," Mrs. James said slowly, as if explaining it to a fool, "Sean wouldn't look at Honora twice, and she thought Mrs. McHugh was the reason. Honora blamed her for being transported and for her broken heart."

If I hadn't seen Sean's face when I told him Honora was back in London, I would've believed her. She was that good a liar. But the way the two women elaborated and bolstered each other's stories told me a good deal.

"So Honora killed her," I said, with a look of sudden enlightenment, as if I were that fool, "because she was bitter over being caught and jealous over Sean Tooley."

Mrs. James and Katie both nodded.

They were in it together.

"Thank you," I said gratefully, though I let them see some exasperation. "Why you didn't tell me this right off, I'll never know."

"Do you know where to find Honora?" Mrs. James asked.

"No," I said. And then, as an afterthought, I added, "Do you?"

They both shook their heads.

"No ideas where I might find her? You're sure?" I asked again. They'd have been suspicious if I didn't push.

Katie spread her hands.

I left and walked down the street until I found a constable and showed him the house to watch. "If anyone tries to leave, take them to the Yard."

His eyes wide, he nodded and took up a post at the corner, where he could see the door.

ᚪᚪ

Leadership of the Wrens went by inheritance, I knew. But even if Alice was a few years older than Katie, she'd still have been too young to take over from their aunt Jacinta years ago. So Maggie, second in command, had been made leader. Given that Maggie had no children, Alice could certainly make a legitimate claim.

Putnam Street was only three streets away, and I found number twelve with no trouble.

The woman who answered the door looked a good deal like Katie, to be sure, but older and a bit careworn. A small boy clung to her skirts. "Aye, what is it?" she asked. "Who are you? Police?"

I wondered when I'd taken on the air of police so clearly that I couldn't pass for Whitechapel Irish anymore.

"I need to talk to you about the Wrens."

She laughed as if I was ridiculous and showed me her left hand. It was badly burned, with skin that was puckered and scarred. Her fingers moved stiffly. There was no possibility she could thieve with it. "I was never a Wren and know naught about it."

I winced. "When did that burn happen?"

"I was eleven," she replied.

It was unfortunate, but it was a sure guarantee that she was telling the truth.

She bent to pick up the boy and settled him on her hip. "I don't need to be thieving, or any of the rest of it. My husband earns a fair living."

"What does he do?" I asked.

She looked sorry she'd mentioned him. "He's a tackle porter, weighin' goods at London docks."

I raised a reassuring hand. "I'm not going to cause him any trouble. I'm just asking. I worked the docks myself for a while. Lighterman."

It's funny how sharing that could make a difference. She stepped away from the door and gestured for me to come in. I took a seat at the tiny wooden table and sat catty-corner from her.

"How long has Katie been a Wren?" I asked.

She went still and used her son tugging her curls as an excuse to avert her gaze.

I set my forearm on the table and leaned in, my voice frank. "I grew up here, and I know how it is. One of my friends was a Wren. For some, it's either that or being a prostitute. I don't blame her. I'm just asking. When did it start?"

Her eyes met mine. "'Twas after our parents died. Katie was fifteen." She sighed. "She's always felt cheated. She's younger 'n me and don't remember what it's like not to have a decent house and new dresses. But after our parents died, we had to sell most everything. Katie hated it. So she went to Maggie and asked to join. Maggie let her, 'specially when she saw…"

"Saw what?"

"Katie was talented," she said simply.

"Maggie had to know Katie might want to lead the Wrens eventually, as Jacinta was her aunt."

"Well, o' course," she said. "Katie's been loyal to Maggie for years, and she was sure Maggie would reward her. With Maggie havin' no daughters, Katie would 'a been the natural choice. But a few months back, Maggie told her she was thinking of giving it to someone else."

"Thinking of?" I asked. A few months was a long time to keep someone on tenterhooks. Plenty of time to make someone feel fidgety and impatient.

She nodded. "Maggie said she was worried Katie had too much of a temper. Clever hands, but too impulsive." She sighed. "She's right, so far as that goes."

"Who was this other person?" I asked, an uneasy feeling settling in my chest.

"I don't know." Alice's son reached toward the loaf of bread on the table, and she leaned over to hand him a slice of bread, which he took happily. "Just she wouldn't be able to make her choice until later in the year."

*Perhaps October*, I thought.

"What's the matter?" she asked. "You look peculiar."

"Nothing," I lied.

For now, I could guess who Maggie had intended to name her successor. Perhaps Maggie thought she could make up for some of what she'd done by offering Honora leadership of the Wrens. The extra seven years Maggie had cost Honora might be compensated by a good income for life. Had Maggie made the offer and Honora refused it?

I thought of what Honora had said when I'd asked who else might have a reason to kill Maggie. She'd told me to look at any other friends Maggie had betrayed.

I could imagine Katie feeling betrayed. I knew what that did to a person. Hurriedly, I left Alice's house, turned my feet once more toward Maggie's house, and began to run.

∞

I found the constable up front. "Anyone leave?" I asked breathlessly.

He shook his head. "Been watching the whole time."

I banged on the door. No answer. Banged again. "Mrs. James! Katie! Open the door!"

No answer. By this time the constable had come up next to me. "No one came out, I promise!"

"Stay here," I told him and ran around the back, peering in a window. No lights, no movement. I took out my lock picks and opened the door. The house was silent. I raced upstairs and found no signs of them.

Where the devil had they gone? Where did Wrens fly when they were about to be caught?

And would they try to silence Honora before they left? She wouldn't be on her guard. Was there any chance Katie knew where to find Honora?

*Damn Honora's distrust*, I thought. *I wish I knew.*

∞

Swearing under my breath, I ran straight for Ma Doyle's house. I prayed Honora was staying close by, and I took the outdoor stairs two at a time and hammered on the door. "Ma! It's me!"

The door jerked open, and Ma stood staring up at me. "Mickey! For goodness's sake!" My eyes went beyond her to the empty room.

"I need to talk to Honora, to warn her. Where can I find her?" I demanded. "Do you know?"

"I'm here," Honora said, emerging from the hallway, with what looked like a wedding veil in one hand and a needle in the other. "What's the matter?"

My heart jumped in relief before beating again, all out of normal rhythm. "Honora, when you confronted Maggie about not coming to your trial, did she offer you leadership of the Wrens? As a way to make it up to you?"

Honora tucked the needle into the hem and set the sewing on a shelf. "You ask that like you already know the answer."

"What did you tell her?"

She hesitated. "I said I'd consider it. Not because I really would, mind you, but I …"

"What?"

"She was …" Honora shook her head. "She wasn't like I remembered. It was like … she resented me, which felt absurd because she was the one who injured *me*. At first, I refused outright, but she came at me, her face full of scorn and anger and asked how could I of all people turn it down? I was already a convict." She shrugged. "She frightened me, the way she looked, beyond reason. So I said I'd think about it and left."

*That equivocation was why Katie thought she might say yes*, I thought. *Why she thought Honora was a threat.*

A groan escaped me. But at least everything was coming clear.

"Mickey, what's happened?" Honora asked.

I rested my hands on the top rung of one of the wooden chairs tucked around the table. "The day you were arrested, Maggie sent you out with

Eliza on purpose because she knew you'd be caught. She told Eliza not to put anything in her pockets, and one of the men who worked in the shop was Maggie's neighbor. He knew to look for you."

Her face paled. "But why?"

"Nearest I can figure, she was in love with Sean Tooley. She thought with you out of the way, she'd have a chance."

"Sean!" Her eyes were wide with shock.

"When I went to see Maggie's maid and housekeeper, they said that Sean loved Maggie, you loved Sean, and that's the reason you killed Maggie. Because you felt that she stood in your way with him all those years ago."

Her green eyes flashed. "That's not true!"

"I know," I said. "I saw Sean's face when I told him you were here."

Now her hands reached for the top rung of a chair, in imitation of mine. But hers trembled.

"I told him you'd returned, and he asked how you were, if you were healthy and safe," I said. "He wouldn't have asked those questions if he didn't love you sincerely and still. I doubt he ever gave Maggie a second's thought."

She scraped the chair away from the table, sat down, and rested two hands, palm down, on the wood surface.

My heart clutched, for I knew where she'd learned to do that, and why.

"I told you he'd find the truth," Ma murmured and settled a gentle hand on Honora's shoulder.

She looked up at me. "You believe me now, that I didn't kill Maggie."

"I think Katie Wells heard you arguing and thought she could—pardon the expression—kill two birds with one stone."

"She could take leadership of the Wrens *and* pin the murder on me," Honora said hollowly. "What a little ..." her voice faded then became bitter. "It makes me think I should've stayed in Swan River."

"Why?" Ma asked.

"At least there you knew to expect people lying and cheating! This maid don't even know me, and she's aimin' to have me hang for what she's done!" Tears rose to her eyes. "I just want to live and work and … try to find a decent life for myself here. Why can't I just do that?"

"You can and you will, Honora," I insisted, leaning over the table to face her. "But right now, Katie and Mrs. James have disappeared. At first, I was afraid they might try to kill you before they left—that's why I ran in here the way I did—but now I think they just want to get away. I'm going to the Yard to ask constables to go to the railway stations and keep their eyes out for two women, traveling together, looking as if they're leaving town. I can give descriptions, but do you have any idea which direction they'd go? What would they consider a safe place?"

Honora thought for a moment, her expression intent. "Look for trains going north. Jacinta Wells had family in Liverpool, along the Mersey," she replied. "And tell them to look for two women *without* bags or trunks or even satchels, Mickey. They have pockets. That's all they'll use, if they're running."

I nodded and left.

∞

Katie Wells and Mrs. James were caught at Liverpool Station, on a northbound train. Just as Honora said, they carried no bags, just reticules, with their valuables stowed in their pockets. Katie drew a knife on the constable who approached, but I'd warned everyone about their dangerous hands, and he escaped with only a scratch.

Honora began her stint as a dressmaker and married Sean Tooley in a quiet ceremony two months later. I stood up with them, and as I handed her the silver ring she had chosen for Sean, she laid her hand on my arm and smiled up at me, her green eyes bright with something like mischief. "Thank you," she murmured. "You're a good man … for an inspector."

That evening, in my room, as I removed my coat, an ace slid out of my sleeve onto the floor. Grinning, I picked it up and tucked it into the frame of my mirror.

# AD 1901

## The Canadian: Death in the Chinese Darkness

### J. F. Benedetto

*The foothills west of Peking, China*
*The Autumn of 1901*

There's something foreboding about the night here in China.

It's not the darkness that bothers me. I've ridden across half the British Empire in darkness while fighting for our late Queen Victoria, God rest her soul. In Canada, I chased wanted criminals by the Northern Lights. In the Orange Free State, I rode against marauding Boers by moonlight. In the Transvaal, I hunted railway saboteurs by starlight alone. No. It's not the shadowed darkness that bothers me. It's something else about the night here in China that makes me wary.

The natives say in hushed whispers that it's because demons rule the night.

Maybe they do. But sitting in Bolt's saddle near the torches with my Magazine Lee-Enfield rifle in my hands, I was certain demons were not what the Manchu Lady over there feared.

She'd told me of her intention to venture outside the walls of Peking tonight to 'receive something,' and that I would get $100 in trade silver for making sure nothing happened to her. That's all she would tell me. But when you're out of work and someone offers you two months' salary for one night's work, you don't inquire too closely about the job.

I could guess why the Manchurian Lady had hired me, though. Great Britain had crushed the Boxer Rebellion, and our troops now occupied all of North China, along with soldiers from the other foreign powers who'd lent England a hand: the Empires of Germany, Austria-Hungary, Russia, and Japan; the Kingdoms of Spain, Italy, Belgium, and the

Netherlands; and the Republics of France and the United States of America. These 'foreign devil' troops were everywhere, imposing their will at gunpoint on the natives around them. As for Great Britain, we were currently busy putting things right in Peking; there was even talk of absorbing China into the British Empire, just as we had India.

Given all that, any despised member of the Manchurian ruling class outside the walls of the Forbidden City *required* an armed guard. Preferably the foreign kind.

Like, say, a former army officer of the British Empire?

The young Manchu noblewoman sat waiting in her mule litter: a chair inside a box with a roof and windows, carried between two mules, one in front and the other behind, led by a walking muleteer. All of the litter's bamboo-grilled windows stood open as the Lady inside smoked her gold-inlaid water pipe. Her exhaled tobacco smoke mixed with the cool night air, bringing memories of that surprisingly expensive night at Van Wyks Vlei a year ago. Some things never—

*Uh-oh.*

I automatically squared the flat brim of my Stetson level with my eyes. "Someone's coming."

"What you see?" the Manchu Lady asked in sing-song English.

"It's too dark to see anything. But they're out there." What I didn't tell her was that Bolt's ears had swung around to the right for no obvious reason. Horses hear sounds that humans can't, so they can sense something coming sooner than a man could. And growing up in the wilderness surrounding Fort Smith, I learned to trust a horse's instincts.

The Manchurian Lady's silent skepticism was palpable until the old Chinese muleteer pointed out a trio of distant torch-fires coming toward us. The Manchu barked an order, and her silk-clad maid — like the muleteer, a Han Chinese native — got off her mule and hobbled over. 'Perfectly' flat-chested (the Chinese think a flat bust is attractive), she also had bound feet, her bones broken and crushed down to a length of just 4 inches. Their foreign Manchurian rulers had outlawed the hideous practice, but for some reason the native Chinese men consider tiny feet on a woman to be a mark of the greatest beauty, and so Chinese women continue inflicting such agony on their children.

The hobbling maid opened the door of the litter and got down on all fours. The Manchurian stepped out onto her, her wooden 6-inch platform shoes digging into the Chinese girl's back. Watching the Manchurian lady use her Chinese maid as furniture explained why the native Chinese have no love for these foreigners from Manchuria who have ruled over them for the past 250 years.

The uncaring Manchu stepped off onto the ground, her hair tied in a bun behind the big bow-tie shaped wooden panel all Manchu women in the ruling class wear on their heads, its ornateness showing her status. She looked up at me and pointed at the ground.

Holding onto my MLE rifle, I swung down out of the saddle, ground-tied Bolt, and looked down at her. Even with her half-foot high wooden shoes, she was still shorter than me.

She turned toward the approaching torches. "You A-meer-i-caan," she said, drawing out the syllables. She'd learned English from someone who overemphasized saying names correctly. "Why you called 'The Ca-naay-dee-an'?"

"What makes you think I'm an American?"

"I study two year with Methhh-o-diist priest. You sound like he. He A-meer-i-caan, you A-meer-i-caan."

*You are an American.*

I fought not to react.

Should I tell her that I was born in Fort Smith in the **Canadian** North-West Territories? That I'd tracked criminals as a constable in the **Canadian** North-West Mounted Police? That I fought against the Boers in South Africa as a sergeant in the **Canadian** Mounted Rifles? That I volunteered to serve a second tour of combat as a lieutenant in the mounted **Canadian** Scouts?

*Or would that not be clear enough?*

The arrival of the approaching strangers saved me from having to answer. Of the four Chinese men, one was bald and the other three had the shaved foreheads and hanging pigtails required of them by Manchurian law. Two of the three torchbearers, Baldy and Hairy, looked dumb as fence posts, but definitely not the third, Fancy-shirt. Neither did their boss-man, who glared at me. "Who is this foreign devil?" he asked the Manchu Lady in Chinese.

I gave no sign I understand spoken Chinese.

*"He is none of your concern!"* the Manchu ordered.

*"Send him away. I do not wish a barbarian here."*

She pointed at the ground right next to her. Gripping my MLE rifle tight, I stepped in close like the guard dog I was being paid to be, and pointed "Emily" at the boss-man with my finger on the trigger.

*"Well?"* the Manchu Lady declared.

Boss-man sneered at me, and tossed a little blue silk pouch into the dirt at our feet.

I ignored it, keeping both my gaze and my gun on Boss-man.

The noble Manchu Lady was above such manual labor as bending down and picking up things, so the maid retrieved it and gave it to her. The Manchu looked inside, then gestured. The old muleteer staggered past us with a heavy wooden chest, which he dropped in front of them. Boss-man sent Fancy-shirt to open the box, and the clinking of silver coins told me all I needed to know. Boss-man had Hairy and Baldy pick it up, and led them away.

Once they were out of sight the Manchu noblewoman ordered the Chinese muleteer to snuff our torches, and the Chinese maid got down on her hands and knees again. The Manchu dug her 6-inch wooden platform shoes into the Chinese girl's back and climbed aboard the litter. Wincing, the maid dutifully stood up and closed the door for her. The Manchu waved her away, and gestured for me to come close.

I did so, and she pulled me halfway through the open window, pushing her lips to mine in a kiss that knocked my Stetson back. She tasted of tobacco and something else, something warm and sweet I'd never tasted before, and I was so surprised that I didn't stop her when she put her other arm around me. I kissed her back, and—

She let go of me, so suddenly that I fell back out the window.

As if nothing had happened, she rapped on the window frame for us to get moving.

Being just a little bit taken aback by that, I footed my stirrup, climbed aboard Bolt, and our tiny group turned back for Peking.

We were not that far down the road when the muleteer jerked his animals to a halt. A cart, just visible in the moonlight, sat abandoned in the middle of the road.

"*What is it?*" the Manchu called out in Chinese.

It had 'Boer trap' written all over it, and I swept both my gaze and my rifle across the moonlit ground out beyond my side of the road. "It's—"

◁◦▷

I woke up on my back on the cold ground, in hideous pain, a trip-hammer using my skull as an anvil. The lightening sky held the color of false dawn, and Bolt loomed over me, whinnying.

What...

*I was down.*

**And I didn't have my rifle!**

I flipped over and ducked low, the sudden movements making me vomit. Spitting my mouth clear of the foulness, I drew my Webley .455 revolver as I threw my pained gaze across the grey landscape around us, searching for the Boers who had attacked me, before remembering this was China. My head throbbing, I got up to my knees, and the vomitous nausea returned, joining the savage pounding inside my skull.

I tenderly touched the lump on the back of my bare head, winced, and looked around. Where was I? The distant foothills looked closer, and nearby Peking further away. *And where was the Manchu I was guarding?* There was no sign of anyone, let alone the three mules, the Manchurian Lady, and her two Chinese attendants.

I holstered my revolver. Bolt and I were very much alone.

I'd been hit in the head from behind. *While on horseback?* A thrown rock, maybe. Fell forward against Bolt's neck, and he bolted and just kept going until I fell from the saddle.

So: we had been ambushed, and they took out the armed guard first. As I fought through the pain in my head, something nagged at me. Something important, regarding the ambush.

Bolt gave me a concerned snort; I still had not gotten back to my feet.

"Thanks, Bolt," I said, wheezing, looking up gratefully into those big, pained eyes. I worked my way unsteadily to my feet, and, grunting through the pain, steadied myself against Bolt—

—and nearly fell over when he went down.

"Bolt!" I dropped to my knees, and only then discovered his bleeding bullet wounds. How he'd managed to gallop this far with me on him, out cold, was nothing short of a miracle. "Just hang on, Bolt! I'll ..."

But he was already gone. His whole body lay still, the only movement being the wind flicking his lifeless mane.

I shoved my head against his hot neck, digging my fingers into his sweaty, lathered hair. *He'd killed himself, to save me.* I lay against him for a long time, holding onto him, not letting him go, my eyes squeezed shut against the tears, suffering in a way I hadn't known since that day at Rietfontein, when the Boers shot my mount Nightfall out from under me and took me prisoner.

But I escaped ... and I got my revenge on them for murdering Nightfall.

With a torn breath I let Bolt go, and stood up, gritting my teeth, to assess the situation. We'd been ambushed. My rifle was gone. The Manchu and her people were equally gone, and Bolt was dead. I was a dismounted Mountie, who'd lost not only his mount but also the people he was supposed to be protecting.

My Stetson lay in the dirt. I put it back on, squared the brim level with my eyes, and retrieved Bolt's saddle before starting back to Peking on foot.

I hiked a good mile before I came upon the dead muleteer. The mule-litter's crimson satin cushions and ebony water pipe lay in the road, but the litter itself was long gone, along with the Manchu and her maid. A few moments' scouting turned up the mule tracks as well as the footprints of four men on foot, the tracks all headed east, back to Peking.

I kept going.

⊠⊙⊠

I left Bolt's saddle at the livery stable the Australians had opened near Peking's Chang Yi gate. A few pence got me a *jen li ch'e* — a rickshaw — which took me along the base of the massive wall dividing the Chinese City from the Tartar City, and on to where I lived, on Book Street. I slumped out of my jacket and hauled myself up the stairs to the second floor, unlocked my apartment door, and opened it.

A fist smashed into my face.

Reeling, I got hauled into the apartment and the door slammed shut behind me.

Hairy and Baldy held me tight between them. I got a fleeting glimpse of my ransacked apartment before the third man of the foursome, Fancy-shirt, stepped up and gave me an open-handed punch to the face, using that weird fighting style that proclaimed him to be a Boxer rebel.

I spat out blood. "*Ch'un huo!*" I cursed.

He drove his hand into my stomach, doubling me over. Gagging, I got hauled back upright by Hairy and Baldy as Boss-man stepped up to me. "Where is it," he said.

"Where is what?"

Fancy-shirt punched me in the stomach again.

Retching, I got hauled upright once more. "Where is it," Boss-man repeated.

I just coughed and stared at him.

"*Give me his pistol,*" he ordered the bald thug on my right.

Baldy took my Webley from its holster, but stared dumbly at the attached lanyard, so I gave him a closer look at it, slamming his hand with the gun in it up into his face. As he lost his grip on me, I grabbed hold of the Webley and gut-shot him. The roar of the .455 was like a cannon in the little room, the 'manstopper' bullet punching a hole right through him in an explosion of blood and flesh.

Hairy, still hanging on to me on my left, grabbed for the gun, turning it away from him before I could fire. I kneed him in the groin, but before I could drop the muzzle and shoot him Fancy-shirt threw a knife. It sliced through the lanyard, and then he jumped at me, kicking the revolver out of my hand, sending it skittering into the corner where my Columbia Graphophone stood. Before I could move, Fancy-shirt drove his foot into my stomach, almost crippling me. I punched wildly and missed, taking his next foot-strike in the chest, heaving me back against the door.

Hairy came at me. Gasping in pain, I pulled over the coat rack, catching him in the face with the hooks, and shoved him into Fancy-shirt.

I lunged for my Webley.

Fancy-shirt's foot caught me in the back, pinning me against the wall, and he looped a strangle-cord around my neck. Thrashing for air, I collided with the Graphophone. The motor spun up the wax cylinder and a chorus singing *The Maple Leaf Forever* arose from the speaker horn. ♫ "In days of yore, from Britain's shore—" ♫

"AIEEYAAA!" Fancy-shirt howled, recoiling from the magic box that spoke.

Clawing the cord free, I grabbed my stone bust of General Wolfe and smashed it into his face.

♫ "—Wolfe, the dauntless hero came—" ♫

As Fancy-shirt fell, I rammed the stone bust down into the back of his head.

♫ "—and planted firm Britannia's flag—" ♫

Hairy charged me, howling. I backhanded him in the face with the stone bust.

While the Graphophone played on, I slammed the bust down against Hairy and Fancy-shirt over and over again until they were both dead, and General Wolfe, the Hero of Quebec, dripped with blood.

♫ "—may peace forever be our lot—" ♫

I slammed the bloody bust against the Graphophone, silencing it.

Boss-man, now trembling, backed away from me. I dropped the stone bust and picked up my revolver. He whimpered, shaking his head.

I didn't care. "You killed Bolt."

The Webley boomed, stopping his whimpering permanently. The .455 "Dum-Dum" bullets I use were outlawed last year by the Hague Convention as being inhumane, but at that moment, inhumane was *exactly* what I wanted to be.

In a room filled with dead men, I was the only one still alive. Panting, I dropped the Webley, barely managing to catch myself against the wall. My legs stopped working and I slid down to the floor, where a thought illuminated my mind, all too late: I'd just killed the only people who could have told me where the Manchurian Lady was.

☙❧

It was a good while before I could stand up again. The stench of spilled blood and torn guts turned my thoughts back to the war in South Africa I had so recently left behind, but I shoved those ugly memories back into the closet of my mind and forced the door shut.

A quick search of their bodies turned up a piece of paper with some Chinese neatly written on it, over-written with some bigger Chinese characters. It might be a vital clue, or a laundry list; there was no way to know. As to money, they all had *wen* — Chinese coins — and a total of $35 in foreign trade silver, which made no sense. The chest of silver had been far too heavy to have just $35 in it.

That's when I realized my clothes were splattered red with blood. I washed my face and hands, then changed clothes. As I got dressed, I fell back on my training as a Mountie and opened the warrant book in my mind. *Make an assumption, Constable, and work from there.*

Why had they ambushed us? Probably to get back the thing they sold the Manchu.

They tried to kill me, but Bolt got me out of there, at the cost of his own life.

They killed the muleteer and grabbed the Manchu and her maid.

Since only the muleteer was dead, they had taken the Lady and her maid with them. That said that they were both still alive.

But the four had not found the whatever-it-is on her, and so figured I must have 'it.'

They came here to get 'it' from me, but I wasn't in. They ransacked my apartment—

And then all this.

But I was missing something, some important clue regarding the ambush. I still couldn't pin it down, though. I closed the warrant book in my mind and rubbed my chin. Better to take care of this first, and hope that it would come to me while I worked. I went out into the hallway and tripped on my jacket, where it had fallen when I got punched opening the door. I put it on and opened the window overlooking Book Street. My whistle brought one of the local urchins running.

I held out a coin. *"This is yours, if you bring Master Li Feng here,"* I told him in Chinese.

He took off.

By the time Li Feng arrived, I still hadn't found my answer. At his knock I opened the door and stepped out into the hall with them. I tossed the urchin the coin I'd promised, and he took off. "Li Feng," I said, greeting the old man but also not inviting him inside.

The former Imperial Mandarin spoke in an emotionless monotone. "I have offended you some way?"

"Not at all. I just don't want you to get blood all over your shoes."

"Ah. You have ... had 'rats' in abode? You wish it 'cleaned' and 'pests' removed?"

"In a way that won't have anyone asking any embarrassing questions."

"Ah," he said again. "Such a thing be ... expensive."

I had fully expected it to be. I handed him my rent money.

Li slipped it up the voluminous sleeve of his brown cotton jacket. "I shall see to it."

"Oh, just one more thing." I handed him the paper I had found. "What does this say?"

Li Feng read it. "Ah. Large letters over small say, 'This debt forgiven.' This be bill from gambling den of Ho Chou. It say Wen Yu Lin owe debt of 114 *liǎng* of silver for his losses at *ma chiang*."

"What's 'mah-jong'?"

"*Ma chiang*," Li Feng repeated, correcting my pronunciation.

I still did not know what mah-jong (sorry, '*ma chiang*') was. But *liǎng,* I did know. Chinese money is valued by weight. Since silver of one *liǎng* is worth about 1.4 dollars, his debt was over $150, some three months wages for a foreigner like me. I didn't want to think how long it would take a native to raise so much money. But that explained why he'd sold the whatever-it-was to the Manchu.

And the dead Boss-man now had a real name: Wen Yu Lin.

I opened the warrant book in my mind again.

He had almost no silver on him, but did have a note saying his huge debt was paid off. *Assumption*: he went to the gambling den and used the chest of silver to pay off this Ho Chou. What would he do with the two women prisoners, though? He had to put them somewhere to question them about the 'it,' then leave them there while he tracked me down to retrieve the 'it.' Did he leave them with Ho at the gambling den? Keep them alive, at least until he had his hands on the 'it'?

I closed my mental book. "Li Feng, where can I find this Ho Chou and his gambling den?"

The address was in the part of the Chinese city where no foreigner goes, because they are often never seen again.

Peking is actually three 'cities,' each one surrounded by its own protective wall. The southernmost section is the Chinese City, where the natives live. North of it, on the other side of the high wall, is the Tartar City, where the ruling Manchu live. And in the heart of the Tartar City, enclosed by towering red walls, is the Forbidden City itself, a hive of palaces for the Manchurian Emperor of China.

The rickshaw stopped in front of a run-down tea shop, whose smell drew my gaze up to the second floor. Opium has a unique, rather sweet smell, not at all unpleasant, and at that moment a heavy odor of it drifted down from the open upstairs windows.

So, opium den, as well as gambling den? I paid the rickshaw man, who left as fast as he could. I squared my hat's brim level with my eyes, and strode into the lion's den.

The aroma of hot noodles and tea mingled with the stink of cheap tobacco and unwashed bodies. The noise — natives talking in Chinese, the clacking of tiles coming from a half-dozen games of what was, presumably, 'ma chiang,' the click of cups and bowls – died off into silence as everyone stared at me.

"I'm here to see Ho Chou."

At mention of his name several heads turned, leading my gaze to a table in the back of the room, where a fat Chinese man sat with two flat-chested Chinese girls, one on either side, backed by a pair of obvious bodyguards, all glaring at me. I strode over to the table where the 'honorable' Ho Chou sat with his whores and his roughnecks, and tossed the canceled bill in front of him.

He glanced at it. "What you wish here?"

"Wen Yu Lin stole something from me. I want it back."

"I not have it."

"I haven't even told you what it is yet." I rested my hand on the butt of my holstered Webley. "He owed you 114 *liǎng* of silver. He stopped by a few hours ago and paid off his debt. He had a Manchu Lady and her maid with him. Left them here. I want them back."

"They belong Wen Yu Lin. They his."

"Wen Yu Lin is dead. I killed him. The women are **mine** now."

At the news I'd killed Wen, Ho folded like a house of cards. "I know nothing what him do! Here no Manchu. Maybe, at house of Wen Yu Lin? Yes! You wish go, house of Wen Yu Lin?"

I raised one eyebrow. "Yes. I wish to go to Wen Yu Lin's house."

"I send these, them show you where Wen Yu Lin live." He raised a couple of fingers to the waiting toughs. "*This arrogant foreign devil came to steal the Manchu away from me. Lead the fool outside into the alley, kill him, and go feed his corpse to the pigs.*" He switched back to pidgin English. "I order them, take you house of Wen Yu Lin."

"Thanks." I whipped out my .455 Webley and gunned down both of my would-be murderers.

The two whores screamed.

I grabbed the fat man as his kept women ran, joining the crowd of fleeing gamblers. Terror distorted his face. "For shooting, military police come!"

"Of course they shall come! Whom do you think I work for?" It was a bold-faced lie, but he didn't know that. I shoved the muzzle of my Webley up into his flabby chin. "*I have four bullets left,*" I told him in Chinese, his eyes widening at the realization that I had understood every word of his order to have me murdered. "*Now, you are going to tell me where Wen Yu Lin put the Manchu and her maid, because if you do not, I will send you to join your ancestors.*"

Now he folded for real. "Up...up stair," he said, gesturing to the staircase on the far side of the now-empty shop.

"Show me!"

Ho swallowed, looked around, and tried to stall. I shoved him toward the stairs, jabbing my revolver in his back. "*Move!*"

The fat man hurriedly waddled his way up the stairs to the opium den on the second floor.

It consisted of little open rooms, inside which Chinese men reclined on their hips, tilting the doorknob-sized bowls of bamboo pipes over the yellow flames of little oil lamps. No one rushed; the few men who spoke did so in soft voices. The air itself tasted of opium and seemed languorous, like I was in someone's dream. A Chinese serving girl carrying a steaming teapot paused and gazed at the two of us with languid eyes, showing no reaction. Did she smoke opium, or was she just a servant who breathed in opium fumes all day? I motioned with my head for her to keep going, and with no worry and no hurry she drifted along.

I shoved Ho. "*Where is the Manchu woman?*"

He pointed, and I pushed him down the hall toward that door. When we reached it, he just stood there.

"Open it!"

He rattled the doorknob. "It locked. From inside! I no have key."

"Damn it!" I cursed, stepping away from him. He turned around to look at me ... and I threw myself into him shoulder-first, bashing him into — or rather, *through* — the locked door. Ho went sprawling on his back and I followed him in, stepping on his belly like a Manchu.

The virtually empty room smelled of fine tobacco smoke, its only furnishings being one small chair and a table bearing an iron teapot, a wooden cup, and a cheap tin water pipe. The Chinese maid cowered in one corner; her Manchu mistress sat in the other, her head locked inside a wooden box punctured by a few air holes.

Ho was out cold. I helped the Chinese maid up, then went to remove the wooden box from the Manchu Lady's head. It had some kind of Chinese lock—

I blinked.

*This room was locked from the inside.*

In a flash I remembered the missing piece of the puzzle: I'd been looking forward, out at the countryside, with my back to the Manchu and her attendants, when I was hit from behind. Which meant the one who threw it was—

I ducked.

The heavy iron teapot just missed the back of my head, the force of the swing pulling the Chinese maid forward off her tiny bound feet, sending her down in a heap.

I savagely booted the iron teapot out of reach and leveled my Webley at her. *"The door was locked from the inside by someone smoking that water pipe, and you are the only person in the room who could do that. Ho would never give you a water pipe, tobacco, and matches, let alone the key to lock the door, unless you were working with Wen Yu Lin the whole time."*

She had a *ho pao*, a pouch, tied to her belt. I yanked it free. It held a small key.

I got the box off the Manchu's head, and she blinked hard in the light, a look of complete helplessness painted across her face — until she saw me.

And Ho, lying unconscious on the floor.

And her cringing, 'loyal' maid.

The Manchurian picked up the iron teapot with both hands and smashed it down on the maid's head. She lifted it high a second time and swung it down on the bleeding maid again as she tried to crawl away. Then a third swing, and the Chinese maid lay unmoving on the floor. The pot dropped out of the Manchu's fingers, and she stumbled over into my arms.

I held her close. "It's all right. You're safe now."

She kissed me, deeply, and I returned the favor, holding her tight. When our lips parted, she pushed me away ... *with the 'it' bag in her right hand, and my revolver in her left.*

How—?! My gun I could understand, but where had she gotten the 'it' bag from?

She cackled at me. "Jade necklace belong me now!"

Then I knew. *She had pulled me that close only once before.* "That first kiss you gave me was only to distract me, so that you could slip that little pouch into one of my jacket pockets."

"Yes. Now jade necklace belong me now!" Her dark eyes glittered as she switched hands. "You are fool!" she said, her singsong voice full of revealing hate. "You think Manchu wish love foreign devil? Ha! Now I pay you, for help me."

She put her finger on the trigger.

I blinked.

*"You see?"* I snapped at her in Chinese. *"It will not fire, because you are but a foolish girl that knows nothing."* I pointed at the left side of the Webley. *"Your finger is on the trigger, but you did not first push the lever on the side! That is why it will not shoot, YOU STUPID GIRL!"*

Grinning at my foolishness in telling her that, she shoved the lever hard with her thumb.

It did exactly what it was there for: it unlatched the two halves of the pistol and broke it open at the top for reloading. In a single second, the thing in her hand went from being a lethal weapon to just an unfolding hunk of metal.

I punched her right between the eyes and sent her sprawling.

*Damnation!* Flexing the damn pain out of my hand, I retrieved my Webley, latched it shut and made a mental note to replace the lanyard as soon as possible. I also picked up the little blue silk pouch. "You still owe me $100. I'll just take the jade necklace as compensation."

My would-be murderer snarled ... and pulled a knife on me.

The boom of my Webley stopped her. Permanently.

As the smell of cordite enveloped me, I glanced over at the bloody, moaning Chinese maid, not yet fully dead, and the now-groaning fat man. Both of them were killers, and both of them had tried to murder me. And after what I had done to them here, given even half a chance, they were certain to try again in the future.

One shot each was all it took to remove the two killers from the world of the living. Maybe it was an act of violence that would yet make the world a better place.

No, it wouldn't. The war in South Africa had taught me that.

As I turned to leave I eyed the lifeless Manchu Lady whose name I had never even learned. *Ten people dead, over a lousy piece of jewelry.*

I stuffed the cursed thing into my pocket.

⟨⊙⊙⟩

My apartment had been completely cleaned, as promised. But I'd spent the rent money to do it, so I needed some cash, and right quick. I took out the necklace: a string of jade beads bearing an Imperial jade pendant showing a curled-up Chinese dragon. Holding the pendant in my hand, it felt strange, in some way I couldn't explain. Well, whatever; it was obviously valuable. Once I sold it, I—

*The last person who sold it died, along with nine other people.*

I blinked.

Stepping over to the shelf holding the canisters of wax cylinder recordings for the Graphophone, I pulled one out at random. I removed the lid, dropped the cursed necklace inside, put the lid back on and blindly shoved it back in amongst all the other canisters. Then I dropped myself as well, into my chair.

Screw it. The rent could wait.

I closed my eyes, and let myself slip off into an exhausted sleep.

# AD 1922

# *The Problem of the Disappearing Heart*

## *S. B. Watson*

The Heart of India was a very large diamond. It came from the depths of Golconda, mined from the mud in the 10th century. For two hundred years, the kings of India fought over the stone, trading it back and forth between bloody fingers, cutting and reshaping it with each transfer. It was never formally weighed, but is believed to have sat in the range of 170-200 carats by the time it took its final, formidable shape — an uneven rose cut, with a wavy base and domed crown of glittering, triangular facets.

The empires of medieval India rose and fell, and the stone was lost. For nearly two centuries it existed only in legend and myth, until it was discovered in the pocket of a dead lapidarist in Italy. It eventually found its way to the Medicis, but was lost again when the family was banished from Florence.

And so, every century, the stone was lost and found. It was owned by rich and poor alike, was gifted to harlots and stolen from princesses, was purchased by blood and sold for love.

On the eve of the Great War, it fought at the Battle of Liege in the pocket of a Belgian Lieutenant. It was never heard of again, until…

〇〇〇

Major Alexander MacLean moved briskly along the hallway of the second floor of the theater, checking the door numbers on the private boxes as he went. Dougal Grieve followed, at a more leisurely pace, leaning heavily against his blackthorn cane with every other step.

Grieve was a large man; beneath the starched implacability of his black-and-white evening suit the sinewy movement of brawn and thick bone was evident. He walked slowly behind the major, looming down the hall with the measured stride of a prize boxer rearing into the ring. If it weren't for his crippled leg, he would have cut an imposing figure. As it was, the cold glint in his eye gave him an air of quiet melancholy rather than heat and vigor.

"They keep regular season tickets," the major said as he opened the heavy mahogany door and stepped into the red-velvet gloom of Box 31.

"Then why are we here, and they aren't?" Grieve asked, following the major into the box and shutting the door, enveloping them in the velveteen dimness.

"The old boy isn't seeing that well," said Major MacLean. He leaned over the back row of seats and read the brass-plated numbers fixed to the backrests. "Stepped out in front of a taxi yesterday." He slipped into the row, leaving the aisle seat for Grieve. "Says he didn't hear it coming at all."

"He's alright?" Grieve asked as he sat beside the major, propping his cane between his knees.

Major MacLean laughed. "May be old, but he's strong as an ox. He's offered me the seats tomorrow, but he's planning on being back the day after that. Which reminds me, are you free tomorrow?"

Grieve shook his head. "I leave for Java tomorrow morning. First leg of the journey."

Below them, the theater basked in the amber glow of the chandeliers. Only the long stage, stretching obliquely away from the box, was illuminated by a brilliant flood of overhead lights. The towering crimson curtains cast a blood-red luster across the churning milieu of theatregoers.

Grieve turned to look at the box. It was spacious. Five rows of bench seats gently sloped down towards the front. Great curtains were fixed above the box, but were drawn back to the walls, framing the view of the theater. All the other seats were empty.

"Is it normal," Grieve asked, turning to Major MacLean, "for box seats to be empty?"

The major smiled. "No, it's not," he said. "Apparently, the chap who sits up there," he pointed towards the front, "has tried to buy out the rest of the box for years. Wants it completely private. But my uncle and aunt like Box 31, Nelson Kline be damned." MacLean shifted in his seat, to talk to Grieve more directly. "Dougal, I'm keen for you to see the act tonight. I've seen Tadmendri perform twice this week already — sitting out there, of course — and I think I may have an idea how it's done. You've heard of The Heart of India?"

Grieve nodded. "I'm aware of its history. I'm aware The Great Tadmendri owns it, and I am aware, in a general way, that political groups in the Foreign Office want it given back to India."

"Quite," MacLean said.

The door opened. Grieve and MacLean both turned into the light as a tall, young man in evening dress walked past them and down the aisle to the front row.

"As I was saying," MacLean continued. But the door opened again, and in a sudden commotion a young woman tripped across the lintel, collapsing to the floor behind Grieve and MacLean.

"Oh, *scheiße*, I've fallen again," she hissed, as she pulled herself back up. She froze as her gaze rose to the faces of the two men directly in front of her. "Oh! I'm sorry, excuse me. Excuse my language, please." She brushed golden curls from her face and tucked them behind her ear. They fell back across her brow. With a sigh, she smiled at Grieve and MacLean, and shrugged. Her eyes glittered in the low light. "I apologize," she said. "I'm not used to… all *this*."

MacLean waved his hand dismissively. "Never you mind, dear. Enjoy the show."

The woman nodded at the men and walked up front. The young man leaned his head into her as she sat, and for a moment they sat close as she whispered in his ear.

"Nelson Kline," MacLean whispered to Grieve.

Grieve raised his eyebrows. "I see now why he wants a 'private' box."

MacLean smiled wryly at Grieve, just as the great curtains swept open across the stage below, and the show began.

The Great Tadmendri was tall and lean, dressed in simple, tattered Indian robes and a dirty turban. The stage was darkened behind him, and empty. He stood alone, commanding attention beneath the spotlights by some strange charisma. When he spoke, it was with an accent so thick Grieve felt the need to lean forward, to bend his ear to discern what the man was saying.

First, Tadmendri made his props appear on the empty stage as if from thin air. Human-shaped boxes, a table, a cage. He produced his assistant from the cage — a young, English woman in music-hall lingerie with fiery red hair. She helped with the act, occasionally changing her attire in a blinding instant, one moment lingerie, the next an evening gown, the next hunting wear, the next a man's suit.

The acts were good, but not unique. They were not why everyone had come. The theater had filled to see the Heart of India.

"Here it is," MacLean whispered to Grieve, as Tadmendri made the props, and his assistant, disappear from the stage in the same manner he had produced them, eventually leaving only himself, again, alone.

In a blaze of light, an enormous idol appeared behind Tadmendri. Shiva, encircled by a ring of arms blossoming outward. Two arms stretched out before her, holding a small, domed altar. It was empty.

Tadmendri reached up into the air and pulled the diamond from nothing. The entire theater was silent, completely still, concentration fixed on the gleaming chestnut of light the magician held between his fingers. Slowly, he moved to the altar, and placed it on the peak of the dome.

"Now, watch closely," MacLean said, leaning in to Grieve. "It liquifies, and melts off the altar, and an item of a woman's handbag is left in its place. The woman is located in the crowd, and she finds in her handbag the diamond."

Grieve leaned to the side. Whenever Kline leaned in to speak to his companion, part of his head occluded Grieve's view of the stage.

Tadmendri took a small, golden kerchief from the pocket of air to his left, and draped it across The Heart.

Kline leaned again, heavily into the woman. Grieve frowned and craned his neck.

The young woman looked at Kline, and spoke into his ear. He seemed to press against her. She grabbed his shoulder, and pushed him back up. In the light from the stage, Grieve could see the furrows on her brow. Kline tottered, and fell away from her, hitting the chairs with a heavy crash.

Grieve and MacLean leapt up.

A distant scream cut the silence of the theater, pulling Grieve's attention briefly to the stage as he rushed forward to Kline.

A dark matter sat on the idol, which appeared drenched in fresh blood. Tadmendri stood looking at it, as if dumfounded.

Kline lay on his back across the chairs, motionless, his eyes fixed open in a deathly glare.

"He just suddenly went stiff," the woman said as they knelt beside him.

"Is that blood?" MacLean asked, pointing to the chest of Kline's shirt.

Grieve ripped the shirt open.

Beneath the shirt, Kline's bare skin was rent, from beneath his neck to the top of his belly. The fissure was deep and gaping, splitting the sternum clean through. Grieve found himself staring into the surprising depths of the moist cavity, past the opened breast bone, and into the nest where the heart should lie.

But Nelson Kline's heart was gone. In its place, sat The Heart of India, glittering beneath the lights of the theater that suddenly glared to full illumination.

◙◖◗◙

Grieve and MacLean stood in the corner of Box 31 as Detective Inspector Bedlow moved quickly around the body of Kline, scrutinizing every detail. He was a short, bulldog-faced man, perpetually scribbling in a police-issue notebook with a broken pencil.

Bedlow eventually snapped his notebook closed and angled through the crowd of police that filled the box.

"My sergeant tells me you two are more than simple witnesses," Bedlow said.

MacLean pulled his warrant card from his breast pocket and held it out to the inspector. "Chief Constable of the Inverness-Shire County Constabulary, Major Alexander MacLean," he said.

In the dim lighting at the back of the box, Bedlow's bulldog face blanched slightly. "I see," he said. "And this man?"

"This is Dougal Grieve," MacLean said, putting his hand on Grieve's shoulder. "A personal friend, as well as professional freelancer. He consults for us on particularly difficult cases."

"Your statements have already been taken?" Bedlow asked.

"Yes," Grieve answered.

Bedlow nodded. "Good, good," he muttered. "Well, we'll try to make this investigation brief, but I don't think I need tell you where things lie. For the moment, you both must stay in the city."

Grieve leaned against the wall of the box and groaned. "I leave for Java tomorrow," he said.

Bedlow shrugged. "I'm sorry, sir. There's nothing for it."

"Is there any way we could help, Detective?" MacLean asked.

Bedlow tumbled the broken pencil stub around in his fingers. "You say," he said, looking at MacLean, "this man specializes in these sorts of cases?"

"Yes."

Bedlow turned to Grieve. "I'll have a contract drawn up for you tonight. Where do you want to start?"

◦◦◦

Grieve walked around the body of Kline, surveying the box. Under the raised theater lights, Box 31 was largely denuded of its mysterious gloom, but was still far from brightly lit.

Kline's body lay out across the seats, shirt ripped open across his chest, the rent diving deeply into his chest cavity.

"There isn't much blood," Grieve said to the constable standing next to the body.

"No, sir," he said, "we noticed too. Seems to be very little. Coroner's still on his way. He can shed more light on it, sir."

Grieve leaned against the banister and looked to where he and MacLean had sat. Then he turned, looking down towards the stage.

The theater was mostly evacuated, but some pockets of theatregoers were still being held for questioning. They sat below in huddled masses among the red-velvet seats.

On the altar of Shiva the red lump sat, the altar drenched in blood.

Grieve pushed off the banister and began to leave, but stopped. Turning, he walked to the large, ornamental curtain draped along the side of the box. It was a thick material, its hem perfectly grazing the floor. Grieve pushed it with his fingers. It moved about three inches before hitting the wall.

"Find something, Dougal?" MacLean asked from behind him.

Grieve kneeled. About two feet up from the hem a narrow, wooden dart protruded from the weave of the fabric. Grieve gripped it between his forefinger and thumb, and carefully pulled it out. It was three inches long, sharpened at both ends.

"What is it?" MacLean asked.

"Devil if I know," Grieve said, placing the dart back in the puncture wound it had left in the heavy fabric.

Grieve rose, pulling himself up on his cane. "It's time to speak with the magician," he said.

∞

The Great Tadmendri was a man name Lowell Kaur. He rose from his seat as Grieve, MacLean, and Bedlow entered his dressing room, beneath the stage. On a wardrobe rack, near the wall, hung multiple robes, all tattered and colored to give the appearance of filth. Kaur himself wore a trim grey suit and spats.

"Mr. Kaur," Bedlow said, "Do you understand the position you find yourself in?"

Kaur stood very still, his dark eyes moving from one man to the next. He thought carefully before he answered. "I understand," he said, all traces of the heavy Indian accent now gone, "that a man has died, and it was made to look as though my effect killed him."

"Did you know the deceased?"

"What was his name?" Kaur asked.

"Nelson Kline."

Kaur shook his head. "No, I did not."

"Then let's start with the trick itself," Bedlow said. "How does it work?"

Kaur shrugged. "It's very simple. Before the show, my assistant, Mary Fowles, takes one of the diamonds, and — "

"Wait," Bedlow interrupted. "You said 'one' of the diamonds? There's more than one Heart of India?"

Kaur's lips crept into a subtle smile. "There are *no* Hearts of India," he said, moving to his dressing table upon which sat a small, square box with a hinged lid. "If that stone ever existed in the first place, I'd be amazed." Kaur raised the lid of the box. It was filled with large, brilliant stones, each an exact copy of the other, each recognizably formed to the shape of the nearly mythical gemstone.

"I'll be damned," murmured Bedlow. "So, there isn't a *real* stone involved?"

Kaur shook his head. "Of course not," he said. "If there was, I'd be a fool to do such a trick, wouldn't I?"

Grieve moved across the room and examined the stones, comparing one to another.

Bedlow scribbled aggressively in his notebook, then looked back to the magician. "All right," he said. "Tell us how the trick is done."

"Mary," Kaur continued, "takes one of the stones into the auditorium before the performance, dressed as a theatregoer. She selects an easy mark for pickpocketing, pilfers something from the lady's bag and replaces it with the stone, as well as a brief note telling the individual to 'play along,' as it were, if they should discover the stone before the reveal. Mary brings back the item and loads it into a compartment on the idol's altar, along with a small sac filled with a mixture of crushed glass and water. When I place *my* copy of the stone on the altar, I place it on a small hinging pedestal that you can't see from the audience. I cover it, at which moment Mary triggers the contraption. The top of the altar sinks, and slides to the side, while a second pedestal rises from below, bringing the woman's item with it. The sac is punctured on the way up, and spills when the platform moves into place, giving the illusion that the diamond has melted."

Grieve cleared his throat, and looked up from the box of fake diamonds. "There are always two stones in play?" he asked.

"Yes."

"Have you recovered the second stone? The one Miss Fowles planted before the show?"

Kaur shook his head. "No," he said.

Grieve looked at Bedlow. "Have *your* men recovered it?"

Bedlow scribbled in his notebook. "I'll find out soon enough."

"One more thing," Grieve continued, looking back to Kaur. "Your name. 'Lowell Kaur.' Not very… Indian, is it?"

"I was born in Paris," Kaur said. "My mother was French. Apparently, 'Lowell' means 'wolf.'"

⚙

Mary Fowles was backstage next to the idol, both guarded by policemen. She was prancing back and forth, arms crossed, as the men approached. She had appeared very young under the theater lights, but as Grieve drew near he could see the lines of age beneath her makeup.

"I set the trick up just like every other night," she told the inspector, pointing at the idol. "Picked a proper nice mark, this time, I did. Proper lady. I came backstage, loaded the idol, and left to get ready for the rest of my bit. That's the last I saw of it, I swear."

Grieve looked at the altar, a large dome of gold-painted metal. Upon the peak of the dome sat a human heart, darkened with exposure to the air. Dried blood had poured over the metal, staining most of the altar dark brown.

"Are you are saying the idol sat unattended," Grieve asked, "backstage, for a time?"

Fowles' head bobbed back and forth. "Well, yeah, there's only two of us, me and Lowell, we can't both watch it the whole time, now can we?"

"Anyone could have accessed it?"

Fowles shrugged. "They *could* have, sure," she said. "But they'd need to know how the idol worked…"

"Miss Fowles," said Bedlow, "does the name 'Nelson Kline' hold any significance to you?"

Fowles frowned, thinking for a moment, then shook her head. "No," she said. "Who is it?"

"The man who died," Bedlow said.

"Oh," said Fowles.

Grieve looked up from the bloody altar. "How long has Kaur performed this trick?" he asked.

"We've only done it this season," she said," but he's used the altar mechanism for years, at least three."

Bedlow's pencil scratched across his notebook before he spoke again. "Concerning Mr. Kaur… You've worked for him a little less than a year?"

Fowles turned to Bedlow and looked him up and down, her sharp eyes glittering beneath the spotlights. "He pays fair, if that's what you really want to know," she said. "Not many jobs for quick-changing pickpockets, other than the streets, now are there?"

⟡⟡⟡

The next morning, Grieve and MacLean met on the steps of New Scotland Yard and walked together into the towering brick building on the Victoria Embankment.

Detective Inspector Bedlow sat at his desk when they entered, chewing on the end of a pencil, staring at a large map of London that hung posted to the wall by tacks. His desk filled most of the small room, leaving just enough space for three filing cabinets and two old mahogany chairs across him his. The cabinets were stacked with tottering papers and files. The odor of cigarette smoke hung thick in the room; the ashtray on the edge of the table was heaped with ash and old butts.

"This is how it stands," Bedlow said, still chewing on the pencil as Grieve and MacLean sat across from him. "Nelson Kline. Private Secretary to the Undersecretary of the Foreign Office. Aged 37. Parents deceased, no siblings, no wife, no children. Incidentally, no real heirs to speak of."

Grieve pulled an old black pipe from his breast pocket, snapped a match across the back of his shoe, and began puffing great billows of smoke up into the air of the tight room. Bedlow glared at him for a moment, but Grieve puffed away, impassively.

"We spoke with his household," Bedlow continued, still chewing on the pencil. "Kline was apparently well known to women. Turns out, the young thing with him that night, Cora Connor, was a distraction from his latest fling, a wealthy, middle-aged woman named Catherine Burgess. Catherine apparently took the breaking of their relationship poorly…" Bedlow lifted a crinkled sheet of letter paper from the table and read, "'And so,' she writes here, 'I will not rest until I tear your heart out, as you have torn out mine.'" He placed the letter back on the desk.

Grieve shrugged. "Such words aren't uncommon between angry lovers," he said.

Bedlow sighed. "You're right, very right. Burgess has an alibi. She was fitting a dress, three miles away, when Kline was murdered."

Bedlow chucked the pencil onto the table. "Next is Miss Cora Connor," he said. "Pretty girl, well spoken. Irish and German, apparently. Here as a student. Met Kline four days prior to the murder, when they both entered the same cab. They'd already slept together, twice, by the night he was murdered. Your testimony, Grieve, is of importance here."

"I clearly saw them talking, during the show," Grieve muttered, through the pipe smoke.

"Yes," Bedlow said. "Which is helpful, and infuriating, at the same time. Then there's Mary Fowles," Bedlow continued. "Picking pockets at seventeen, prostitution at nineteen, fell in with a travelling magician at twenty, worked on her own for a few years, met Kaur in a bar one evening a year ago. A quick operator, but no motive to kill him, that we can find."

"And what of Kaur, himself?" Grieve asked.

Bedlow pulled a cigarette from the desk drawer, and lit it. MacLean coughed, and fanned the air.

"Lowell Kaur," Bedlow said, a snide tone creeping into his voice, "entered the country five years ago, and brought his brand of magic with him. Mostly cheap tricks he'd learned from a stint among the magicians of Cairo. His first year here, he played bars, nightclubs, opium joints, and brothels. His first assistant left. He found another, and somehow moved up to small stages at variety shows. Each year it seems he's moved a rung up the ladder. Last year, however, he leapt up. The Heart of India came from nowhere, and he became famous overnight."

Bedlow opened a thin file on the desk, and turned it towards Grieve and MacLean. "Coroner reports," he said. "The heart on the idol was verified to be Kline's. The blood, however, is chicken blood." Bedlow leaned forward, and tapped a hand-drawn schematic of the cut found in Kline's chest. "Coroner says this is barely possible, by the way. This cut, through the sternum, isn't known to science."

"Impossible," MacLean growled through the smoke.

Bedlow shrugged. "Just like the rest of the case. But you want to know the real punchline?" Bedlow grinned across the cigarette. "The fake diamond in Kline's chest?" He shook his head. "Wasn't fake."

Grieve pulled the pipe from his lips. "What do you mean?"

"It's a real diamond," Bedlow said, the words slithering from his lips. "It's *the* real diamond. It's the Heart of India."

The smoke swirled around the ceiling, yellowed in the office's dim light.

"You're sure?" Grieve asked.

Bedlow nodded. "We told Kaur this morning. He went pasty as a sheet. Kept saying, 'How could that be? But how could that be?'" Bedlow puffed a billow of cigarette smoke into the haze. "At the moment," he said, "we've succeeded in keeping all this from the papers. But…" he shrugged. "I'm sure that won't last long, at this rate. Just like my sanity."

⊂⊃⊂⊃

Grieve closed the passthrough window of the taxi as it swept through the streets, a scant rain crackling irregularly against the pane windows.

"Do you have any idea, Grieve, what we're dealing with?" MacLean asked, brushing the frosting of rain from his pea-coat.

"None whatsoever," Grieve growled. "My ship sailed two hours ago, you now. My harvest won't wait, for heaven *nor* hell, and if I don't get my ass on a ship for Java soon…"

They were silent for a moment.

"Where are we going?" MacLean asked.

"A quick stop," Grieve said, looking out the window, biting the bit of his empty pipe. "Then a doctor friend of mine."

"You don't have faith in the coroner's conclusions?"

"Driveling conclusion, if you ask me. *Not known to science?* Pah! Foolish thing to say… It's known to *somebody*! They did it to Nelson Kline, apparently beneath my very nose… Fool…"

⊂⊃⊂⊃

The taxi slowed as it entered the alleys of Rotherhithe. Cautiously, the driver crept deeper into the mazelike complex, the streets becoming thinner and tighter, the buildings reaching higher overhead. The taxi stopped at a crooked elbow in the road, next to a gated corridor. A mossy courtyard reflected the rainy gloom beyond the iron gate.

"I'll be back," Grieve said, slipping from the taxi.

MacLean watched as he moved quicky through the gate, the brass ferrule of his blackthorn cane tapping along the cobbles.

He returned in less than five minutes, and the taxi sped away.

⊄⊃⊄⊃

"Straight down the sternum, you say, cutting the cartilage?" Doctor Joseph Gatton repeated, running his finger down the breastbone of the skeleton in his office.

Grieve nodded.

"Very unusual," Gatton murmured.

The doctor's offices were large, with doors accessing a waiting room and small surgery, as well as his secretary's office. Overcast light streamed in through tall, bay windows on either side of the bookshelf behind the doctor's desk, and mixed with the soft, amber light of his floor lamps.

"The Met's Coroner termed it *unscientific*," Grieve smirked.

Gatton shook his head. "No," he said. "That's not correct, but it's not far off. This procedure *is* done, but it's extremely rare. There are only a handful of practitioners in the entire world who would be capable of performing it... You say you saw the victim *talking*, right before this happened?"

Grieve nodded. "I did," he said.

"If anyone other than yourself told me this, Grieve," Gatton said, thrusting his thumbs into the sleeves of his vest, "I would say they were crazy. But, coming from you..."

Grieve slowly shuffled away from the skeleton and looked out the window. "I'll be the first to admit," he murmured, "*something* in my own story must be incorrect. What I saw simply *cannot* be true. And yet, I saw it."

Doctor Gatton coughed, and moved to the bookshelf behind his desk, frowning at the titles along the shelves. "Let me get back to you,

Grieve," he said. "This procedure, performing a mediastinal cut, is very rare indeed, but it *is* documented… somewhere… I have it here, somewhere. Give me a day and I'll bring you more information."

❧

Grieve and MacLean dined at The Samaritan. Across the street was a small newspaper stand. All the headlines read some variation of the same concept: Impossible Murder at The Emporium Theatre! Nelson Kline Found Dead, Heart Missing! Heart of India Found in Dead Man's Chest!

Halfway through the meal, MacLean could stand it no longer, and ran across to purchase an edition. They read it together as they ate. It contained all the details of the case, including the authentication of The Heart of India.

"I wonder how the devil they acquired *that* information," MacLean muttered.

❧

The next morning, Grieve met MacLean early and they took a taxi back to Rotherhithe.

The rains had stopped during the night, but dark clouds still covered London as they walked through the corridor and into the small, mossy courtyard Grieve had entered the day before.

Grieve led the way up the stairs of an old, crumbling landing to a dark door, and knocked. A stooped woman opened the door, her graying hair falling from its hasty bun in messy streams. She took them through a gloomy hall, passing the shadows of disused furniture, and opened a heavy oaken door. Light streamed from the room, pouring from two enormous windows that looked out onto the street. The man at the desk between the windows stood as they entered.

Pietr de Graaf was portly, short, with dark hair and twinkling eyes. His mustache drooped from the corners of his mouth in a sad fashion, contradicting the constant joke his eyes seemed to be laughing at.

"I received your message late last night," Grieve said, moving to the man and slapping his shoulder in familiar greeting. Grieve looked at MacLean. "We served together, in The War."

De Graaf frowned at MacLean. "Is he a policeman?" he asked. "He looks like a policeman. Or a soldier."

"Of sorts," Grieve said as they sat at De Graaf's desk. "But he's out of his jurisdiction here, my friend. In either regard, you have my guarantee."

De Graaf nodded, and opened the drawer of this desk, taking out a large, flat box. He opened the lid towards himself, and turned to pull a worn velvet mat from the shelf behind him.

"This is the one you gave me," he said, pulling a glittering Heart of India counterfeit from the box.

MacLean stiffened. "Dougal," he groaned. "You stole this from Kaur's box?"

Grieve shrugged dismissively. "I only took one. He has plenty," he said. "I wanted to learn more about his fakes."

"This is a *very* good fake," De Graaf said, turning the stone on the velvet mat. "Very good indeed, very high quality. Similar quality to this one…" From the box he withdrew an identical stone, and placed it next to the first.

Grieve frowned at the second stone on the table, glittering brilliantly next to the one he had given De Graaf the previous day.

"What the devil?" MacLean murmured as Grieve lifted the stone to the light, turning it between his fingers.

"Both those stones are similar quality," De Graaf said. "But *this* one…" He placed a third stone, again identical to the Heart of India, on the mat.

Grieve sat in silence, the second stone still held between his fingers, looking at the third stone on the table.

"This stone," De Graaf said, "is among the highest quality gemstone fakes I've ever encountered."

"Three stones," Grieve murmured. "Two I can understand… But *three*?" He looked at De Graaf and placed the second stone back on the mat. "Where did they come from?"

"The first was given to a... dealer... near Aldgate."

"By whom?" Grieve asked.

"A young man," De Graaf said. "Looked well to do, in a simple suit, dark brown hair, small mustache. Raised no concerns, my associate said. Gave him the stone to find a discrete buyer."

"And the second?"

De Graaf frowned, and shifted in his chair. "The word spread quickly, Dougal, that I was a searching for stones matching The Heart's description. This exquisite specimen," picking up the third stone gingerly between his stubby fingers, "was entrusted to a very, very reputable dealer from the North of London, whom I have occasion to do business with. This contact is very confidential, you understand. However, he did tell me the man who delivered the stone was merely an emissary of the stone's owner. He had been instructed to sell it, for as high a price as possible, as soon as possible. My associate took the stone, recognized it as counterfeit, and threw the emissary out."

"Three stones..." Grieve murmured.

Pietr de Graaf slipped each stone into a small, velvet bag, and placed them back on the mat.

Suddenly, Grieve sprang up from his seat.

"We have to leave now," he snapped, grabbing the stones from the table and hurrying towards the door. "Kaur is in danger."

&#9763;

"What is the significance of the third stone?" MacLean asked as the taxi weaved through the morning traffic. "For that matter, what is the significance of the second?"

The Victoria Embankment came into view, Scotland Yard's roofline visible above the trees.

"The second stone," Grieve said, "is the stone that went missing from Kaur's act."

"The stone Mary Fowles planted before the show?"

"Just so."

"And the third?"

The taxi stopped. Grieve paid by throwing a clump of notes into the driver's window, and hobbled up the steps.

Bedlow was sitting, hunched over his desk with his head in his hands. Cigarette smoke curled and hovered in the room. He looked up briefly as Grieve entered, followed by MacLean, but dropped his head back. "Tadmendri is dead," he growled through his hands. "Shot in the back of the head by a contract killer as he breakfasted this morning."

❧

Grieve poured more coffee into the China mug at The Samaritan. He topped his cup, and then poured for MacLean.

"Well," said Grieve, "at least we can cross Lowell Kaur off our list of suspects."

MacLean frowned as he sipped the coffee. "Grieve," he said, "have you ever suspected The War may have soured your disposition?"

Grieve sighed and shrugged, looking at the blackthorn cane that sat propped against the table. "More than just my disposition, Alex."

MacLean put the cup down. "Alright, then, what of this third stone?"

"It occurred to me," Grieve said, "when we interviewed Kaur that his dismissal of the stones as trivial may have been misdirection. A box of fake gemstones…" Grieve shook his head. "It invites so much opportunity for trickery. Pietr and I served together at Mons. As I'm sure you know, Major, you'll tell a man surprising things when you think you might die next to him. De Graaf had been a significant force in the fencing of stolen gems for years, even before The War. I have on occasion used his services in my investigations, and he was my first thought when I saw that box full of Hearts of India."

MacLean shook his head. "As a Chief Constable, Grieve, I find this difficult to accept."

"As my friend, I expect you to forget his involvement," said Grieve.

MacLean sighed.

Grieve continued. "If Mary Fowles planted a fake diamond for the act, where did it go? We know it couldn't have been the diamond found in Kline's chest, because that diamond was real. So where was it? Apparently, still in the murderer's pocket, because he tried to move it the next day."

"Isn't that foolhardy?"

"Very, which is interesting."

"And the third stone?"

"That confused me," Grieve said, "But if you accept that Kaur lied to us, and *did* own the original, it makes more sense. Kaur's rise to fame had brought him up from the gutter. Look at his associates — criminals, petty thieves. It's inevitable the man had many dirty connections. Assume, for a moment, that he came into possession of the heart. He had copies made, and devised a highly public performance to publicize his ownership. Then, say, he sells the 'original' stone — a high quality, special fake — to select buyers, multiple times. Only to discrete buyers, mind, who are easy marks to fool.

"Then," Grieve continued, "a man is murdered and the *real* stone found in his chest. It hits the news. His buyers must realize they have been duped... Someone attempts to sell their stone, but the fences are too clever, and won't take it. So, they exact revenge, throwing yet more money at Kaur, only this time to have him killed."

"Conjecture," MacLean said.

"As yet," Grieve conceded. "However, once Bedlow examines Kaur's personal finances the truth or falseness of it will be clear. I expect Kaur to have moved a breathtaking amount of money over this stone. That will be impossible to hide."

"Then, this young man who pawned the first stone," said MacLean, "must be the killer."

Grieve turned his cup in the saucer, his eyes narrowing as he chewed on his lower lip. "Perhaps," he said.

⊰⊱

Lowell Kaur had lived in a little apartment in the East Side. Grieve knocked on the door with the knot of his blackthorn cane. After a moment, it was opened by Mary Fowles.

"Just you?" she asked, looking out onto the landing.

"Yes," Grieve said. "Major MacLean is following the police in their hunt for Kaur's killer."

The woman shrugged. "Good luck, I say. They'll never find 'im."

Grieve smiled. "I regret to admit I agree," he said.

She led Grieve into the small flat.

"Now that he's dead," she said, "I'm left to clear out all the papers."

"Does the magic act pass to you?"

Fowles shrugged. "Passes to nobody," she said. "So, I'm just doing it anyway."

"The police don't mind?"

"Said I was free to do whatever I needed. They been through it all this morning."

Grieve shrugged. "Simple of them."

Fowles laughed. "When aren't they simple, though?"

"They have their moments."

"What was it you said you was looking for, again?" she asked.

"Kaur's employee records."

Fowles nodded, and brushed a loose strand of hair from her eyes. She wore a faded pair of slacks and a comfortable blouse, her hair tied messily by a kerchief. Her sleeves were rolled up.

Papers littered Kaur's rooms. Fowles moved to a filing cabinet and pulled a small sheaf of papers from the top drawer.

Grieve took the papers and leafed through them.

"You worked for Kaur for one year," he said.

"That's right."

"Before you, Malcom Castelbrook. Three years. Then Sarah... just 'Sarah,' for two. Then John Evers, for one."

Fowles shrugged. "If that's what it says..."

Grieve put the papers down and looked up at Fowles. "I want to ask you clearly, Miss Fowles. Did Kaur ever make advances towards you?"

Fowles laughed, and leaned against a cabinet. "All the time," she said. "All the bloody time. But he wasn't my type, you see."

"But you were his?"

Fowles' eyes twinkled. "Every type was his," she said. "Very peculiar man. Very queer."

⊷⊶

Grieve met with MacLean at The Samaritan for supper.

"Nothing," MacLean said. "They found nothing. The killer was highly professional. They were unable to track down a single thing about him. He merely appeared beside Kaur's table, shot him dead through the skull, and walked out the door into the street."

"What about Kaur's finances?" Grieve asked.

"Yes, well," MacLean muttered. "You were right. Kaur recently paid off upwards of one-hundred-thousand pounds worth of gambling debts," he said quietly.

Grieve raised his eyebrows. "That's royal."

"Quite."

⊷⊶

The next morning, a knock sounded upon the door to Grieve's hotel room.

Grieve was sitting at a small table in his slacks and shirtsleeves, grimacing at the bill for the rooms. He hadn't originally planned on staying there more than a day, but the murder had changed that.

"Come in, it's open," he snapped.

Doctor Joseph Gatton opened the door and stepped into the room. Grieve dropped the bills and rose to meet him, his frown turned to a smile.

"Morning, Grieve," Doctor Gatton said, pulling a small stack of periodicals from beneath his arm as he hung his hat and coat on the rack next to the door. "I brought you this," he said, handing Grieve one of the journals.

"*The Lancet*, 1897," Grieve read.

"Yes," Gatton said. "In it you'll find an article entitled 'Mediastinal Surgery' by Herbert Nelson Milton, M.R.S.C., England. An incredible practitioner, if obscure. He still operates, I believe, out of Cairo."

Grieve turned the pages, stopping at the article. After a moment, he looked up. "This is legitimate?" he asked.

"It's *The Lancet*," Gatton said, smiling. "It's as legitimate as it gets." Gatton pulled a single sheet from the pages of the other periodical in his hands. "Also, I dug this up, from a friend of mine. A picture. There's Dr. Milton, himself… in the middle."

Grieve took the picture and froze. "Who are the rest?"

"His fellows, nurses, associates…"

Grieve looked at the other periodical that Gatton still held. "And that?"

"This? Oh! This is mine. Fresh from the morning news stand." He held up that morning's edition of *Punch*.

Grieve fell back against the table.

"I've been blind," he hissed. "Blind, as well as crippled, damn my eyes!"

⊰◌⊱

The smoke from Grieve's old, rusticated pipe curled into the billowing haze that filled Bedlow's claustrophobic office. He sat, in Bedlow's chair, a great book opened on the desk in front of him. Slowly, he drew the fingers of both hands down the wall of un-illustrated, small-type text. Bedlow sat across from him, next to MacLean.

Grieve had sent three telegrams, all to Cairo. He had received two back; now, as evening drew near, he awaited a third, and final, response.

Bedlow pulled his cigarette case from the pocket of his jacket, slung across a heap of papers on a filing cabinet next to the wall, and lit a cigarette. "Grieve," he said. "We've waited all day, and you still haven't explained — "

Grieve raised a finger. Bedlow stopped talking.

Slowly, Grieve dropped the finger to the open page, and looked up. "Here," he said. "I found it. It's here."

Bedlow sat forward and began to speak, but the door opened, interrupting him. A secretary entered. Grieve jumped up, leaning across the table to take the telegram. He read it twice, then looked up at Bedlow.

"I know who killed Nelson Kline," he said.

"Who?" Bedlow asked, chewing on the butt of the cigarette as he smoked.

"You must make two arrests," Grieve said, rushing around the desk and reaching for his cane. "Cora Connor and Malcom Castlebrook."

"*Who?*"

"Castlebrook was Kaur's last assistant, before Fowles," Grieve said, grabbing his coat and rushing through the door. "Castlebrook will be easy to find," he said, leading the men down the hall. "I suspect he's an idiot, frankly. Connor, though… Her real name is Elsa Kinneman. You may have your work cut out for you there, Bedlow…"

◖◗

"What do you mean, she's gone?" Bedlow snapped into the telephone. "I don't give a damn how many men were there when she disappeared, Sergeant! Find her, and do it quickly!"

Bedlow slammed the phone back against the receiver and looked up at Grieve and MacLean.

"You were right," he said. "She slipped away from my men not two hours ago."

"And Castlebrook?" Grieve asked.

"I have men searching for him," said Bedlow. "He's on the move too, but left a trail. I expect we'll have him by morning."

"Excellent," Grieve said, turning and striding down the hall towards The Yard's front desks.

Bedlow and MacLean followed him.

"Are you going to explain?" Bedlow hissed.

"I know *who* killed Kline," said Grieve. "*How* is still a puzzle, requiring one final piece. A piece I need to find for myself."

"Where are we going?"

"Back to Box 31."

◄○►

The police cruiser lurched through the foggy evening traffic towards the theater. Grieve, Bedlow, and MacLean sat in the back seat.

"There is one conceit in these crimes that must be elevated above *all* others," said Grieve, "one truth you must keep utmost in your mind as I explain the death of Nelson Kline, and the destruction of Lowell Kaur: The murderer *left* the real Heart of India inside the body of his victim. The minute we verified this all hope of a rational, mathematical, logical motive evaporated, and all that was left was fanaticism. Fanatic love, fanatic hatred, fanatic passion... The only motive that could justify leaving a king's ransom of a gemstone must be one of these."

"Now, let me tell you a story," Grieve said. "Forgive me, Bedlow, if there are gaps. Those are for you, to fill in later. Nearly twenty years ago," he continued, "a middle-aged woman went to work for Doctor Herbert Milton, in Cairo. She had a daughter, Elsa Kinneman. Also in Cairo at this time was our friend, Lowell Kaur. He and the daughter fell in love. Or, rather, she fell in love with him. You see, Kaur had a talent for inducing pretty people to love him. Pretty people, of *both* sexes, apparently."

"When Kinneman became pregnant, Kaur left her. The child died in labor."

Grieve pulled the telegrams from his pocket, and handed them to Bedlow. "The brief tale is told there, by the director of the Kasr-El Aini Hospital, in Cairo." Grieve then pulled the picture from Dr. Gatton from his breast pocket, and handed it to Bedlow and MacLean. It was a group photo. Standing next to Dr. Milton was a woman who looked exactly like Cora Connor. "The mother," Grieve said, pointing.

"The problem with sleeping around so aggressively," Grieve

continued, "is that one runs the risk of 'hitting' a psychopath. For Kaur, this was Elsa Kinneman. She followed him to Europe, seeking revenge.

"How Kinneman and Castlebrook met will likely need to be explained by them, when they're caught. It's enough that they *did* meet, a year ago, after Castlebrook left Kaur's employment, and devised a plot."

The cruiser pulled up to the theater. The doors were locked, but staff moved about inside, preparing for the next program. Bedlow flashed his badge against the glass of the door and the men were quickly ushered inside.

"Castlebrook knew of Kaur's diamond," Grieve said, limping towards the stairs to the second floor. "He knew where he kept it, and he knew Kaur's side hustle selling fakes as the real stone. What's more, Castlebrook must have had similar qualifications to Fowles. He stole the diamond from Kaur's rooms the night of the performance. He followed Fowles as she planted the fake, and stole it back from the mark. He manipulated the idol to produce Kline's heart, *after* Fowles had set it before the show. Only an employee of Kaur could do these things. In a foolish gesture, Castlebrook attempted to sell the fake stone the next day, immediately clearing Fowles from suspicion in the process."

"But why did he do it?" MacLean asked.

"Love," said Grieve. "Fowles told me herself. Kaur was very open in his tastes. The term she used was 'queer.' She fully intended the innuendo. Kaur and Castlebrook were lovers. Just as Kaur loved, and left, Kinneman."

"But what of Kline?" Bedlow asked.

The men reached the second floor. The door to Box 31 lay directly ahead, down the hall.

"The secret to that, Bedlow, is that Kline himself was unimportant. Box 31 was important. Kinneman and Castlebrook followed Kaur for months. I have no doubt the effect we saw was inspired by the circumstances. You see, Box 31 is regularly occupied by an aging couple---"

"My aunt and uncle!" MacLean interrupted.

"Exactly," said Grieve. "The box is occupied by a couple that are hard of hearing and vision, and a younger man, who usually sits alone or with few guests.

"Castlebrook and Kinneman recognize the opportunity. They kill Kline and implicate Kaur. His act will be ruined, any chance he has of moving up destroyed. By producing the real diamond, they all but guarantee everyone who bought Kaur's fakes will eventually be alerted to the scam, ensuring Kaur lives the rest of his life in fear of those he'd cheated.

"Of course," Grieve said, as he opened the door to Box 31, "it backfired. Kaur was killed very quickly. I'm sure they would have preferred he live a little longer, to wallow in the dread of being hunted."

"You seriously suggest they would carve a man's heart from his chest, simply because he sat in Box 31?" asked MacLean.

"Remember, Alex," Grieve said, stepping into the box, "this crime is that of psychopathic fanaticism. It's the only explanation. Kinneman lured Kline, simply to get into Box 31 with him."

Bedlow and MacLean followed Grieve into the box. The lights were turned full upon the stage below. Grieve walked down to Kline's seat.

"All this is well and good, Grieve," Bedlow said. "But you yourself admit the impossibility of the murder. *How* did they remove the heart, both *before* the performance as well as *during* it?"

Grieve moved to the curtains along the wall of the box, and knelt where the small, wooden dart still stuck from the heavy weave. "If I am correct," he muttered to himself, running his fingers down the fabric, "there should be a second hole…"

Grieve's fingers stopped two inches from the carpeted floor. He gripped the hem, and lifted it up to Bedlow and MacLean. The fabric was stiff, and lifting it made the curtain shift and buckle against the wall. Grieve pointed to the second hole that dimpled the weave, near the hem.

"The night of the murder," Grieve said as he stood, "Kinneman and

Kline arrived early to the box. Kinneman injected Kline with a paralytic and cut him open, here, on these seats. I expect she exsanguinate his blood, during the operation. It would be as simple as cutting one artery, and connecting it to a catheter and bag, letting the dying heart pump it out for her. Hence his 'bloodless' body.

"Kinneman removed the heart, which she gave to Castlebrook. She then laid him out, on his side, with his butt planted on Kline's seat. She left the box. Then, to their surprise, instead of the old couple, two men arrived: Myself and Major MacLean. They had no choice, however, but to proceed. The heart, and a bladder of chicken blood, had already been loaded into the idol. There was simply no other option.

"Castlebrook entered first. We assumed he was Kline, because there was no one else he *should* have been. Kinneman came shortly after. Castlebrook waited until she fell all over us to prop the body of Kline upwards. He held it up, from below the waist, while Kinneman completed her distraction. Everything below the top of the seats, you see, is hidden from the back row of the box.

"Elsa went to her seat, and sat next to Kline's corpse. She held him up by his arm. Castlebrook crawled across the floor and lay along the wall. You saw how stiff the curtain is? This wooden dart pierced the curtain twice, holding the hem upward, removing any necessity of bending the curtain up to access the hiding place. All he needed to do was pull the dart back, until it slipped from the outer layer of fabric, dropping discretely over his body. During the performance, he could work at standing up. At that point, the displacement of the curtain would be nearly imperceptible. After the body was discovered, he simply slipped out from behind the curtain during the commotion in the box."

"But *we saw them talking*," said MacLean.

Grieve shook his head. "No," he said. "We saw *her* talking. In silhouette. She spoke. She *acted* as though she listened. Our attention was focused on the stage. We *saw* what a reasonable person would expect to see. It occurred to me when I saw Dr. Gatton, this morning.

He had a copy of *Punch*… Punch and Judy. They're puppets."

"Damn," said MacLean.

"She timed her own act with Kaur's. When he and Fowles revealed Kline's heart on stage, she allowed the corpse beside her to fall."

"You're forgetting one thing," Bedlow snarled. "How could Kinneman remove a man's heart, in a manner so arcane it's virtually unknown to science, on theater seats no less?"

Grieve pulled the copy of *The Lancet* from his coat pocket.

"The procedure is known as Mediastinal Surgery. It was pioneered by Doctor Herbert Milton, at Kasr-El Aini hospital, in Cairo, 1897. Kinneman was very aware of it, since her mother regularly assisted Dr. Milton. Allow me to read you from Milton's own words. 'So easy is this incision of execution, and so considerable the power of exploration thereby obtained that one is most induced to hope that future experience may justify the normal application to it of the term *normal thoracic incision*.' You see, Bedlow, the procedure is easy. You cut the cartilage of the sternum, and rent it apart. The heart is just there. If you don't care about your patient's life, if could be done in a matter of minutes."

⊠⊠

Grieve was organizing his clothes upon the bed, placing them quickly into a large trunk that lay open on the floor when MacLean entered.

"Leaving soon?" MacLean asked.

Grieve looked at his wristwatch. "Two hours," he said.

"They found Castlebrook."

"Oh?" Grieve said, absently.

"Trying to board a train for France."

"Another clever decision… I wonder if Elsa didn't utilize him simply for his stupidity, as a cover for her own escape." He placed a stack of trousers into the trunk. "She is still at large?"

"Yes," MacLean said, watching as Grieve shuffled the stacks of clothes around in the trunk.

"Look, Dougal," MacLean said suddenly, "there's one thing you never explained. What about those great dictionaries you were pouring over, in Bedlow's office."

Grieve smiled. "When I heard her name, I remembered something. 'Cora,' in German, means 'heart.'"

"The devil it does," MacLean muttered.

"Which made me curious," Grieve said, turning back to the trunk. "I decided to look up 'Connor,' as well. It comes from the old Irish word, 'conchobhar,' which means 'lover of wolves.'"

"And 'Lowell' means 'wolf' in French."

"Exactly. Speaking of which," Grieve said, rising from his stoop over the trunk, "whatever happened to the Heart of India? You know, I quite forgot about the actual stone itself, until this very moment."

MacLean flashed Grieve a wry smile. "I asked Bedlow about that myself, this very morning," he said. "He wasn't very happy I brought it up. Apparently, it's gone missing from the evidence room, and nobody seems to be able to find it."

# AD 1941
## Something to Tell
### Hal Dygert

*November 1941.*

Einar Lund rented a room on the second floor of Mrs. Turley's boarding house at the corner of Rosehip and Daniels, walking distance from the docks where he worked as a longshoreman. He'd heard that the heat didn't reach the back of the house but in his room, second from the front overlooking Daniels, he was plenty comfortable. He'd eaten way worse food than Mrs. Turley's, and she served seven days a week. At a lot of places, you were on your own Sundays and in some places on Saturdays and Sundays both.

Tonight, Einar and his fellow boarders were served watery beef stew and boiled green beans. Bread and margarine filled the gaps. Afterwards, Einar went straight up to his room. He unlocked the door, entered, switched on the overhead light, and locked the door behind him. His belongings were hardly worth stealing. Sometimes though, late at night, a boarder would come home drunk and barge into the wrong room. Not if the door to the wrong room was locked.

Pushed up against the streetside wall of Einar's room, under the only window, there was a square table with a fly-tying vice clamped to its front edge and a piano stool positioned in front of the table. The vice was tiny, its jaws sized to hold fishhooks which Einar painstakingly turned into fishing flies. Strewn across the table-top were fly-tying tools and materials: scissors, clips, clamps, hooks of various sizes, thread, glue, metallic foil, small squares of animal hide, and many colorful feathers, some contained within glassine packets, some still attached to dried bits of bird skin. Einar didn't fish himself, but he made a little side income selling his creations.

To the right of the table, an armchair upholstered in nubby gold fabric had been pushed into the corner. A pole lamp, its bulb and shade attached to a swinging arm, stood between the table and chair. Depending on where he planned to sit, Einar pushed the swivel arm this way or that. At the moment, it was positioned over the armchair.

Einar dropped into the armchair, raising dust enough to trigger a sneeze. He reached over the armrest to retrieve a magazine, the latest issue of *Dime Detective*. He bought *Dime Detective* and *Black Mask* every month at Ken's News. He read the magazines from cover to cover and then reread the stories he particularly liked.

Two-thirds of the way through a rouser called "The Slippery Slope," Einar jerked upright, reacting to a knock on his door. Too forceful, he thought, for Mrs. Turley. One of his fellow boarders? Unlikely. The current roster wasn't particularly sociable. They'd all been at dinner together and had said what little there was to say. Einar sat tight.

Again, the knock, louder and more insistent than before. The door handle turned and came up against the lock.

Einar closed the magazine and set it aside. "Yeah?" He tried to make his voice sound as if he'd been asleep. "Who is it?"

"Keith Green."

Keith Green? It took half a second for the name to register. Christ on a crutch. Keith Green, better known as Pinkeye, was one of waterfront boss Nolan Hedgepeth's enforcers, as Einar and the rest of his longshore crew were reminded only yesterday.

Einar wrestled the urge to turn off the lamp and crawl under the bed. He cleared his throat. "What?" Though he'd seen Pinkeye and others of that lot around town, he'd never once spoken to any of them.

"Open up."

Einar owed money, a gambling debt. Knowledge of what he owed and his inability to pay gnawed at him constantly, sometimes nibbling, sometimes biting down hard. Two hundred dollars? They'd come after him for two hundred dollars?

"Got something on the stove. Just a minute." There wasn't a stove in the room, only a hot plate.

Einar hastily surveyed his enclosure, the four walls, the ceiling and floor, as if in search of a previously undetected escape hatch. Nothing doing. He could elude Pinkeye in one of two ways. If he could somehow persuade the thug to wait downstairs, he could exit his room, tiptoe down the hall to the back of the house, and flee by way of the fire escape. Otherwise, he'd have to jump out his window. A ten-foot drop. Rain-soaked earth underneath. Easy enough.

"Coming," Einar called out.

The corner streetlight cast shadows of tree branches against the brown paper shade drawn over his window. Einar leaned across the table and pulled back one side of the shade just enough to peek out.

A man in an overcoat and dark fedora stood under the corner streetlight. From this vantage point, he could see the boarding house's front door and every one of the windows overlooking Daniels, Einar's included. The man looked up at Einar, looked right into his face, and showed his teeth in what was more grimace than grin. A four-door Dodge sedan idled at the curb. Fat raindrops fell through the headlight beams and spattered on the pavement. Einar let the shade fall back.

Another knock sounded high up on the door. "Open up you lunkhead, or we'll bash the door down."

We? Pinkeye in the hall and who else? For two hundred dollars.

Trapped.

Feeling as if he might heave up his dinner, Einar crossed the room, unlocked and opened the door.

The tails of Pinkeye's dark overcoat reached almost to the floor. Both the overcoat and the suit-coat underneath were unbuttoned. A short tie the color of tapioca pudding lay twisted against an orange shirtfront. "What took yah?"

Einar looked up and down the hall. It was only Pinkeye, thank goodness. Einar prayed that he wouldn't look inside his room for the stove that wasn't there. How would he explain its absence? He did his best to fill the doorway. "What can I do for you?" Trying to sound upbeat, like a man beholden to no one.

A gaping yawn delayed the reply. Einar smelled tooth decay and a day's worth of cigarettes on Pinkeye's breath. His eyelids were inflamed and flaky.

"Get your coat," Pinkeye said. "Mr. Hedgepeth wants a word."

"About what?"

"How should I know? Get your coat or come without it. Makes no difference to me."

Einar pulled his jacket from a hook on the back of the door and slipped into it. He closed and locked the door. Descending the stairs on jelly legs, he extracted a cloth cap from his jacket pocket and pulled it on. He went out the front door and down the steps with Pinkeye following close behind. At Pinkeye's direction, he turned right and followed the sidewalk along Rosehip, then turned right again and followed a newer, broader sidewalk along Daniels to where the sedan was parked mid-block.

The man on the corner had relocated to the sedan's back seat. He sat on the passenger side with the door closed and the window open. Looking down from the second floor, Einar hadn't recognized him. But Einar now saw him up close. Liard Seeley, Pinkeye's senior partner. At some level, Einar had known all along.

Pinkeye opened the rear driver's side door, shoved Einar into the back seat, and slammed the door closed behind him. Settling into his seat, Einar tried not to look at Seeley. He couldn't help himself. Seeley was looking steadily at Einar through half-closed eyes, his head tilted back.

A rat-and-snake situation. Einar was the rat.

Pulling away from the curb, head half turned, Pinkeye spoke to Seeley over his shoulder. "Any stops?"

"Straight on." Seeley spoke without taking his dead-looking eyes off Einar's face.

Einar could feel Mrs. Turley's watery stew winding up his gullet.

From the time he was a kid, he'd had a nervous stomach. He felt as if he might have to heave at any moment. Should he say something? What would they do to him if he heaved in the car? He swallowed and swallowed again.

He pressed his hands to his thighs, working to keep his eyes fixed on the oily ringlets of Pinkeye's rust-colored back-hair. They were headed toward the river. A direction? Or a destination, a watery grave?

Einar's peripheral vision was drawn irresistibly toward Seeley. He watched his captor lean to the right and slide his left hand into the pocket of his overcoat.

I'm either gonna heave, Einar thought, or crap my pants. Maybe both.

Seeley jerked his hand from the pocket and swung it toward Einar, who, as if pushed, banged against the car door. He crossed his arms over his stomach and pulled his head in between his raised shoulders.

A blunt, stubby object stuck out of Seeley's fist. He pointed it at Einar.

"Gum?" he inquired.

&#x221E;

They crossed the Columbia River on the Interstate Bridge from Vancouver, Washington, on the north side, to Portland, Oregon, on the south. They tooled south along Interstate Avenue—pole-studded, wire-strung, cinder-specked, busy—and turned toward the smell of water, following Going Street down the long slope onto Swan Island.

At the base of the Going Street slope, the main road, built wide enough to carry freight trucks coming and going, angled left, leading to dry docks and shipping terminals on the Willamette River. Einar had worked jobs at the Swan Island terminals and knew the main road well. A second road, North Basin Avenue, angled to the right and ran parallel to a foul-smelling slough that was choked with flood debris and scuttled watercraft.

The main road was brightly lit and well-traveled at all hours of the day and night. It figured that Pinkeye would turn instead onto North Basin Avenue, which was ill-lit, narrow, little-used. Buildings, mostly derelict, stood here and there along the road. Seeley's chewing gum was Beeman's Pepsin and for a few minutes, before the flavor leeched out, it had settled Einar's stomach. Now he chomped the tasteless wad faster and faster to no avail.

A half mile on, Pinkeye veered off North Basin onto a weedy acre of cracked and broken concrete. He bucked and bounced across the slab and then slipped in behind an abandoned two-story warehouse. A second building huddled behind the first, out of sight of the road. It looked more like a house than an industrial building. Who would want to live in such a dismal setting? Not Einar, that was for sure.

Two cars were parked nose to tail along the near side of the house. Pinkeye parked in front. The three men got out of the car and walked single file along a dirt path and up three steps onto the porch. Light showed around the edges of curtains drawn across the windows.

Suddenly and without a beckoning knock, the front door was yanked open from within. The light blinded Einar for a moment. Inside, with his eyes adjusted, he saw that the doorman was hollow-cheeked and skeletally thin, aged about fifty, scowling. He wore shiny, cinnamon-colored slacks and an open-necked, green silk shirt, clothing Einar associated not with a chilly mid-November evening but with summertime at the horse track.

The doorman's hair, long thin strands combed over a nearly bald scalp, somehow reminded Einar of his hat, which he peeled off and crammed into his jacket pocket.

It turned out that what from the outside looked like a house was really the shell of a house with a few vertical beams supporting the roof and all the interior walls removed except in one corner where, Einar guessed, there might be a bathroom. Dare he ask to use it? Best not. Besides, he wasn't sure if his urge to pee was genuine or only a symptom of acute distress.

Einar had never set eyes on the notorious Nolan Hedgepeth, but the man who sat at the head of the long narrow table that divided the cavernous space had to be him. Of the five men in the room, he was the only one seated. He wore the sort of shirt Einar had seen in the movies but never in real life, white and stiff and pleated in front, and also a black tie with butterfly ends hanging down either side of a muscular neck. There was a reddish-gold tone to the skin of his long unlined face. Thick, wavy blond hair was brushed back from either side of a high part.

"Trouble?" the man in the chair asked Laird Seeley.

"Nah," Seeley said. He dropped onto the seat of a couch, draped in a purple slipcover, that had been pushed to the back wall of the room next to a breakfront cabinet.

Einar stood exactly where Pinkeye had first planted him, trying to get his bearings without looking too obvious. He'd heard stories about guys who'd pissed off Nolan Hedgepeth. None ended happily.

Apparently responding to some signal Einar had failed to notice, Pinkeye gave him a shove. He staggered forward and regained his balance near the head of the table, standing uncomfortably close to the man in the chair. Paring an apple, the man worked methodically, taking the skin off in one long continuous strip.

The fellow in the green silk shirt stood two steps behind the man in the chair. His scowl seemed a permanent fixture. He looked like one of those guys who'd carry a grudge long after most others would've decided to forgive and forget.

Still occupied with the apple, the man in the chair introduced himself—Nolan Hedgepeth, none other—and added, "I appreciate your stopping by." On the table in front of him were a dish towel and a plain metal plate of the sort common to ships' galleys.

"Sure thing," Einar replied. As if he'd had any choice

"Keith," Hedgepeth said, "I expect our guest might want to rest his legs."

Quickly and with a magician's flourish, Pinkeye whisked away one of the mismatched chairs that surrounded the table and swung it around behind Einar who, without looking, backed up until he felt the edge of the chair seat against the backs of his knees. He sat down. Good thing. He felt ready to collapse.

"Drink?" Hedgepeth asked.

Einar, who rarely drank anything stronger than beer, might now have said yes to a snort of something more potent. With his stomach churning, however, he was afraid a snort might trigger the heaves. "Best not. Thanks, though," he hastened to add.

Hedgepeth glanced over his shoulder. The fellow in the green silk shirt answered with a slight constriction of his eyes, nostrils and mouth, and an almost imperceptible shake of his head.

"No?" Hedgepeth said. "Alright then, Scotch for me."

Pinkeye poured two fingers neat from a bottle retrieved from the breakfront cabinet. He settled the glass in front of Hedgepeth, backed up two steps and stood more or less at attention, with interlaced fingers joined at the belt.

Hedgepeth had finished paring the apple. He lay aside the unbroken peel, cored and quartered the ghostly fruit, then wiped his hand with the dishtowel. "First thing," he said, "I wanted to thank you for yesterday."

"Sure," Einar said, thinking, yesterday? What about yesterday?

Hedgepeth seemed to sense Einar's puzzlement. "The warehouse accident. Longshoremen swarming our office. Your timely intervention."

"I was there, yeah."

"You gave our man Ordway a hand up after he fell."

"He tripped over himself. Went down in a puddle." Did Ordway appreciate the assistance? No. In fact, when Einar first offered the ingrate a hand, he'd batted it away.

"At the office, you helped us there too."

Einar recalled yesterday's stand-off inside Hedgepeth Marine's dinky north shore office, seeing Laird Seeley reach under his coat for the gun. He recalled restraining little Jimmy O'Leary, the union shop steward, grabbing the back of his belt and dragging him outside. He'd just done it. Nothing he'd thought about. He supposed he didn't want anybody getting shot, not even a loud-mouthed rabble-rousing pissant like little Jimmy O'Leary.

Hedgepeth spoke as if Einar was supposed to feel good about yesterday. Hedgepeth Marine and its rotten warehouses? Bischoff, a kid who'd only just started working the docks, lying dead underneath collapsed shelving and cartons of canned tomatoes? He didn't feel the least good about yesterday.

Hedgepeth sucked in a mouthful of Scotch and inspected his glass while he swallowed, seemingly a teaspoonful at a time. "So, there's that." He re-settled the glass on the table and, for the first time, looked directly at Einar. "Now…"

Nothing different in Hedgepeth's expression, every aspect of every feature unchanged. Tone of voice? Just the same. And yet, in an instant, Einar went from feeling appreciated, even welcomed, to feeling as if he were sitting on the edge of a cot in a holding cell on death row.

"I understand you have something to tell me," Hedgepeth said. He snapped the Scotch glass with his middle finger. It pinged.

Einar felt the vibration from the crown of his head to the tips of his toes. "I'm late paying back the two hundred bucks," Einar blurted out. "Believe me, I know. I'm good for it, though, every dime." He glanced at the man who hovered behind Nolan Hedgepeth. With his gaudy clothes and sullen expression, he looked like a big parrot. Even a small parrot, Einar had heard, could seize a man's finger in its beak and bite it right off.

"How did it happen?" Hedgepeth inquired.

"Playing blackjack. Won seven hands in a row. Feeling lucky like I'd never felt lucky before. I was feverish, though, coming down with the flu."

"You were sick. You kept playing. Your luck didn't hold."

Einar's head and shoulders rolled forward. He looked at a spot between his shoes and then lifted his head, addressing Hedgepeth in a tone he imagined Catholics must use when confessing their sins. "An hour later, something like that, I come to my senses, such as they were. Dropped what money I'd brought to play with, my back-up roll, and two hundred more that I owe on the markers." Einar held up his hands as if to fend off a blow. "No, not two hundred, two hundred and ten."

"A working stiff like you, Bitsie took markers for all of that?"

"He knows me. I'm at his place at least once a week. I been into him before, and I always made good. Same as this time. He'll get his money."

Somehow affiliated with Hedgepeth Marine, Bitsie Warnick's place was upstairs of a chop suey joint, north of Burnside, near Portland's Chinatown.

"Why come to Portland?" Hedgepeth asked. "Plenty of action on your side of the river. Alvin Ames runs a clean operation."

"I like Bitsie's. The girls treat me good." Once there had been one who treated him good, who he hadn't seen before or since. Really, the girls just tolerated him—so long as he had the money to pay for their favors. No dough, and they wouldn't even let him light their cigarettes. Hedgepeth looked steadily at Einar, who dropped his head and muttered the truth. "I don't like people on the other side of the river knowing my business, the gambling or the girls either."

"You been in to Bitsie before," Hedgepeth said. "And you always paid up. Meaning, you paid when the markers came due. Not this time."

"Never been in quite so deep."

Hedgepeth nodded. To Pinkeye he said, "I'm guessing our friend here is a rye man. Why don't you fix him up?"

Hedgepeth was right about the drink. How could he know? But that was beside the point. Einar didn't want a drink, wanted it even less now than before. This time, however, Hedgepeth hadn't asked.

Pinkeye placed a glass filled halfway with an amber liquid in Einar's hand. Everyone in the room was watching him, and he understood that he was expected to drink. He cleared his throat. He took a swig and swallowed—the burning liquid along with his chewing gum. Was this why they'd brought him here? He remembered Raymond Chandler's book *The Big Sleep*. He especially remembered Harry Jones, the grifting little private eye who'd provided Marlowe information that helped him solve the Rusty Regan case. Harry Jones, yeah. Lash Canino had laced the little man's whiskey with cyanide and wished him bottoms up.

The faces around the room told Einar he wasn't done drinking. He sipped again and lowered the glass, holding it in his lap with both hands. He waited for the poison to close his throat and knock him retching from his chair. He drew a couple of deep breaths. He felt like retching all right, but in the usual way. Nervous stomach. Maybe the drink wasn't poisoned after all. Cyanide-laced whiskey was supposed to smell like bitter almonds, and this stuff just smelled like whiskey. He took another sip. This time he savored before swallowing. Best whiskey he'd ever tasted.

"This business yesterday," Hedgepeth said, "we can't allow it. We can't have our people worrying about attacks any time some little problem crops up."

A man crushed to death under canned tomatoes? Some little problem? Jesus Christ. These people wouldn't think twice about killing a guy who crossed them or interfered with their business plans.

"We need to know when trouble's brewing," Hedgepeth said. "We were lucky yesterday because when Ordway called, the boys here were twenty minutes away. Gave 'em time to cross the river, to even up the odds."

Einar was startled to hear a rapid tsk...tsk...tsk, the scolding sound a squirrel makes when annoyed. He traced the sound to Seeley, who'd drawn in his legs and was sitting at the very edge of the couch, hunched forward, baring his front teeth. His tight-fitting suitcoat, though buttoned, luffed a little around the chest, and Einar could see the butt of his pistol.

"If the boys here hadn't arrived when they did," Hedgepeth continued after draining the last of his Scotch, "hard to guess the outcome, notwithstanding your efforts."

"Another?" Pinkeye asked.

Einar peered into his glass. Plenty left. About to decline, he realized

Pinkeye was speaking to Nolan Hedgepeth and not to him.

Hedgepeth shook his head without looking at Pinkeye. Rather, he stared fixedly at Einar who felt the weight of the man's words, the pressure of his unblinking gaze. Sweat trickled from Einar's armpits into the dank folds of his T-shirt. Doomed by debt. For Einar, two hundred and ten might as well be two thousand and ten.

"In your present financial circumstances," Hedgepeth went on, "I can't imagine you'd want your workplace disrupted. No work, no pay. Your debts run, and your creditors lose patience."

Seeley made the squirrel sound again. Hedgepeth glanced at his watch. "Here's a proposition you'll want to consider. Across the board, we're looking to keep a tighter rein on port operations. Especially with war on the horizon, as it seems to be. We're looking for people to help, to let us know if some hothead on the docks is nursing more than the usual grudge. And we want to know right now about right-now kinds of problems."

Hedgepeth raised his hand as if to silence whatever response Einar may have been contemplating.

Einar's allegiance, even his heart—if not with every man jack of them—was one hundred percent with his crew. He'd never rat them out. Under present circumstances, however, he sure wouldn't say so out loud.

"While you're thinking things over," Hedgepeth continued, "say for a week, I expect Bitsie will carry your debt interest-free. And, who knows? If this works out, I could see him wiping it clean off the books."

Einar swirled the contents of his glass, raised it partway, let if fall back. Good as the whiskey tasted, he was afraid that consuming even a sip might make it look as if he were toasting Hedgepeth's idea.

"We'll be in touch," Hedgepeth said.

Einar understood that he'd been dismissed. He rose to his feet, unsure what to do with his glass.

"Set it on the table," Pinkeye said. "And let's make for the car."

Einar followed Pinkeye across the room and out the front door to the porch. Making his squirrel sound, Seeley brought up the rear. Einar jumped as the door slammed shut behind him.

They returned to the same seats in the Dodge sedan that they'd occupied on the way over: Pinkeye at the wheel, Einar in the back seat behind Pinkeye, Seeley to Einar's right. Pinkeye fired the engine and set off, spraying gravel as he spun the car around and headed north, retracing their earlier route.

Some combination of the liquor's intoxicating effect and the relief he felt at treatment more forgiving than he'd expected emboldened Einar. "How did Mr. Hedgepeth know I owed Bitsie the two hundred bucks? The two ten. The guy in the green silk shirt?"

"Nah," Seeley said. "He doesn't play any part in the gambling. He's got bigger fish to fry."

"Then how did he know?" Einar persisted. "Mr. Hedgepeth, I mean?"

"He didn't," Seeley said. "He didn't know."

"He asked me."

"Not about money, he didn't. He asked you what you had to tell him, and you told him about the two hundred, and then you owned up to two ten. He didn't have any idea what you had to tell him. He just knew you had something. If you work or drink or screw anywhere near Hedgepeth Marine operations, you'll always have something to tell Mr. Hedgepeth. Because one way or the other you're gonna have stolen from him or cheated him or insulted his family name. With you, it's welshing on the two ten."

"Then it isn't like he cares about the two ten in particular, I mean about me owing it, or about him or Bitsie getting it back?"

Up front, Pinkeye chortled.

"Two ten?" Laird Seeley scoffed. "Mr. Hedgepeth wouldn't stoop to pick up two ten if he saw it laying in the street. That's on the one hand. On the other hand, if I were you, I'd make sure Mr. Hedgepeth gets what he wants. If he doesn't, well…I'm sure we'll be paying you another visit."

"Two ten, two ten." Pinkeye bounced in his seat and banged the dashboard with the flat of his hand. And then he tilted his head back and sent a high-pitched laugh toward the roof of the car, a laugh so loud and shrill that it hurt Einar's ears, the way the noon whistle did when he was standing too close.

# AD 1942

# On the Side of the Angels

## Merrilee Robson

Donovan's partner was driving when they saw the suspect hurrying down Main Street.

The kid had timed it well, like all the others in this string of robberies. This one was pulled off just before the siren sounded for the blackout drill, when everyone else was already safe at home or hurrying to get there.

"Just a boy, the little devil!" the jeweler had said, his voice trembling.

Of course, everyone in Vancouver, and along the whole west coast, was jittery these days. The talk of a Japanese aircraft carrier off the coast had people worrying about an air raid like one on Pearl Harbor a few months ago.

They didn't need armed robbery on top of war. The jeweler was shaking as he described the robber. "Didn't even look old enough to shave — had a face like a baby — but he pointed that gun at me like he didn't have a care in the world."

His description of the robber matched all the others. The man told them how the thief had grabbed the contents of the cash register and filled the pockets of the too-large overcoat with jewelry.

Donovan was lucky to have caught sight of the figure. With no streetlights and the car headlights masked to just slits, it was hard to see. But the clothes — the jaunty angle of the fedora and the overcoat that reached almost to the ground — matched the description the jeweler had just given. Like a kid dressing up in his father's clothes, he'd said.

Donovan jumped out of the car to check the suspect out.

Well, jumped was hardly an accurate description. Clambered?

Lumbered, maybe?

The suspect ducked into an alley, surely not a sign of innocence. Donovan signaled to Blake to meet him at the other end of the block.

The fog had started creeping up from the harbor as the sun dropped. Tendrils of mist were already draping the alley. A shadow seemed to leap into the air.

Or jumped over a fence into one of the back yards, Donovan realized when he followed and came up against the boards.

He let out a deep sigh.

Maybe he should have let Blake go after the kid. Blake was as old as Donovan, both of them coming out of retirement to fill the spots of men off to the war. But Blake was noticeably thinner and he had been spared the shrapnel wounds from the Great War.

Early on in Donovan's time with the police, jumping the fence would have been a piece of cake, even with his war injuries.

Now he could feel the cold and damp deep in those wounds, as if the fog was seeping through his scars.

So he slid his hand along the fence until he found a change in the width of the boards that seemed to indicate a gate, and reached over to the other side, searching for a latch.

It was unlikely the kid was still there when Donovan finally made it into the yard. If he was, Donovan couldn't see him. He couldn't see anything, really. The fog was heavier now. It felt like he was wrapped in a thick, wet blanket.

Well, he *was* wrapped in a blanket. He'd walked straight into the laundry hanging on a clothesline and planted his face into a soaking wet sheet.

He hoped some housewife wouldn't be cursing him in the morning for dirtying her laundry. He scanned the darkness, searching for a cellar door or shrub that might have provided a hiding place. But the yard was a square garden that must have been lush with fruits and vegetables in the summer but was now just a large expanse of mud, with only a potato or two and a few stalks of Brussels sprouts still standing. He found the gate again, and hurried down the alley, hoping Blake might have picked up the suspect at the other end.

Like the suspect, the big Ford was more a shadow, an absence of light than anything he could actually see.

"I lost him," he said, when Blake said he hadn't seen anyone. "But I have an idea of who our robber might be. A young tearaway who lives just around the corner. Let's leave the car here and go see if he can account for his whereabouts."

Blake fussed a little about leaving the car where someone might run into it in the blackout. Finally he found a spot on the side street where he thought it might be safe.

"Better than trying to drive in the fog," Donovan assured him.

"I know the family," he told Blake, as they navigated the dark sidewalks. "They go to my church and it's always a pleasure to see the children looking so neat and well-behaved on a Sunday morning. The father signed up early in the war but I think they were doing all right until the mother died early in the year. Now I think they're struggling a bit."

"And you think they're involved in these robberies?" Blake asked.

"There's a boy. I suppose he's about 15 or 16. It's him I worry about. He's sung in the church choir for years and been the altar boy. But since the mother died, he's gone a bit wild. I caught him trying to syphon gas from cars. Good thing he was stopped. The young fool didn't know what he was doing. He could have killed himself.

"He lost his job as a grocery delivery boy for stealing a few things from his deliveries. That'll be hard on his family. They need the money he was bringing in."

"A bit of a jump from stealing apples, or even gas, to armed robbery," Blake murmured.

Donovan shrugged. "I agree. It's just how that jeweller described the robber … about the right height, that baby face, and the shock of gold hair he saw sticking out from the fedora. I don't know any other thief in the city who looks like that."

Blake still sounded doubtful and Donovan hoped he was wrong.

"There's a widowed aunt that moved in to help after the mother died but it's the oldest girl, their Mabel, who's holding it all together. She's a pretty little thing. She should be out having a bit of fun, not looking after those kids."

He led Blake to a two-storey house on the hill, overlooking the railway flats. No lights were showing and Donovan nodded in approval. The yard and house were generally tidy but, even in the dark, Donovan could see signs of disrepair here and there. A shingle missing on the siding. A shrub in need of pruning.

A small boy answered their knock, opening the door to a dark hallway.

"Who is it?" he asked in a small voice.

Blake answered him. "Police," He held up his badge although the kid looked too young to read and it was too dark to see it even if he could.

"Is something wrong?" the boy asked. "It's not Dad, is it?"

"Nothing like that," Donovan replied in a gentle voice. "It's Billy, isn't it? I've seen you at church. Is your brother Frank at home?"

"No, he's not home from choir practice. Do you want to talk to Mabel? She's in the kitchen."

Donovan and Blake followed the kid through the dark, cold hallway.

At least the kitchen was warm, heat radiating from the large black stove where Mabel was stirring something in a pot. The smell of fresh-baked bread and whatever was in the pot filled the kitchen with a smell that made Donovan's mouth water.

He was used the seeing the girl in her Sunday best, her hair neat under her hat. She looked like an angel then, with the sun shining through the stained-glass window lighting up her pretty face and making her hair shine like a halo. But she looked just as pretty here in the kitchen, with wisps of yellow hair clinging to her damp forehead, wearing a faded blue housedress and old, patched lace-up shoes.

For a moment, seeing her turn from the stove with a smile on her face, she reminded him of his Rose, when they were both young. Gone these four years now, and his baby daughter even longer. Would his own girl have looked like this one, if she had lived?

"Mr. Donovan? What a surprise" Her forehead wrinkled. "Nothing's wrong, I hope."

"It's Sergeant Donovan these days. I'm back in the police."

A dimple flashed in her cheek. "Oh, is that why we haven't seen you in church lately? I was imagining you were enjoying your retirement at your favorite fishing spot."

Donovan flushed at the thought that she had even noticed he was missing. In truth, although he had worked some Sundays, he was usually just too tired to get up on a Sunday morning. He was happy enough to do his bit while younger men were off fighting the war but he wasn't the man he once was.

Once, he would have been able to keep up with a suspect.

"We had a few questions for your brother Frank. Do you know where he is?"

She frowned at that. "Frank? Why do you need to talk to him?"

When Donovan didn't reply, she glanced at the clock on the sideboard. "He...well, you know he isn't delivering groceries after school anymore." She flushed a little as she said that.

Donovan looked down, avoiding her gaze. He'd had to look into the grocer's complaint but he couldn't help feeling like that policeman in the book — the one who had pursued that guy all his life for stealing a loaf of bread. The kid shouldn't have stolen from his employer but he could understand how a hungry boy might be tempted by the fruit and vegetables in the basket of his bicycle.

"He'll be at choir practice now," Mabel said. "He planned to go to the church right after school. The minister asked him to do some work around the church, putting up some plywood to protect the stained glass and adding some new coverings on the other windows for the blackout. You could catch up with him there." She smiled at him, the dimple flashing again. "He'll be meeting Aunt Irene there." She looked at the clock again. "Or they should be home in an hour or so.

"Unless … I heard the siren. I assumed it was just the drill they talked about. It's not a real air raid, is it? I'm afraid we don't have a radio anymore, so we're a bit cut off." Her face reddened a little as she said it and Donovan imagined the radio might have been sold off once Frank had lost his job with the grocer.

"No, as you say, just a drill, a precaution now. And you've done very well. I couldn't see a glimpse of light so you won't be hearing any complaints from the warden. Your aunt and brother should be able to make it home without a problem."

Her dimple flashed again. "Well, that's a relief. I know we should be practicing sheltering in the cellar but the damp makes Billy wheeze and the baby carries on something dreadful if I move her when she's sleeping. But I wouldn't like to think I was cooking supper when bombs started falling on our heads."

Donovan knew he should tell her that was the whole point of the practice — to learn what to do in a real raid. But here he was gallivanting around the city.

Still, he had a reason. Crime had dropped during the war but the blackouts sure made it easier for the criminals who were around.

"Would you like to wait?" she asked. "I have some tea left and I'm sure Aunt Irene would be happy to see you."

Donovan looked down at his polished shoes. It was true the widowed aunt was a very pretty woman, with the same yellow hair as her niece, But it didn't seem fair to the memory of his Rose to think about another woman. Besides, he had a vague memory that there was something iffy about the aunt's late husband. Not anything they'd ever been able to pin on him but rumors. Probably not the fault of the aunt but still….

But the girl was all right. He'd told Blake she looked like an angel. She really was the most beautiful girl he had ever seen. He could picture her in church, golden curls peeking out from under that cute little round hat, brushing against her round pink cheek.

But she was much more than a pretty face. He admired the way she'd stepped in to look after her family after the mother died with the youngest still a babe. Mabel had left school and was doing her best to keep the baby alive and the two boys in line.

"No, we won't wait," Donovan told her. "We'd best get the car back to the station before some fool runs into it in the dark. Tell young Frank we'd like to talk to him. Can he come to the police station after school?"

Mabel shook her head. "He's found new work." Her face lit up. "It's good news, really. Aunt Irene got taken on at the shipyard and she's making much more money than she did at the shop. And then they hired Frank too. I know he's young but he's strong and he does work hard. He's starting tomorrow. It will mean him leaving school but it will make such a difference to us all."

She looked down at the scuffed toe of the shoe. Donovan thought he saw a speck of mud on edge of one of them.

"Sergeant Donovan," she said, "Frank thought for sure the grocer would want him to be charged for theft. Was it you who persuaded the man not to make a fuss? Because…."

The apples and carrots the boy had taken hadn't been worth much. The small amount of money Donovan had given the grocer was certainly worth saving a young boy from a criminal record.

But armed robbery was another matter.

Mabel looked up and Donovan met her eye.

"Frank was lucky that time," he told her. "I'll check with the church to confirm he was there. I may not need to talk to him if the minister says he was at the church at the time when…." He gave her a steady look. "I hope this new job will keep him on the straight and narrow now."

∽○∾

Supper was ready and the kitchen was warm and inviting by the time Aunt Irene and Frank were back.

"We had a visit from the police," Mabel told them. "I told them you were at the church after school." Her voice held a worried note.

"I was. And the Reverend was with me every minute," Frank said.

"And then the entire choir can vouch for me."

"It felt a bit odd to be singing hymns and listening for the air raid sirens," Aunt Irene said. "But I suppose the church is a safe place to be, if it came to an air raid."

"The police didn't search the place, did they?" Frank asked.

"No. That nice Sergeant Donovan from church followed me down the alley but I managed to get away from him. I was in the kitchen stirring the soup when they arrived. Billy did a good job of looking after it while I was gone. My hair was a bit of mess but I think the police assumed it was just from housework. I was worried my shoes were very muddy from cutting through a garden to get away from him but they didn't seem to notice it."

She looked at her aunt. "We'll need to get rid of the stuff right away. Can you take it to your friend, the pawn broker, tomorrow before you go to work?"

"Yes, he's always there early." She looked around the kitchen. "I could pretend I was just visiting my husband's old friend but I guess at that hour I'd better take the clock so I'll have an excuse to be there. Shame we have to pawn it, and our radio too, but we've got to keep the family going until your father can come home."

"Is there a lot of stuff?" Frank asked.

"Yes, and there's some money, too," Mabel said. "I think we should leave it where I hid it at the bottom of the diaper pail until Aunt Irene can take the jewelry to her friend. Just in case the police come back."

"That was a super idea you had, Mabel," Frank said. "It would take a pretty dedicated cop to think of looking there."

Mabel started to ladle out the soup. "It has worked so far," she said. "But you know I don't like leaving Billy and the baby. And Sergeant Donovan...."

Mabel looked at her aunt. "I think you should take the gun back to your friend. With you both working at the shipyard, I don't think the baby-faced bandit needs to make another appearance."

⌈⊂⊃⌋

After they left the house, Blake grabbed Donovan's arm.

"Listen, when we were in the hall just now I brushed against that old coat hanging there," he said. "It was soaking wet. I think we should go back and ask some more questions."

Donovan kept walking to the spot they had left the car.

"Well, the girl was making something for the family's supper. She must have gone to the shed to get more wood for the stove or to fetch some potatoes."

"But it was a long coat like the jeweler described," Blake insisted, reaching out and pulling Donovan to a halt. "And her shoes were muddy."

"There you go then…she popped out to the shed to get more fuel for the stove. The coat's probably some old thing belonging to the father that she uses for chores."

Blake went on grumbling but Donovan kept walking through the dark and the fog, back to the car. He sighed, thinking of his Rose and their baby girl, thinking it would be nice if he had a family at home waiting for him, with a meal ready.

"I'll check with the Reverend in the morning," he told Blake, "but I think I was wrong about young Frank being the culprit. As I said, they're a good family.

# AD 1946
## *Cold in Chicago*
### *John G. Bluck*

Joe Nelson lived in the big city of Chicago and was dead broke after World War II ended. He didn't want to shave at six o'clock on this Monday morning in the frigid winter of 1946. But he knew he couldn't appear desperate when he went looking for a job. After rubbing a wet bar of soap in the YMCA communal bathroom to make a lather, he hacked away a three-day growth of beard with his dull razor. While he shaved, he felt hunger pangs. Three days before, he had used the last of his money to rent a closet-sized YMCA room.

Though Nelson now faced hardship, it was nothing compared to the daily confrontation with death he'd had when he fought German Waffen-SS troops in Czechoslovakia during the last weeks of the war in Europe. Not long before the conflict ended on that continent, an enemy artillery shell had exploded near him. It was a miracle he'd survived, though he still carried shrapnel embedded in his legs.

He had refused medical treatment and continued to fight, though four of his ribs had broken. He couldn't keep food down and lost thirty pounds. After more than two weeks, his commanding officer ordered him to report to the medic for evacuation by airplane to a hospital in France.

During the flight, Germany unconditionally surrendered to the Allies on May 8, 1945.

A month later, after he'd been released from a French hospital, Nelson returned to the United States, and fully recovered from his wounds. Then he received orders to take part in the invasion of Japan. When his troop ship was halfway across the Pacific Ocean, A-bombs fell on the cities of Hiroshima and Nagasaki on August 6 and 9 ending the war in the Pacific. He had once again beaten the odds against him. He'd survived.

Nelson had learned that in 1942, researchers at the University of Chicago had secretly constructed a nuclear reactor underneath the spectator stands at Stagg Field and had created a fission chain reaction. The scientists' nuclear experiments were the beginning steps in the development of the first atomic bombs. This had happened in his hometown, the windy city–Chicago.

Nelson believed the two A-bombs that had detonated over the two Japanese cities saved him. Otherwise, he would've been in the first wave of American soldiers to assault the Japanese beaches.

Despite today's biting cold, Nelson smiled. He was free, and he was not in mortal danger. Ready to begin his search for employment, he stepped outside into the frigid, high wind. It took his breath away. The sky was gray. He passed tall, massive, stone, concrete, and brick buildings. He tried not to look upward at them because he didn't want to appear to be a country bumpkin. The city of big shoulders gave him the cold shoulder. A speeding car splashed a mixture of salt and icy water onto his thin jacket. After slapping the slush away, he trudged onward.

By midmorning, he neared the mammoth Union Station, which occupied a full city block. Located on Canal Street on the edge of the Loop, it was the city's major rail terminal. As the cold winter air bit deeper into his skin, it sucked heat from his body. The super frigid air smelled of smog, like a blend of coal smoke, automobile exhaust, and scorched steel. He figured breathing Chicago air was like smoking two packs of cigarettes a day. Defiantly, he inhaled the polluted gases through his nose and filled his lungs. He willed himself to soldier on as if he were on a forced march.

He had to step around dirty, icy slush and cold puddles when he crossed streets. His cheap jacket, scarf, and stocking hat only gave him partial protection from the icy conditions. He'd recently lost weight, but his muscles were still strong like those of an emaciated alley dog that had the gumption to survive in spite of adversity.

When he entered the huge railway station, he found it was gratefully warm inside. The slight odor of oil, carried by steam emitted from radiators along the walls of the open space, spread within the edifice. Did the aroma of lubricants come from diesel locomotives and train cars? What did it matter? The humid heat made him feel at ease. The inside atmosphere welcomed him and was a refuge from the glacial, unforgiving city.

Footsteps and an occasional voice echoed loudly in the Great Hall, where massive, stories-high, Roman travertine columns surrounded the expansive, wide space. He glanced up at the hall's barrel-vaulted skylight two hundred and nineteen feet long, and more than one hundred feet above him. Across the wide floor rows of varnished, dark wooden benches stood with ample space between them.

It was past rush hour, and the crowds of people scurrying to work were gone. Nelson spotted a copy of the thick *Chicago Sunday Tribune* on one of the benches.

When he grabbed the paper, his stomach protested, yearning for food. The mouthwatering scent of hamburgers and coffee from a food stand along one wall masked the smell of oil and beckoned him. He wished he had a least a dollar, but he knew he didn't have folding money.

Nelson sat heavily on the bench, kicked aside a cigarette butt on the stone floor, and saw a headline, "Conrad Hilton's Money Remodels Hotel."

Nelson scanned the article. He learned that during the war, the US Army had purchased the Stevens Hotel at 720 South Michigan Avenue to use for barracks and classrooms for the Army Air Force. When it first opened in 1927, it was the biggest hotel in the world. Recently, Conrad Hilton bought the hotel for nearly five million dollars. The article stated the hotel was expected to become an important asset of the Hilton Corporation.

Nelson wondered how long it would take the economy to reenergize after the war's end. Hilton must've had confidence things would improve. He'd risked big bucks.

After Nelson grabbed the Want Ad section of the *Trib*, an advertisement for manual workers seized his attention. He didn't want dirty work, like shoveling muck or cleaning a building, but this ad stated the pay for a laborer was $35 a day.

The address was in the 6600 block of South Wentworth Avenue, a long trek away, especially in the wind and cold. Nelson automatically felt in his pocket for carfare. He didn't discover any coins, only fuzz and a hole in his trousers.

"I'll need to walk it," he said to himself. He tore the ad from the *Trib*, crumpled it, and shoved it into his shirt pocket.

He saw warm breath steaming from his mouth, as he walked into the frigid air outside the station. The reality of the relentless, freezing climate hit like a splash of ice water slapping his already chilled face.

Hours later, Nelson's feet were numb with cold when he arrived at the Wentworth Warehouse and found a help wanted sign near its door. The structure appeared abandoned. It was a block long and had lots of windows – some boarded up, others broken. Those still intact were thick with sooty dirt, nearly opaque. The wooden doorframe of the main entrance had been painted dark blue years ago, but most of the paint had flaked away. The gray cast of the deteriorating wood was depressing.

Nelson pushed the door open, which was swollen and stuck a little. He stepped into the dark interior, and his eyes began to adjust to the low light.

"Hands up, sucker," a deep voice echoed. Nelson saw the long barrel of a gleaming, silver pistol that seemed to pop out from the gloom. The weapon appeared too clean for the forlorn scene. It was out of place.

Nelson raised his arms. "Look, Mister. I'm broke." Nelson saw a half dozen men sitting against a filthy brick wall with crumbling mortar. A second thug with a heavy black beard aimed a shotgun at the six prisoners.

The man with the silver pistol waved it toward the captives. "Throw your watch in the bucket, and sit with the rest of the job applicants," he said, smirking.

Lowering his hands a little, Nelson walked toward the man with the shotgun. The robber swung the weapon's stock at Nelson.

Nelson jumped back, grabbed the gun's rusty barrel, and jerked it aside. A big boom sounded. Buckshot sprayed the area.

"Joe Nelson!" the man with the shotgun yelled.

Nelson's eyes bugged out when he focused on the gunman's face behind his thick whiskers. "Roger Katinsky, is this the best you can do to make a living?"

Nelson eased his grip on the gun barrel.

Katinsky let it fall to point at the floor.

"I can't believe it, Sarge," Katinsky said. "Sorry, I didn't recognize you without your uniform."

"If you would have shaved today, Private, I wouldn't have had to grab the barrel," Nelson said, smiling.

When Nelson and Katinsky hugged, one of the men against the wall stood and ran through a side doorway. The rest of the prisoners scrambled away in seconds.

Katinsky shook his head. "They're getting away." He turned toward the man with the silver pistol. "Hey, Ernie..." Katinsky's forehead wrinkled when he saw Ernie lying on his back.

Nelson and Katinsky rushed to Ernie, whose face was pale white. A dribble of blood had leaked from a small wound on his left temple. Nelson felt for a pulse, but detected none. "He's dead, Roger," Nelson said.

"Let's get out of here," Katinsky said, as sirens began to wail in the distance. "Somebody's called the cops."

Nelson snatched his handkerchief from his back pocket. "I'll wipe down your shotgun."

"Okay, I'll grab the loot." Katinsky picked up the galvanized bucket that held watches, small change, and four one-dollar bills.

"Leave it, Roger," Nelson said.

"You want to eat, Joe?" Katinsky asked.

"Come on, Roger! Let's move," Nelson yelled. He dropped the shotgun near Ernie's body.

The two men fled to Katinsky's dented sedan. A child could've pushed a finger through its rusted fender. Katinsky fumbled for his car key, jammed it into the ignition, and fired up the engine. It spat, sputtered, and then rumbled to life. It was as noisy as a motorcycle. "The muffler's shot," thought Nelson.

"I got a place in a basement four blocks away," said Katinsky. He guided his rust-heap jalopy in a zigzag route through five alleys and turned onto a side street. "You're welcome to have dinner. You look like a scarecrow."

"I'm starving. But I'm not going to eat the food you buy after you pawn those watches and take the money from the bucket."

"I've got food already–bread, peanut butter, soup, Spam, and coffee."

"I'm too hungry to ask how you got the money to buy it."

Katinsky parked the car in a vacant lot near an ancient frame house. "The widow who lives here is nice. I don't pay much, so I help her when she asks."

"When you're not robbing people, you help old ladies?"

"Mable needs me. She's eighty."

"If you spent as much time working in a store as you do figuring how to commit perfect crimes, you'd be ahead."

Katinsky unlocked Mable's house. "So, if you have a steady job, why were you answering our ad?"

The smell of hot vegetable-beef soup wafted up from the basement, which was spotless. Katinsky had always been a neatnik, Nelson remembered, as he glanced at a large pot of soup simmering on top of a tiny white gas stove. He began to salivate like a hungry wolf.

"I keep soup cooking all day, every day," Katinsky said. "You keep adding water and any food you have. That's what my mother did when

I was a kid. You gotta try my soup, Joe."

"I'd like to," Nelson said, as he followed Katinsky toward a card table. Katinsky grabbed two chipped bowls, ladled soup into them, and sat.

"I'm tired of dodging cops," Katinsky said as he rubbed his hands together over the hot soup, drawing warmth into his fingers.

Nelson blew on the soup puddled in his big spoon. Then he sipped the broth and chewed on a chunk of beef. Its flavor was wonderful. He heard his belly rumble as his body rushed to absorb strength into his malnourished, skinny frame. Logic told him any food tastes great when your body demands it. Then again, this soup was better than any other thick stew he'd enjoyed.

He greedily dipped his spoon into the old chipped bowl for more. "Tastes great, Roger," Nelson said. "You should go into business."

"Yeah, Roger's Soup and Salad. The only customers around here are old folks, bums, and criminals."

"Older people like Mable may well go for a bowl of soup for a quarter."

"Mabel likes my soup. She gives me a dime and a potato or a carrot for a bowl of it."

"Kidding aside, Roger, you could peddle soup and salad, eat well, and make some dough." Nelson winked. "You could set up shop in the abandoned building next to where you park your car."

"Could work," Katinsky replied. "Nobody around here knows who owns the place. There's running water there, which I've used to wash my car. And believe it or not, the gas is still on. I've lit a stove in there."

"If you need a partner, I'm game," Nelson said. "That is, if you want to go straight, and shave so the police don't ID you."

"I agree, for now, Joe, but I'll have to pay off cops and food inspectors," Katinsky said.

"Deal," Nelson said. The men shook hands and then talked until midnight. They decided to call the place *The Soup and Salad Trading Post*. Besides money, they would accept vegetables, cans of paint, bags of nails–anything that would grow their business.

Katinsky smiled. He stood. "I better shave before a patrolman sees me in the street."

A sense of relief coursed through Nelson's whole being. He felt at home at last.

Late one summer night, after six months of illegal operation, Nelson and Katinsky sat at one of the eight tables in their makeshift eatery.

Nelson took the lid off the large coffee can where they'd hidden their bundle of cash. He began to count it, laying the bills in neat piles. When he finished, he guided his eyes to gaze at Katinsky. "We got enough jack for the down payment."

Katinsky stood and slapped Nelson on the back. "Joe, if it weren't for you and your idea, I'd be in jail or dead," Katinsky said.

Nelson shrugged. "If you didn't know how to make soup like you do, we'd both be in the clink."

Katinsky laughed and nodded.

The two men stepped out into the night and stared at the stars. Nelson felt the warm, humid, Chicago evening air soothe him. All of a sudden a fresh breeze carried with it the sweet smell of flowers and began to cool the air. "Roger, the best thing we got is each other, friend," Nelson said.

Katinsky grinned in the light of the moon.

By fall the two pals had bought the distressed building for a song, and *The Trading Post* became the best eatery near Ogden Park on Chicago's Southwest Side.

# AD 1948
# Itching Hands and Aching Hearts
## David Hagerty

The scandal ruined him. Not anything he did, which never hurt anybody. Not the lawsuit, which never came to judgement. Not the criminal case, which never convicted him. The scandal alone did it.

Because at that time, if a woman accused a man of seduction, it branded him. Before the Kinsey Report, before Masters and Johnson, before the liberation of the sixties, everyone believed that sex only occurred within the confines of marriage, and outside of those bonds we all lived like scared school girls.

But before I tell you about the scandal, I want to tell you about him.

&#9731;&#9731;&#9731;

Stanley Willard Duggins — Stan to his girls — owned a small photo studio in Gladstone Park, a squat of immigrant Poles, Irish, and Germans on the northwest side of Chicago. He shared walls with a butcher, a baker, a dress maker — respectable businesses.

On the first floor facing the street he showed off family portraits and adverts for the local papers. Just behind it sat his studio, which held the usual props and backdrops — fuzzy earth tones and soft focus landscapes — the kind you see in people's living rooms. He specialized, though, in debutante photos: glossy black and whites of young women with dramatic lighting. Every deb on the Gold Coast and the North Shore wanted him to immortalize them, with heads turned just so, eyes seducing the camera.

Farther back, behind a thick, black curtain, lay his darkroom, with the enlarger and the sinks and the films — and his second studio. A red light by the doorway warned away peepers. Nobody went back there except him — and his girls. On one wall hung a velvet drape, and that's where he'd take the "money shots," as he called them. Because even then you couldn't make a living off family keepsakes. So he'd pay cash to working-class girls who needed it, outfit us with whips and chains, or make us up as belly dancers. No full on nudity, no actual violence, just costumes and acting. He'd sell the prints to pinup mags — the detective series or fetish houses — but never direct to customers — no men in raincoats walking out with brown paper bags. That part of his trade he kept secret — except from us.

⧉

Of course I was nervous as a virgin the first time he brought me there, unsure what this little man with the limp intended. All I knew was what I'd read in the ad — amateur models wanted — but he talked me through it beforehand, helped me relax. "Modeling is just playing dress up," he said. Then he put on some Sinatra and mood lighting, decked me out in a slacks chemise and stilettos. He had a whole wardrobe for us girls — everything from pencil skirts to leather corsets.

He led me into his private office, as he called it, where lights surrounded me like guards — to keep me in or others out, I couldn't tell. The first time they flashed, I flinched, but I liked the heat they put out, as warming as an incubator. I couldn't help notice the smells — not just the usual photo chemicals, but something else: sausage. It wafted in from the meat shop next door. Most girls found it repulsive, but I loved it — making something tasty out of parts nobody else wanted.

For my debut we skipped the bondage. Instead he posed me on a swing hung from the ceiling, like some little girl. Look angry, he said, with a voice soft but firm. Bossy, I thought, but I did what he said, and we play acted, made it fun. With the makeup and lighting, I felt like glitterati — Lana Turner or Betty Grable.

Afterward he gave me an extra five bills and asked me back the next week. How could I refuse? In one hour I made more than for a day of "respectable" work.

It was only after I saw the prints that I understood his vision. Those snaps — good as the ones in fashion magazines or film noir — transformed me into a real woman. The crab patches called his pictures smut, but I never looked so glamorous. He could have been Herb Ritts or Helmut Newton if he wanted — he was that good — but he liked the pulp presses better.

Those first pictures made me a local celebutante. Everyone wanted me to pose — all the camera clubs and nature films. The moralizers say I was exploited, some sad sack who didn't know she was being taken for a ride. Because I appeared in my unmentionables or had my headlights showing, they assumed I was some charity girl. But the men all treated me like a starlet: blushing when I looked their way, asking me to autograph their pictures, speculating if I was rationed. Back then no one made stag films or peep shows — not legal ones, at least — which meant that a man without a baby doll needed to risk arrest to see an attractive female.

I never did anything I didn't want, never had anyone talk crude or crass to me. I dated who I liked and posed when I wished. I just modeled, with no add-ons.

A total about face from my life before. I was nothing: a seamstress sharing one room over a tailor's shop, working ten hour days six days a week, till my fingers literally bled from needle pricks and my eyes crossed from hemming and buttonholing. I can still smell the mothballs, hear the whirr of the sewing machines.

But within a couple months after that first sitting, I had quit the dressmaker and earned yards as a model. I had my hair done at the beauty parlor and bought my makeup from a department store. I even put those old skills to use, stitching my own outfits once I'd used up all of Stan's.

Without his pics, I'd be some factory girl or someone's fat, pregnant wife. For a country girl from Peoria, there's no other choice. Which is why I left home at sixteen: to escape all the farm boys, leering at me, pawing at me if I consented to ride with them to the town's passion pit.

Compared to Chicago, downstate was licentious, as the preachers would call it, with nothing to do but plow and propagate. People there called it earth's heaven, but to anyone with ambition it was pure purgatory. I heard far more propositions from the Bible-thumpers than the photographers.

They tried to warn me against leaving, told me of the wicked ways of the Windy City. My pastor quoted 2 Peter, 2: 18

> *For when they speak great swelling words of vanity,*
> *they allure through the lusts of the flesh, through*
> *much wantonness, those that were clean escaped*
> *from them who live in error.*

I always preferred Matthew 12:36-37

> *But I tell you that everyone will have to give account*
> *on the Day of Judgment for every empty word they*
> *have spoken. For by your words you will be*
> *acquitted, and by your words you will be*
> *condemned.*

Even though the Bible tells us not to, people rejoice in judging each other. The curfew keepers want to tell us all where to live and how. Which is why once the lawsuit surfaced, the news made a sermon of it.

&#10048;

I can only imagine how Ruth felt about all the attention. The papers branded her the "Chicago coquette." Her lawyers claimed Stan had "importuned" her with gifts of clothes and jewels until she couldn't resist his lascivious advances. Only that's not how he worked. He told you straight up what he wanted, never underhanded, never forced. He dressed you, posed you, then paid you. One of the few honest men I've ever met.

I only saw her once at his studio. A real plain-Jane. If you met her at a bar or club, you'd never think she could be beautiful, with her weak chin and lank hair, her feet too big and splayed so she walked like a duck. She even smelled ordinary, of bar soap and talcum.

That's how sharp he was — with makeup and lighting, he could make any girl glamorous. In some shots Ruth looked curvaceous and confident, in others frail and meek. I guess that was her true talent, a fickle quality that could mutate to whatever guise he needed.

I always thought her father pushed her to it, that he wanted to defend his little girl: her youth, her honor, her innocence. Because she grew up in the church, a Catholic school girl, the kind who can't consent before marriage. Once dad heard her being called a strumpet, harlot, hussy, he felt compelled to defend her from the unholy world.

So they sued, for seduction. Claimed that Stan had corrupted an innocent child into "virtual prostitution." Shows how much they know about the profession, that they'd confuse such degradation with having your picture taken. That's all it was, just a bit of titillation.

Titillation. That's a word I learned from her jackleg lawyer. He wanted to interview me, asked if Stan tried to seduce me, too. As though his photos offered nothing more than arousal.

Stan called her his succubus, which isn't what it sounds like. It's a woman who seduces a man in his dreams and steals his soul. It's all made up, of course, but not far from true.

Despite what Ruth and her father did to Stan, I pitied her — seventeen and pregnant, with no man, no job, and a priggish family who tried to pray the sin out of her. Her knees must have ached from all the kneeling she did, her nostrils burned from the incense. The Catholics are competitive that way, services all day and night, seven days a week, like God is keeping count. Really, her biggest sin was not knowing about birth control.

What did they expect from it? Money? Fame? A husband? For Ruth to become some brevet wife? As though that would offer her heart balm. As though that could restore her reputation, her respectability. How can you restore what you never had?

Because we all got heckled. His girls. All girls. The fore castle lawyers who don't know how to talk to women instead call us cheesecakes and sweater girls. The only difference between her and me is I accepted the cracks. In fact, I embraced them, gave them a big kiss, lay down and made love to them.

◐◑

I don't know how the scandalmongers found my name — probably from studying the photos in the pulp press — but one morning a half dozen of them were lurking outside my apartment, asking about my "corruption." Like dogs to a bitch in heat, they followed me, hoping to get lucky. At first I ignored them as I did the randy teenage boys from downstate, but they persisted more than the farmers, marking me with their inky hands, taking my picture without asking or paying me.

So I talked to one, Maggie, a society columnist for the *Herald-American*, which Mr. Hearst owned. She modeled too once, then wrote about fashion. She dressed like it, too, all silks and satins, the latest New York styles from Bloomies and Saks, her hair done in waves, her makeup airbrushed. She even smelled upscale, of cold creams and leathers.

She asked how I felt in the fetish clothes. "Beautiful," I said, "especially when you compare them to the frumpy house dresses that most women walk around in."

That day I had on a good swing skirt and cardigan from Marshall Fields, so Maggie posed me in my easy chair. Only half my leg showed and none of my torso. Still, people commented on my tight top and my short dress, like they'd never seen a woman's knees before. Really, the whole reason anyone wanted to read about the scandal was as an excuse to look at his photos. The hacks were selling sex to prudes too sanctimonious to buy my pictures direct.

At least Maggie got it. "These kind of lawsuits disguise itching hands as aching hearts," she wrote. In private she told me about some of the come-ons she'd heard when she worked the runways, from men who assumed she'd be of easy virtue because she liked to dress up. "They didn't understand that clothes merely disguise our true selves."

Maybe, but after her article, I had even more muckrakers on my doorstep, begging for an interview, a date, an invitation inside my lair. They smelled of cabbage and stout, as though they'd just escaped a beer garden, and shouted in the shrill cries of newsboys. Only they published condemnations from the local preachers and civic leaders, people who'd never met me, who'd turn me out if they saw me in their congregation, who'd labeled me a "fallen woman." Fallen from what? I asked. My cell above the sweatshop?

Then the politicians got involved, questioning my character, and his. They talked like they'd never heard of speakeasies, couldn't remember Prohibition. If they needed reminders, they could've walked down Rush Street any night, including Sundays, to see how real working girls worked. Instead, they talked. Talked about public morals. Talked about vice. The aldermen claimed they wanted to save the city and its citizens from "degradations," all while taking bribes from the Outfit that organized them. Even the press got smeared by one who said, "Stories of this kind corrupt the public morals and induce a sordid image of illicit affairs in the minds of the immature."

Pretty quick, the gossip killed Stan's "legit" business. No upper crust types wanted their daughters glamorized by him anymore, as if he were tarting them up to walk the streets. They didn't understand — he was no pimp, only a man who appreciated female beauty.

Once his respectable clients left, he doubled down on the scandal shots. Had to pay for his food and rent somehow. He'd work two or three of us a day. Sneak us in through the back alley. Then he started selling mail order, risking an indictment by the postal service, he said. All to survive.

Even with the hubbub, he still treated us like starlets. Claimed to be getting calls from Hollywood producers and New York agents. I knew what he was doing — lying to put us at ease — and I loved him for it. He promised us it would fade away like an old photo, and it almost did.

◖◗

They didn't expect the paternity test to clear him. Ruth's dad insisted on it, as if he counted on a shotgun wedding. I heard they strapped poor Stan to a chair when they drew his blood, so he could "see how it felt" to be tied down. Only the blood didn't match, which left him scot-free but every sailor on leave in the Great Lakes as suspects.

That torpedoed the civil suit, and it should have finished the story. Except after that much attention from the press, the law couldn't fake ignorance anymore. Plenty of beat cops knew what Stan did. He paid them $50 a month to "protect" him. That's the way business was done back then. If you wanted anything in the City that Works, you paid a tribute to City Hall. Truth was, you couldn't get a business license or a loading zone without tipping out the civil servants.

Only this time it wasn't the city that came after Stan, it was the G-men. I guess after they'd finished with Al Capone and John Dillinger, they needed new targets. He made an easy one, without lawyers or gunmen to protect him. They accused him of white slavery under the Mann Act, claimed that he'd transported underage women across state lines for "immoral" purposes. As though Illinois didn't breed plenty of poor, working girls from its own loins.

First, they searched his studio, took all his equipment so he couldn't even use the back room any more. Then they locked him up, dressed him in stripes and chains, treated him like a street criminal. What he actually did didn't matter.

In the papers they portrayed him as a gimp too lame to fight in Europe. True, he limped due to polio as a child, but he had no problem getting around the studio. As for keeping him out of battle, I'd count that a blessing. I knew plenty of farm boys who deployed as heroes and discharged as cripples.

"They persecute what they covet," he once said.

I think they feared our freedom. Because they couldn't control someone like him, someone who thought for himself, who didn't adhere to conventional morals. Uncle Sam wanted conformity, not beauty. People wanted someone to make them feel superior, someone to be the scapegoat of their own desires.

ᔓᔍ

They jailed him for six months. Six months while the lawyers bickered, while his bills accumulated, while his shop sat empty and unprotected, while thieves took what little equipment the police had left.

In the meantime, I moved by night, a virtual vamp, working only after hours for other photographers, and most off avoiding the police. Because they pursued us girls with more passion than even the news hounds, banging on our doors after dark, following us to our day jobs, informing our supervisors about our "corruption." They wanted us to testify, to affirm that he "seduced" us the way he did Ruth.

None of us wanted to tattle, so they threatened prosecution: for public indecency, solicitation, depravity. One told me he'd "ruin me for marriage," like that was life ending. The way most men act, who wants to be legally bound to one?

Stan's lawyer assured us he would win. Given time the feds would fold, once they realized no one would back up their story. All they had were the photos, which proved low morals but not seduction. So long as we stayed loyal to Stan, he'd be out in months.

A couple of the girls wavered, though. They had boyfriends and brothers and bosses to worry about. What would the men say if their girl Friday backed a pornographer?

"Say nothing," I told them. "If you talk, they'll use your words against you later."

Still, when the cops detained several of them overnight for questioning, like common streetwalkers, they panicked. One took a midnight train out of Union Station and never returned. Another married a soldier then hid behind her husband when the cops came knocking. I brushed them off like you would a horny dog trying to hump your leg.

As Stan's trial date loomed, all of us wondered: Who'll break on the stand?

ᔓᔍ

A week before, my mom called. Her minister had told her about the case, showed her clippings from the *Tribune* and the *Daily News*. I should've expected as much. In small towns, nobody misses a chance to point out the faults of their neighbors.

Mom asked me to move back home, told me she'd kept my old room waiting. "Everyone misses you," she said.

I didn't tell her that I never missed them. Even with my wages cut in half, I'd rather starve in Chicago than grow fat and old in Peoria. Or be catcalled by moralizers.

"Thanks, but I've got friends here who need me," I said.

⧉

The trial started with another free-for-all of the libel makers. I'd outfitted myself in my best wrap dress, fishnets, and stilettos, camera ready. When they spotted me outside the courthouse, the flashbulb boys started pushing to get a good view, nearly knocked me off my heels. The cops had to hold back the mob with shoves and billy clubs.

In the hallway, I sat next to Ruth, who looked even younger than before — bulbous and bloated, with acne breaking out on her weak chin. She didn't even nod at me, probably ashamed more by her betrayal than her condition. I whispered to her that it wasn't too late to recant, to defend Stan, but she ignored me until they threw open the doors to the judgement chamber. When she stood, I felt truly sorry for her — her duck walk had turned into a full waddle.

Inside the courtroom smelled as stale as a butcher's back alley, compacting all manner of raw flesh. Not one window let in fresh air while a single ceiling fan circulated the stench. With the doors shut and so many people crammed in, I feared we'd all molder.

When they led in Stan, he looked ready for a chain gang. The guards had shackled his feet and arms like he was some dangerous murderer, which caused him to limp even more than usual, made him look clumsy and frail. I couldn't bear to see him that way and lifted my chin. He didn't smile or wink, only shook his head sadly and looked away.

The first day of testimony starred a platoon of federal agents, who showed off our photos like booty from a war. The jurors — all milquetoast types wearing three-pieces and long dresses — leaned in to see them up close, then looked at Stan, mercilessly. After they displayed one snap of me in leather and chains, he smiled and shrugged as though to say, "See, we're both bound up."

On day two, the girls got put in the box. Ruth started it, playing the patsy even though Stan never killed her rabbit. Then Selma, daughter of an insurance salesman from Gary, teared up when the prosecutor asked what Stan had done to lure her from Indiana to the big city. She looked to Stan like she expected advice, lowered her head, then said, "He didn't do it," silently indicting her father. Another girl from Wisconsin stared at the stenographer the whole time, as if her freedom were at risk, but couldn't bring herself to say anything useful.

Finally, they called me. Plenty of times I'd been interrogated by the cops without turning over, but the shyster was crafty, setting me up for one question by asking another, like a verbal version of the shell game. Did I take off my clothes willingly? Yes. Did I get paid? Yes. Did I consider it immoral? No. Even if the law forbid it.

He tried to chasten me, but I sat tall and proud, like my parents taught me to do in church, answering his questions without shame or guilt. Even when he held up a picture of me menacing another girl, I didn't feel embarrassed. Because I didn't care what they thought. I cared for Stan.

At one point, I looked at him and smiled. Right off, the shyster asked me to explain the meaning of that smile, like it was some secret code. "Have faith," I said.

"Are you sure, miss, that you're not still under his influence?" he said. "Because it appears to me that he can control you even in handcuffs."

"No one controls me."

"So he didn't recruit you, train you? You and the other girls? To his kitten house." He smirked as though he'd invented the phrase.

Which is where I saw his weakness. "No one recruited me. I wanted to work. Same as the other girls. They came to me, asked how I got started, so I told them."

The courtroom went silent, the only sound the fans swirling dead air overhead. Even that grandstanding lawyer couldn't think what to say — for a moment at least — then tried ten different ways to back me off. Asked didn't Stan prey on poor working girls?

"He made me into a woman," I said and stared him down.

In his summation, the government's mouthpiece claimed that photographers were always on skirt patrol. He said that Stan led a "sad, lonely life" as a cripple who shacked up over his studio and paid women for company. He showed the most salacious shots to the jury, the comical ones with us all trussed up. He never talked about the art Stan made, the beauty of his photos.

After days of the vice squad trying to humiliate us, to embarrass us all into confessing, which none of us did, Stan's lawyer asked for a dismissal on account of the government failing to prove its case. The judge leaned back in his plush chair to ponder, then called for a conference by the bench. Meantime, we all waited hushed and wary, murmuring to each other while the lawyers did the same. I told Selma the feds were trying to end this while saving face.

When they broke their huddle, we sat on tenterhooks, watching for some tip to what they'd agreed. Stan's defender whispered in his ear, waited until he nodded, then looked to the bench and did the same. The judge panned the audience like a preacher searching out sinners in his congregation, then launched into a long explanation about the laws of indecency and the court's definition of it: "to deprave or corrupt those whose minds are open to such immoral influences, and into whose hands a publication of this sort may fall."

What all of it meant none of us could tell until the judge asked Stan to rise like some chained ghost. "How would you plead to a lesser charge of public indecency?"

Stan nodded, then in a small voice said, "Guilty."

Another hiss passed through the courtroom until this Solomon interrupted to say, "On that basis, I hereby sentence you to six months incarceration, with credit for time served." He banged his gavel, thanked his jury, and ordered his courtroom cleared, while all of us sat in wonder at what had just passed.

Stan's attorney shook hands with his client, who could hardly lift his arms with all the iron weighing him down. Then the bailiffs picked him up by the elbows and carried him toward the back entrance for inmates.

"Where's he going?" I heard myself say, still trying to comprehend it all.

"To be processed," said his lawyer, "for release."

〰️

Even if you never heard about his life, you probably read about his death. That made national news. No doubt, you saw the picture of him on the perp walk, surrounded by guards, and a man in a trench coat leaping out of the crowd with a gun. Ruth's father hated Stan so much, he put himself in a cell. Really, I think the G-men wanted Stan dead and set up the whole thing so they wouldn't have to watch him walk free. Otherwise, why parade him in public like that?

Stan died before he reached the hospital, even though the doctors claimed they used all their tricks to save him. Then they insisted on an autopsy, even though everyone saw what had happened. They planned to bury his desecrated body in an unmarked grave out behind the prison until me and some of the girls chipped in for a headstone and a hole at Graceland.

Now, years after, strangers visit his plot. He lies next to a bunch of muckety mucks — George Pullman and Allan Pinkerton, Louis Sullivan and Cyrus McCormick. People can see him for what he was: a victim of public prudery. They sacrificed him so they could feel better about themselves, atone for their own lechery. Otherwise, why persecute someone who fulfilled their desires?

〰️

Once, years later, I stopped by his studio, which still sat empty. Someone had taken down his sign, papered over his windows, erased all traces of him. The glass had been scraped clean of his name, but at the right angle, I could still see the faded outline of it. I guess even sanitized no one wanted to inherit his infamy, as though the scandal had tainted the space.

Probably, it's better that way. I'd rather remember his work, which you can see now in magazines and galleries. *Playboy* ran a retrospective of it, and some people collect the originals, display them in their living rooms next to the Vargas girls. Funny to think that I'm an object of art, like the Mona Lisa or the Venus de Milo.

I guess it's like they wrote in the Bible: one man's sin is another man's salvation.

## AD 1950
## What Lies Buried
### Avi Sirlin

From atop the steps outside Luxor's train station, Lester Huxley squinted at the evening's peculiar fog. In a cone of light above the taxi stand, airborne particles twirled and danced. Across the roadway he could make out the base of a stone obelisk easy as pie, but higher up the monument dissolved. The back of Lester's throat finally caught a taste. Sand. Shouldn't have been a surprise, an entire desert out there in the dark, always shifting, who could say how much of it was launched skyward at any one time, blurring this and that? What he did know was if he stood there any longer he'd likely be brushing it out of bodily crevices till kingdom come. Clutching his duffel, everything he owned at his side, Lester descended onto the roadway and struck out in the most promising direction.

Not a motor vehicle in sight, only a mangy grey-marbled cat, its torn right ear covered in congealed blood and lowering its body to growl at him, Lester marched down the middle of the thoroughfare. The pavement reeked of horse piss, its gutters filled with sand drifts that'd track a man's bootprints. While shuttered storefronts and homes hid it from view, Lester knew that nearby flowed the Nile. And due west beyond the great river, in a desert valley not too distant, good old King Tut and the rest of the pharaohs, sleeping cozy in their crypts. Finding a quiet bed for the night was exactly what Lester also had in mind.

Signs of life, a roadside café, yellow light spilling over sidewalk tables where conversation and spoons tinkling against glass subsided as he approached. Lean working men lounging in their *galebayas* sipping tea, their creased, sun-baked faces betraying no expression, eyes trailing as he passed. Further along, a half-dozen soldiers materialized, chatting and kicking a wadded up cloth ball. They paid him no mind, rifles casually slung or lazily gripped at their sides. Kids, Lester sized up, none old enough to have seen action before the armistice five years ago; their mothers would have been packing them off to school each morning, home cooking waiting at the end of each day. How easy to snatch a gun and turn its muzzle around so they'd shit their pants, wise them up to real soldiering. He fixed his eyes forward until he could no longer hear their scuffing boots.

Pavement turned to dirt and a wafting odour of raw sewage. Wondering if he'd do better trying the other direction from the train station. at his back, Lester heard the throb of hooves and edged aside before a caleche taxi rolled past, wheels muttering over the ground. The carriage abruptly halted not fifty feet past and a man leaned out from behind the canopy, black cape hanging off his tuxedo. He raised his top hat and a lock of pomaded hair fell against his forehead.

"Good evening, sir," the man called out. "You are an Englishman?"

Catching hold of the clipped German accent, Lester's gut tightened. This being 1950, your typical Kraut didn't simply strike up idle chit-chat with a fellow who would've obviously been lighting a cigar on V-E Day.

"American."

Nothing in his tone encouraged further talk, but if the curt reply bothered the man, he failed to show it. "Delightful! Few Yanks in Egypt these days. Myself, I am from Switzerland. May I ask the reason for your visit?"

Swiss. Now that figured. Sit out the fighting, nothing to do except make their cheese and chocolate—maybe hoard some German gold—thinking you're everyone's friend, poking your nose into everybody's business. Well, not his.

"Only here for a quick look-see at the tombs."

"A grand adventure! Such a shame so many burial chambers have been plundered, yes? How can people learn history without all the facts?"

Lester said nothing, hoping the fellow would take the hint and shove off already. Instead he prattled on like they'd met at a strawberry social.

"The Valley of the Kings is a spectacle I have always wished to see, but the afternoon heat is unbearable and mornings impossible, late hours being an unfortunate aspect of my trade." A sly grin as the fellow tugged back a sleeve to flourish his hand, fingers spread to indicate nothing hidden. Lester understood he was to keep watching. The man's hand curled into a fist and when the fingers unfolded, a silver flask lay cradled across the palm. There'd been a feint, that much was plain, but it'd defied Lester's powers of observation. The illusionist signalled his driver to remain in place and descended onto the road where he strode to greet Lester.

"How very rude of me, I am Roland Steiger. I presently return from my nightly performance at the Winter Garden Hotel where, on stage, I answer to The Great Carnavale."

Lester introduced himself as they shook hands. At six feet, it wasn't often in these parts he found his eyes level with another's. He made Steiger for late thirties, roughly ten years older than himself, but with a younger man's bearing, cockiness coming off him like steam from a kettle. All of it a warning.

"Say, I don't mean to hold you up."

Steiger clucked. "Mr. Huxley, I have had the pleasure to perform in Tripoli, Cairo, Istanbul and Damascus. We are in *Luxor*! Any diversion is most welcome! And if I may say without giving offence, by your appearance, I assume you have just arrived on the regular passenger train, yes?"

Lester needed no reminder of his ragged state. From the wary looks he encountered everywhere, he could tell two years of nomadic existence had carved hard edges into him. This past season the only work he'd been able to scrounge meant toiling in the orchards west of Malaga, shoulder-to-shoulder with African migrants, thin desperate men who wanted nothing to do with him, accurately calculating that any white man picking fruit must be a fugitive.

Steiger cast a re-appraising eye, then grinned conspiratorially. "I am presently en route to my quarters, a hotel where I have hardly seen a soul. Plenty of cheap rooms and I would be most happy to share my evening apertif." Steiger jiggled his silver flask.

Lester desperately ached to end the man's inquisition, find himself a bed. But he'd also rattled his keester all the way from Cairo, fifteen hours on a hard-slatted bench crammed among natives stinking of wood smoke and clay and sweat. All of that for this exact opportunity, an out-of-the-way encounter with a fellow traveller. A passport bearer like Roland Steiger. But there was a rub. Steiger was no average Joe. Strapping build, eager chumminess with a vagrant like himself, and that magic bit with the flask? Just like the town's air, it made his throat catch. Still, as with the rest of his self-imposed exile from home, trying to confront and at the same time control his fate, Lester understood predicament created chance.

This in mind, Lester clambered aboard the caleche's upholstered seat next to the magician. Behind a swayback chestnut mare with protruding ribs, they clopped through the soupy night, merging onto a more significant road where they passed other caleches and donkey carts, and men on foot destined for home, judging by their reluctant gait. To Lester's consternation, everyone crossing their path turned to stare. The Great Carnavale and his surly tramp companion, a one-float parade.

❧❧❧

After the war, he'd returned to Albany where he didn't leave his mother's house for two months. Twenty-four years old, camped out in his childhood bedroom, emotions tamped deep into bone. "War, ma," he said. "Just tired as hell. I'll be all right soon."

One evening he whispered through the door to Susan, his youngest sister, requesting a writing pad and envelope. Later, knees pressed against the underside of his old school desk, pen hovering above the paper, he waited an eternity for the words to come. Wartime faces flashed before his mind's eye like night tracers until one, and only one, lingered. Her moist brown eyes and thick, expressive eyebrows, the slightest shadow of hair on her upper lip. Olive skin trembling and warm to his touch, glistening. His sweat. He'd been dripping onto her as she lay beneath him, his creased knuckles lined black with rifle grease clamped over her mouth.

He started writing:

*Dear Lucia, I am the American soldier who raped you.*

Her northeastern mountain town had looked no different than other towns and villages they'd cleared as they made their way up through Italy. Waffen-SS, they'd been warned, but they were nothing if not cautious now anyhow. Six months, a year tops, and the war would be over. Survive, that's all, they repeated. Inside the first minute they took sniper fire. Two dead, four moaning for help and Georgie, Lester's best friend, his lower face shattered, a stomped red tomato. The medic waffled over whether Georgie would survive medivac to Monghidoro, eventually giving in to the little bastard's plea for another morphine. Georgie, who'd escaped the bloodbath in Sicily with nothing more than scalded lips, too dumb to cool his hot coffee, predicting then how he'd live to a hundred; not getting it even a quarter right.

After they'd secured the town, Lester and the other men, khakis rimed with salt and encrusted in dirt, listlessly reclined on the bare ground in the shade of the town hall, waiting for orders. That was when the first locals turned up, pointing bony fingers. The Germans' puppet mayor was holed up in the basement of the town hall. Captain Kershaw, a married man who worked for an advertising agency in Chicago found a functioning water tap, finger-combed his wetted hair, then accompanied the howling residents inside. Rumour had it that during college Kershaw studied art in Florence; he could make do in the native pigeon-talk. He persuaded the man to surrender, and drew him out into the square. The old mayor, a corner of his rumpled white shirt untucked, collapsed when through his thick glasses he noticed the firing squad Kershaw assembled. Participation in special duties being the most reliable way to avoid Kershaw's doghouse, and maybe assignment as platoon scout with its high extinction rate, Lester took his place. They had to prop the mayor on a chair.

The rifle reports had barely faded before eight young women, the eldest no more than twenty-five, were hauled forward. Shawls tightly wrapped around tear-streaked faces, they strained against their captors, a mob of house matrons garbed head-to-toe in black, and a couple of toothless hobbling men. Amid all the caterwauling, Kershaw lit a cigarette and studied the young women from beneath his heavily lidded eyes, then muttered a few words in Italian. One of the braying old crones went round tearing the shawls off each girl's head. Lester and the other men, dead to the world a few minutes ago, stirred.

Kershaw crushed the cigarette under his boot and explained the situation to the unit. Local men burrowed in the mountains, fighting with the partisans, while these women slept with SS officers, receiving food, clothing, wine and luxuries for themselves and their families. Italian and American blood on their hands. The mob's leader, a stocky middle-aged woman, expected the same justice meted out to the mayor, but Kershaw wasn't about to execute women. Whores and traitors, he judged. Punishment should fit the crime.

Lester had no time to process the task, the stocky woman shoving in his direction the tallest girl who, even as Lester caught her by the elbow, traded curses with the woman. Amid the barrage of insults he plucked out the name Lucia.

Inside the town hall, broken glass crackled beneath Lester's worn boots as he tugged the girl into the first empty office. In the back corner, behind the overturned desk, a grandfather clock stood, works missing, clock-face empty. Lucia kicked him in the thigh, missing her target by a few inches. He pressed her down onto a dusty rug speckled with broken plaster. She turned her head from him, staring at the clock. It flashed through his mind how the German officer she'd been fucking was certainly more handsome and more cultured, and she likely didn't care if goddamned fascists ran the whole planet much less her town. She sure as hell didn't care about Georgie. He felt an urge to squeeze all the oxygen out of her whorish lungs and she seemed to register this, letting out a scream. He covered her mouth. She squirmed and in response, though he told himself at the time there was no pleasure in the task, he felt his blood surge. He finished quickly and left her quivering on the floor. Another uniform brushed past into the office before he'd made it through the doorway.

He wrote:

> *When I was young my father died and I was raised at home by women, their hard work and sacrifices invisible to everyone but me. Now I can't look them in the eye. I allowed myself to believe my actions were a form of justice, even though a piece of my heart said different. I carry this shame in my soul and will never forget the harm I inflicted upon you.*
>
> *Sincerely,*
> *Lester Huxley,*
> *Albany, New York*

Without a word to his mother or sisters, he left his bedroom the next morning, hiking clear over to the downtown post office where no one would know him. On the envelope, along with the Italian town's name, he marked: *Lucia c/o General Post Office.* Uncertain the letter would ever reach her, let alone be read and understood, he never expected a reply. He told himself a response wasn't necessary.

A local lumber yard hired him, finding him reliable, even if he tended to keep to himself. More than two years after his confessional letter he came home one afternoon to find an envelope bearing an elaborate Italian seal. He got furiously drunk that night, then called in sick to work next morning. While his mother and sisters were out, he packed his duffel, then cleaned out his bank account and took a bus to New York. He checked into a Bowery flophouse where an ex-GI directed him to a lighting showroom on Mott. At the store's loading dock, Lester's face burned as the warehouseman, Italian-American a few years his senior, but hair threaded grey and stooped like an elderly librarian, unscrewed the cap on the bourbon Lester slipped him and haltingly translated, sneaking surreptitious glances at him. In addition to the arrest warrant in Italy, Italian police were requesting an American military investigation and court martial.

Lester phoned his mother to explain what he couldn't say to her face. She urged him to return, saying war did awful things to people and she would take a loan if necessary to hire the best lawyer. He told her that quite aside from his own fate, implicating other men in his squad was out of the question. He caught a steamer to England. Nearly every day he thought about surrendering himself to justice. It would be as easy as presenting his passport at the Italian border. Instead, he kept moving.

∞

The starving mare sighed when the caleche stopped in front of the Nile Sphinx Hotel. Steiger spoke French with the one-eyed desk clerk, his other socket a pale divot of flesh. The clerk glanced quickly at Lester, then under illumination of a faux-candle chandelier, he focused his working eye on the register and entered the information Steiger provided. Steiger accompanied Lester to the second floor and reminded him of the nightcap waiting one floor above once he'd refreshed himself. After washing up, Lester trudged upstairs, wanting to get on with it, the brass tacks.

Steiger answered his door in shirtsleeves and calico trousers. The curtains were drawn and the magician's garments folded at the foot of a neatly made iron bedstead. On the wall opposite, in a mirror above a rust-streaked porcelain wash basin, Lester glimpsed himself, the worry in his deep-set eyes, lips drawn tight as if half-formed words had curdled. Battle experience taught him a man who looked like that would waver, even with a bayonet pointed at his belly. Kershaw used to say, *You hesitate, you die.* So Lester eased the tension out of his jaw and reminded himself why he'd journeyed all the way from Cairo, then tried to figure out where in the room Steiger likely kept his Swiss passport.

The magician had circled to the bureau where his silver flask stood alongside a half-full bottle of Bols, two tumblers, and vials of what appeared to be cologne. Leaning against the wall, a small framed photo of a young boy with dark features. Steiger filled an empty tumbler and passed it to Lester, who eyed the brimming glass.

"Mighty generous amount."

"Befitting a man who travels five hundred miles in third-class." Steiger raised his own glass in salute. "To adventure!"

Lester let the liquid float upon the paddle of his tongue before easing it down. His first drink since Malaga, after the harvest. Outside a tavern, he'd ended up in a drunken brawl with a squat fellow whose sour face took the brunt. Naturally, come morning someone would be looking to even the score—maybe the injured man's friends or family, possibly the police. So by the time the sun rose, Lester's elbows were leaning on the portside rail of the ferry taking him to Tangier. North Africa turned out a good decision: his money stretched, alcohol was hard to find, the locals kept to themselves, and fellow wanderers were few. Heading east from Tunisia, he didn't come across another Westerner until Cairo, giving him time to sort out his thinking, make the hard decisions.

Steiger was eyeing him curiously. Lester remembered Kershaw saying he had a tendency to drift away on his thoughts, how that could get him killed. The Captain was always focused—Lester doubted he would have fallen for the magician's earlier sleight of hand. With his Swiss passport and handsome showman's flair, Steiger must've had a very different wartime experience. Probably had his pick of lonely women. That would explain the picture of the young boy on the bureau. Sunken eyes too large for his narrow bony face, Lester would bet the kid had been born during the war years amid the food scarcity. Maybe Steiger sent a token sum each month for upkeep. Lester wondered if the boy's mother had sacrificed herself in the same manner as Lucia.

It'd crossed his mind more than once over the years that maybe Lucia had loved her German officer. Would it have been so wrong for her to seek happiness—even if happiness was tinned meat purchased with the only currency she possessed? Hadn't he and Georgie repeated to each other that survival was all that mattered? Broken-faced Georgie, setting off an animal whimper as the morphine carried him away, leaving Lester no way of saying goodbye.

What he'd figured out in North Africa was that two years of drifting had changed nothing inside him. By the time he arrived in Cairo, he'd finally worked out his way forward. First he'd have to go back.

Lucia could have had nothing to do with the arrest warrant. His written confession would have needed a translator, someone capable of putting matters in motion. She might just as likely have wanted the terrible incident suppressed. But he could also readily imagine the opposite—he remembered the way she'd writhed beneath him, legs stronger than he'd expected, her hatred fuelled by contempt. She'd seemed a woman quite capable of grabbing the nearest knife and plunging it into his chest.

"Another schnapps?" Steiger indicated Lester's empty tumbler.

"Much obliged." He had no intention of getting liquored up, but one more would do no harm. Then down to business.

Lucia. Would she forgive him? To find out, he needed to enter Italy under another name. But at the souk in Cairo, all his earnest enquiries about acquiring a passport yielded only suspicion or mocking laughter. Later, watching pigeons tussle over discarded bread crusts in Tahrir Square, a bespectacled man dressed in white clerical robe sat next to him on the bench. The way the man cradled his cigarette, cupped hand never straying more than a few inches from his lips as he spoke his heavily accented English, led Lester to believe he was no cleric.

Accompanying the man to a nearby apartment block, Lester was instructed to wait in the foyer. Lifting the corners of his robe, the man climbed the stairs and disappeared from view. A quarter of an hour later he returned and motioned Lester outside. Careful to match the man's languid strides, Lester learned that for the sum he could afford, he'd be guaranteed a flawless photo substitution and expertly forged particulars that would pass muster. But Lester had to furnish the passport himself. And to ensure local police remained uninterested, it couldn't be traceable to anyone in Cairo.

No money to buy a stolen passport, he needed to poach one. Immediately Luxor made sense. He imagined his American or European victim wealthy, a man of leisure who would nicely recover on a thick mattress in a luxury hotel from the bruising he received. Meanwhile Lester would be sweating it out on unforgiving hardwood during his long rail journey back to Cairo. Fate then presented him Roland Steiger, a show-off, a womanizer, and owner of a Swiss passport somewhere in this room.

Lester raised the glass to his lips, eager for the brandy, enjoying its sweet jolt. "Did you perform magic during the war?"

Steiger eyed him strangely, up and down as if examining livestock. It was then Lester noticed his legs faltering, muscles gone slack.

"Prior to the hostilities," Steiger said, "I performed throughout Europe, including England, where I'd been educated. But after war broke out, I felt called upon to ensure survival of my heritage. So then my only magic trick was making people disappear."

Lester found his mind going fuzzy. "I don't follow."

"I joined the Waffen-SS."

Trying to sort out the implications of Steiger's confession, Lester found his legs crumpling, crashing him to the floor. Steiger crouched over him, studying him before reaching into Lester's shirt pocket. Lester locked onto Steiger's wrist, but the magician worked his hand loose, extracted Lester's passport, and leafed through its pages.

Lester struggled to rise, but his muscles failed. He noticed a bitter taste in his mouth. Unable to speak, he felt a clamp inside his throat, narrowing his air passage.

"Won't be long now, Lester," Steiger said. He retrieved the empty glass tumbler from Lester's fingers and carefully rinsed it at the basin before placing it on the dresser. "Unfortunately, activities in service of my ancestral homeland attracted severe scrutiny when the war concluded and I had to flee Europe. I deeply desire to return. A son I have not seen for over five years, his mother pleading. But how? I asked her. I face immediate arrest."

In the brief silence that followed, Lester heard the clicking of wind-borne sand against the window, the desert surrendering part of itself. His lungs seared, every pinpoint of muscle blazing heat, incinerating him from within. His chest convulsed.

Steiger nodded, as though he'd been waiting for that sign. He lifted one of the vials from the bureau, unscrewed its cap for a sniff, then closed it. "Not so terrible, cyanide and apricot brandy. A much kinder fate than many soldiers, yes? Now I must seek out someone who can replace your passport photo with mine." He chuckled. "How do you Americans describe it—a switcheroo, yes? Regrettably, I cannot return to my beloved Fatherland where my face is well known. But do not be sad for me, Lester Huxley, for I remain a fortunate war criminal! At last I shall reunite with my son and his mother in Italy."

Upon hearing of Steiger's destination, Lester exhaled his final breath and, barely visible upon his lips, as if exhumed from a vault, a long-buried smile emerged.

# AD 1954
## A Rehanging at Nine
### Karl El-Koura

Sheriff Jeremy Martins didn't get home until well after ten o'clock that night. He'd stayed late talking with the Governor, both of them sitting on the scaffold, their feet dangling below like Ernie Johnson's feet should've dangled. Martins was explaining — well, trying to explain — what had happened with the execution, and negotiating — or trying to negotiate — to not have to rehang Ernie at nine the next morning.

As he pulled into the long unpaved driveway of their newly built farm house on two acres of land about thirty miles outside the town of Elam, one more time Sheriff Martins played out the scenario in his mind of how he was going to explain everything to his very pregnant wife. He'd promised her a trip into town the next morning, which he now had to cancel unless her ideal outing involved getting up early to execute a twenty-three-year-old rapist and murderer and then bury his sad, lanky body in the prison cemetery.

The storm door creaked as he pulled it open, and he remembered again that he needed to oil the hinges. He unlocked their wooden front door and stepped into their home. "Honey?"

"In here." He could hear the TV playing Jackie Gleason in the living room, the live audience responding heartily to one of Jackie's jokes.

His wife, wearing a nightie, once white but now almost see-through with sweat, craned her neck so he could kiss her lips across the back of the couch. He reached down to pat her nicely swollen belly, their eight-month-old baby growing away in there like a champ.

"Dinner's in the fridge," Leslie said, turning back to Jackie's rotund image on the black-and-white screen. "Want me to get it?"

"I got it," he said, moving into the kitchen. He grabbed the plate with two chicken breasts, barbecued to perfection, and steamed broccoli florets and carrots.

"There's gravy on the stovetop," Leslie called out.

"Got it," he said. It had solidified, but he gave it a quick stir and poured a generous helping over everything.

He brought the plate back to the living room and sat next to his wife.

"Heat it up for you?" she said, turning her pretty little blues to look at the cold meat and veggies smothered in cold, chunky gravy.

He shook his head and used the fork to shovel carrots into his eager mouth. He felt the ravenous hunger start to abate.

"I'm sorry you ate dinner alone," he said when he came up for air.

She shrugged her slender, almost naked shoulders. "I figured — tough day for you." One of her hands was resting on her belly. "May he rest in peace."

"Ernie Johnson?" He always hated that expression she said about the criminals he had to execute — who wanted any of these guys to rest in peace? — but today he felt he had her. "He ain't dead." But immediately he felt a twinge of guilt at the pleasure of correcting her assumption.

Leslie turned her head to look at him again. "Pardon?"

Martins swallowed the piece of chicken he'd been chewing. "He ain't dead."

"I was asking if he got a pardon."

Martins shook his head. "Execution got postponed." He swallowed half-chewed veggies during pauses. "To tomorrow morning. I was dealing with all that."

"Tomorrow morning?" she said. He couldn't resist that puppy dog voice, those puppy dog eyes, and hated the Governor (or his wife, really) for making him stay late that night, for making him come in on his day off, for making any of it necessary when it could've all been over and done with.

"Maybe we can have our day on Sunday?"

"Church on Sunday." He was always trying to get out of the long service and sermon by Pastor Bob, and the even longer pot-luck lunch right after. Why couldn't the Governor have postponed the hanging to Sunday morning?

"We can still go out for dinner on Saturday," he said, picking up the cold chicken with his hands and biting off a chunk.

"Why'd it get postponed?"

"The hanging? The Governor's wife became hysterical. Listen, honey, you know I think a woman can do anything a man can do, and can do most things better. But I don't think an execution is any place for a woman, if you ask my honest opinion."

"Why'd she become hysterical? What happened?"

"They didn't reweigh him, that's what happened. And I didn't double-check because I trusted Clint to do it."

"Ernie Johnson?"

"Yeah, they used the measurement from when he was first arrested."

"So?"

"So he lost a bunch of weight while in custody. You're supposed to reweigh him and adjust the height of the drop. Clint didn't do that, and don't ask me why. But, listen, do I have to double-check every single time? Can't I ever just trust that people are doing as they're supposed to?"

Leslie got up and turned off the TV, cutting Jackie off in the middle of a ripper. "What happens if the height isn't adjusted properly?"

"If the guy put on a bunch of weight — some do, you know, some have never eaten so good — then their heads can come right off their bodies."

Leslie made a face and pulled back from him a little.

"Don't ask if you don't want to know," he said, biting off another chunk of chicken.

"And if they lose weight?"

"The fall isn't enough to kill them right away. Takes time for them to strangle to death."

"But — ?"

"The Governor's wife started to have a nervous breakdown, so the Governor gave the order to stop the execution. 'Pull 'im up!' he yelled. 'Get 'im off that thing!' And he has this booming voice that cut right through his wife's high-pitched shrieking, and made stupid Deputy Clint jump to follow the order without even a sideways glance at me."

"You would've told him not to?"

"I would've made him take his time. Instead, like a shot he was by Ernie Johnson, wrapping his big bear arms around the twisting, jerking body, pulling him out of the drop, raising him up until I got there and onto the step stool and removed the noose from around that scrawny little neck."

"What happened after that?"

"I told Clint to get him out of there. We could hear him weeping like a baby under his hood. Clint slung him over his shoulder. Then I told Steves to clear everyone out. Then it was pandemonium. Tim Lester was at my side, grabbing my arm, yelling at me over and over 'What you go and take 'im down for?' Lester's wife was weeping in the bleachers while her two boys and her daughter, the one that's left to her, surrounded her and comforted her. Then, if you can believe this, all of that happening, and Williams comes up and asks me what he should record in his book!"

"That poor man."

"Williams? Poor nothing, his stupid records could keep—"

"Ernie Johnson."

"What do you mean, Ernie Johnson?" Now Martins was mad and had to take a moment to make sure he didn't raise his voice. But really it had been too long a night for him to have to explain to this soft-hearted woman why Ernie Johnson was anything but a poor man.

"Ernie Johnson," she repeated. "Can you imagine having to go through something like this, not once, but twice?"

"I don't have to imagine," he said. "I'm not planning on raping or killing any children."

"Calm down," she said, placing her hand on his thigh.

"I am calm," he barked. "And if we'd let him die on his own, he wouldn't be facing anything. He'd be dead and buried by now and you and me could've had our day together tomorrow."

"How long would he have strangled for?"

Martins shrugged. The Governor had asked him the same thing. "Just another couple of minutes," he'd said then, and said the same thing now.

"What's a couple?" the Governor had said, as they sat on the scaffold and watched the sun go down.

"Another five minutes, sir. Maybe ten."

"Son, you wanted me to sit there and watch that man twist and turn like a fish plucked out of water for another ten minutes? You wanted Mrs. Brighton to experience that sight for another ten minutes?"

"No, sir. I just meant that he would've died on his own."

"After ten minutes."

"At the most, sir. Probably less."

His wife was staring at him.

"What's that?" he said.

"I'm going to bed," she said. "I'm tired."

"I'm sorry about tomorrow," he said again. "I'll make it up to you."

She craned herself up; he jumped to his feet to help but she pushed him away gently.

"Don't stay up too late," she said.

"I won't." He couldn't; Saturday was his day off, but he still had to wake up before six and be at work by seven-thirty at the latest. They had to reweigh Ernie Johnson to make absolutely sure and readjust the drop height, then get everything ready for the rehanging, because the Governor had promised Tim Lester that Ernie Johnson would be dead first thing.

Leslie turned to look at him at the foot of the stairs. "Can you imagine what that poor man is going through tonight?"

Martins pushed aside the feeling of annoyance that welled up inside of him. Ernie Johnson deserved whatever he was going through, but —

not to be selfish about it — what had Martins done to deserve having his Saturday plans ruined?

His wife smiled sadly at him, then started making her way up the stairs.

The next morning was difficult, but everything worked out. Ernie Johnson struggled when they tried to weigh him, and it was Martins who had to step up and slap him and explain what would happen if Ernie didn't stand still so they could weigh him ("Same as happened yesterday," he said. "You want to go through that again?") Martins himself supervised the setting of the drop to the correct height, and double-checked everything else on the scaffold. Then he'd told the whimpering Ernie Johnson before they led him out that if he made a sound, he'd feed his body to their dogs at home (Martins and his wife didn't have dogs) and Ernie Johnson nodded and started whimpering more quietly. But then, when Martins thought the coast was clear, Ernie Johnson soiled himself while waiting to be led up to the scaffold, and again it was Martins who noticed and ordered them to carry him away and change him into fresh clothes, which they were able to do before anyone saw what had happened.

The rehanging took place at a few minutes after nine, Ernie Johnson falling into the hole that appeared under his feet, snapping his neck instantly. The calculation was perfect.

Tim Lester and his family walked down the bleachers and left; the Governor shook hands with some people and then he and his wife left too. Martins could finally breathe once they were gone.

When everyone had left, Martins and his deputies brought down the body and took apart the scaffold until the next execution. Everything was done, and Ernie Johnson buried, by noon.

No one had thanked Martins for coming in on his day off, for taking care of everything, for getting the job done. And although he hadn't received anything from anyone, he still had to pass it on.

"Good job, boys," he said. "It was a fine execution." He even allowed his glance to pass over Clint, who'd started this whole mess. He thanked

Steves and Plate, who'd come in on their day off too, and told them to go home.

By two in the afternoon, he was on his way home as well, wondering if there was a way to rescue this weekend. And he promised himself, if he had any say in the matter, no more executions on Fridays ever again.

# AD 1957

## A Good Judge of Character

### Penny Hurrell

I think I finally grew up that day. You'd have thought I couldn't have learnt anything new, but life is full of surprises.

I'd boarded the bus at 7.45am from an area of London north of the city. It would wend its way down the A10 and I'd alight at Old Street, close to where I worked.

This was the late fifties in November, so everything was grey. The streets were always grey, rain or not, especially the city, imperious with old stone and iron. Victorian red brick buildings with their pomp, or the red buses, could not compete with the rain.

Even people were grey back then. Raincoats were always grey or dark khaki. Only the well-off would wear beige because they could afford to get their coats cleaned after brushing against the grime of the city or the grubby upstairs level of the bus, the smokers' area, which even when empty had a non-lifting fug about it. I did wear a beige trench coat, or rather, lighter than khaki at least, but only because it was left-over from working at the bank all those years ago, and it was therefore not bad quality.

Outside the bus a post-war landscape passed by.

I sat on the bench seat downstairs, by the entrance platform. These seats were raised higher than those at the front and I liked to see people as they boarded or left. I entertained a notion that I was a good judge of character and would assign personalities and lives to the people that passed by. I also liked a good detective novel and would imagine what crimes these people could have committed. Maybe that's why I favoured my old trench coat, slipping into a Phillip Marlowe state of mind whenever I put it on.

Once seated, the cold damp of the rain started to creep through my trousers onto my skin. As I warmed up, the texture of the seat nap prickled my skin through the fabric. I remember it well, I was uncomfortable and started to fidget. I straightened my tie — needlessly — perched my almost empty briefcase on my lap, and tried to settle. The briefcase was my father's. A slim buckled type, similar to a school satchel. It contained my sandwiches, pencils, a notebook, the newspaper.

A wet diesel mist wafted in through the open doorway.

I thought ahead to the day at my desk, stamping incoming post with a big rubber date stamp, distributing it, collecting up post to take to the post office. A world away from the responsibility of my bank job but needs must. It had started to fall apart when the house was bombed. We were lucky that our house escaped the Blitz, but not so much in '44. The V bombs. Irene lost the baby and went a little loopy. We stayed for a while in whatever was empty, made available or had a couple of walls still standing, like many others in the same situation. Neither of us had family nearby to go to, and I had my job to think of. Lost that however trying to look after Irene.

Nobody wanted to break the law, most people didn't have it in their nature. But they were very difficult times, food was scarce, money scarcer. The bank understood why I took it but had to let me go. I understood too. I was conned anyway, there was no empty house available for a 'consideration'.

The clippie stalked up and down the bus. "Fares please! Any more fares!" A late arrival jumped on the moving platform shaking his umbrella out. A young man, very smart, the world at his feet. He took off upstairs, followed by the clippie.

Opposite me sat a wiry man I hadn't seen before wearing a trilby and reading the sports pages. He was about my age, early fifties, and I wondered what he had done in the war. He looked like he could have been useful and had probably risen to the rank of Sergeant. He had a keen energy about him and I think after the war he would have dabbled in trade of some description, maybe utilising his war chum contacts. He certainly looked tidy, smartly dressed in newish clothes. I imagine he didn't suffer during rationing.

Further down the bus sat the woman with the expensive looking skirt and jacket under the coat with the astrakhan fur collar, in her usual place. She was probably in her forties. She was very smart but plain. I don't think I would have liked her for a boss as she seemed very efficient and cold. I thought she might have been a secretary to someone very important, keeping all his secrets, his dallying and financial complexities. Yes, she would have learnt a lot during the war, making herself indispensable in the War Office. Just as reliable now, if compromised.

Childish I know, but at the time it put my own nagging troubles and doubts to the back of my mind. We had a nice flat however, of the new style of the time. I expect because of Irene's 'problems' we were fairly high up on the housing list. Irene had never been the same after the war.

The narrow streets were choked with traffic but we moved steadily. The windows had started to steam up but I could see out through the open doorway. People walked purposefully about, or maybe just mechanically, one foot in front of the other. They passed the yawning gaps in housing or shop parades without a glance, rubble gone but memories of those that lived or worked there still in the air, the gaps a constant reminder, as if we needed it. On the larger patches children would run about playing. Shouldn't have really, everyone knew there were unexploded bombs burrowed deep into the ground.

After a few stops she boarded the bus. I wouldn't have noticed her except for the perfume and the make-up immaculately applied, if a little heavy. It didn't chime with the drab coat that was clearly more than ten years old, like mine. She wore a headscarf — common back then — and I could tell that underneath it her hair could have been bright and shiny, but it seemed she had been unable to make it so.

Perhaps she wore something smart and unexpected under the coat? I couldn't tell, it was buttoned up to the neck. Her shoes were ordinary and certainly not of the time. She was probably in her early thirties but not an obvious follower of fashion, unless the coat concealed good clothes. Was she off to a 'do' and wore the old hand-me-down coat to protect her clothes? Unlikely in those days, being off to a 'do' at 8 o'clock in the morning.

As she slipped past me to the seats at the front I noticed her eyes were ablaze. At least one of them was. In the other she had what we used to call a 'lazy lid' it seemed. She looked incongruously happy. I watched her take her seat, a vacant spot by the aisle. Maybe she'll talk to the elderly woman beside her. I could possibly catch a word here or there.

But she sat upright and still, her head didn't move and she seemed to concentrate on what was in front of her, which was the back of someone else's head, so she clearly wanted to keep herself to herself. I watched for a couple of minutes but nothing changed. She sat just as still, just as upright with her small, plain handbag on her lap, her hands folded across it.

Maybe she has a new boyfriend she is going to meet? Or her husband? I searched for her ring finger but couldn't see from this angle. I suppose any of these scenarios were too unusual as it was so early in the day. Her face and aroma were meant for the evening. So, I imagined that she was a spy. She had been working all night attracting the attentions of a known enemy collaborator on the run, in order to lure him to a trap. It wouldn't have surprised me in the slightest that the Government still had tidying up to do. The mission had been a success, but she had been abandoned by colleagues in the ensuing chase to find her own way home. And no, the success of the mission did not rely on her crossing any boundaries of morality.

Unusually, I hadn't imagined that she could be involved in anything shady or criminal. She didn't seem the type. If anything, she looked a little naïve, childlike even, with the make-up and scent that women didn't usually wear at this time of day. Maybe I made up a heroic scenario for her because it's what a child would like. It was quite nice, believing her to be an innocent. I was definitely disenchanted with most people by then and it wasn't often I would see anything good in anyone.

People came and went through the bus and I sat waiting for my stop, and she hers. When my stop arrived I stayed in my seat, as she had too. I had to buy another ticket off the conductor although I wasn't sure how much to pay; I didn't know where she would get off.

I expect about now you'll be wondering what I was up to. So was I, believe me. At my age I was too old to expect this young lady to be interested in any advances I might entertain. Anyway, I had Irene.

I'm not the type you might now call a pervert, not now, not then. I can't explain what was going through my mind just then, except that it might have been curiosity. I travelled on that same bus route to and from work for the best part of a decade and little changed. Everyone looked the same. Fashions changed of course and younger people would pass through the bus with shorter skirts (the women) or longer hair (the men) and the old would tut and scoff quietly, maybe looking for a little too long to exhibit their displeasure.

And we had our occasional disturbances, not everyone was as well behaved as you might think. Someone down on their luck might have had an early drink or two and grumble to their embarrassed neighbour about the injustice of it all. Or — especially as the sixties wore on — groups of the young and trendy would board in the morning after being out all night, still in high spirits, making sure the whole bus knew they'd had a good time. We rarely got the gangs, not on the commuter shunts. I imagine they frequented the late-night buses.

In my defence I can only say I was a little concerned about the lady. If I'm honest she didn't look quite … all there.

I'd seen it before, in Irene, the dazed expression of otherworldliness, disbelief; shock. I'd seen it in men too, returning home, medically discharged. We'd had a chap at the bank for a short while, very menial duties, but he would fly into rages unexpectedly. I don't mind admitting that it broke my heart to see it. From my position of safety — not willingly I might add, I was deemed medically unfit to join up — I used to shudder at where it would all end. I dared not imagine the realities, the mud and the blood, and the fear.

I looked out of the window as the unfamiliar passed by. I knew the route, knew this part of London well enough, but it was more than the different neighbourhoods outside that made me look with some anxiety. I was on edge. I'd never done anything like this before. What would my boss say? I'd have to telephone in as soon as I could, say I'd had a funny turn on the bus or something, which wasn't far wrong anyway.

Eventually, as the bus turned to head east close to the river, she stood from her seat, rang the bell cord and walked towards the back of the bus. As she grabbed for the upright handle I could see the wedding band. Her face hadn't changed. I stood also and, at a polite distance, hopped off the platform behind her. She didn't walk fast, but she had a definite purpose and destination in mind. I followed as best I could. Something told me I should.

My mood kept fluctuating between concern and embarrassment. She's probably on her way to work! What was I thinking? But it really didn't seem likely, especially through this area. The overall impression I had before, of her being in shock or a trance, hadn't left me. Although she looked happy, it was as if in a dream, a dreamlike state. And she walked with care as if her feet hurt, or the ground was uneven and she might fall. Was it drugs? What did I know about drugs? Absolutely nothing. I was being absurd, what would Irene say?

I continued through the blackened backstreets of Wapping, close to the river, concerned about my footsteps in the silent decay, but she didn't look back. This was not a place to be on your own and every doorway presented danger to me, although there was no one else to be seen. There was a community here somewhere, but the filth and disrepair of bombed and abandoned businesses and housing darkened the soul. I could smell mould and brick and held my sleeve over my nose in case I sneezed. Occasionally, jagged glass framed a window opening into the detritus of what had once been a home. Rebuilding was still ongoing, some areas being left behind a little, and gentrification was not in our vocabulary. She didn't seem to notice, and eventually the river loomed ahead.

She walked right up to the edge and stood against an iron rail looking down at the river. It was grey and sludgy below her, moving languidly at its own speed, with its own power, its own memories of centuries of death and punishment. I was standing slightly behind her and quite a few yards away, sheltering in a boarded-up doorway. Curiosity was now a distant frivolity. I was struck immobile at the very real possibility of her tumbling into the river.

I stirred myself, this was no time to be discrete or polite or mindful of someone else's privacy. But I didn't want to force her to act, so I approached slowly, still slightly behind so that she might not see me. Maybe I stood a chance of grabbing her?

She hadn't heard me. She looked down to her bag and lifted it up to undo it. From it I could see her take something. I was close enough to see she'd taken a knife from the bag. I was also close enough to see that the knife blade was coated in dried blood.

I couldn't move. I couldn't think or make sense of it. Had she stabbed someone? Had someone stabbed her? Would she stab me?

She extended her arm over the rail until her hand was above the river, and then she opened her hand and dropped the knife. It was a short while before it plonked into the miserable waters, but I did hear it. She stood for a while longer, her arm extended out as if unwilling to end the act too suddenly.

From where I stood I could see that the sleeve of her coat had ridden up. She still hadn't seen me. I think she was somewhere else at the time. Part of her arm was visible, just a small part, but enough to show that fierce and obscene bruising extended beyond the edge of the sleeve. Was it under the make-up too? She lowered her arm and lifted the other. Her hand opened slowly and what looked like a military cap badge fell from it.

I looked at her fully, saw her completely. It filled me with guilt and shame. I had no right being here, the uninvited witness to what her life must have been like, what life must have been like for both of them.

She was still but dropped the arm slowly. I couldn't move, I wasn't even concerned that she might see me. But she didn't. She turned away from me and started to walk along the river. She seemed to come awake, her gait quickened albeit with a limp, her headscarf came off and she shook her hair free of some burden, and then she stopped and sobbed into her hands.

# AD 1958

## *Only a Story*

### *Kai Lovelace*

*Striker hitch-hiked the last seventy miles to Galveston and had to listen to a born-again Christian in a blue hatch-back prattle on about Jesus Christ until he'd had enough and told him to go to hell.*

*"Out of the car, Mister," the driver's voice quavered as he pulled over. "Nobody talks to me like that."*

*Striker thought about the .38 wedged into his waistband and the 30,000 in the duffel bag between his legs, calculating the risk of making any moves a hundred yards from the quaint rest stop and gas station shimmering down the road like a toy set.*

*He pulled out the .38 and set it on the dashboard. The driver started to shake.*

*"Please, sir. I've got a family."*

*Striker smiled. "Yeah," he said. "So do I. We're all one big happy family."*

*He picked up the revolver and aimed it idly towards the driver's seat. The man whimpered. No winks of sunlight signaled approaching cars in the rearview mirror.*

*"You ought to be happy," Striker said. "This way you'll get to heaven a whole hell of a lot faster."*

Henry lowered the paperback when sweeping headlights disturbed the stillness of the lobby. A troupe of shadows rippled across the stucco siding, gray columns drifting between bands of golden light growing larger until they dissipated. An engine groaned like a giant turning over in its sleep. He waited; if it died down the vehicle was heading south on Alston Road and would bypass the motel.

The bands of light merged and brightened. The motor got louder and slowed, underscored by the smooth crunch of tires on gravel.

Henry inserted his tattered bookmark and set the book down. A brilliant flash of orange-yellow bathed the lobby before the vehicle angled away and slowed to a stop. He waited for the engine to cut but it kept on growling, headlights cutting into the scraggly woods past the parking lot. Through the glass doors the back half of a long, boxy, squared-off sedan idled, rocketship wings flaring off the rear corners. Nobody made a move to get out and Henry inclined his head for a better look. The left tail light was cracked and the fender badly dented.

It was going on 1:30 AM. Before the dark blue Lincoln Continental showed up it was another boring night, seconds oozing by like drops from a leaky faucet.

Henry liked the graveyard shift because it gave him time to get ahead on homework and read his crime stories, but sometimes the boredom was murder.

It wasn't that people never showed up in the middle of the night. They were just too exhausted for chitchat, complaints, or questions. Cash for the room key and a scribble in the log book. Traveling salesmen dead on their feet, road tripping couples hauling comatose children who'd gotten lost or bit off more than they could chew on a day's run.

Occasionally someone with a different look in their eye would arrive who Henry would have to think about. No luggage or companions. Quiet, self-contained, furtive. Secret agents laying low, hitmen tracking unwitting targets; even G-men and assassins needed sack time.

A couple years ago in junior high comics like *Crime Doesn't Pay* and *The Long Arm of the Law* were his favorites. He'd pick them up at the drug store on Wilmot Street downtown by the train station. Then he discovered *Tales of Suspense* and *Corruption of the Innocent*— racier, edgier, more convincing.

When he was younger he idolized the heroic lantern-jawed policemen stolidly pursuing their prey. Compared to the upstanding officers, the degenerates who shot a prison guard while escaping a chain gang or kidnapped the mayor's wife and dragged her on a cross country spree appeared subhuman. Ugly, pinched faces, squat or spindly physiques, each disfigurement a stamp of their fate.

Around his twelfth birthday a creeping suspicion became undeniable, starting as a passing notion quickly dismissed but growing stronger every day like a moldy odor.

Fearless, noble cops versus sleazy scum-of-the-Earth became as stale and thin as the educational Saturday morning cartoons he'd outgrown around the time he spat out his last baby tooth. It wasn't just the repetition or the pat endings where the convicts, feral with self-destructive greed, met justice. It was the *lessons*, like Mrs. Florsheim's sermons against the evils of drugs, alcohol, premarital sex, and race music.

Henry paid attention and remembered things. Officers lurking by the squad car on his way to school, chewing tobacco and hawking viscous brown strands. A wolf-whistle at the library assistant, the strained smile stabbing a pang of heat into Henry's chest, reminding him of school yard bullies patrolling for lunch-money shakedowns. Bright scarlet flecks under the summer sun tarmac when they'd stomped a vagrant outside the bowling alley, ducking his mother's fingers trying to shield his eyes. They never showed that in *Tales of Daring Crime Fighters*.

He also knew Officer Tim, hero to every child and housewife in the neighborhood. He found that missing girl in the brambles by the golf course over in Stratford that one time, dirt-streaked and frightened but alive, heard the story a hundred times. Why did his mother call him "roguish"? Henry thought the Roman nose and receding hairline made him look gawky, but he accepted the fact that he was a good guy, upstanding. But heroic? Not exactly.

Then last year he'd borrowed a battered paperback of *The Postman Always Rings Twice* from the library and dumped his heap of hero cop comics into the waste bin. *The Secret Agent* and *Red Harvest* lead him to Walter Delaney's *Striker* series, wherein the taciturn anti-hero escapes prison and embarks on a cross-country odyssey centered around revenge and financial gain.

He had new heroes now. Down-on-their-luck drifters, desperate gamblers, icy killers, weary private eyes, slicing through life like rusty blades because the straight and narrow was a fool's dream.

His mother worried.

He'd said the words many times: "It's only a story, mom."

Always that skeptical face as she angled her head away and exhaled smoke sideways from a puffed up cheek, plumes dissolving under the hanging kitchen bulb's anemic glow. "These things really happen, Henry."

How could he explain the difference between loving villains and being one? The biggest jerks in his school idolized TV lawmen and treated their classmates like Jack Palance in *Shane*. Henry got straight B's and had never been in a fight, even when the bigger guys harassed him with questions when he had nothing for the Father's Day presentations. The next year he just skipped it. Going the extra mile for A's would have cut into his reading time.

The latest *Striker* book had come out two days before, and the title —*Three Strikes and Out* — made Henry nervous. Surely this couldn't be the end of the road for that raw-boned bastard; he needed peace and quiet so he could find out.

That's why he liked working the graveyard shift at his uncle's motel.

The phone wouldn't answer itself, nor would the ashtrays tap themselves out. Someone had to be in charge of these responsibilities.

The Cozy Road Motor Inn was a long single-story complex with the office at the far end, tucked in a weedy lot far enough off Interstate 684 to be easily missed between the clustered maples and oaks lining the exit to a lonely stretch along the border between New York and Connecticut. The drab beige stucco was lined with a slash of mint green along the base. The roof extended over the pathway to the rooms, dark green paint chipped on the doors, brass numbers reflecting gold winks from the arc sodium lights at the gravel intersection off the highway. Of the eight units about half were typically occupied on a good night.

Between midnight and 6AM the lobby was quieter than the downtown library or the Chester Arthur High cafeteria. Tidy the seating area, sweep and dust. It was seven extra hours for reading and homework.

Sometimes he'd have to switch peoples' rooms if these new Magic Fingers beds stopped working, haul luggage, or dust off the road atlas under the front desk and help with directions. Anything more complex got passed off to the errant handyman Chuck, limping around half-drunk ever since he got back from Korea, or better yet, jotted on the clipboard and shunted to the next day.

His uncle gave him the night shift twice a week. It was an easy job. If he could barely keep his eyes open the next day in school he'd catch up later. Most nights he passed absorbing a lurid paperback, sometimes cover to cover without interruption. His uncle dismissed them with a sneering wave as trash and Henry didn't mention the Tijuana bibles in the back office filing cabinet, wanting to keep the shift.

Usually nothing much happened, which suited Henry fine. But some nights the boredom got to him no matter how good the book was. A barrage of floor lamps lit the maroon carpets, mismatched armchairs, and wooden rack of outdated travel pamphlets. A canopy of maples swayed outside the bay window overlooking the quarry beyond the parking lot.

Was this really it? There had to be more to life than waiting out the clock in the dingy lobby of Uncle Ansel's pride and joy.

A middle aged couple had checked into room 6 and had not emerged since. Another younger guy had lounged by the coffee table, leafing through an issue of *Life* for about an hour before someone came to pick him up.

Since then the phone hadn't even rung. It was too late in the season for crickets and the stark silence thrummed a phantom tone. Henry turned the portable radio next to him on low to a local station that was normally off the air from midnight to 6AM but had recently started piggybacking off an overnight DJ in New Haven– a godsend. The dials and speaker on the compact turquoise box formed a surprised face and a driving brassy voice crackled from the wide mouth: Billy was begging Stagger Lee not to take his life.

He tugged at a loose thread on the sleeve of his frayed brown corduroy shirt, worn at the elbows and thick with a musk of mothballs and his mother's cigarette smoke, humming tunelessly along to the music. When his uncle was around it was usually a baseball game, maybe some Mantovani or Andy Williams. No chance staying awake all night to that crap.

*Striker ditched the Bible thumper's sedan in the bus station parking lot.*

Henry was forcing himself to pay attention to the words when the visitor arrived. Just sitting out there on the muddy patch of gravel damp from last night's rain, engine humming, going on five minutes now.

The boy was sliding off his stool — maybe the driver was elderly and needed assistance, he realized belatedly — when the engine cut and the entrance dimmed, lit only by the highway light at the turn-off and the buzzing sign's crimson aura. A door clicked open and a tall, slim shadow shuffled across the tarmac to the trunk of the car. The lid slammed and the figure approached the doors, dusty denim gaining definition as he neared, toting something on his shoulder which threw off his stride.

The doors swung open. A pair of wild eyes darted from a gaunt, haggard, coldly handsome face. His lips were parted and his teeth clenched. He stood surveying the lobby as if expecting a wild animal to jump out any moment. Then a miraculous change came over the visitor, serenity descending from the top of his dirty blonde head down to his soles as his whole body relaxed and his face settled into a pacified smirk, lids lowered over the large hazel eyes.

His scuffed denim jacket was a few shades lighter than his jeans and the top few buttons of a faded Hawaiian shirt were undone, wisps of curly hair matted on his tanned chest. He locked eyes with Henry and crossed the room without breaking contact, not quite limping but favoring his right leg as he approached the front desk and slid the duffel off his shoulder.

"Welcome to the Cozy Road Motor Inn," Henry muttered. They were the first words Henry had spoken in several hours and his voice cracked.

The guy leaned his elbows on the edge of the desk and exhaled deeply like he'd been walking for days.

"Hey, bud." The man's voice was a clear note from a bass guitar. Sweat beaded on his creased forehead as he inspected the boy. "You're a little old to be doing this kinda work, aren't you?"

Henry blinked at him. "I'm fourteen," he said. The guy looked him over for a moment, a skinny kid cutting an absurd figure all alone in the dead of night but carrying defiance in the set of his shoulders. The broad forehead was speckled lightly with acne but his lips were set in a surly twist, curled like a sideways bracket with a slight overbite revealing slivers of two front teeth. The ungainly adolescence ended at the eyes, reserved and cool with the stoicism and suspicion of a young man.

"Oh yeah?" said the visitor. "You look like you're barely out of diapers."

"I'm fourteen," Henry repeated.

"So you're fourteen," the man answered. "I'm forty. Good for us. Who else you got working tonight?"

"It's just me."

"Bullshit," he said, a hint of his former tension coiling tight. "You can't run this place on your own."

Henry opened his mouth to protest, then caught himself and pulled it back, lacing his fingers. "I'm in charge until six AM," he said calmly.

The sandy head bobbed backwards and the thin lips quirked down, impressed under a layer of offhanded irony. "Head honcho, huh?"

"That's right. You want a room?"

The man winced, rolling his left shoulder and throwing shifty glances around the lobby. "Busy night? I saw a couple more cars out there."

"Not too busy."

"Lotta action since you came on?"

Henry hesitated. "What do you mean?"

"Forget it. Listen, bud. You got a first aid kit?"

"Uh, yeah. In the back."

"Grab it."

"Was there an accident?"

The visitor shook his head. "I had a little scrape a while ago and need to rest."

Henry leaned forward. Something dark stained the bottom of the man's pant leg and his colorless face was slick with sweat.

"You're hurt?" Henry asked. "There's a hospital a few miles over in Kitchawan."

Flash of nicotine-stained teeth. "I don't need a hospital, kid. I asked you for a first aid kit."

"You sure you're okay, mister? I can call you an ambulance—"

A white-knuckled fist slammed against the countertop and rattled the pens in the mug by Henry's elbow.

"Don't need a fucking ambulance either. Get the goddamn kit."

Henry eased off the stool and pushed through the swinging doors into the back office, glancing back to see the man's hand resting in the pocket of his denim jacket.

The room was cluttered with filing cabinets, folding chairs stacked against a mini-fridge, and a standing coat rack draped with unclaimed lost-and-found items. Henry rummaged through a cupboard until he found the dusty green tin box and brought it back to the front desk. The visitor laid his hand on it reverently.

"Thanks," he said. "Sorry about that. I've had a hell of a day."

Henry nodded. "So have I."

That got a raspy chuckle. "I bet you have. You even allowed to do this?"

"I can do anything my uncle can. I calculate the books at the end of the night."

The man tapped the lid of the first aid kit with a fingernail. "Well, look out," he said, "kid's going places," squinted eyes roving across Henry's workspace and lingering on the paperback, chewing on his lower lip as if solving a math problem in his head.

After a minute Henry slid the log book over, cleared his throat and asked, "Do you need a room?"

The visitor's gaze snapped up. "Yeah. Hey, that one of those Striker books?"

Reaching under the desk alcove for the cash register key, Henry stopped. "You know them?"

"Read every single one. Delaney's a genius."

A grin lit up the boy's face. "He's the best. Striker's my favorite character of all time."

"Which one you like best?"

Henry gestured indecisively. "Oh man, that's tough. *Striker's Score*, probably. No, actually it's *Lucky Strike*."

"With the riverboat casino."

"Yeah!"

"Ever read Black Mask or's that before your time?"

An enthusiastic nod. "I got a pile of them cheap from the pharmacy. My mom wants to throw them out but I told her I'd skip school if she did."

"Smart man."

"What about Hammett? And Chandler?"

"Sure. You know a good one? *The Stranger*. Camus wrote it after reading James M. Cain."

Henry's expression clouded and he grabbed a notepad to jot it down. "I'll get it from the library," he said. "But man, Striker is tougher than all of them. He could probably take Philip Marlowe in a fight."

"Tough call. But you want my advice, stay away from Delaney's stand-alones. The covers make 'em look like crime stories but they're domestic melodramas." The shaggy locks dipped and he snored loudly.

Henry laughed. "Sounds boring."

"You said it. Probably as boring as this job."

"Oh no," Henry said, more animated than he'd been all night. "Nothing could *ever* be as boring as this."

"I know how that goes. Waiting for something to happen. What's your name, pal?"

"Henry Haldane."

The man pursed his lips. "Good name. Would look good on a cover. You should write some of these yourself, you're such an expert."

The boy shook his head and his face felt hot, but he couldn't help smiling. He spun the log book around with a flourish so it was facing the man. "I'll get you number eight down on the end so you can have a queen-size bed, just sign here, Mister, uh—"

The man drew squiggles in the air over the line for a moment before the pen started scratching. "Name's Frank."

Henry looked down. *F. Jones* was scribbled messily in the log line. He dug underneath the desk and came up with a small silver key attached to a plastic oval with an 8 on it.

"Here you go, Mr. Jones."

"Frank, please."

"Okay. Thanks for staying at The Cozy Road, Frank."

"Trust me, you saved my ass." Frank pocketed the room key and stuck the first aid kit under his arm. He hefted the duffel and was turning to go when he cringed sharply and staggered, dropping the bag and sucking air through his teeth.

Henry leapt up from his stool and started around the partition but Frank raised his hand.

"I'm alright." He recovered and took another deep breath. "I'm thinking, Hank. Anyone ever call you Hank?"

After a moment Henry murmured, "Sometimes."

A smirk quivered on Frank's lips. "Henry it is then," he said. "Listen, seeing as how you're the boss tonight, I'm gonna level with you." He toed the duffel. "See this bag? It's gonna change my life."

Henry stretched over to take a look. "What's in it?"

"Don't worry about what's in it. All you gotta know is, it's mine. I got it…*won* it fair and square. I laid everything down on the line and it paid off bigtime. Understand?"

The boy's brow furrowed and he nodded tentatively.

"Good. You're smart. See, bud, not everyone understands something like that. You know about sore losers, right? On the playground, or the dugout?"

"I don't play a lot of sports."

Frank stared at him for a moment, gray eyes unblinking.

"Yeah," Henry sputtered. "I know about them. Bullies."

The smile returned and lit some life into the craggy face. "Exactly right. Well my point is you got them out there in the grownup world too. And it just so happens some real nasty folks weren't too happy with me the other night. Wanted to take what's rightfully mine. Get me?"

"I think so."

"So I've been laying low til the heat dies down." Frank shifted his weight, crossed his arms and leaned over on the desk. His voice dropped into a quiet, rumbling purr. "Don't worry, I got away from the pricks. I'm on the home stretch now. But I'm tired as hell. I gotta rest and patch up. Get some shut-eye."

Henry eyed the man up and down and the hairs on the back of his neck tingled. Flecks of brown dotted the right arm of Frank's denim jacket. Besides the stained and frayed cuff of his jeans, streaks of dust and grime mixed with foul sweat dampened the material of his tattered Hawaiian shirt.

"It's not polite to stare, Henry."

The boy started fiddling with the log book.

"What are you smiling at?" A sharp edge to his words, deliberately paced.

"Nothing, sir. Frank. I was just gonna say there's a couple extra parking spaces out back if you take the dirt path by the trees down at the other end."

"What's wrong with the spaces out there?" Frank jerked a thumb towards the front doors.

Henry shrugged. "You can't see the ones out back from the road."

Frank considered the boy behind the front desk and cocked his head. "Is that right? You know, I might feel more comfortable with a little…" He twirled his hand in the air searching for the word.

"Discretion?"

Frank's smirk widened. "Discretion." He chewed his lip, glanced down at the cover of the paperback, an illustration of a scowling, muscular, rough-hewn man tearing across the desert behind the wheel of a black Cadillac with dollar bills blowing in the wind. "I'll do that, Henry. Thank you." He crooked a finger and beckoned the kid closer. "One more thing, bud. Since you're real smart and all, I got a favor to ask."

Henry's face became serious.

"I don't want to make trouble," Frank said, "but on the off chance someone comes by asking for me, or about someone might fit my description? Well, I'd appreciate it you kept—" Frank mimed zipping his mouth shut.

The boy's jaw set and he nodded vigorously.

"Thanks kid. Like I said, I left those friends of mine way back in the dust. But they're wily. You can't trust anybody in this world, you know that? Not your teachers, your parents, or your friends. Not even the police. Especially not them."

*Striker knew the flat empty eyes of a cop; he'd seen the same grim look on lifers in the prison yard.*

Henry nodded again slower, enrapt.

"Not everybody who pulls a dime-store badge is who they say they are," Frank said. "You got no idea what people are capable of."

"I have some idea," Henry said.

Frank snorted and rapped his knuckles on the desk. "I bet you do.

You and me are alike. Not asleep like most of them dinks out there." For a moment the man's face clouded and went nauseously slack. Then it cleared and he gave a tired smile. "Do me a favor, you see anything looks suspicious, you let me know, understand?" A sinewy hand dug in the pocket of his jeans and he slid his palm across the desk.

Henry hid his excitement. "I won't let you down."

"You're my eyes and ears." Frank lifted his hand, revealing a brand new fifty dollar bill. "This is for you, bud. I'll settle up for the room in the morning, alright?"

"Sure thing."

"Thanks, kid." Frank sagged and squeezed his eyes shut, shoulders tensing. He rubbed his face and heaved a deep breath. "I gotta hit it."

"Want me to carry your bag?" Henry asked.

"I'll manage, but thanks," Frank said, rallying. "You're a good kid."

Only after Frank had pulled the sedan around and disappeared behind the main building was Henry aware of the syrupy country ballad seeping from the radio. He clicked the dial off and sat in silence. His heart raced and deep down a pit of fear gnawed his stomach, mingling with the exhilaration that he'd gotten away with something, but he couldn't say exactly what. Gravel crunched and floorboards creaked distantly as Frank ducked into Room Eight, a lanky shadow with a jerky stride passing through the night.

After a few minutes Henry opened the book again but quit after three sentences. The pit in his stomach was crawling up his throat. Something hazy in his mind was coming into focus. In a daze he dropped the folding card onto the counter — *We've Stepped Away From The Desk, Be Right Back!* — and flicked on the light in the back room.

Under the coat rack was a pile of newspapers wrapped in twine. Henry sawed through the string with his house key and unfolded the first paper, dated the day before. He leafed through the front pages, scanning headlines. Unrest in Birmingham after the Bethel Church bombing last summer, marches, riots, scary stuff that seemed to come from another planet. He skipped sports and the cartoons, moving with a graceful indolence as if underwater or taking care not to damage the flimsy paper. When he got through the first one he laid it down and took another, dated two days ago. The itch in his brain was almost unbearable even if he couldn't believe or accept what he was really checking for, keeping an ear out for any activity in the lobby. He didn't usually read newspapers but they helped pass the time and Uncle Ansel had a habit of letting them accumulate creased and coffee-stained in the back room until Henry started tying them up for the garbage. Nothing in the second paper either. Or the third. Doubt crept in— he was just tired and letting his imagination run away. One more paper, crinkled and checked cover to cover. Nothing. Give it up, he thought, you're being stupid. The itch was subsiding, replaced with flooding embarrassment. Dumb kid thinks he's in a movie, sitting in the back room under humming fluorescents next to a pile of old newspapers. Get back to the desk. Show's over.

On the second to last page of the seventh newspaper he found it.

A small item, four or five inches in a single column under a grainy black and white photo of several men in dark suits and hats standing outside a bland brick building. Another man in a police uniform crouched and pointed to something on the ground out of frame.

'*Police Track Robber of Hillsborough County Bank*' by Sheila Kenton.

Feverishly his eyes poured over the story and the words swam together.

'*...FBI, state, and local police are close on the trail of a man who escaped with $28,000 from the Parkville Branch of the Hillsborough County Bank...*'

'*...shouting, "I want the money now, up against the wall," according to Head Teller Martina Harris...*'

'*...wearing a black ski mask with slits over the eyes but described as a tall, lanky man with a slight limp...*'

'*...fired three shots, injuring veteran security guard Lloyd Calhoun* *before making his escape in a stolen 1953 Chevy Impala, later found abandoned several miles to the east...'*

Henry's hands were shaking as he carefully tore out the article and folded it into his pocket, crouched in the stuffy office. He retied the messy pile of newspapers, swallowed the lump in his throat and wiped sweaty palms on his jeans, then stood slowly and braced himself against the wall as his vision dimmed into a gray churning void of TV static. Only his shallow breathing kept him tethered to reality. After what seemed a long time it cleared. He shut the lights off and returned to the front desk.

⟨∞⟩

It was impossible. Or was it? Hillsborough County was in New Hampshire. Wouldn't he have made it farther south in over a week? Maybe it wasn't a straight shot, he'd had to make stops, rethink his route. Maybe—

No, there's no way. Nothing so exciting could ever happen out here, least of all to him. He smoothed the fifty dollar bill on the countertop. Crisp, clean, new, like you'd get from a bank. Henry's chest swelled and he giggled, smacked his hand on the desk and shook his head in wonderment. It was a hell of a story either way. He couldn't wait to tell his friends the next day in school. Couldn't wait to tell Mom.

His cheeks flushed with a torrent of guilt. She'd be furious. She'd ask him why he didn't call the police if he was so sure. Because he *wasn't* sure, that's what he'd tell her.

But he was.

The giddy weightless feeling hit him all over again. He spread the article on the desk and reread it. It was like the time he'd seen Lee Marvin in Midtown when his mom had taken him into Manhattan. But more than that, as if Lee had come up to him, singled him out and asked him to keep a secret, help him out, making them buddies.

A protesting voice deep down spat a fragment of the article back at him: fired three shots, injuring veteran security guard...

Did real pros fire their guns? Didn't they keep things under control?

Henry shook his head to clear the confused thoughts. Alan Ladd shot the cop in *This Gun For Hire*. He was the bad guy and Henry loved him. But that was just a movie, this was real life. Veteran meant old. Would the guard live? He couldn't start calling around in the middle of the night to check.

He shivered with another surge of excitement, wishing there was someone who'd understand that he could call and tell right now. Then the roller coaster stomach-drop again: was he protecting a real criminal? A killer? Was the stolen fifty a piece of evidence? He was breathing quickly, fidgeting, staring at the bill, chewing and licking his lip, when a wave of exhaustion pressed down on him. His eyelids were heavy. He looked at the clock on the wall by the rack of travel guides.

2:15 AM. Almost four hours to go.

Adrenaline was retreating from his muscles and he felt limp as a ragdoll. He blinked and his eyes stayed shut, his head lolled, then snapped back up. Stretching his arms up until his shoulders cracked, he yawned massively. Make some coffee, he thought, it's the only way you'll get through it. All these late nights catching up.

He'd make coffee right after he rested his eyes. Just two minutes. Two minutes until he had to get up for school because he was still in a dream, *wow* what a dream — that he'd been on the night shift at the motel and a real life bank robber came in, spoke to him. The lobby of the hotel swam, contracted, oozed like a lava lamp; cycling in a psychedelic police siren of orange, red, green and purple.

*The stool behind the desk was a leather driver's seat, reclining as the desert landscape sped by him. The Bible-thumper was dead, and that was good.*

Wasn't it? Or was he really dead, a real person murdered? Had *he* done it? Terror squeezed him in a vice grip: his mother would never speak to him again. He'd go to prison. What had he done? Think, think, as the little gas station grows on the arid horizon. He could remember if he just concentrated, and yes, here it came. Black and white and grainy, running with words like a newspaper headline, like the old James Cagney movies but no, it was more recent than that, color film like *Rear Window*, here it played out again in front of the judge and the jury, exactly what he'd done.

*In an instant, the peace of a Tuesday morning is shattered like a plummeting chandelier. Shouts echo off the marble pillars and glass partition where Martina at counter 3 sees it happening in slow motion before it happens, always the way she thought it would, when the man is just a blooming, quivering silhouette refracted through pebbled glass. Moving too fast, jerky but purposeful. No, it can't be. She's seen too many bad TV shows. It can't be, but it is. They have to base those shows off something. She's nowhere near the alarm button in the vault room when he bursts in and starts yelling.*

*The man is tall and lanky and moves with a wild grace as he fires a shot into the air, the short hot pop of a firecracker paralyzing the room. Screams, everybody down now, nobody move or you're dead. Pacing and sweeping a short-barrelled pistol across the meager, huddled crowd, bright angry eyes burning holes in the black cotton mask as his head darts, cataloging his surroundings like a speed-reader while the barrel holds steady.*

*"Where's the old man?"*

*Martina is nowhere near the alarm in the vault room. Her feet are bolted to the carpeting and her knees are shaking, adrenaline thrumming through her slight frame. The two other tellers on duty are frozen stock still, shooting-gallery ducks lined in a row behind their windows. Where the hell is Lloyd? Usually propped half-asleep by the restrooms from opening to close, rooted to the same spot for twenty-four years it seems but now when they need him vanished into thin air, daydreaming about retirement, close enough for him now to taste. Or maybe not.*

*"Where is he?" Striker screams as the beige-uniformed wisp of a man, sixty-two come August, elbows his way out of the men's room, adjusting his thick frames and gawping at the intruder while his liver-*

*spotted hand slaps at his side holster. "I want the money now, up against the wall!"*

*No, Martina thinks. This isn't what we're trained to do. Stay in the bathroom, you old fool. Don't go for it.*

*Lloyd goes for it. The short barrel swings smoothly and discharges. After that it's easier.*

*Mountains, phone lines, brown smudges of clouds wisp across the moon through the cell's tiny window. Silence and cold like the loneliness of a rotting pine box clogged with earth. Rusty hinges squeal as the lawman marches in, a shadowy face and billowing jacket as he raises the double-barrelled shotgun and fires. The explosion of light and sound is a shrill clang that freezes Henry's blood, worse than any gunshot or tearing of flesh and fabric.*

*Another high searing note like a bell, tolling for him and it won't stop, it rings again and—*

Henry mumbled incoherently as he jerked up from the desk. His forearms tingled with pins and needles, damp from the tiny puddle of drool.

"Oh I'm sorry, did I wake you?"

The man at the counter silenced the reverberating service bell with a fingertip. He stood very still, broad-shouldered and stocky with two deep lines running across his small forehead, beady eyes and a wide thin-lipped scowl incongruous on the squared-off face. His curly hair was coiffed up with pomade and he carried the stench of cigar smoke, rough sun-baked copper skin like sausage casing. The slate gray suit jacket was tight-fitting and bulged at the hip, top button undone on the wrinkled white shirt and the thin brown tie with beige stripes tugged loose.

Henry blinked around blearily and checked the clock: 4:42 AM. His mouth hung open. Asleep for over two hours.

The man with the slick hair frowned. "No child labor laws out here in the sticks, huh? No wonder you were asleep on the job. What's your name, son?"

Henry wiped his mouth and composed himself, looking the new arrival up and down and folding his arms. "Can I help you?"

The man stared at him for a moment. "Uh huh, nice to meet you too. My name's Daryl Geddes, I'm a Deputy U.S. Marshal." He waited a beat but got no reaction. "You know what that is?" His delivery was a quiet, evenly staccato monotone.

A shrug and a nod from the blank faced kid behind the desk, playing it cool.

Geddes' thick eyebrows twitched. "Okay then." He glanced around the lobby and yawned, fillings in his back molars nestled like burnt kernels of popcorn, then smacked his hand on the desk and shook his head. "This job," he sighed, "the hours are a bitch. You probably know what that's like."

The silence between them grew until Henry cleared his throat and said softly, "Where's your badge?"

Geddes exhaled impatiently, lifting the front of his blazer to reveal tarnished gray metal, a squat shield with an eagle perched on top clipped to his belt. "Satisfied? I'll get to the point," he said dryly, "because I can see you're a busy man. Manager around?"

Henry shook his head.

"Handyman?"

"No, it's just me tonight."

The marshal grunted and appraised the boy with a new grudging sympathy. "That so? Well okay then, tell me. You had any customers come in tonight, tall, rangy, sandy hair? Driving a blue Lincoln?"

Henry's chest flared with heat. "No, nobody like that." Geddes stared flatly and waited for more. "A couple older folks checked into number six earlier," the boy continued, "that's it." His voice wavered slightly and he clenched his teeth.

Geddes watched him. "No one else at all, huh? Nothing unusual?"

"No."

"You seem pretty sure."

"I am sure."

The marshal squinted off towards the window where the dark willow branches swayed. "Damn. Thought I was close this time. What about yesterday? Anyone stay even just for a few hours, or stop by and decide to move on instead? You hear about anything?"

"I said no," Henry snapped.

Geddes looked back at the boy deadly slow and his brow furrowed. "You know why I'm out here at this hour? A bank up in New Hampshire got robbed last week. The perpetrator killed a guard and stole a woman's car two days ago after another dust-up in Massachusetts."

Henry's mouth hung open and a glazed look came to his eyes. "The guard died?"

"You saw it in the paper?"

"No. I mean, yeah I did, but…"

The scowl deepened as the square-faced man studied the boy. "We've been trailing him east, state and federals all over the county. Thought I'd spotted his car earlier tonight but I lost him. You better believe I'd rather be home in bed but I can see you're a working man too, you understand. I can't sleep when I'm this close, my nerves are a little frayed and for that I apologize. But I'm eager to bring this matter to a conclusion and any help you might provide would be… appreciated."

Henry looked down and tried to do something more natural with his hands than tugging nervously on his fingers, a childhood habit that reappeared in times of stress.

Geddes surveyed the desk, the crime novel, the article. He reached and turned the scrap of paper around with a hairy knuckle. Little spasms played across his frown.

"If it comes out that you saw something," he said slowly, "that you know anything, you're going to be in a lot of trouble, you understand? This whole place," he gestured around with his chin, "we'll shut it down. For letting a damn twelve year old work the desk. For a hundred other violations too I'm sure, judging from the look of this dump."

Henry's heart was pounding and his back ached. "I'm fourteen. The guy you're looking for isn't here. He never was. Now get out."

The man straightened and tugged on his lapels, adjusting his jacket before he brushed the tails aside and stuck his hands in his pockets. "Well I'm sure you won't mind if I just take a look around, will you? Being a good citizen, what with nothing going on and nothing to hide." For a moment they stared at each other, Henry simmering and Geddes' beady brown eyes flashing.

"You got a warrant?"

The marshal stopped and regarded the boy like some unknown specimen. "You read too many of those books, junior."

"Is that the law or isn't it?"

Geddes' bemused squint turned meaner.

"Those cars out front the only ones here tonight?"

Henry hesitated only for a heartbeat before saying, "Yes."

"So if I were to follow the tire tracks in the mud out there round back, I'd find what, a fancy outhouse?"

Henry said nothing and forced himself not to look away.

"As I said," Geddes drawled, "I'm going to have a look around. That alright with you, boss man?"

"Go ahead," Henry said.

The marshal was gone barely ten minutes. Henry didn't leave his post. A feeling of unreality washed over him as he shifted objects on the table and thought about what he'd say to Geddes about the car out back. His mind leapt wildly through different possibilities, each one leading to a dead end, so he kept still, unwilling to break this delicate balance. It would work out, he told himself, it would be okay. An idea came to him and before he was consciously aware of it he'd hopped off the stool, ducked into the back office and returned, turning over what he'd done dispassionately. It was the only way to keep things as they were. Any change carried the ominous disquiet of an approaching cyclone. He folded his hands and shut his eyes. For thirty more seconds there was peace.

Then Geddes shouldered the door open and crossed to the front desk with tense, short steps. His jaw was set and his nostrils flared; a forelock of his greased coif had come undone and lay plastered to his forehead with sweat.

He snapped his fingers at Henry and whispered, "Phone. Now."

"It's not working."

The marshal's face contorted as if inhaling a whiff of open sewage. "Are you fucking with me, boy?"

Henry gestured helplessly to the phone and pushed it forward. Geddes snatched it up and listened, then swore and set it down again. He took a deep breath and spoke quickly and quietly: "Did he threaten you? Is that why you covered for him? Is someone else here in trouble? Nod your head if the answer's yes."

The kid was frozen, not like a frightened deer but with a deeper blankness, a color photograph that blinked. Geddes slid the log book over and his eyes darted across the page.

"Which room? When—" He stopped at the most recent entry. "Eight, is that it? He's in room eight?" When Henry didn't respond the marshal clutched a handful of his shirt. "*Which one?*"

The boy's wide-eyed nod was more like a lurch in the set of his head on his scrawny neck while his Adam's apple bobbed. "Eight," he croaked.

Geddes let go of Henry, unbuttoned his suit jacket and unstrapped the holster on his right hip, but didn't draw the service revolver. His eyes flashed to the phone and he swore again.

"Stay here."

He was turning to leave when Henry said, "Wait."

"What is it, goddamnit?"

"If you call it in you might scare him off. He's asleep."

"Leave it to the pros, junior."

"Don't you want to get him yourself?"

The marshal glowered at the boy. He left quietly, easing the door shut and stepping gently down towards Room Eight. The vestibule light threw sharp shadows in the gloom, hues of blue just beginning to brighten. When the marshal was out of sight Henry dashed into the back office and plugged the phone extension back into the wall socket.

He felt sick to his stomach; what was he thinking? Back at the desk he scooped up the phone. The hum of the dial tone was a universe of choice. 9-1-1 was just three numbers, couldn't be simpler. Internal calls were only two digits. His finger moved to the dial.

The marshal tread carefully on the walkway, heel-toe silent, palm on the butt of his service pistol.

The front-desk phone swung in a hanging pendulum, dancing a crazy jig at the end of its chord.

Henry cleared the door too quickly and stumbled into the support pillar, shivering in the chill dawn. Geddes was down in front of Room Eight with his revolver drawn and held down by his leg.

Inside the room, the phone rang.

Geddes froze, senses tightening as he whipped his furious gaze from Henry back to the door, teeth gritted, and considered his move with frantic calculations. Rustling and knocking inside the room made the officer step back. He cupped the butt of the service pistol with his free palm and brought his arms up.

"Open up, Hanson," he shouted, "I know it's you."

A series of thunder cracks tore the night. The door frame shook, spitting splinters and popping holes. Geddes jerked backwards, arms pin-wheeling as his pistol spun in the air. He cleared the edge of the wooden slatted porch and fell hard on his back, sending up a puff of dust and a spray of gravel.

*An enormous whip had lashed the world, shattering its fragile composure.*

Henry dropped to his knees. Duck and cover.

The fractured door burst open, brass screws and wood shards scattering as the frame rebounded. Frank lowered his booted heel as he sprang out, hair a wild mess, eyes burning over a feral grimace. A short barrelled black pistol dangled from his fist as he took three long strides towards the fallen man. Geddes was trying like a feeble infant to roll himself over. His right hand scrabbled blindly in the dirt for his revolver.

Then the bank robber shot the marshal in the head.

Air drained from Henry's lungs and he collapsed like a punctured balloon, clinging prone and spider-like to the carpet of the vestibule as he watched Frank standing over the marshal's supine body, gun outstretched, staring down into... what?

*Into the heart of an impenetrable darkness.*

The man snapped out of it and reeled back into the room drunkenly, crashing and tinkling glass resounding. A moment later he reemerged, hefting the duffle bag and skirting along the walkway towards the gravel path like a fox chased out of a hen house, jaw set gravely as he rounded the end of the building.

Henry was alone with the corpse.

The marshal's right foot jittered twice and was still. Henry found himself on his feet, crossing the parking lot with quick, calm steps, heart throbbing painfully, passing a tan Buick he hadn't noticed before parked on an angle. The echo of a motor sputtering to life carried on the crisp cordite and iron-tinged air, the rumble getting louder as the front grill of the Continental rounded the gravel path, rear-end fishtailing as it made for Alston Road.

As the sedan neared the turn-off Frank hissed "*shit*" and slammed on the breaks. The marshal's .45. The cash in his wallet. No time to get sloppy. He leapt from the car leaving the driver's door ajar and stopped short. Fifteen feet away, next to the body, Henry held the heavy .45 caliber straight ahead in both shaking hands. The boy's feet were splayed and tears danced in his eyes.

Frank straightened, a cautious glare easing into the old smirk.

"What are you gonna do with that, kid? I thought you were on my side. Thanks for the call, by the way."

Henry coughed raggedly but kept the gun steady. "You can't do this," he managed. "You can't go around killing people."

Frank's smile soured and he spat onto the gravel. "Shit-for-brains child."

"Stay where you are. Don't move. The police will be here soon." Henry squeezed one eye shut and the heaving chest under the Hawaiian shirt hovered out of focus beyond the sighting notch. His arms burned but the barrel barely quivered.

"Oh yeah, cowboy?" Frank sneered. "You can't even squeeze the trigger."

"I'm warning you," Henry croaked, a shaky note through a broken reed, "If you take another step, I'll shoot."

A ripple of hesitation flashed across Frank's haggard features, then he scoffed and turned towards the Olds.

Henry pulled the trigger.

An explosion ripped the air. Henry's feet left the gravel and the ground slammed into his back. His wrists bent sharply and the heavy weapon was snatched from his hands by the force of the discharge.

"*Jesus Christ!*" Frank cried through the ear-splitting whine of the shot and Henry felt the ground vibrate with heavy footfalls.

*The slim figure approached through purple and pink crepuscular pastels, kicking the fallen pistol out of reach and towering in his vision. Cords stood out on his neck and the black bore of the pistol stared into Henry like a phantom eye. The boy lurched to his elbows and crab walked backwards until his shoulder blades hit the wooden edge of the walkway.*

"You're dead, you little fucker," Frank growled, an amused note swimming in his tone.

Henry closed his eyes and silence stretched. Odd that in this final moment he shouldn't feel fear but only profound sadness, a tired lament at the broken beauty of an undiscovered world.

He waited. Moments or years passed.

*His eyelids raised gradually, surreal shades on the figure of the outlaw with the pistol aimed, eyebrows furrowed. The slightest hint of a smile curling the cruel, thin lips and a hard cold glint flickered behind the eyes. Slowly the susurration of the wind returned, the distant wail of a police siren leaking into the tranquil dawn.*

The barrel lowered.

"How much you got left on that new Striker book, kid?"

"Fifty pages."

Frank stuffed the pistol into the band of jeans. "Well, then," he said, "Wouldn't be nice of me, would it? You'll like the ending."

*The outlaw turned and scooped up the marshal's gun, ducked into the car, revved the engine and burned rubber in a wide arc across the gravel before bouncing onto Alston Road. Tires shrieked in a hard right and the rocketship fins disappeared past the row of bushes out of sight. The thrumming of the engine died away with the siren still a faint suggestion on the breeze.*

Henry's shallow breathing filled the quiet morning as the whine in his ears began to fade.

A black pool was spreading underneath Geddes' ruined face, his arms tangled awkwardly across his chest and legs spread.

The door to Room Six snicked open and a pair of slippers shuffled out followed by the padding of bare feet. The old couple stood gaping, the wife speechless through gasping breaths and the husband murmuring, "It's okay hon it's okay the kid's alright, just hang tight hon it's okay…"

The phone in Room Eight was still ringing.

❈

The motel was crawling with cops. Three cruisers were parked at obtuse angles surrounding the marshal's body, now covered with a white tarp, patches of sticky dark red seeping through like stains on a picnic blanket. An officer stood snapping photographs while three more combed the area around the motel, nosing around the back lot and barking into car radios.

A rookie cop with thick glasses interviewed the old couple on the lobby couch, the husband rubbing his wife's shoulders while they talked over each other. In the back office Henry slumped glassy-eyed on the swivel chair with two more officers standing over him. On his left was Officer Tim, stern faced and remorseful. On his right was a shorter, stout man he'd seen on his way to school, auburn hair cropped in a crew cut, beetle-browed, grimly chomping gum and glaring at the boy like he'd just caught a shoplifter. His badge read "G. Woods." Ansel Haldane paced behind them gray-faced, hair ruffled, pajama top buttoned wrong beneath his overcoat.

"He wouldn't have gone in alone," Woods said. "He knew the protocols and who he was dealing with. Something's not right here."

"Go easy on him, Gene."

Woods ignored that and leaned down in Henry's face.

"Tell it again from the beginning. What time did Hanson arrive?"

Henry's gaze wandered, hovering between the officers like he'd been drugged. Finally he shrugged slightly. His lips parted but nothing came out.

Woods snapped his fingers in Henry's face and the boy blinked nervously.

"Wake up, kid. Help us out here."

Officer Tim winced but folded his arms, waiting for a response.

"Problem with the phone," Henry finally murmured.

"That's a goddamn lie," the stout officer snapped. "It's working fine now."

Officer Tim observed the boy pensively. "Son, are you sure you're thinking straight? You want a sodapop or something?"

"He doesn't need a can of soda," Woods said. "We need to haul his ass down to the station for real questioning."

Tim kept his voice level. "You're not helping. He's in shock."

Woods shook his head, scowling. "Doesn't smell right. I think this punk played dumb and got a good man killed."

Smoldering beneath a stray lock of hair, Henry glanced up at Woods and held his eye.

"Why would he do something like that?" Tim asked quietly.

"Cause these damn kids don't respect the law. His story doesn't make sense and you know it. I'm not buying this routine."

Tim smoothed back his lank brown hair. "Geddes may have acted unprofessionally," he said. "We won't know until forensics comes back with the full report."

Woods shot Tim a disgusted look, then noticed Henry eyeing him and bent down further, his face inches from the boy. "What the hell is wrong with you, kid? You know we can try you as an adult for aiding and abetting robbery and murder, don't you?"

Ansel gave a choked cry and stepped forward before Officer Tim grabbed his shoulder and patted the air to soothe him. He turned to Woods. "Step outside, Officer. You're out of line. Let me handle this."

Woods' glare lingered contemptuously on Henry, who had lowered his head and sunken back into a passive daze, then he marched out of the office, slamming the door behind him.

"I'm sorry about him," Tim said. "He's just upset. Geddes was a good man."

Henry raised his head. "How do you know?"

"Excuse me?"

"Did you know him?"

The officer hesitated. "Not personally, no. But I know what this badge represents, the respect it demands and the responsibility it carries. Do you know about that, son? That it's the lifeblood of our community?"

Henry shook his head and hissed a sharp derisive chuckle. "It's only a story."

The officer shifted his weight uneasily. "Listen, I think what you did was right. You kept your head and probably prevented more bloodshed. You knew who it was when he showed up, didn't you?"

Henry pressed his lips into a thin line and kept quiet.

"I believe you were brave, son. I know you and your mother, she's a lovely woman and she's done a fine job raising you. It's my job to keep this town safe, do you understand? We can try tomorrow, you should get some sleep, but it would be very helpful if you could recall as much as possible and walk us through what happened thoroughly. Could you do that for me?"

Henry's gaze was steady and his voice came through deeper and resonant: "I got nothing to say to you."

Muscles twitched beneath the taut skin of the officer's face as the warmth drained from his eyes. "Stay put," he said, "We're not done here yet," and left the lobby.

Henry stared blankly into the middle distance, fished in his pocket absentmindedly and came out with the folded fifty. The bill showed a bit of wear now and was creased diagonally. "Evidence," he whispered, then crumpled it in his fist and went into the back to flush it down the john.

# AD 1963
## Cop and Robber
### Maddi Davidson

Ricky emerged from The Cowboy Diner to an overcast sky of concrete gray. His stomach fluttered, not from the late breakfast, but from what awaited. In a few hours he would conduct his fifth bank robbery.

The day had not begun well. His scrambled eggs were dry, the toast burnt, the coffee acrid, and a clumsy waitress serving the neighboring table had fumbled a plate onto his lap. Sunny side up eggs became yolk side down pant stain. Ricky didn't make a fuss, not wanting to draw attention to himself. He'd used wet paper towels in the men's room to blot the stain, hoping it wouldn't be detectable when dry.

During his years with the Philadelphia police, Ricky had arrested several robbers. His easiest collar was the idiot who jumped into his getaway car, drove around the corner, parked, and took a nap. The guy worked night shifts at a local factory and was exhausted from staying up past his normal bed time in order to knock over the bank. He fell asleep with the bag of loot, emblazoned with "Citizens and Northern," lying on the front seat in sight of all who passed by. Equally stupid was the man who needed cash to pay his rent. He robbed the savings and loan a few hundred yards from his apartment, went home, and handed the money to his landlord. In Ricky's experience criminals, at least those who were caught, were dumb, dumb, dumb.

After eight years working the streets, a back injury forced Ricky off the force. He railed against the mind-numbing jobs available to him: shoe salesman, filling station attendant, and factory guard. His wife hadn't enjoyed being married to a cop and detested even more having a husband who worked dead end jobs. She left, freeing Ricky to turn to the one profession he knew well: crime.

His first holdup had been The Quaker Bank in Bethlehem, Pennsylvania, disguised as an old man, complete with a gray wig, baggy sweater, and cane. Better than the money — Ricky netted $4,800, more than a year's salary for a cop — was the adrenaline rush during the robbery. After that, he could never return to a conventional life.

He headed south and then west, choosing institutions in larger cities rather than small towns where strangers stuck out. Ricky knew that with every job the risk of being arrested increased. The FBI was quick to profile and catch serial criminals. To stay off their radar, he adopted different costumes for each job: khakis, blue shirt, and the steel helmet of a construction worker; the tweed and a bow tie of a university professor; and a gas jockey's shirt and cap bearing the Shell logo. He avoided speaking to anyone, instead passing the teller a note, which could be hand written, typed, or constructed from paste-on letters.

Leaving the diner parking lot, he drove his 1960 Ford Falcon into town. Although the car was three years old, it was new to Ricky. He'd changed cars after hitting a savings and loan in New Orleans. His target this time was the Third National Bank in Oak Lawn, Dallas. He was counting on the planned hoopla in downtown Dallas to keep every law enforcement officer in the area busy with security and crowd control.

Ricky parked several blocks from his destination. The gritty area had the virtue of easy access to U.S. 75, a direct route out of the city. To reach the bank, Ricky took a circuitous route passing night clubs, bars, hair dressing salons, pawn shops, small apartment buildings, and houses. The cool sixty-three degrees was punctuated by a slight wind carrying the aroma of chilies and fresh herbs from nearby restaurants. Occasional gusts of wind picked up bits of old newspapers and grocery store coupons, sending them skittering along the ground. Emerging from behind the clouds, the bright sun reflected off the windows and highlighted the broken glass scattered on the streets. Near Third National the neighborhood was cleaner and Ricky saw more Whites and fewer Negroes and Mexicans.

The fresh-faced teller smiled as he entered the lobby. Medium height, sturdy, and a shade under six feet, Ricky wore a dark suit, white shirt, maroon-pattern tie, and sunglasses. Copious amounts of Brylcreem held his wavy, blond hair in place, and he looked every inch the typical office worker, except for the grayish-white stain on his pants.

"How may I help you, sir?" The girl starred at the large, dark mole Ricky had painted on his cheek after leaving the diner. Good. He wanted the mole to be the defining characteristic of her description. He placed a medium-sized paper bag on the laminate countertop and pushed a note toward the young woman: "I have a gun. Fill this with twenties, fifties, and hundreds and you won't get hurt."

Hands shaking, she withdrew cash out of her drawer and stuffed the larger denominations into the bag. When Ricky snatched the note and money, she didn't look up.

Leaving the bank, Ricky took an immediate left into a narrow alley between the single story buildings. He removed the cash, jamming it into his jacket and pants pockets. The folded-up bag he stuffed into his belt underneath his shirt, and replaced his maroon tie with one bearing blue stripes. The used tie he rolled up and stuffed in his pocket. His last act before leaving the alley was to rub his face with a scrap of fabric soaked in makeup remover. Ricky stopped outside a hardware store to check his reflection in the window. Satisfied no trace of the mole remained, he sauntered along the sidewalk, his hands in his pockets like he hadn't a care in the world.

Ricky's demeanor belied his feelings. He was most afraid during the ten to twenty minutes following a heist when the police were likely to appear. Despite the note he'd given the teller, Ricky was not armed. He could never shoot a fellow officer, or anyone who wasn't committing a crime. He had no chance should someone confront him holding a gun.

Head up and constantly observing his surroundings, Ricky became aware of a growing crowd of Whites and Negroes up ahead. They huddled around a late-model Impala. He considered crossing to the other side of the street; however, no one seemed angry or restless. Since he didn't sense any danger he went on and soon heard the blasting of the car radio.

"…in time to see a policeman standing behind one of the fire poles, looking around as if for some place to shoot, or someone to shoot at. Ah, I'd like to remind you here that as the news comes into the newsroom we will be on the air, we will have our eyewitness people here in just a moment."

A shooting? In Dallas? Ricky slowed his steps. He knew he should be making a beeline for the car. No doubt the alarm had been sounded and the police would be on their way by now. However, when a sobbing Negro woman in an olive green suite slipped out of the group and brushed by Ricky, he stepped forward to take her place.

"Ah, Vicky," the voice on the radio continued. "Will you see if they need some coffee or something. These people are shaken up. They've come awfully close, they were in the line of fire. Now, Jerry?"

"I remember, Jay," said a second voice, "you said, 'I thought that was a firecracker.' Then a second or two later, another shot, and another second, a third one."

"What's happened?" Ricky whispered to a young man similarly attired, but sporting a red tie.

"President Kennedy and Governor Connolly have been shot," he replied in a soft drawl.

Ricky was stunned. God! The President. Although he shouldn't be surprised. This was Dallas. Several weeks earlier the United National Ambassador, Adlai Stevenson, had visited the city and been jeered at, called a "Communist" and "traitor," spat upon, and whacked on the head by a placard. When Ricky checked into the Best Western on the outskirts of Dallas, he discovered pamphlets denouncing Kennedy and accusing him of encouraging "Communist-inspired" race riots.

Ricky was jostled, breaking his reverie. He realized more and more people were pressing in to hear the radio. He should be on his way, yet the need to know what happened, like an invisible force, held him to the spot.

The announcer stated the President, shot in the head, and the Governor, shot in the chest, had been rushed to Parkland Memorial

Hospital. Both were still alive. Murmurs of "thank God" surrounded Ricky, but he was oblivious. At the mention of a head wound, he'd flashed back to Korea: his platoon commander lying in the mud with a shattered skull. He'd survived the bullet, although was never the same man.

A boy riding a bike approached, short legs pumping furiously. His high-pitched yell broke Ricky's trance, although he couldn't make out the words, due to the blaring radio, until the boy stopped a few feet away.

"Dixie's TVs are in the window. Cronkite is on!" he said, flinging his arm back the way he had come. At once three men began running along the street. Others followed in a veritable stampede. Women, hobbled by their tight skirts and heels, hurried behind.

As Ricky trailed the herd, he became conscious of a dull pain radiating from his lower back; a sign he'd been on his feet for too long. If he didn't sit soon, he'd experience painful spasms. Fortunately, the car was less than five minutes away. He could listen to news reports on his radio while he drove out of town.

Reaching the intersection where he should turn north, he noticed a large group milling around a half block to the south. Dixie's? Ricky hesitated. He still had seen no sign of pursuit. All the men in blue must be searching high and low for the shooter, and Dixie's was not far out of his way. Besides, he wanted to know what Walter Cronkite had to say.

A crummy looking store, Dixie's advertised new and used appliances. Two beat-up television consoles in the window had been turned on for those in the street to watch. Parallel Cronkites stared somberly out of the tubes. The shop's front door was open, allowing viewers to hear the commentary. By the time Ricky arrived, people were stacked six deep in front. The clerk turned on several more sets in the store and beckoned people to enter. Ricky remained outside and was able to secure a better spot after the crown thinned, although he had to peer over two heads to see Walter.

As Ricky watched, Cronkite reported that the President had been given blood transfusions and two priests had been called into the room. He also played an audio report from the local station claiming a man had been arrested in the assassination attempt. A few moments later, Cronkite stiffened as he was handed a piece of paper.

"We just have a report from our correspondent Dan Rather in Dallas. He has confirmed that President Kennedy is dead. There is still no official confirmation of this. However, it's a report from our correspondent, Dan Rather, in Dallas, Texas."

Murmurs ran through the listeners. Ricky felt a stone settle in the pit of his stomach. Sirens echoed in the distance. Time to go. Easing his way out of the crowd, he felt a sharp pain as his back spasmed. Ricky took a few tentative steps toward his car. He heard a siren wailing over his shoulder, then the sound of screeching brakes. He didn't need to turn to know the police had arrived. He continued moving.

"Hold it right there, mister!" yelled a voice from behind. "Put your hands up!"

A patrol vehicle rounded the corner in front of Ricky, stopped, and a cop emerged with his weapon drawn. Ricky stopped where he was and raised his hands.

Grabbed from behind, Ricky was thrown against a building. Two cops seemed to be working on him, cuffing his hands and searching his pockets. More cars arrived. Bystanders threw questions at the police.

"Who is he?"

"Did he kill the President?"

"It's not official. Kennedy could still be alive."

"Not if the priests have been called."

Hustled over to the patrol car, Ricky observed patrolmen holding back a throng of onlookers. Alongside the car, a sergeant stood next to a woman: the teller.

"This the man?" he said.

She nodded. "I was on my way home and saw him joining the crowd at Dixie's. He looked a lot like the robber: dark suit, too much Brylcreem, and that gray stain on his pants. He didn't have the mole, which I knew was fake when I saw him up close. The tie is different though."

"Found his pockets full of cash," said the man holding Ricky's arms. "And this." He handed a maroon tie to the sergeant.

"Well, well, well. An hour after stealing all that money, you're still hanging around. Not the smartest guy I've met," the sergeant said, smirking. "But then, in my experience all criminals are dumb."

# AD 1966
# Shake Hands with the Devil
## J. Aquino

The portion of Route 95-South on the way to Aberdeen, Maryland was always the loneliest stretch south for Grahame Shannon. He was on the cusp of completing his tepid trip from Manhattan. As he and his Ford Galaxie V8 passed the grey and skeletal military facilities, he cursed his business situation that forced him to accept the case from Marion Cannon's parents to find her. She wasn't lost. She was running from the man from whom she had stolen three quarters of a million dollars. Grahame was supposed to get there first. He felt no sympathy for her nor drive to help her.

The man was Tony "the Claw" Tanney. He used to be nicknamed "Two-Ton," which was alliterative, but he'd slimmed down on the advice of his doctors and at first adopted the moniker "the Shredder." But his financial advisor found that a little too explicit, preferring the more ambiguous "claw." In 1964, Tony even did a television commercial for Vic Tanney's Gyms, no relation, promoting his weight loss through exercise.

Grahame carried a gun, a Smith and Wesson 39, and so he felt capable of dealing with Tony's ambassadors. But he'd also asked around among his network of friends of friends of mobsters and determined that Tony's search was just beginning. Grahame had a head start. And, of course, the cops weren't looking for her because neither her parents nor Tanney had told them Marion and the money were missing.

Grahame instinctively tapped his jacket pocket where he had the polaroid photo her parents had provided to have it ready to show around. Marion was a redhead with green eyes that looked wholesome in the photo where she was laughing. From experience, he guessed that they could appear wicked when aroused or crossed. As to height, Mrs. Cannon had gestured that she herself came up to her daughter's shoulders, which would put Monica at about 5'7", maybe 5'9" in heels. At a stop light, Grahame tilted the rear-view mirror to assess how he looked. He made a disapproving face. He could lose about ten pounds and should wear a hat more often to cover his balding pate. He wasn't only lonely on the road.

Grahame was going to Aberdeen because Mrs. Cannon had mentioned they had lived there ten years earlier when Marion was eighteen. A friend of his with the New Jersey Division of Traffic Safety who just completed his Vietnam service had also put the word out, and a toll guard matched her license plate to a vehicle leaving the turnpike from the Holland Tunnel going south. But by Elizabeth, there was no trace of the car. Being familiar with the city and its car lots, Grahame decided that Elizabeth would be an ideal spot to trade in and buy, so he continued south to Aberdeen.

He had no sense from what the parents had told him that Marion had any military connections. Grahame instead followed his thirst and instincts to a large bar named "Clancy's," although the bartender's name tag reading "Sergio" suggested that Grahame shouldn't try out his childhood Gaelic on him.

"Hi, Sergio! Guinness draft. And, while I'm here, I want to ask you if—"

"There's just one movie house in town," Sergio preempted him, assuming the question. "The movie starts at seven. It's *What's New Pussycat* ! First run!"

"That opened a year ago!"

"Not in Aberdeen."

"No," Grahame laughed the confusion away. "I wanted to ask if you've seen this woman." He slid the photo towards him, avoiding the wet marks on the bar because there was no copy of a polaroid. Grahame sensed his reluctance and read him the drill. "I'm not a cop. I'm a P.I. She's not in trouble," he kind of lied. "Her family is searching for her."

Sergio looked the picture up and down with obvious pleasure. "Wish it were full length," he cackled. "She had good looking legs." He slid the photo back to Grahame. "Yeah, she was here. Three nights ago. We called her the 'babe.' I wouldna made a play for her myself if she'd stayed." Grahame held his tongue but wondered whether Sergio ever looked at the mirror behind him like Grahame had in the car. He could have lost forty pounds. "But then it became pretty clear she swung the other way—if you know what I mean," Sergio confided.

Grahame acted as if he didn't understand and shrugged. Her parents hadn't mentioned it. Perhaps they didn't know.

Sergio knitted his brow and explained. "A lady soldier sat down next to her, and they hit it off. Started playing footsie—or whatever—and they left together."

"Where'd they go?"

"Next door to the motel where the 'babe' was staying." Sergio felt the need to explain. "You see, the women outnumber the men here two to one, mostly Women's Army Corps. The WAC soldiers get lonely, so you see some of that stuff here, and nobody cares."

"You get either of their names?"

"Not the 'babe.' I heard another soldier—a guy—say to the WAC, 'Hi, Ballantine' like the whiskey. I asked him why, and he said it was her nickname because she had quite a kick. Given her romantic choices, I assumed he meant as a fighter."

Grahame went to the motel and found out Marion had checked in as Althea Gibson. The clerk looked barely eighteen and unaware of the tennis connection of the fake name or that the real Gibson was black. The young man was unable to provide more about Marion's whereabouts except that she had checked out the next morning—alone. He asked around about Ballantine and learned she was Private Ann Spitz, who had a reputation as a troublemaker and thief. She was assigned to a training program reporting to a Sgt. Joan Hood.

The facility where Spitz was stationed was sterile and cold on an otherwise beautiful July day. Grahame was admitted to the base after showing his business card and still active bar membership. Grahame thought Sgt. Hood would be brusque with him, but, when she emerged, her manner was calm and attentive. Her appearance, however, was what he had expected: a face that could have been chiseled by the ancient Greek sculptor Phidias of the goddess Medusa. She looked as if she was stone herself with eyes that could do the same to males of any species. Her black hair was tied in a ponytail.

"I'm sorry," she responded without meaning it, "but Private Spitz is being held on charges of drunk and disorderly. If you leave me your contact information, I can call you when she's released. Will there be anything else?"

Grahame sighed overdramatically and began a move towards the door. "Look, Sergeant," he bluffed by choosing his words carefully, "an attorney has an obligation to his or her client to use every measure available to represent them properly, even if the client is someone with an extensive criminal past. Now, I can force the issue of an interview with a court order or by going through your military chain of command." He omitted that he had abandoned the practice of law, or rather that the law had abandoned him.

Sgt. Hood's face remained stone, but her eyes widened, not with anger, but with fear.

Twenty minutes later, Grahame was sitting in a windowless interview room that didn't even have a clock let alone a bulletin board or anything else on the walls to divert attention from their dinginess. Suddenly, without fanfare or escort, Spitz entered. A guard closed the door behind her, but Spitz remained there like a lost child. Her left eye was bruised and half closed. The skin on her chin was broken with red blotches as if burned. She wore an orange jumpsuit that appeared two sizes two large, although her height may have appeared reduced by her timidity.

"Please sit down, Private Spitz." She did on the chair opposite him, giving the impression that she could bolt at any time and return to the door where she felt safer. "Private," Grahame began with an apology, "I see that you are in some discomfort, and I am sorry to involve you in this. But I really have no choice. You evidently are the last person to see Marion Cannon, and I need to find her and talk to her. Can you tell me where she went?"

An eon seemed to pass while the young woman considered what he thought was a direct and simple question. Finally, she asked in a child's voice, "Why do you want to see her?"

Relieved that she was able to make sounds, Grahame continued to be direct. "Her parents hired me to find her."

Spitz's mouth opened in preparation for speech, but it did not close, as if she were frozen in thought. Suddenly she asked, "How—do I know—that?"

"Ah!" Grahame shifted in his seat as he weighed the best options to convince her quickly. "Well, I have a folder that has her parents' authorization letter back in my car. But I didn't think I'd need it."

"What kind of car?"

Grahame grappled with the question, thinking for a moment that perhaps beatings had scrambled the woman's brains. "A new and blue Ford Galaxie V8. But as for the proof you asked for, her parents provided me with information to give to Marion to show that I had talked to them. Her mother said Marion had told her she had made a— withdrawal from Mr. Tanney; that her favorite doll was Wonder Woman and that her date to the junior prom was Skippy Schneider, that—"

His recital was broken by Spitz abruptly shouting out, "I—." but then she stopped. She swallowed as if summoning up courage and continued, "I am Marion Cannon."

In that instant, as Grahame gazed at her face, mentally removing the bruises, and replacing in his mind her short black hair with the red, soft wave cut from the photograph, he concluded aloud, "Yes. Yes, you are. What the hell are you doing here?"

She looked down at the hands in her lap. "It's a long story. And I don't know that she'll give us the time."

"Yes, she will," Grahame insisted. "She wanted to set a time limit, and I wouldn't let her, threatening—. Well," he spared her the details of his bluff, "threatening things that she clearly didn't want to happen. Go ahead. Tell me. First, why did you take the money?"

"Well," Marion started slowly, "because Tony was dumping me, and I figured he owed me."

"You didn't think he'd come after you?"

"He had too much to lose. I left him a note telling him that I had written out all the bad things he had done that I knew about to be sent to the D.A. if I got killed."

"Giving him *two* reasons to go after you, only more carefully. Did you write such a note?"

She shook her head as if slightly embarrassed. "No."

Grahame grinned appreciatively. He always admired a good bluffer. "Then what happened?"

"I switched cars and made for Aberdeen. I was sitting in this bar when a woman soldier sat next to me. 'You look as if you need company,' she said. 'How can you tell?' I asked. 'You send vibes,' she said,' and brushed her hand against my bare thigh" Marion cleared her throat as if compelled to give a lecture to explain her actions. "You see, I've dated both sexes."

"That's okay. You can preserve my fantasies and spare me the details. Next?"

"We had a few drinks and then went up to my room. It was quite exciting and exotic. Suddenly, an embrace turned into a choke hold. I tried to pull away, but she was muscled as if she pressed weights, and I passed out. I woke up when I felt something being put around my neck. When my eyes cleared, I saw that she was wearing my dress and had dyed her hair to match mine. My own hair was wet. I felt it and pulled away my hand to see it black with dye. Spitz was putting her socks on my feet. My breasts were still uncovered, but she'd pulled her boxer shorts halfway up my legs and I could see her dog tags sticking out from my neck. I started to scream, when she looked up, reared back, and chopped her flat hand into my neck. I was out again. Later, I started to come to, but then I felt her wrapping something around my face. It smelled of cleaning solution—."

"Full of ammonia, no doubt, to keep you unconscious. She probably found it under the bathroom sink. That explains the burns around your lip."

Marion instinctively touched her fingers to her mouth. "Is my face burned?"

Grahame brought her hand down for her. "It's not bad. Go on."

"Through a haze, I sensed her putting her blouse, pants, and boots on me and then pouring what smelled like whiskey over me. Then she dragged me outside and leaned me against some building."

"Hence the drunk and disorderly charge," Grahame explained, mostly to himself.

"I heard Spitz say, 'Sleep tight. I'm sacrificing you to Hood, the goddess of darkness.' The next thing I remember was waking up after being doused by a bucket of water by Sgt. Hood. I was lying on the floor of what looked like a prison cell."

"Spitz must have called the military cops with an anonymous tip."

"I tried to explain to Hood what had happened. 'I know you're not Spitz,' she snapped at me. 'You think I don't know my own women. And I can guess what she did to you. Drugged you and changed clothes She was running from me. And,' she explained in a reasonable manner, 'she's put me in a bind.'"

"Her in a bind?" Grahame asked.

"Yes. She said, 'If you think I'm going to let everyone know she's AWOL and ruin my chance for promotion, she—and you—are out of your minds. I also know who you are. I made some inquiries. Evidently, there are some well-connected people looking for her—you. Something about money.'"

"Swell!" Grahame snorted. "If you had a head-start, you don't have one anymore."

"Yeah. Hood went on about how she assumed Spitz had the money I'd taken. I said I assumed so too. Then Hood told me, 'I have some people looking for her without knowing why. If I get her back and I get the money, tell you what, I'll let you go.'"

"She sounds like a Russian at the negotiation table."

"Then she added, 'I'm keeping you here in solitary. How hard it is for you depends on how nice you are—to me.' She helped me up and then moved in to kiss me. I pulled back, and I guess I looked horrified. I mean, you've seen her. Her eyes filled with hate. She reached behind her and pulled a thick baton from her belt in the back. She swatted me in the face, knocking me back onto the floor. Reaching down, she spun me over and pounded me on the back with her big, black stick." Marion was crying now. "She did it two more times. I don't want to look at my back now."

Grahame's attitude about having no sympathy for Marion had made a U-turn. Before him sat a helpless creature. At the same time, even with her bruises and plastered black hair, her beauty made his heart beat faster and deeper. He was also changing his mind about his weight. Maybe he really didn't have to lose ten pounds after all. He went to a gym when he could. He worked out. Overall, he looked pretty good.

He took her hands and tried to calm her. "Okay, okay. Marion, my name is Grahame. And I promise you, I'm going to do everything I can to get you out of here. I'm going to go to the court and work through military channels. Although I realize I can't tell them everything. It wouldn't help you with Sgt. Hood. I'm going to give her, the court, and her superiors the story about your being a witness in a case about a New York mobster and refusing to talk. By the way, did Spitz say anything at all to suggest where she was going?"

Marion thought about it. "I think that before the lights went out, she had mentioned something about taking the train."

"Train," Grahame snapped his fingers. "The PB&W stops in Aberdeen going both north towards Philadelphia and south to

Washington, D.C. Of course, after that she could change trains. But that could still help us find Spitz and the money. But first, we have to get you out. I'll be back this evening, and I'll tell the sergeant that so she'll be careful what she does to you. Okay?"

"Okay," Marion sniffed. "Thank you—Grahame."

Outside, he recited his story about the New York mobster to Sgt. Hood. Hood was her usual stone face and just nodded. As he was leaving, he heard through the walls Hood shouting at Spitz, demanding to know what she had told Grahame, making him think Marion was going to get another beating. "I gotta work fast," he told himself.

Grahame spent the rest of the afternoon trying to make some headway with the U.S. district court and base administration. The lack of interest he encountered in what he was doing was made more difficult by helicopters coming and going that were distracting the audience for his spiel and making it difficult for them to even hear him.

By seven, he'd really gotten nowhere. He returned to the base as the sky began to darken. He asked to speak to Sgt. Hood.

"I'm sorry, sir," said the guard. "She's not available."

"I told her I was coming back with a court order for the release of Private Spitz into my custody" he lied and bluffed at the same time. "It's essential that I see her."

In response, the guard turned to confer with other guards. Grahame heard whispered words and hushed phone calls and was soon escorted to the office of Col. Elmer McBath.

The colonel, who looked extremely fit and very much in command, asked, "What's your business with Sgt. Hood?

Grahame told him it was about Private Spitz and a court order for her release.

McBath's façade of command vanished, and he took on the appearance of a humble and uncertain colleague of Grahame's. "Mr. Shannon, I'm sorry to have to tell you this, and I'm embarrassed for all here, but Private Spitz is dead. She was apparently beaten to death. She was with Sgt. Hood, who left before Spitz was found. It is assumed that the sergeant lost her temper and—accidentally, I'm sure—killed her. Hood has disappeared, and we are looking for her with helicopters for as long as it's light. The local police have been informed. Since you were working for her release, you were clearly fighting on her behalf, only to have this happen. All I can say is—I'm sorry."

Grahame left the commandant's office as if recovering from a collision with a Mack truck. He went to his car, got in, and wept. "So," he said aloud, "Hood did kill Marion after all. Beat her to death. But I promised I would get her out. 'Alive' was implied. I failed. No daughter, no money returned for the reward. And a naïve, young woman, admittedly a thief, is dead. What a bonehead you are, Shannon! I boasted 'I'll take care of you! I'll just spin Hood the old New York mobster witness story. That always works!' What a smug, stupid, talentless bastard you are. You don't have the stuff to be a lawyer! You don't have the smarts or the guts to be a PI!"

Still grieving for a woman he barely knew, Grahame drove to the gate, showed the guard his pass, and left the base. As he halted at a stop sign just outside the walls, a figure came out of the shadows and pointed what looked like a German luger at him, gesturing for him to roll down his window.

Grahame put up his hands and prepared for the worst. "Sgt. Hood? Out for revenge, are we?"

"Think again!" shouted a woman's voice he recognized.

She walked into the beam of his headlights. Her hair was red, and she was wearing a simple blue dress. It was clearly Marion.

Striding over to the passenger's side, she perused the vehicle from hood to trunk. "Blue Ford Galaxie. Just like you said. Easy to spot in the dark too. Good choice." She plopped into the passenger seat, all the while keeping her luger aimed at him. Leaning forward, she removed his gun from the holster under his jacket. "Drive."

"Where?"

"Back to Aberdeen. I have to pick something up."

He waited until they were back on the highway before declaring,

"You killed her!"

"Hood?" she responded nonchalantly. "You could put it that way. I just think I pulled her stick away and used it. Then, I thought that if it worked for Spitz, it would work for me, so I changed clothes with her. Once in her uniform, I mashed her head some more, blood streaming around her, until she was unrecognizable. They won't know that goo is her for a couple of days. They'll continue to think it's Spitz. I even broke all the bones in Hood's hands thinking they won't be able to fingerprint her with limp digits. I dunno. Maybe they can."

Grahame tried to mask his amazement that the helpless girl had turned into an even match for Tony the Claw. "Had you counted on switching places with her?"

"Her or someone else. I was happy for it to be her. I was able to just walk out of the cell in her uniform and right out the front door. It was perfect."

Grahame let it all sink in for a moment. "How'd you get off the base?"

"I walked to her lodgings just like she would have, used one of the keys on her belt to get in, and washed out all the dye Spitz had poured on my hair, becoming a redhead again. Then I found the one non-military dress Hood owned. I looked for a weapon and found this old thing, a luger from the Second World War, in her desk. It was probably loot taken home by her father," she waved it around for emphasis and then noticed that Grahame was tensing as if he were going to grab for it. She pulled it back and aimed it carefully at him. "Don't be fooled by its age, though. It's loaded and has been recently cleaned. She probably used it for target practice. You know," she said as she appeared annoyed if not bored, "I'm getting tired of pointing this thing at you. And your driving is making me nervous. Pull over. I'll drive. Over there under the moon."

Once parked, she ordered him to slide over and put his hands between his legs, then she pulled his seatbelt across his arms to tie him in. "Nice accessory, seat belts! Ford really knows had to make cars safer.

I always used to make fun of them, saying 'Ford' meant 'Found on the roadside dead.'

"But where are you going to go?" Grahame whined. "You don't have the money. You have no identity. Spitz has it."

"Does she?" Marion asked as she put the car in drive and pulled away. "Grahame, I have a confession to make. I have lied. The way I described my time with Spitz wasn't correct in every detail. She didn't knock me out and switch clothes. All the marks on my face were made by me. She didn't pick me up. I picked her up. We went to the room together, but we didn't become lovers. As soon as the door closed, I suggested my plan that we exchange clothes. I gave her $5,000, which is what I had with me from the $725,000. And I offered her $5,000 more when we rendezvoused in two months."

"And you didn't mention that Tanney might possibly want his money back?"

"Sure, I did! Fair is fair. I told her that's why I needed her, a trained soldier, to stay out of his reach. I appealed to her pride."

"So she'll be waiting for her share and just give you the $700,000?"

Marion pulled off the main road and turned on the brights. "Oh, she'll be waiting and waiting and waiting. For all eternity really. I made a bet with myself that Spitz would only last two days before Tony's men caught up with her. I lost because she lasted three. That was another reason for settling with Hood. When she stormed in screaming at me after you left today, she shoved a newspaper in my face describing how a headless body that had been expertly tortured was found just outside of Wilmington in a creek bed. Spitz couldn't tell them where the money was because she never knew."

"She just had the five thousand."

"Right! Tony's men had never met me. As far as Tony is concerned, I am dead, and the money is lost."

"And Hood?"

"She was angry because she realized she wasn't going to get three quarters of a million dollars."

"Where was it?"

"Not so fast. Let me finish with Hood. Now that I was dead, I could end it with her. I lied to you about her too. She didn't beat me. There are no marks on my back. I was nice to her. Her momentary anger made her vulnerable. What happened to her was what I said Spitz did to me."

"An embrace turned to a choke hold?"

"Followed with my beating her with her baton until she stopped moving."

The road was getting bumpier, and the moon fled behind the trees. "Where are we going?" Grahame asked.

Marion turned to him with the devilish gleam in her eyes he had anticipated when he had first seen her photo. "I gave my folks $55,000, $5,000 of which was your retainer, so I've taken care of them. The rest of the money is in a post office box I rented in Aberdeen. The key is glued to the bottom of a mailbox in front of a deserted house three blocks away. I was just waiting for someone like you to bring me there— like you, whom my folks hired. Of course, as it turned out, I didn't have to wait for you to come for me because Hood gave me the opportunity to escape."

"And so you killed her," Grahame summed it all up. "Unless there's more?"

"Nope. That's it."

Grahame blew air out in wonderment and would have whistled if he could. "Boy, you are one cold cookie, lady."

"Neither Hood nor Spitz were very nice people, Grahame."

"And now you have the money and can buy a new life because Tanney thinks you're dead."

"You made out too. You got $5,000 for asking a few questions and giving me a ride. Which ends here." They pulled in front of a mailbox in front of a deserted house.

"Is this it?"

"This is it." Marion turned to Grahame grinning. "We could share the money. We could find a motel. Didn't we mention something about your looking at my back?" Marion put the car in park and unfastened her belt. She slid over to him, lifted up her leg, and straddled him. "I've decided that I really prefer men. I know that you like me. I can feel it."

"Oh, that's not the question," he moaned, tensing. "Given our current positions, you'd have to be stone yourself not to feel it." She leaned forward and kissed him full on the lips and long. As she pulled back, she frowned because he wasn't smiling. "No, I think I'm done," he announced with finality. "I just don't have the—what would you call it?—zest for robbery and murder to be a good companion for you. Have a nice life. Kill me if you must. And remember that when you pile up the bad karma through bad deeds, the weight smothers you and tilts the scales irredeemably."

Marion sighed, slid off him, undid his belt, leaned across, and pushed his door open. "Out."

Standing in the light of the full moon, Grahame reached for the mailbox. "Is this where it is?"

He fell forward, whacked from behind by the luger.

It was dawn when he woke up. His car was gone. There was no one in sight. He used the mailbox to steady himself as he stood up and saw that there was a folded-over piece of paper inside. It had his name on it and read, "Check your pants. For services almost rendered. Your car will be at the train station. Keys under the mat. Maybe we'll meet again, and you'll change your mind."

Grahame reached into his pants pocket and pulled out a packet of fifty $100 bills. "Private Spitz's second payment that she never got." Surprisingly, his gun was back in its holster. He looked down at his shirt and saw that it was misbuttoned with the edge hanging low. "What the hell did she do! Examine what she missed?" He unbuttoned and rebuttoned so that he could look presentable to anyone thinking of giving him a lift.

As he started to walk back down the rock-laden road to the highway, he decided that it had been a most unusual day. He was $10,000 wealthier and a potential witness concerning Hood's murder. That is, if they ever caught her. He gave an inward smirk, deciding that it was impossible to catch the devil. Remembering the old saying, Grahame was just glad that he hadn't shaken her hand or any other part of her, metaphorically or actually.

# AD 1969

# *The Parking Lot*

## *Kirk Landers*

### *March, 1969*

Jackson kept a mental list of good things happening to him as he was getting ready to ship out to Vietnam, which was probably un-American, but he was doing it anyway, mostly to keep his mind off going to Vietnam, but also because some of the weird shit he was experiencing was kind of fun and might be good to recall when he was in Vietnam.

He was thinking this as the late afternoon light softened on the Fort Lewis, Washington rifle range, where he had to qualify with an M-16 rifle before he could ship out to the war zone. He was the only shooter on the range because all the other soldiers getting ready to ship out to Vietnam had trained on the M-16. Jackson trained on the M-14 a year ago, before clerk school, graduate clerk school, and his posting at Fort Belvoir.

"How many targets do I have to miss to stay home?" Jackson asked the sergeant who commanded the rifle range. He was a staff sergeant with a combat infantry insignia on his shirt, a good guy, kind of happy-go-lucky, not stupid-serious about the spit-shine stuff, and they had been conversing easily.

The sergeant gave Jackson a humorous grin. "You know," he said, "I must be really good at this because I haven't had a single guy fail in all the time I've been here."

Jackson grinned, too. Some Army bullshit really was funny, though in a twisted way.

The easy-going attitudes of the NCOs at Lewis was one of the good things on his list. So was the weather. It was late March and he was in the far north, just a couple hours from the Canada border, and yet the day had been almost balmy and the evening was more of the same. He loved having the mountains in view, and the evergreen forests were so profuse it seemed like the air was saturated with the scent of pine. Jackson was thinking that if he made it back okay, maybe he'd live around here somewhere, fish in the rivers, hike in the mountains, maybe learn to ski, breathe ocean air filtered through the pines for the rest of his life.

The sergeant gave him a choice between firing from the prone position, or standing in an ersatz foxhole lined with corrugated aluminum. "I'll take the hole," Jackson said. "If I shot from the prone position you guys would make me a clerk-sniper instead of a clerk-typist." It was a joke and the sergeant got it.

He positioned himself, locked in the magazine, loaded a round, unlocked the safety, and got ready to fire. The targets would be life-size silhouettes of a man's upper body and head. They'd pop up at distances between 50 and 350 meters away. When Jackson hit a target — IF he hit the target — it would flop down.

Jackson's adrenaline started rising. He liked shooting. He wasn't crazy about the idea of shooting people and he hated the idea of being shot himself, but shooting targets was fun. And he was looking forward to firing the M-16. It felt like a plastic toy compared to the much heavier M-14. The M-16 was also just plain cool. It was black. You could carry it by a handle that housed the rear sight, and when it fired, it made a popping sound instead of the ear-splitting crack of the M-14.

Jackson's first target rose 50 meters away and he nailed it.

"Take your time," said the sergeant who was standing behind him holding an M-16 at port arms. Jackson chuckled to himself. Yeah, this test wasn't about the quick and the dead, it was about getting on a bird bound for Vietnam. It was a test you couldn't fail because the Army didn't care if you could handle the M-16, it just wanted your ass in Vietnam. Fucking army.

He pegged all the targets out to 200 meters. He had qualified as a sharpshooter in Basic, the middle rating, missing Expert mainly because he had trouble seeing the 300-meter targets, and he couldn't see shit at night.

And 300 meters was when the fun began on the Lewis range. When the distant silhouette went up, Jackson saw his first round kick up dirt in front of it. But almost immediately, the sergeant shot, too, and the silhouette went down. From then on, any time Jackson missed, the sergeant knocked down the target with an expertly placed round. When it was over, the sergeant said, "Congratulations, Specialist Jackson. You were perfect."

"Damn, I'm good" said Jackson, "And I didn't even zero in my weapon."

"It's a miracle," said the sergeant.

"But not the one I was praying for," said Jackson.

⋘⋙

The next day was already beautiful when the in-transit people formed up for the head count and work details. Jackson was put in a group of soldiers who would be shipping out the next day. They would spend the morning out-processing, then pull work details in the afternoon.

Jackson made the headcount at the afternoon formation, but he blew off the work detail, thinking to himself, "What are they going to do? Send me to Vietnam?" He gave himself a tour of the post, shopping at the PX, shooting baskets at a gym, sitting under a tree and reading a book.

It was a glorious day until he showed up for the evening formation. During the head count, he was called out to wait after the group was dismissed. The sergeant in charge of the head count, an E-6 named Wilson, called him to attention and got in his face.

"Are you too good for an Army work detail?" Wilson bellowed. He was a young master sergeant with a voice like a drill instructor. It felt like Basic Training again to Jackson, with a DI screaming in your face. There were a lot of smart-ass comebacks Jackson could think of, but he opted to play it straight.

"No, Sergeant."

"Then why were you not present at your assigned work detail, Specialist Jackson?" This was the classic Army game: a question to which there was no right answer, only an opportunity for the respondent to trigger the wrath of the questioner.

"I erred," said Jackson.

Wilson went ballistic. "You erred? You erred? What the fuck does that mean? You erred?"

"It means I forgot to show up," said Jackson.

"You forgot? You forgot?" Wilson ranted for what seemed like a long time to Jackson. It was starting to piss him off, especially since the guy was in his face, and it wasn't like the crime of the fucking century. Jesus, they were just picking up cigarette butts or painting rocks or some other Army bullshit. "Are you going to do that in Vietnam, soldier?"

"If it's an option I'll have to carefully consider it." Jackson knew he was going to pay for his quip, but he was losing the ability to choke back the contempt he had for the Army. Still, as soon as he said it, he wished he'd just gone along with the script.

Wilson smiled a nasty smile and stepped back a half-step and eyed Jackson. "Well, I've got something special for you, Mr. Special-ist." He gave Jackson a "right-face" command and marched him—literally, calling the hup-two-three-four cadence like a fucking drill sergeant— to the transit unit's headquarters. There, Jackson was turned over to the sergeant of the guard for duty. Wilson left, promising Jackson that if he "erred" in executing his guard duty responsibilities he'd spend the next month in the stockade, and then he'd ship out for Vietnam. Jackson kept his mouth shut this time. The sergeant of the guard, a wiry young buck sergeant with a weasel face, made eye contact with Jackson and flashed a cocky, evil grin. Jackson knew it was going to be a long night.

He had thirty minutes to eat, then reported back to the guard house at 1830 hours—six-thirty p.m. to civilians and Jackson. Just before eight p.m., Owens, the weasel-faced sergeant of the guard, drove him to his guard post.

It was a parking lot. A fucking parking lot!

Owens handed him his weapon. It was a baseball bat. Jackson shook his head in wonder. A fucking baseball bat. To defend a fucking parking lot with maybe a hundred cars in it, probably all belonging to lifers who lived on the base. Jackson heard Owens explain that cars had been vandalized in the lot, that's why they were posting guards, and Jackson better damn well stay alert. Jackson heard the words, but he was thinking, leave it to the fucking Army. His last night in the U.S. he was supposed to risk his fucking life defending some fucking lifer's fucking car with a fucking baseball bat.

Even for the Army, this was too screwball to be a comedy.

Owens flashed another weasel smile at Jackson, then left. Jackson shook his head in wonder again, then began a leisurely stroll around his domain. There was no parking lot in America worth defending with a baseball bat, Jackson thought, but this was at least a kind of pretty place for a parking lot. It was in a shallow bowl, open on the entrance side, with pine studded slopes gently rising maybe fifty feet on the other three sides. Green bushes and grasses grew in between the patches of trees, and in the dim evening light, the place took on an emerald glow.

Jackson strolled through the rows of cars, entertaining himself by identifying current-model-year cars and pickups. He figured they belonged to the idiots who just re-enlisted for another hitch in the Army. New lifers. They were famous for blowing their re-up bonuses to buy new cars which lost half their value when you drove them off the lot and the other half by the time you got back from your next tour in Vietnam. If you got back.

Jackson calculated that maybe ten percent of the vehicles in the lot belonged to new lifers. Jesus.

He did his best to play it straight. He spent the whole two hours walking, first the rows, then weaving between the parked vehicles in a serpentine pattern, then figure-eights, then the rows again. He had no idea what he'd do if a vandal came along, but he thought if he stayed visible, maybe the bad guys would wait until some other guy's watch to do whatever it was they did.

He let his mind wander, wondering what his friends were doing now. He thought about John K, his best friend from high school and college, who was sitting out the war on a base in west Texas. He called it "doing time," because it was so boring. A vast wasteland hundreds of miles from anything remotely resembling a city. He was stuck there because the Army trained him in a missile system that was discontinued by the time he finished training. In its wisdom, the Army figured that even though the system had been retired, John K's technical knowledge would be a great liability to America if he was ever captured by an enemy. So he was sitting out his military commitment with the coyotes and snakes in west Texas.

Jackson wondered if Sandy, his last college sort-of girlfriend, had finished her flight attendant training yet, and if she'd ever get to fly international flights, like she wanted. And he thought about Melanie, the Ozarks woman with a husband who wanted to fight in Vietnam instead of being with her, and he wondered how she was doing with her college courses and if her husband had been killed yet. He thought about his high school girlfriend, Bess, and her favorite saying, "Life's a bitch and then you die," the perfect ode to serving in the fucking Army. He tried not to think about Polly B, the one who got away, the college girlfriend he was sure he would marry. He wondered why they couldn't get along, two people who loved each other like that, it was as crazy as guarding a parking lot with a baseball bat. The picture of her floated in his mind's eye—light brown hair framing deep brown eyes and a loving smile--and he blinked, trying to wash it away. She'd be married by now. He'd tried to approach her again after the breakup, but she was done with him and there was no going back.

To get his mind off her, he started counting the vehicles as he walked the rows. One hundred eighteen, give or take, because he'd had some mental lapses in there. He did the rows again, counting pickups and vans. Twenty-seven, including three vans. He was getting ready to count station wagons when Owens brought his replacement and took him back to the guard barracks, for his four hours off. He'd do station wagons on his two a.m. shift.

⧓

By the time Jackson started his graveyard shift, clouds had rolled in making the night as dark as a nightmare and cold. The parking lot had a couple of weak lamps, but they were planted in the middle of the lot and cast light so feeble that half the cars were lost in darkness. The temperature had dropped into the 40s, and it felt colder than that. The air was wet, and night breezes had kicked in to chill Jackson to the bone.

He walked the rows of cars, trying to get his blood circulating, trying not to think about the cold, but his mind kept going back to Lou Rawls's Southside Blues monologue on the *Live!* album, when he talked about "the hawk, the almighty hawk, Mr. Wind." Jackson mouthed the words from memory.

*When he comes blowing down the street about 35 or 40 miles an hour it's like a giant razor blade going down the street.*

Jackson started singing the songs on that album. He had a terrible voice and he didn't know all words to the songs, but it got his mind off the cold and maybe his crappy voice would scare off vandals.

When Owens came by at the end of his shift, Jackson was numb with cold and tired enough to actually sleep, even in a guardhouse bunk. He had turned up just four station wagons in the parking lot, even after doing a recount. And he had tried to imagine what sex would have been like with Sandy and Melanie, and he had absolutely forbidden himself to recall what it was like making love with sweet Polly B, the only true love of his young life.

Jackson knew something was wrong when Owens was the only one to jump out of the Jeep. He walked quickly to Jackson. "Bad news, Specialist Jackson," he said. "Your relief came down sick and I don't have anyone else to take the last shift."

"But Sarge," said Jackson, "I'm shipping out tomorrow."

Owens nodded and flashed a fuck-you grin. "You'll have lots of time to catch some zees on the bird. Twenty-four hours or so." The NCO paused a beat, just so Jackson would know he was getting screwed for ducking the afternoon work detail.

"Don't fall asleep, Specialist," he said. "It can get worse."

Jackson watched Owens leave. He wondered if one of the cars in the lot belonged to him. It would be fun to piss in the gas tank or flatten the tires or maybe even pound dents in the sheet metal.

He let anger drive him for twenty minutes or so, but by then he was so cold he could barely feel his feet and he had to keep his hands in his pockets to protect them, carrying the bat under his arm. It had been a long day and he'd walked a shitload of miles. He found a large old evergreen with a trunk thick enough to block the wind. It was about twenty feet high on the valley wall, and he had a pretty good view of the parking lot. He sat beside the tree, out of the wind, and tucked his knees up to his chest. He'd take a 15-minute break, walk a lap, take another break, and so on. It would get him through the night, and if someone came to check on him while he was resting, he'd be out of sight in the shadows. They wouldn't see him until he entered the pool of light in the middle of the lot, a good soldier braving the dark edges of the perimeter to keep all the lifers' cars safe. The good soldier issuing the stupid challenge. *Halt! Who goes there.* Jesus Christ.

An hour later, Jackson was nestled against the thick tree and his mind was fixed on the stories he'd been told by Vietnam returnees, especially the ones about their flights into Vietnam taking small arms fire when they landed. He figured it was bullshit, but until he'd actually landed and saw for himself, he couldn't really be sure. He was in the middle of imagining what that would be like—would you try to grab your duffel bag before you low-crawled to cover? He had been one of the best low-crawlers in his basic training unit, but he'd never tried it with anything more than an M-14 on his back. Or would you stay by the plane, using it for cover? He was on the part about, no, only a crazy person would stay by the plane with its gallons of aviation fuel still on board, when he heard voices down in the parking lot.

Jackson shot to his feet and scampered down to the tarmac, his eyes peering into the gloom to spot the intruders. He heard three distinct voices. Laughter. Exclamations. An obscenity, medium volume. More laughter. They sounded drunk. Not guard duty people. Maybe revelers fetching the car that would take them wherever they're going to sleep it off.

Jackson headed for the voices. He was still in the dark when he saw them. They were drunk, for sure, staggering now and then, but not fall-down drunk. They wore civilian clothes and military haircuts and they were young, like him. They weaved their way down the center row, heading for a wooden stairway at the end of the lot that led up to another street lined with barracks and administrative buildings.

Jackson froze in the shadows and watched them. They started singing the Airborne Ranger song, loud and off key. *I want to be an Airborne Ranger, I want to live a life of danger...* One of them punctuated the "danger" line by levelling a karate-style kick at a parked car. Jackson saw the headlight of the car shatter and heard the glass tinkle to the ground, followed by the raucous laughter of the three men. They were close to him now, just a couple of rows of cars away, them in the light and unaware of him, standing in the dark.

A different man kicked a car grill. The third karate-kicked a headlight on another car, shattering it. Jackson started toward them, ready to shout the "halt" challenge, when his mind registered how well the karate kicks had been delivered. These guys were way past the two-week basic training course in hand-to-hand combat. They might be Rangers or Green Berets or LURPs or some other form of killing machine. Whatever, they weren't going to be intimidated by a fucking clerk with a baseball bat.

Jackson sank into a crouch behind a car, trying not to attract their attention with movement. They continued laughing and singing. *I want to go to Viet Nam, I want kill some Viet Cong.* He started to get up once and checked himself. What in the hell would he do? One guy with a baseball bat, no communication device. Jackson played the scene in his mind, the trio laughing at him, directing their karate kicks to his balls, then his face, leaving him like a pile of shit in the middle of the parking lot. The sergeant of the guard finding him and thinking it was pretty funny.

Fuck the Army, Jackson thought. He'd stay safe and let the drunks have their fun. What would the Army do to him? Send him to Vietnam?

But as rational as that thought was, he kept coming back to the other thought, the one that said it was his duty. He didn't want to be in the Army and he didn't want to be in the fucking parking lot, and he didn't want to be on guard duty, but that's where he was and he was supposed to defend the fucking lifers' cars with his brave voice and baseball bat, even if it meant getting the shit beat out of him.

When he couldn't stand it anymore, he stood up and screamed, "Halt, who goes there?"

The three drunks froze, then spun in the direction of Jackson's voice. He couldn't see their faces clearly, but the closest one cocked his head, like he was asking a question or wondering if Jackson was just a funny dream he was having. Jackson strode out of the shadows. He didn't know what to say, and they didn't either. They watched him emerge from the darkness and come closer, but when they saw the bat they started laughing.

"Hot damn, man," said the guy closest to him. "Do I look like a curve ball to you, dude?" He was wearing blue jeans and a yellow short-sleeve shirt with a collar. The guy was about six feet tall, like Jackson, and one of the other guys was, too. The third one was smaller, maybe 5-9, and wiry, but Jackson thought he might be the most dangerous of them all. He'd faced off with a guy just like that in pugil sticks in Basic and the guy creamed him in two minutes.

The other six-footer was wearing a blue jacket over an olive-drab army t-shirt. He strutted up to Jackson like he was a meat-eating carnivore and Jackson was a rabbit with a limp. He got in Jackson's face and Jackson braced for a kick in the balls or maybe a karate chop to his face, but the guy just yelled, "What the fuck are you going to do? Are you going to kill us with that thing?"

"Maybe not," said Jackson. He was trying to be a wise ass because maybe these guys were just fucking with him, but his mouth was dry because they were still at the anything-can-happen stage and it was hard to make words.

"Maybe not!" the guy yelled, doubling over with laughter.

"Guy that funny, maybe we should let him live," said the one in the yellow shirt. The shorter guy was just watching, from a distance. He was quiet and alert, like a predator, but he smiled a little.

The blue-jacket guy grinned at Jackson. "You ain't going to turn us in, are you, Mr. Specialist Four?"

"I have to account for the damage you did," said Jackson. "Otherwise they might not send me to Vietnam tomorrow." He managed a smile.

"Fucking newbie with a bat!" blue jacket exclaimed. The guys roared.

"I don't suppose you'd like to give me your names, would you?" asked Jackson. It was an ask, but he was grinning because he knew what the answer was.

"Not this time," said blue jacket. "See, we done been where you're going and you may not believe this, but when you come back, if you come back, you'll want to bust up some shit too. So we earned a pass on this one, right?"

Before Jackson could answer, the short guy completed the picture for him. "Because to get our names you're going to have to beat the shit out of us with that bat, and Boy, I don't like your odds."

"Me either," said Jackson, with a shrug. One of them nodded, another winked. They turned and resumed walking to the back of the lot. He watched them hop up the stairs, still buzzed on alcohol, but strong and nimble and physically fit. They would have killed him easily in a fight. Jackson knew that. But they left him with a terrible problem. When Owens saw the damage to the cars, he'd want Jackson's skin for it. Jesus Christ, he swore to himself, what in the hell do you do when there's no right answer?

He shuffled over to the stricken cars, walking like a condemned man, rehearsing things he could say to the sergeant, and maybe to the judge at his courts martial. There was really only the truth, and there was no way to tell it that didn't end up with Jackson not performing his duty. He was fucked.

There was no visible damage to the car that had been kicked in the grill, but the shattered headlights had tell-tale puddles of broken glass just beneath the damage. Jackson kicked a few larger shards under the first car so no one would step on them. It dawned on him then that with the glass out of sight, the damage wasn't easily visible. He pulled out a couple of shards that remained on the headlight and tossed them under the car. A headlight without its glass shield looked just like a headlight with a clean glass shield. Owens wouldn't notice it. Hell, with a little luck, the owner of the car wouldn't either, not until the next time he drove at night and turned on his headlights. By then, Jackson would be in some shithole in Vietnam and no one was going to haul him back to the States for a broken headlight or two. For that matter, even if someone figured out the damage had been done the night he pulled guard duty, who could say which guard was on duty when the damage happened?

Jackson spent the next ten minutes doing his best to sweep the broken glass under the cars. The bits he couldn't move with the sole of his boots, he tried to pulverize with the end of the bat, then he got on his hands and knees and blew as much of the powder and tiny bits as he could under the cars.

He spent the rest of his watch agonizing over what he'd done and what he hadn't done, but he couldn't find any real alternative to his shameful behavior. Even if he could have subdued the three guys with the bat, really? Three Vietnam vets, surviving the fucking war, then getting the shit beat out of them in a parking lot in the U.S.A.? By another soldier?

As Jackson mulled it over and over, he kept realizing that even reporting them was puke-worthy. After a tour in Vietnam, you get busted for vandalism?

There was a hint of light in the western sky when Sergeant Owens arrived to take him back to headquarters and release him for the day. Jackson had been thinking about the war novels he'd read in college, and how they all showed war as being sometimes heroic but always corrupt, and how he was beginning to understand why.

Ferret-faced Owens didn't even ask Jackson about his watch, so Jackson didn't have to lie. Back at HQ, just before he released Jackson, Owens looked up from Jackson's paperwork and gave him one more mocking grin. "A Personnel Specialist?" he said, referring to Jackson's military occupation specialty. "Not just a clerk, a *personnel specialist*." The sergeant shook his head sarcastically. "You fucking office bitch. I'm glad you pulled double duty last night. Guard duty's all you're good for."

Owens' insults were a tonic for Jackson's tortured conscience. He grinned and nodded to the sergeant. "Be all you can be," Jackson said. And he left.

# The Usual Unusual Suspects

*Gary Thomson* resides in Ontario, Canada where in his rec moments he blows Beatles and blues on his Hohner harmonica. His short fiction has appeared in *Horla e-zine, Wellington Street Review, AgnesandTrue,* among others. He first appeared in *Crimeucopia – The Cosy Nostra* with *Deadly Harvest.*

*Edward St. Boniface* lives and works in London UK and writes across various genres including crime, Science Fiction & Fantasy and contemporary literary fiction. He's always interested in exploring an unusual angle to a story, and is keen to build up a readership. In addition to work freely available on his WATTPAD account he has also self-published several novels and surreal humour pieces available on Kindle. He believes literature like all the arts should start from being Fun, and hopes you enjoyed his story. Ed has had crime short stories in his *Black Hand Incorporated*' series published on the *Mystery Tribune* and *Close2TheBone* websites:
 https://www.close2thebone.co.uk/wp/zero-points-of-articulation.
He also has another Simon Magus Iscariot story, IMPERATRIX ABYSSA on the *Eternal Haunted Summer* website —
https://eternalhauntedsummer.com/issues/winter-solstice-2023/imperiatrix-abyssa-or-queen-of-the-damned-from-the-misadventures-of-simon-magus-iscariot/ — and hopes you will read his madness-inflected forays into those worlds respectively! For Ed's works otherwise available on the Amazon website, go to:
https://www.amazon.co.uk/Edward-St.-Boniface/e/B00JBCZMDS
His first *Crimeucopia* appearance was in *Boomshakalaking! — Modern Crimes for Modern Times.*

*Terry Wijesuriya* has been a published author since the age of seven, though admittedly it was a plotless short story about a butterfly, which appeared in the local children's newspaper....
She reads anything interesting that she comes across, with her favourite genre of fiction being Orientalist adventure. She also runs a very sporadic fan blog dedicated to JT Edson's Floating Outfit series —

https://www.theysabelkid.wordpress.com. She lives just outside Colombo with her family and other animals. Terry also appears in *Crimeucopia – One More Thing To Worry About* with *Murder at the Aragalaya*.

*Frances Stratford* has always been fascinated by the Tudor era. Even as she completed her PhD in medieval literature, she made time to read any work depicting the history and complexity of the sixteenth century. Now she writes in the voices of forgotten women of the Tudor period for all the world to hear. Frances is the author of academic books and essays too baroque for even Cardinal Wolsey to read. She teaches at a liberal arts college in New England. Most days you can find her hiking with her dog Madeleine or scribbling with her favorite flea market fountain pen.

*Dennis E. Delaney*'s short stories have been published in magazines such as Rod Serling's *The Twilight Zone Magazine*, *Night Cry*, *Night Terrors*, and anthologized in *Tales of the Marvelous Machine* (*Creative Computing Press* 1 Jan. 1980) "I know, this really ages me", and others, including several hundred articles in various newspapers.

*Joan Leotta* plays with words on page and stage. She performs tales featuring food, family, and strong women. Internationally published, she's a 2021 and 2022 *Pushcart* nominee, a *Best of the Net 2022* nominee, and a 2022 runner-up in the *Robert Frost Competition*. Her essays, poems, and fiction are in *Ekphrastic Review*, *When Women Write*, *The Lake*, *Verse Visual*, *Verse Virtual*, *anti-heroin chic*, *Gargoyle*, *Silver Birch*, *The Wild*, *Ovunquesiamo*, *MacQueen's Quinterly*, and *Yellow Mama*, among others. Her chapbooks are *Languid Lusciousness with Lemon* from Finishing Line Press and *Feathers on Stone* out now from *Main Street Rag*.

*Hope Hodgkins* grew up in rural Missouri, earned her PhD in literature from the University of Chicago, and taught for years at the University of North Carolina at Greensboro. She has published essays on literary-historical figures including George Herbert, James Joyce, Oscar Wilde, Barbara Pym, Muriel Spark, and Daniel Boone, in areas ranging from poetics and religion to dress style and early-American literacy. Her recent book is *Style and the Single Girl: How Modern Women Re-Dressed the Novel, 1922-1977.*

Her mystery stories appear in *Ellery Queen* and the 2024 Malice Domestic anthology, *Murder Most Devious*.

Hope Hodgkins's novel-in-progress, *Decently*, mixes historical murder with present-day malfeasance in staid small-town Missouri.

She dislikes enclosed spaces such as caves, and she's never been a governess or experimented with poisons.

**Karen Odden** earned her PhD in English at NYU in 2001, writing her dissertation on the medical, legal, and fictional literature written about Victorian railway disasters and the injuries they caused, tracing textual connections to 1910s "shell shock," and what we now call PTSD. She subsequently taught at UW-Milwaukee, wrote introductions for Victorian novels in the Barnes & Noble Classics Series, and edited for the academic journal *Victorian Literature and Culture* (Cambridge UP). She has written five novels, all set in 1870s London; her most recent, *Under a Veiled Moon: An Inspector Corravan Mystery*, was nominated for the Lefty, Agatha, and Anthony awards for Best Historical Mystery 2023. She serves on the national board of Sisters in Crime and is an active member of MWA and the Historical Novel Society. Originally from New York, she now lives in Arizona with her family. Connect with her at www.karenodden.com.

**J. F. Benedetto** is an active member of the *Mystery Writers of America* and has had work published in numerous anthologies and short story collections in both Australia and the United States — the most recent being in the *Colp: Desert/Dessert* short story collection.

**S. B. Watson** lives in Keizer, Oregon, USA — and has had numerous pieces published in *Spinetingler Magazine, The Dark City Mystery Magazine, Mystery Magazine, Mystery Tribune,* and *Punk Noir Magazine.*

**Hal Dygert** practiced environmental law before taking on supervisory responsibilities within the Washinton State Office of the Attorney General. He devotes his free time to writing crime fiction and fishing, especially for bass, and is current President of the Olympia, Washington-based Puget Sound Writers Guild. In continuous existence for more than 30 years, the PSWG provides instruction to novice writers, supports a weekly critique group, and sponsors craft seminars led by, among others, Hallie Ephron,

Robert Dugoni and Allen Eskens, Edgar nominees one and all. Mr. Dygert's taste in literature embraces the hard-boiled crime classics, contemporary neo-noir, especially that set in the classic era, as well as literary fiction. Mr. Dygert is an avid fan of the noir films shown by Eddie Muller, The Czar of Noir, on his Noir Alley series for Turner Classic Movies. For samples of Mr. Dygert's writing (novel excerpts, song lyrics, reviews and blog posts) please visit his website at https://haldygert.com/

*Merrilee Robson*'s mystery short stories have appeared in *Ellery Queen, Alfred Hitchcock, Mystery Magazine, The People's Friend*, and various other magazines and anthologies.

Her first novel, *Murder is Uncooperative*, is set in a non-profit housing co-op. She is working on a historical mystery, *Summer Smoke*, set in Canada at the start of the first World War.

A former director of Crime Writers of Canada, and former vice president of Sisters in Crime – Canada West, she is also a member of the Short Mystery Fiction Society. She previously served three years as a member of the Vancouver Police Board, which provides civilian oversight to the police department.

She lives in Vancouver, with her husband and two very pampered cats, in a house which is over a hundred years old and was first owned by a police officer.

*John G. Bluck* was an Army journalist at Ft. Lewis, Washington, during the Vietnam War. Following his military service, he worked as a cameraman covering crime, sports, and politics—including Watergate for WMAL-TV (now WJLA-TV) in Washington, D.C. Later, he was a radio broadcast engineer at WMAL-AM/FM.

After that, John worked at NASA Lewis (now Glenn) Research Center in Cleveland, Ohio, where he produced numerous television documentaries. He transferred to NASA Ames Research Center at Moffett Field, California, where he became the Chief of Imaging Technology. He then became a NASA Ames public affairs officer. John retired from NASA in 2008. Now residing in Livermore, California, he is a novelist and short story author.

Find out more by visiting his website: http://www.bluckart.com and also his Rough Edges Press webpage
https://roughedgespress.com/project/john-g-bluck/

**David Hagerty** is the author of the *Duncan Cochrane* mystery series, which chronicles crime and dirty politics in Chicago during his childhood. Real events inspired all four novels, including the murder of a politician's daughter six weeks before election day (*They Tell Me You Are Wicked*), a series of sniper killings in the city's most notorious housing project (*They Tell Me You Are Crooked*). He has also published more than 40 short stories online and in print. Read more of his work at https://davidhagerty.net/

**Avi Sirlin** resides in Victoria, Canada – though has a Radio interview available via Australia Broadcasting:
http://www.abc.net.au/radionational/programs/booksplus/avi-sirlin's-novel-the-evolutionist/7405086.
His novel, *The Evolutionist* (Aurora Metro Books (UK) 2014), tells the story of one of Britain's most controversial and misunderstood Victorians, a man Sir David Attenborough called "the most admirable character in the history of science" — Alfred Russel Wallace.
More recently, his short fiction has appeared in *The Fiddlehead*, *The New Quarterly and Grain*, and he is currently completing a new novel.

**Karl El-Koura** resides in Ottawa, with his beautiful editor-wife and their adorable tiny human.
Primarily a writer of fiction, he works in a wide variety of genres — SF, Horror, mainstream and detective fiction — either in short story form through to full length novels. Almost all of his work can be classified as theological fiction—a Christian deeply interested in the "big" questions, Karl's stories explore issues of theology and spirituality even when he doesn't consciously intend them to do so. For those who care to know, Karl is a Greek Orthodox Christian.
Almost seventy of Karl's short stories and articles have been published in magazines since 1998. In 2012 he independently published his debut novel *Father John VS the Zombies*, and in 2015 he published the sequel, *Bishop John VS the Antichrist*.
Karl holds a second-degree black belt in Okinawan Goju Ryu karate, is an avid commuter-cyclist, and works for the Canadian Federal Public Service.
He will occasionally refer to himself in the third person — but then, who doesn't?

*Penny Hurrell* is from Essex, England and has been writing for the last ten years after a lifetime of enjoyment from reading. She first appeared in *Crimeucopia — Tales From The Back Porch,* with *Accidents Will Happen.* When not working on her novel — which she still intends to finish — she continues with short fiction, and the occasional flash fiction competition entry.

*Kai Lovelace* is a freelance musician & writer based in Manhattan.
*Only a Story* is his debut short story, and when not writing fiction he heads up The Lovelace band — a shifting ensemble specializing in jazz, blues, funk, bossa nova & lounge music — along with other music projects. Find out more by visiting:
https://www.klovelacemusic.com/music

*Maddi Davidson* is the pen name for two sisters: Mary Ann Davidson and Diane Davidson. Together they have published several novels, a non-fiction book, and numerous short stories. Their tales range from the murder of a deranged scientist resurrecting the dodo to a spurned wife hacking the pacemaker of an ex-husband who richly deserved it.

*J. Aquino* is an attorney and retired journalist whose fiction has appeared in numerous anthologies. He is the author of *Truth and Lives on Film: The Legal Problems in Depicting Real Persons and Events in a Fictional Medium, 2nd edition June 2022,* https://mcfarlandbooks.com/product/truth-and-lives-on-film-2/ and *The Radio Burglar: Thief Turns Cop Killer in 1920s Queens,* September 2022, https://mcfarlandbooks.com/product/The-Radio-Burglar/

*Kirk Landers* launched his professional writing career in the US Army, writing profiles of his fellow Basic Trainees for the post newspaper to get out of KP and guard duty. After military service, he became a staff writer and editor for special interest consumer magazines, a staff writer for *Time-Life Books,* co-author of the biography of self-help writer Napoleon Hill, and chief editor for several trade magazines. He writes crime fiction under a pen name. His first Kirk Landers novel, *Alone on the Shield,* told the story of Vietnam era lovers who broke up over the war meeting on a wilderness island forty years later.

CRIMEUCOPIA
*Rule Britannia*
BRITANNIA WAVES THE RULES

Features fiction from
Daniel Marshall Wood, Gerald Elias, S. E. Bailey, Alexander Frew,
Kelly Lewis, Carew S. Bartley, Madeleine McDonald, Edward Lodi,
Michaele Jordan, J. Aquino, David Rich, Kelly Zimmer,
Sharon Richards, T. K. Howell, Maroula Blades,
David William Johnson and Harris Coverley

As I best recall, it was one afternoon here at MIP Towers – must have been a touch after the start of tiffin, so around 4.35pm – when some smart young cove decided to politely call attention to himself by saying he had a proposal:

'Why can't we do an all-British Crimeucopia?'

And, bless my soul, after several pots of tea — Darjeeling (mid-season second flush, naturally) the general consensus was a resounding:

'Why not indeed?'

From there was born this anthology, containing, we hope, stories that, were you to cut them in half with a knife, they would flash you their Union Jacks without a moment's hesitation.

### Rule Britannia - Britannia Waves The Rules

features fiction from Daniel Marshall Wood, Gerald Elias, S. E. Bailey, Alexander Frew, Kelly Lewis, Carew S. Bartley, Madeleine McDonald, Edward Lodi, Michaele Jordan, J. Aquino, David Rich, Kelly Zimmer, Sharon Richards, T. K. Howell, Maroula Blades, David William Johnson and Harris Coverley

The fiction ranges from general British cosy, through Harry Palmer and George Smiley territory, before going deep into very British Modern Noir. And as with all of these anthologies, we hope you'll find something that you immediately like, as well as something that takes you out of your comfort zone – and puts you into a completely new one. In other words, in the spirit of the Murderous Ink Press motto:

*You never know what you like until you read it.*

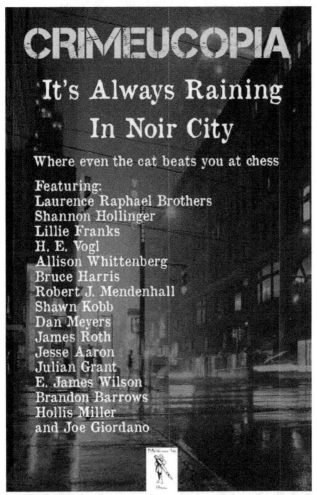

# CRIMEUCOPIA

## It's Always Raining
## In Noir City

Where even the cat beats you at chess

Featuring:
Laurence Raphael Brothers
Shannon Hollinger
Lillie Franks
H. E. Vogl
Allison Whittenberg
Bruce Harris
Robert J. Mendenhall
Shawn Kobb
Dan Meyers
James Roth
Jesse Aaron
Julian Grant
E. James Wilson
Brandon Barrows
Hollis Miller
and Joe Giordano

Is the Noir Crime sub-genre always dark and downbeat? Is there a time when Bad has a change of conscience, flips sides and takes on the Good role?

Noir is almost always a dish served up raw and bloody - Fiction bleu if you will. So maybe this is a chance to see if Noir can be served sunny side up - with the aid of these fifteen short order authors.

All fifteen give us dark tales from the stormy side of life - which is probably why it's *always* raining in Noir City....

Paperback Edition  ISBN: 9781909498341
eBook Edition ISBN: 9781909498358

CRIMEUCOPIA
Crank It Up!

Featuring fiction from:
Ed Teja, John A. Connor, Ruth Morgan, Jesse Aaron,
Scotch Rutherford, Billie Livingston. Robert Petyo,
John Elliott, M.E. Proctor, William Kitcher, R. M. Linning,
Annie Reed, Wil A. Emerson, Dan A. Cardoza,
Alan J. Wahnefried, Sam Wiebe, Jon Fain,
and Mark James McDonough

### *Just An Eight Banger With Big Baloneys*

To honour motor transportation in some of its many roles in the crime fiction genre, we have gathered together a fine collection of short pieces that we feel, in one way or another, will crank up your adrenaline and get your emotions racing without making you blow a gasket or strip a gear.

Featuring: Ed Teja, John A. Connor, Ruth Morgan, Jesse Aaron, Scotch Rutherford, Billie Livingston, Robert Petyo, John Elliott, M.E. Proctor, William Kitcher, R. M. Linning, Annie Reed, Wil A. Emerson, Dan A. Cardoza, Alan J. Wahnefried, Sam Wiebe, Jon Fain, and Mark James McDonough

We hope you'll find something that you immediately like, as well as something that takes you out of your regular racing line comfort zone — and puts you into a completely new one.

In other words, in the spirit of the Murderous Ink Press motto:
You never know what you like until you read it.

Paperback ISBN: 9781909498525  eBook ISBN: 9781909498532

This is the first of several 'Free 4 All' collections that was supposed to be themeless. However, with the number of submissions that came in, it seems that this could be called an *Angels & Devils* collection, mixing PI & Police alongside tales from the Devil's dining table. Mind you, that's not to say that all the PIs & Police are on the side of the Angels....

Also this time around has not only seen a move to a larger paperback format size, but also in regard to the length of the fiction as well. Followers of the somewhat bent and twisted Crimeucopia path will know that although we don't deal with Flash fiction as a rule, it is a rule that we have sometimes broken. And let's face it, if you cannot break your own rules now and again, whose rules can you break?

Oh, wait, isn't breaking the rules the foundation of the crime fiction genre?

Oh dear....

With 16 vibrant authors, a wraparound paperback cover, and pages full of crime fiction in some of its many guises, what's not to like?

So if you enjoy tales spun by

Anthony Diesso, Brandon Barrows, E. James Wilson, James Roth, Jesse Aaron, Jim Guigli, John M. Floyd, Kevin R. Tipple, Maddi Davidson, Michael Grimala, Robert Petyo, Shannon Hollinger, Tom Sheehan, Wil A. Emerson, Peter Trelay, and Philip Pak

then you'd better get

CRIMEUCOPIA - Strictly Off The record

by the sound of it!

**CRIMEUCOPIA**

**BOOMSHAKALAKiNG!**

## Modern Crimes for Modern Times

Featuring: Scott Talbot Evans, Edward Sheehy,
Robb T. White, Robert Petyo, Brian R. Quinn,
Orca Green, Robert Parker, Brandon Barrows,
S. E. Bailey, Edward St. Boniface, Dan A. Cardoza,
Sean Marciniak, Lynn Hesse and Hernán Salvarezza

Boomshakalaking is a variant of the expression Boomshakalaka, currently recognised as a boastful, teasingly hostile exclamation that follows a noteworthy achievement or an impressive stunt — the meaning similar to *in your face!*

Which is why this anthology is subtitled *Modern Crimes for Modern Times*, because most, if not all, are not your 'regular' crime fiction pieces — in fact some quite happily dance along the edges of multiple genres and styles, while others skew it like it is.

Of the 14 who appear in this anthology, 8 are new Crimeucopians, and even we have to admit that this is one of the most diverse Crimeucopia anthologies so far, and still sits under the umbrella of Crime Fiction.

As with all of these anthologies, we hope you'll find something that you immediately like, as well as something that takes you out of your comfort zone – and puts you into a completely new one.

In other words, in the spirit of the Murderous Ink Press motto:

*You never know what you like until you read it.*

Totally — *adverb:* completely; absolutely. Used to emphasize a clause or statement. "He/She is totally bat-shit crazy!"

Psycho — *noun:* an unstable and aggressive person. "Don't you know? My ex is a total psycho!" — *adjective:* exhibiting unstable and aggressive behaviour "There's some kind of psycho nut job on the loose out there!"

Logical — *adjective:* characterised by or capable of clear, sound reasoning. "His/Her logical mind? Are you nuts or something?"

But are all psychos 'nut jobs'?

Laurie Stevens, Jesse Aaron, Patrick Ambrose, Stephen D. Rogers, Wendy Harrison, Jan Glaz, Brandon Doughty, Elena Schacherl, Joyce Bingham, Jeff Somers, Glenn Francis Faelnar, Douglas Soesbe, C.G. Merchant, Daniel C. Bartlett, Richard J. O'Brien, David Bradley, and Kamal M present 17 cases for the defence.

**Paperback 9781909498563 eBook 9781909498570**

Printed in Great Britain
by Amazon

43332363R00199